AN UNOFFICIAL GRAPHIC NOVEL FOR MINECRAFTERS

REVENGE of the ZOMBIE MONKS

CARA J. STEVENS

ART BY DAVID NORGREN AND ELIAS NORGREN

SKY PONY PRESS
NEW YORK

This book is not authorized or sponsored by Microsoft Corporation, Mojang AB, Notch Development AB, or Scholastic Corporation, or any other person or entity owning or controlling rights in the Minecraft name, trademark, or copyrights.

Sky Pony Press books may be purchased in bulk at special discounts for sales promotion, corporate gifts, fund-raising, or educational purposes. Special editions can also be created to specifications. For details, contact the Special Sales Department, Sky Pony Press, 307 West 36th Street, 11th Floor, New York, NY 10018 or info@skyhorsepublishing.com.

Sky Pony® is a registered trademark of Skyhorse Publishing, Inc.®, a Delaware corporation.

Visit our website at www.skyponypress.com.

10 9 8 7 6 5 4 3

Library of Congress Cataloging-in-Publication Data is available on file.

Special thanks to Cara J. Stevens, David Norgren, and Elias Norgren.

Cover design by Brian Peterson
Cover illustration credit Bethany Straker

Print ISBN: 978-1-5107-0727-6
Ebook ISBN: 978-1-5107-0728-3

Printed in China

Editor: Julie Matysik
Designer and Production Manager: Joshua Barnaby

INTRODUCTION

If you have played Minecraft, then you know all about Minecraft worlds. They're made of blocks you can mine: coal, dirt, and sand. In the game, you'll find many different creatures, lands, and villages inhabited by strange villagers with bald heads. The villagers who live there have their own special, magical worlds that are protected by a string of border worlds to stop outsiders from finding them.

When we last left the small border world of Xenos, Phoenix had to leave home to protect her village from her secret identity as an outsider. T.H., a mischievous hermit boy, offered her the protection of his hut until she could safely return. Unfortunately, the monks protecting the border world had been turned into zombies, leaving Xenos and all its inhabitants unprotected.

Our story resumes as these two young friends are about to set out on a journey to avenge the monks and save their peaceful world from destruction.

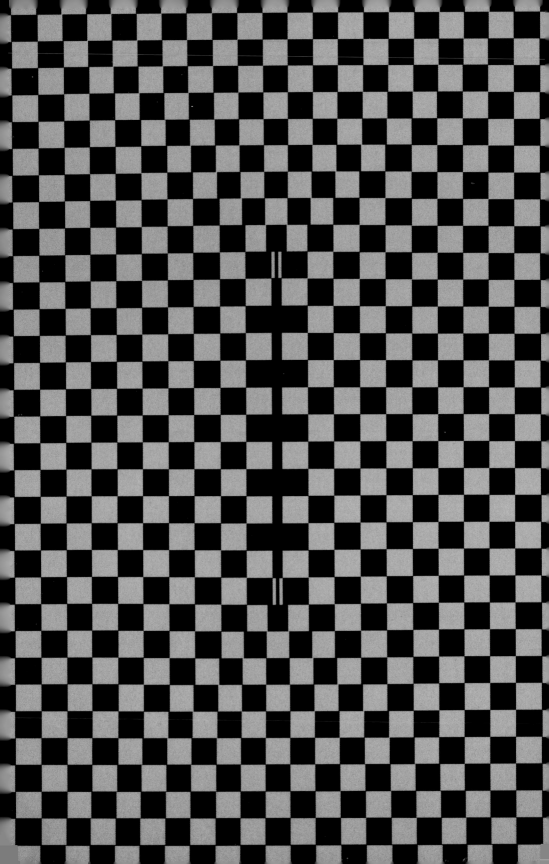

CHAPTER 1

THE HUT

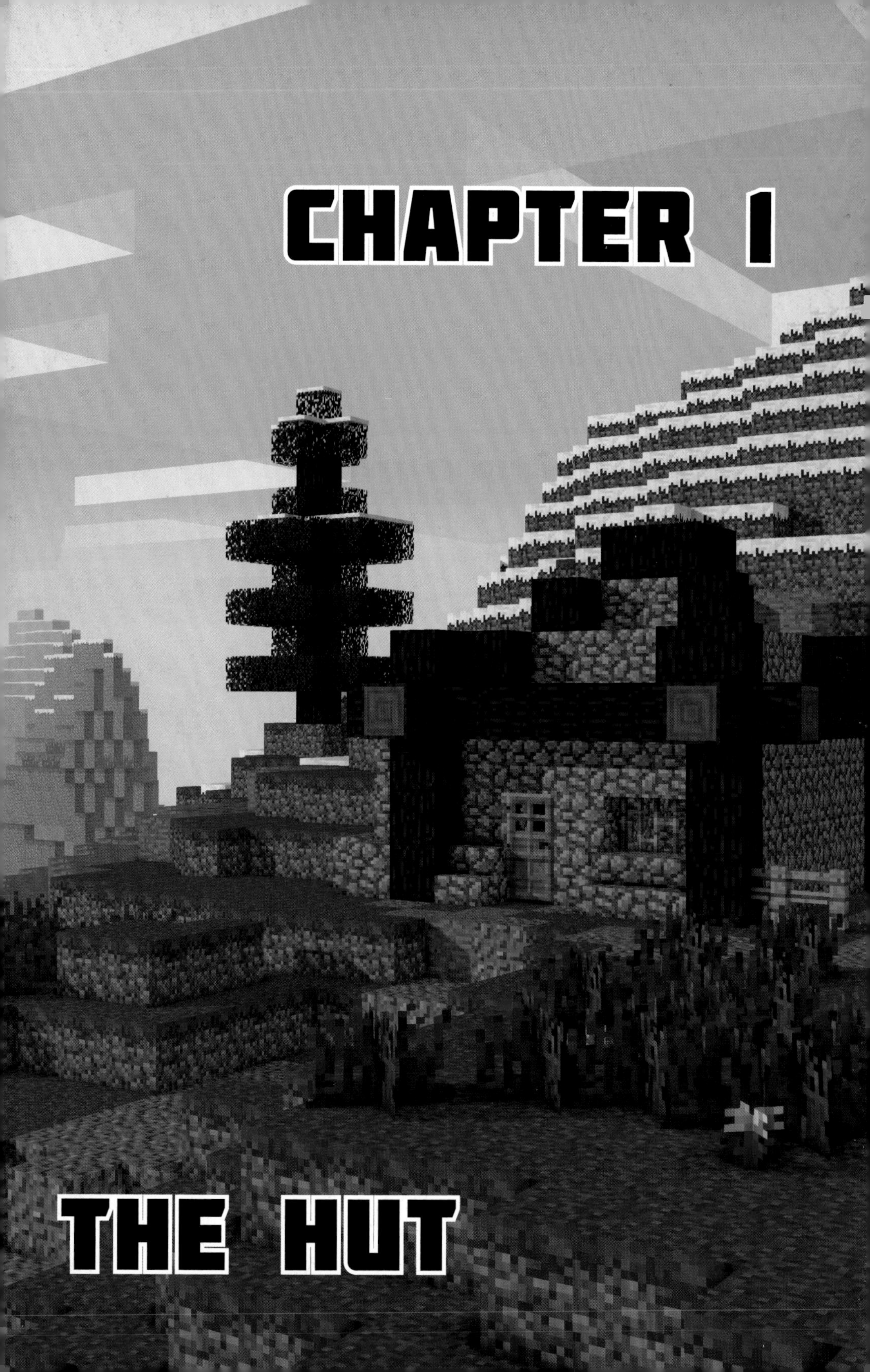

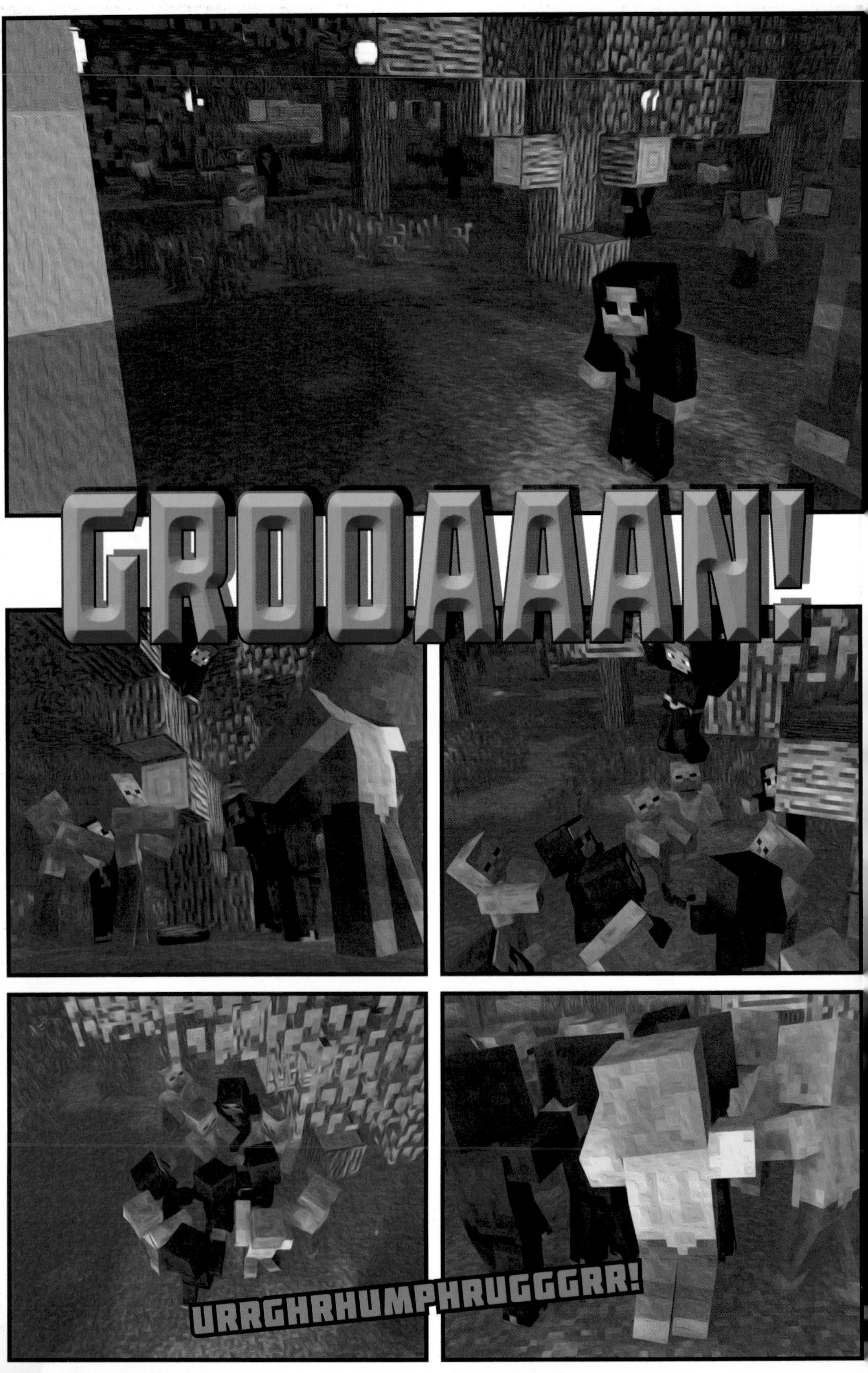
GROOAAAN!
URRGHRHUMPHRUGGGRR!

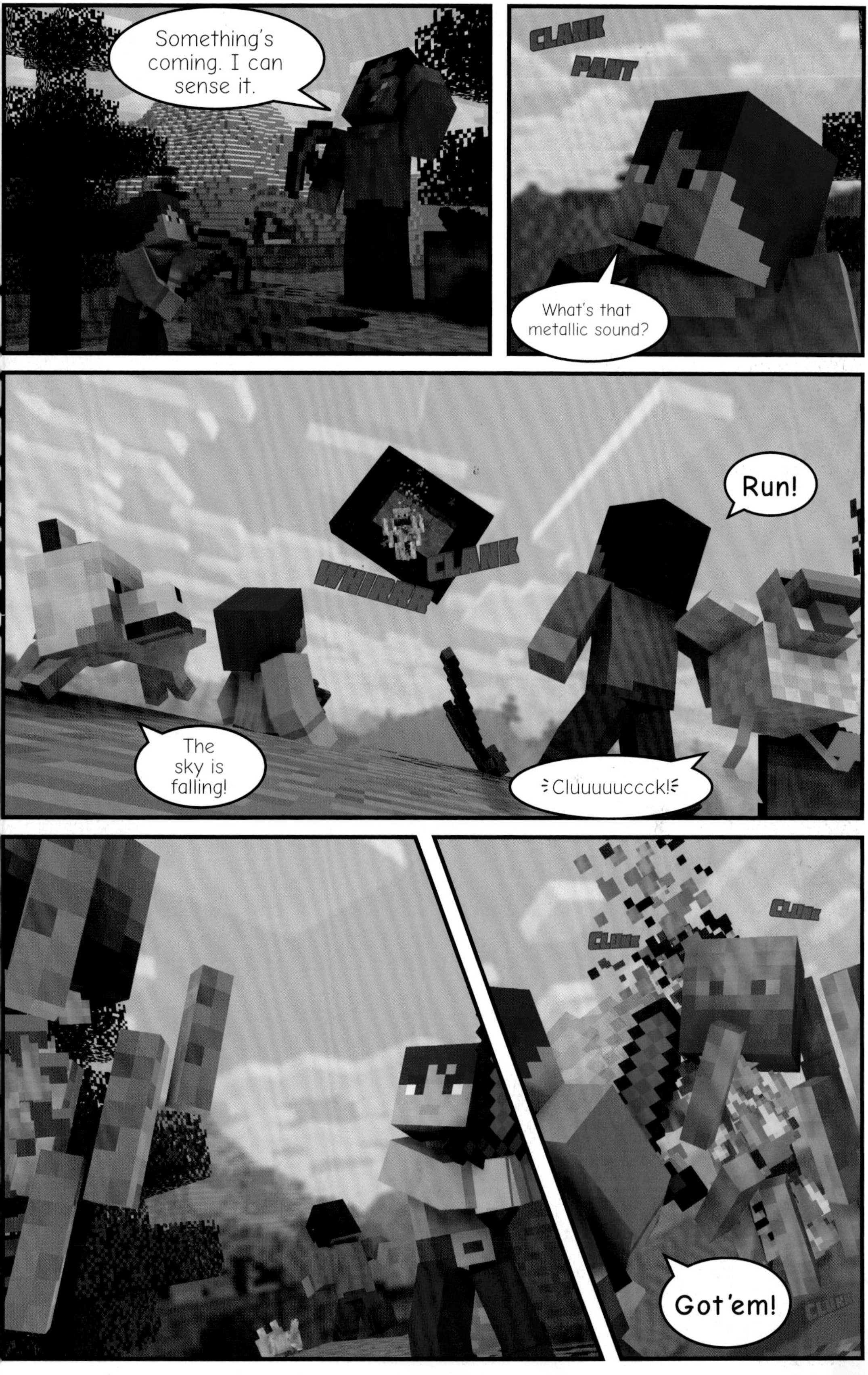
Something's coming. I can sense it.
CLANK
PANT
What's that metallic sound?
WHIRRR
CLANK
Run!
The sky is falling!
Cluuuuuccck!
Got'em!

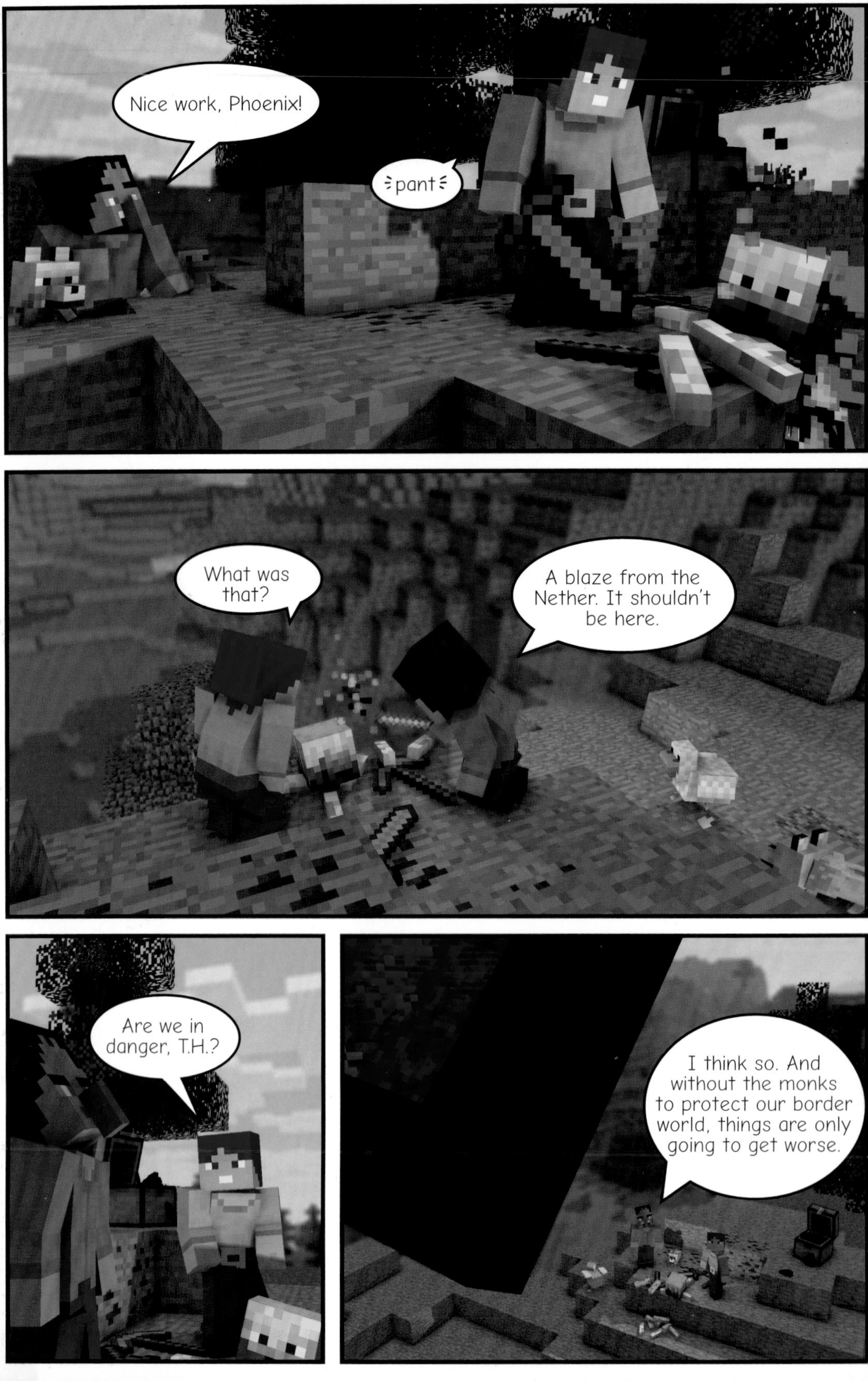
Nice work, Phoenix!
pant
What was that?
A blaze from the Nether. It shouldn't be here.
Are we in danger, T.H.?
I think so. And without the monks to protect our border world, things are only going to get worse.

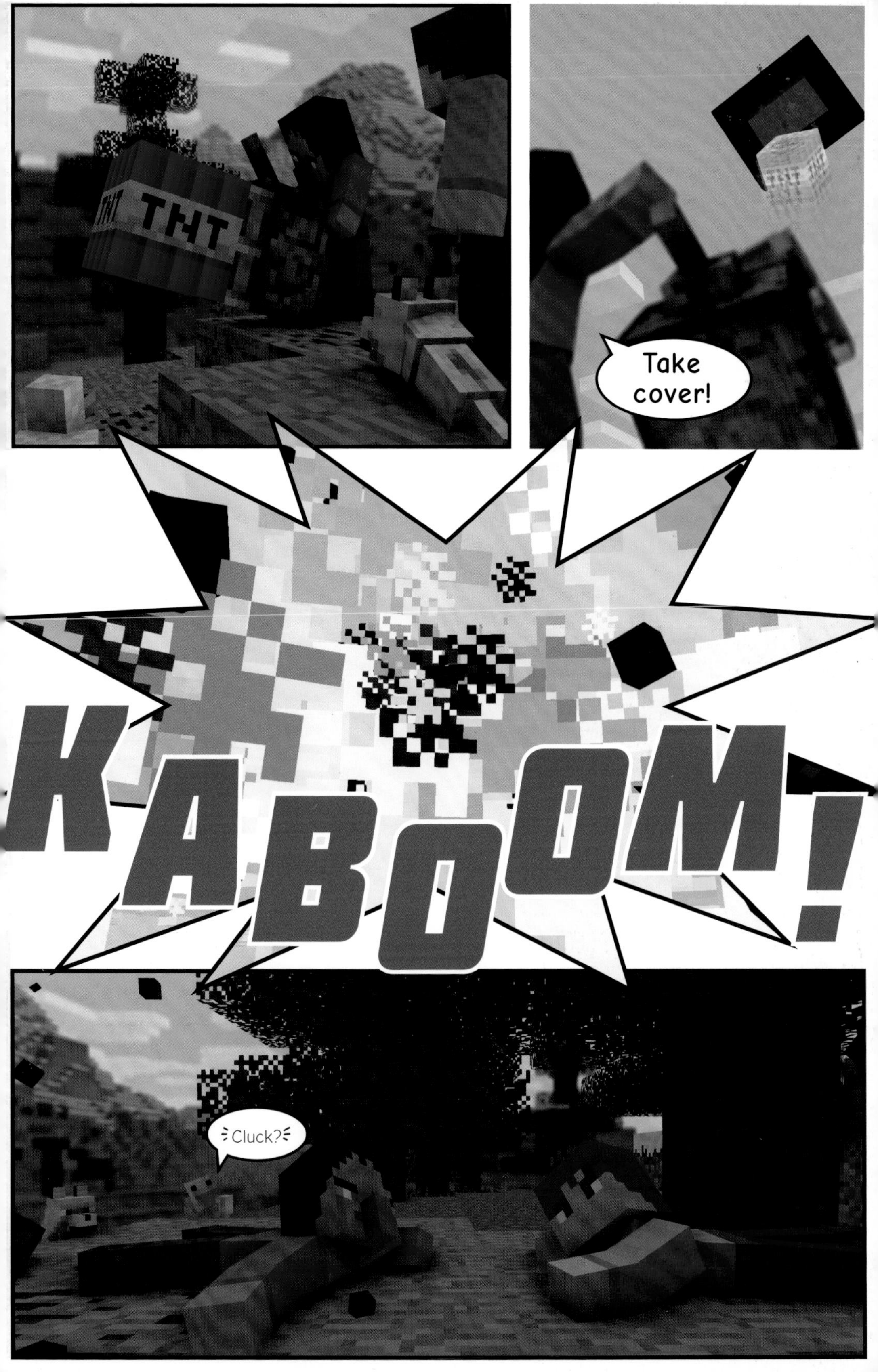
Take cover!
KABOOM!
Cluck?

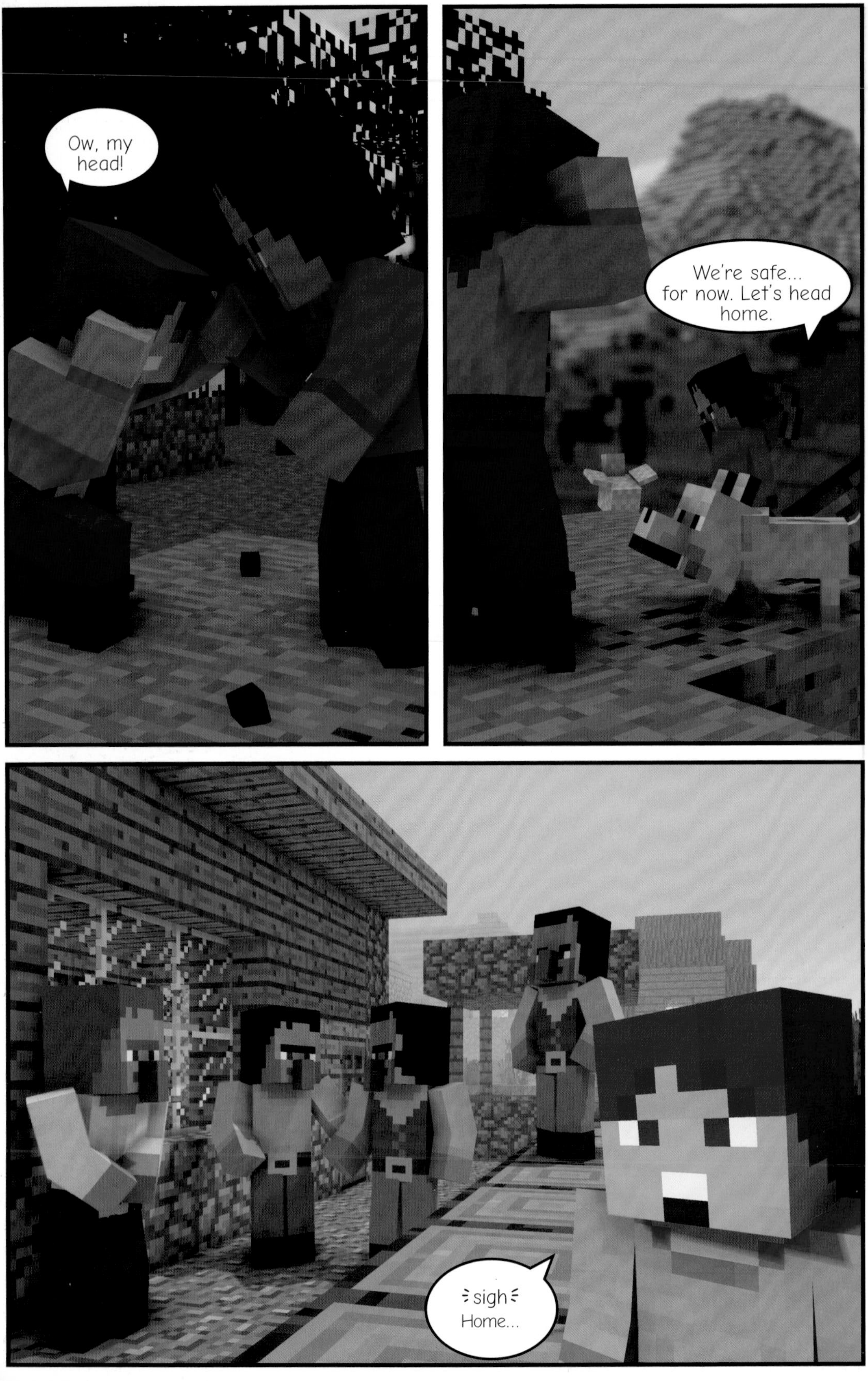
Ow, my head!
We're safe... for now. Let's head home.
sigh
Home...

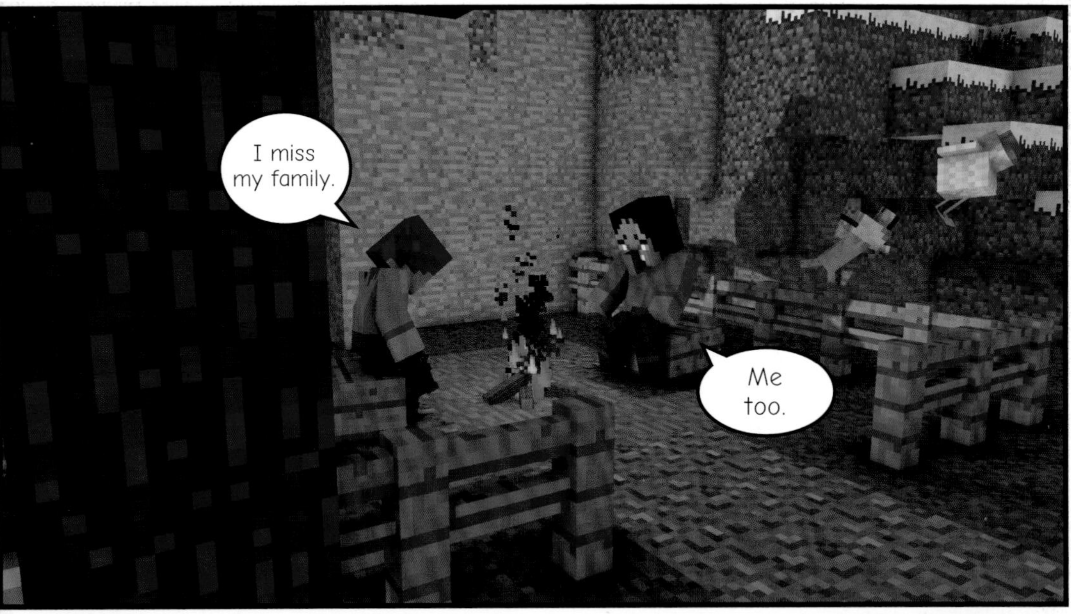
I miss my family.
Me too.

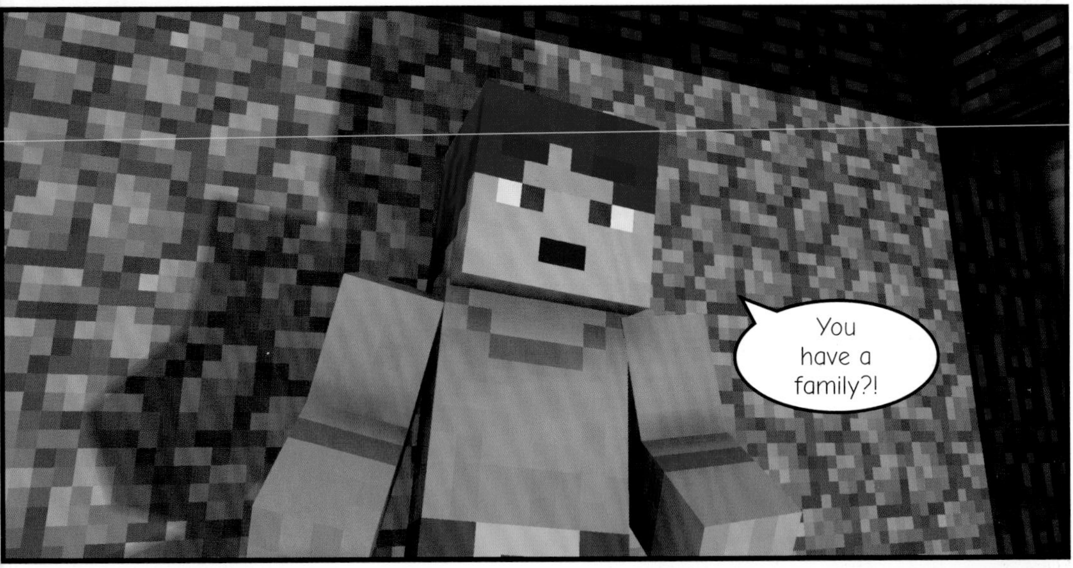
You have a family?!

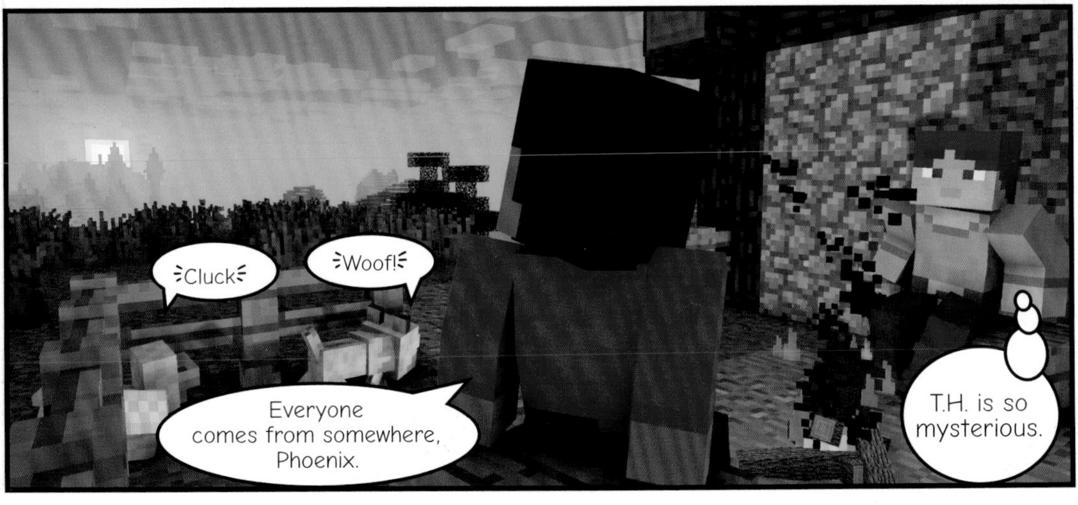
Cluck
Woof!
Everyone comes from somewhere, Phoenix.
T.H. is so mysterious.

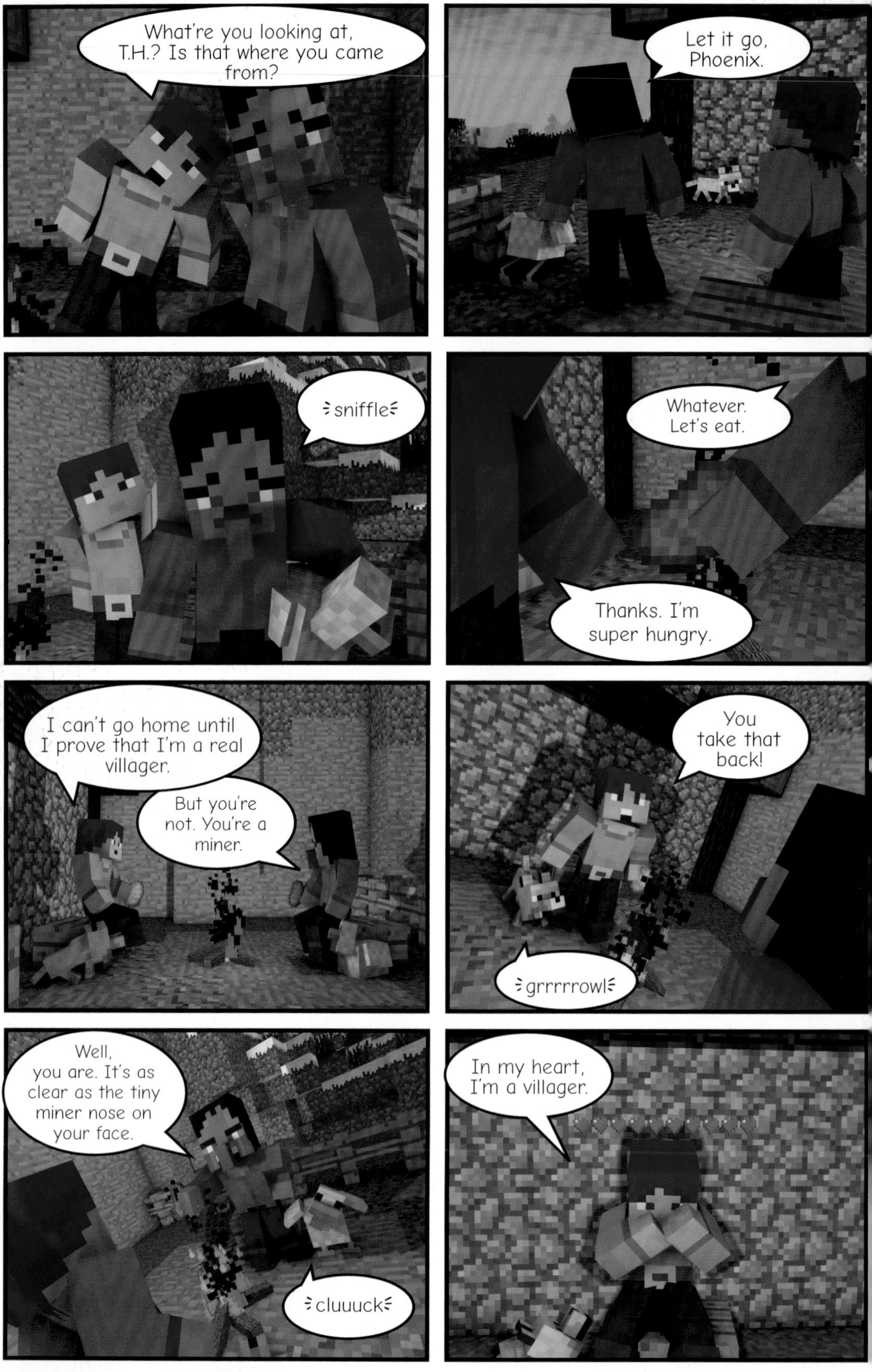

What're you looking at, T.H.? Is that where you came from?
Let it go, Phoenix.
sniffle
Whatever. Let's eat.
Thanks. I'm super hungry.
I can't go home until I prove that I'm a real villager.
But you're not. You're a miner.
You take that back!
grrrrrowl
Well, you are. It's as clear as the tiny miner nose on your face.
cluuuck
In my heart, I'm a villager.

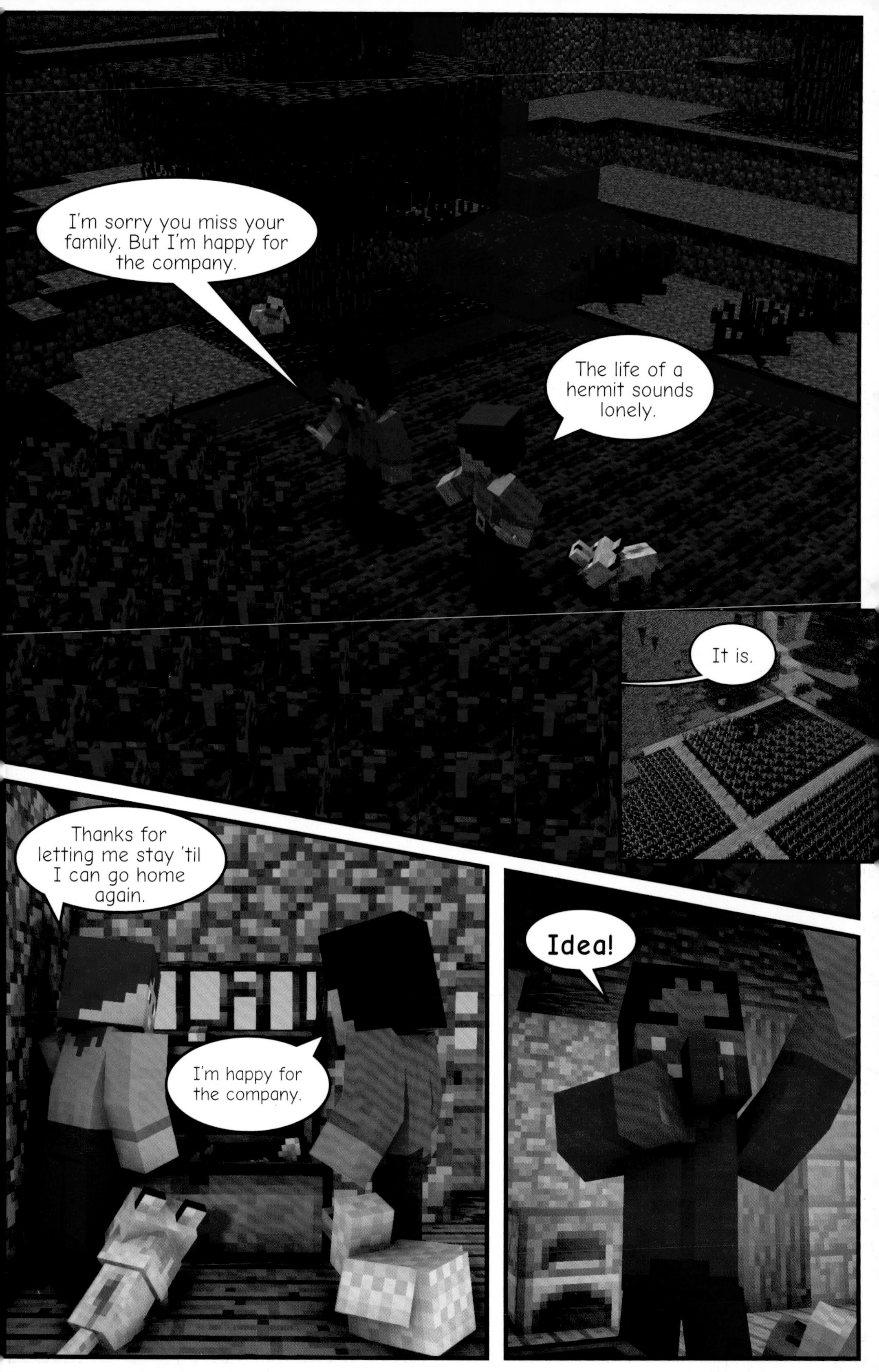

I'm sorry you miss your family. But I'm happy for the company.
The life of a hermit sounds lonely.
It is.
Thanks for letting me stay 'til I can go home again.
I'm happy for the company.
Idea!

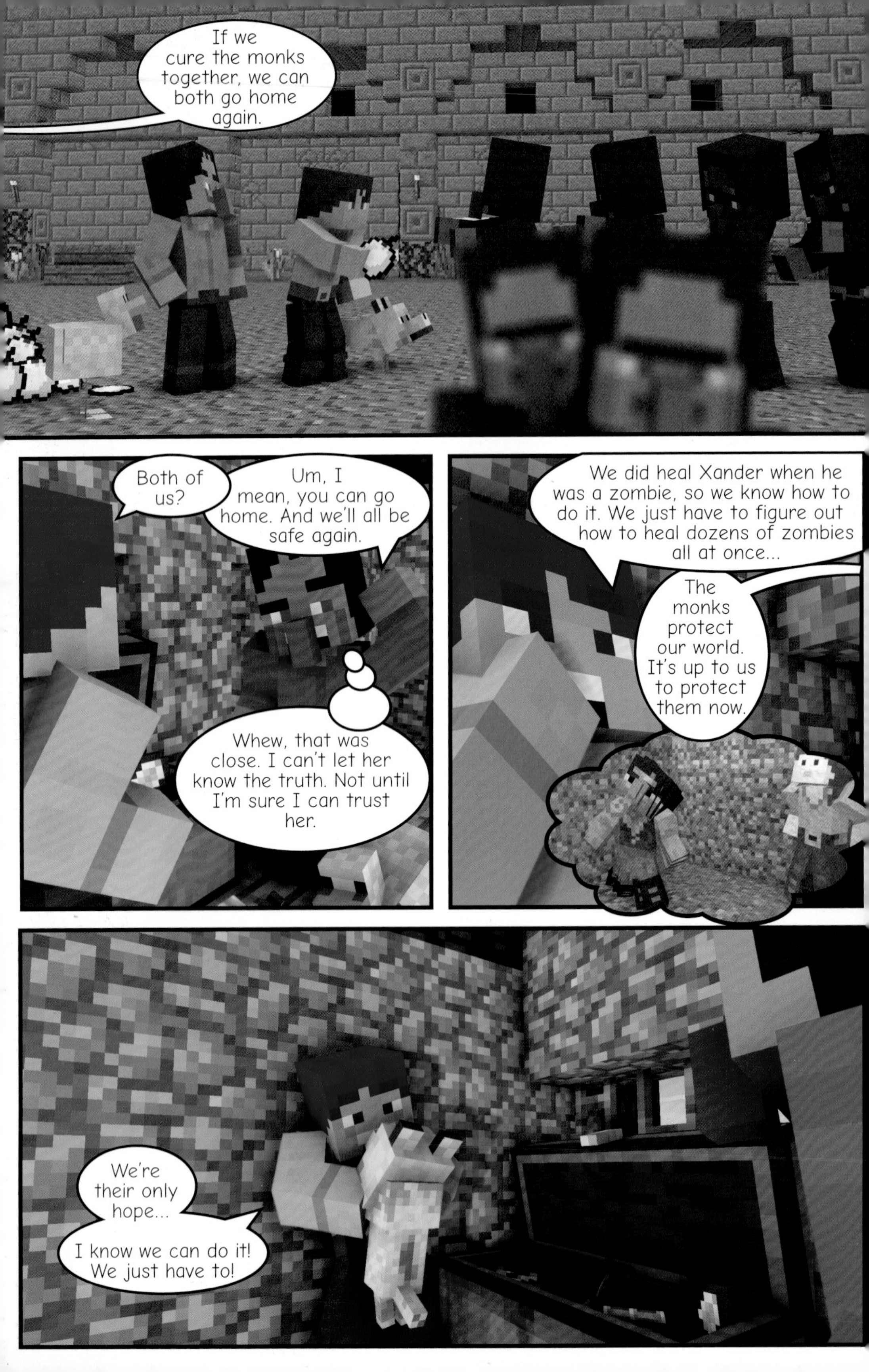

If we cure the monks together, we can both go home again.
Both of us?
Um, I mean, you can go home. And we'll all be safe again.
Whew, that was close. I can't let her know the truth. Not until I'm sure I can trust her.
We did heal Xander when he was a zombie, so we know how to do it. We just have to figure out how to heal dozens of zombies all at once...
The monks protect our world. It's up to us to protect them now.
We're their only hope...
I know we can do it! We just have to!

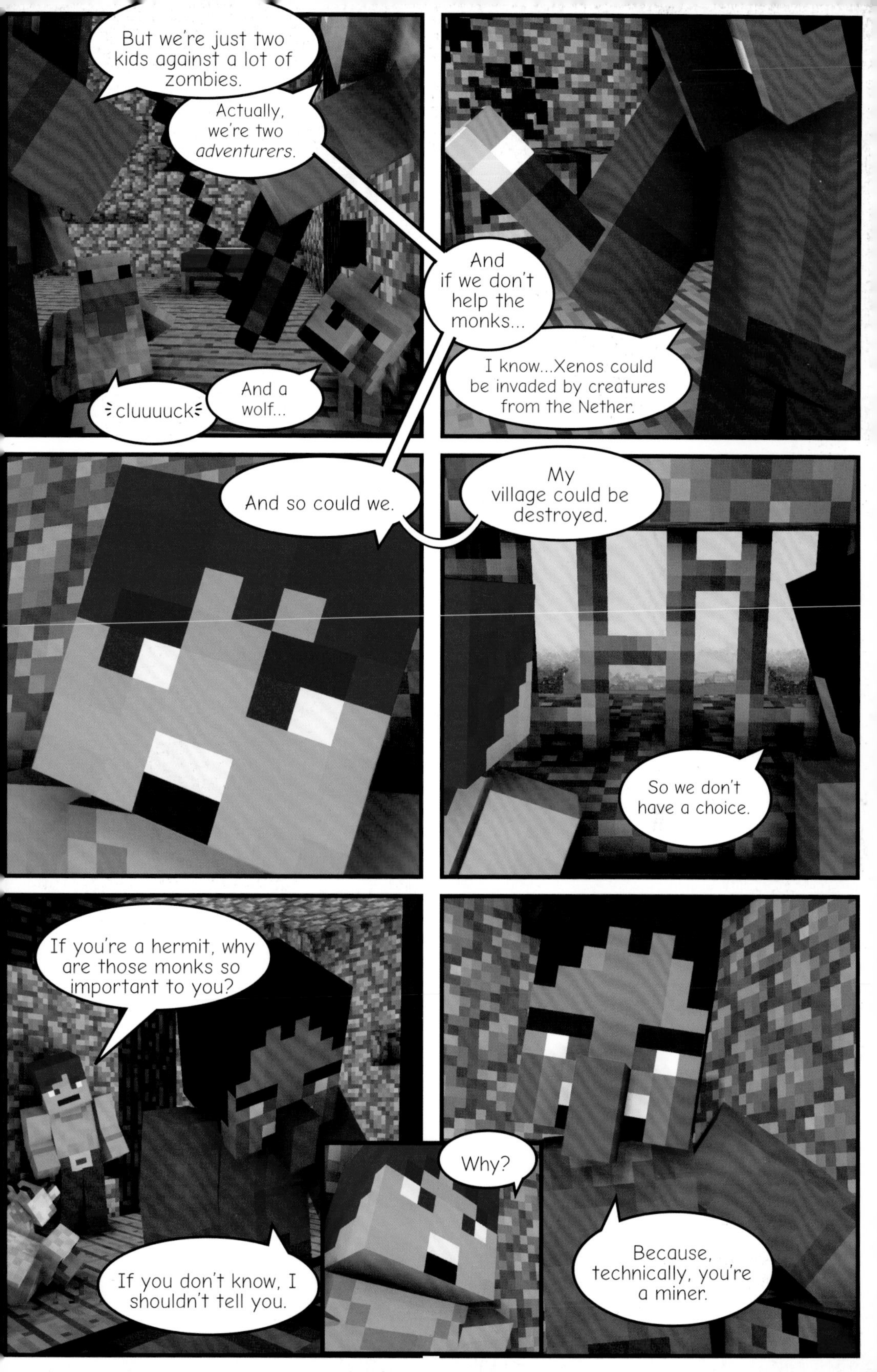

But we're just two kids against a lot of zombies.
Actually, we're two *adventurers*.
cluuuuck
And a wolf...
And if we don't help the monks...
I know...Xenos could be invaded by creatures from the Nether.
And so could we.
My village could be destroyed.
So we don't have a choice.
If you're a hermit, why are those monks so important to you?
If you don't know, I shouldn't tell you.
Why?
Because, technically, you're a miner.

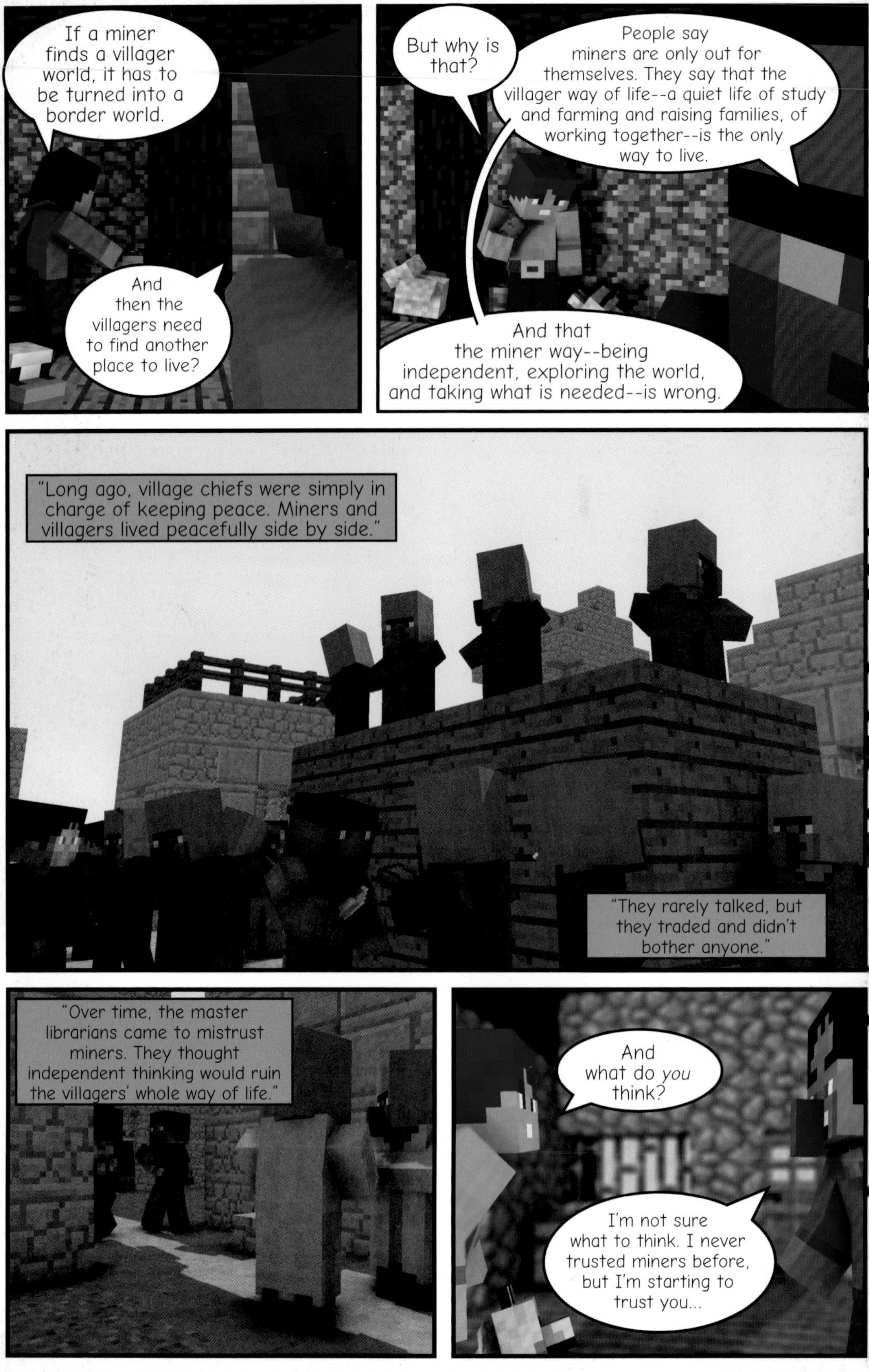
If a miner finds a villager world, it has to be turned into a border world.
And then the villagers need to find another place to live?
But why is that?
People say miners are only out for themselves. They say that the villager way of life--a quiet life of study and farming and raising families, of working together--is the only way to live.
And that the miner way--being independent, exploring the world, and taking what is needed--is wrong.
"Long ago, village chiefs were simply in charge of keeping peace. Miners and villagers lived peacefully side by side."
"They rarely talked, but they traded and didn't bother anyone."
"Over time, the master librarians came to mistrust miners. They thought independent thinking would ruin the villagers' whole way of life."
And what do *you* think?
I'm not sure what to think. I never trusted miners before, but I'm starting to trust you...

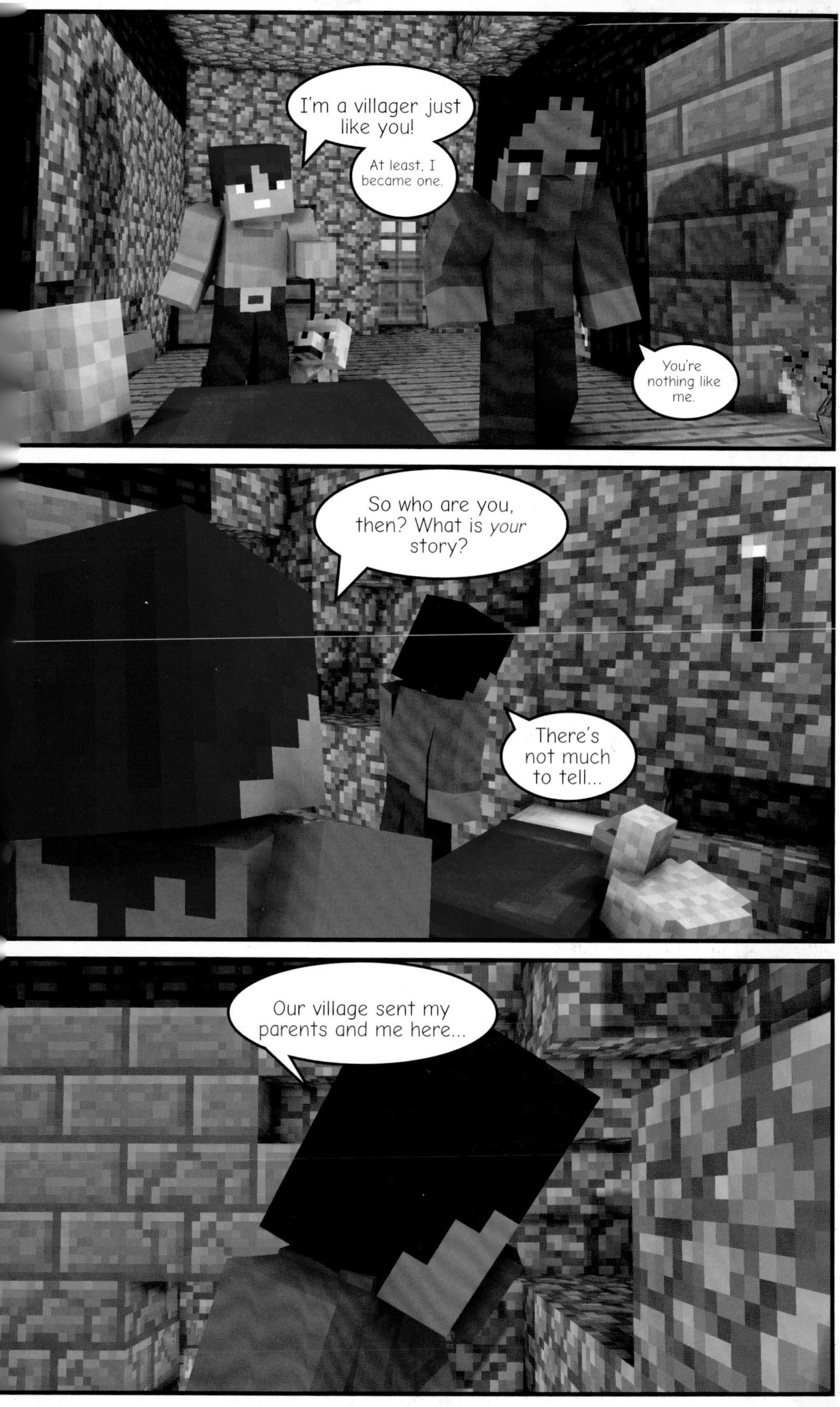
I'm a villager just like you!
At least, I became one.
You're nothing like me.
So who are you, then? What is *your* story?
There's not much to tell...
Our village sent my parents and me here...

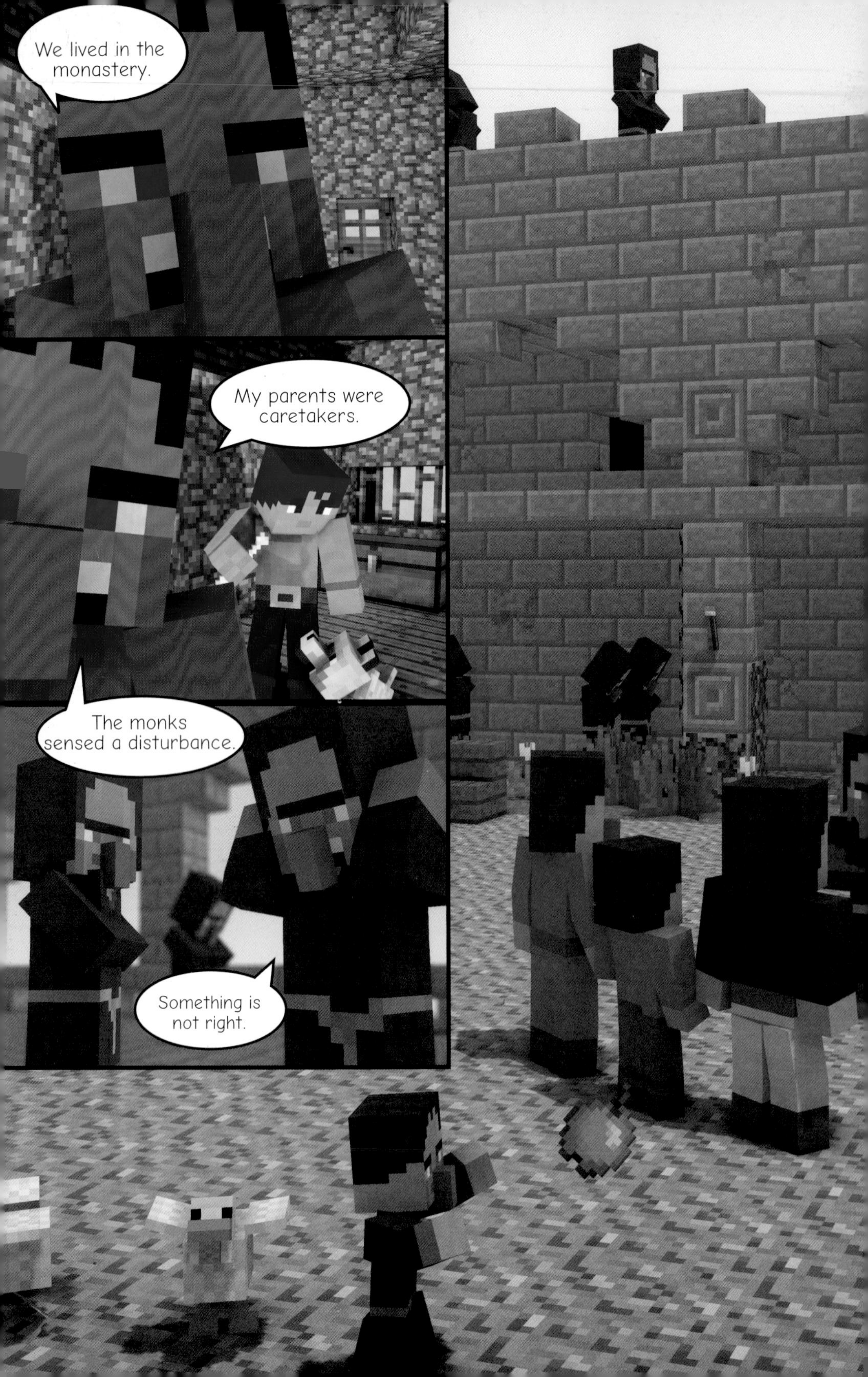

We lived in the monastery.
My parents were caretakers.
The monks sensed a disturbance.
Something is not right.

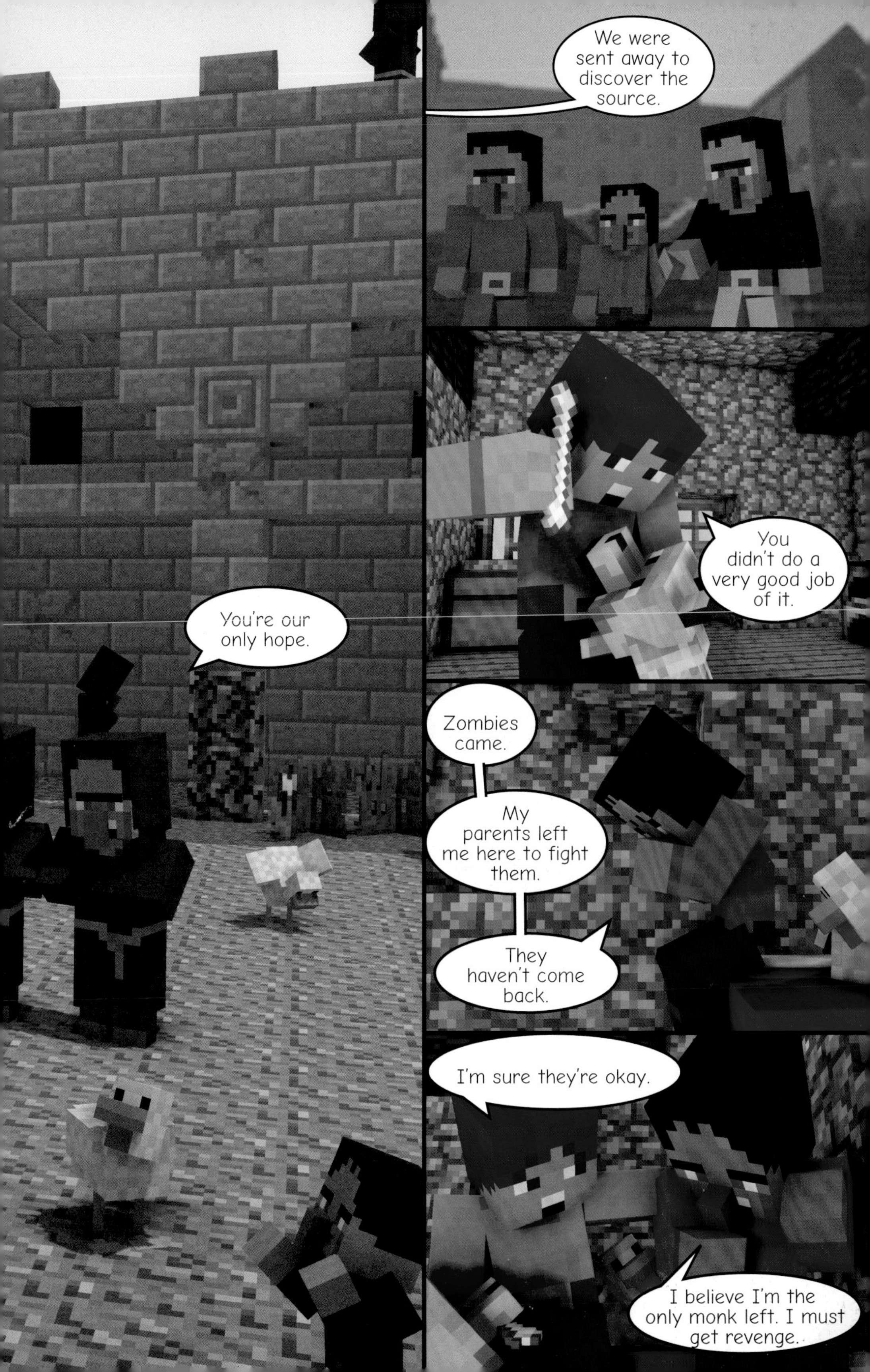
You're our only hope.
We were sent away to discover the source.
You didn't do a very good job of it.
Zombies came.
My parents left me here to fight them.
They haven't come back.
I'm sure they're okay.
I believe I'm the only monk left. I must get revenge.

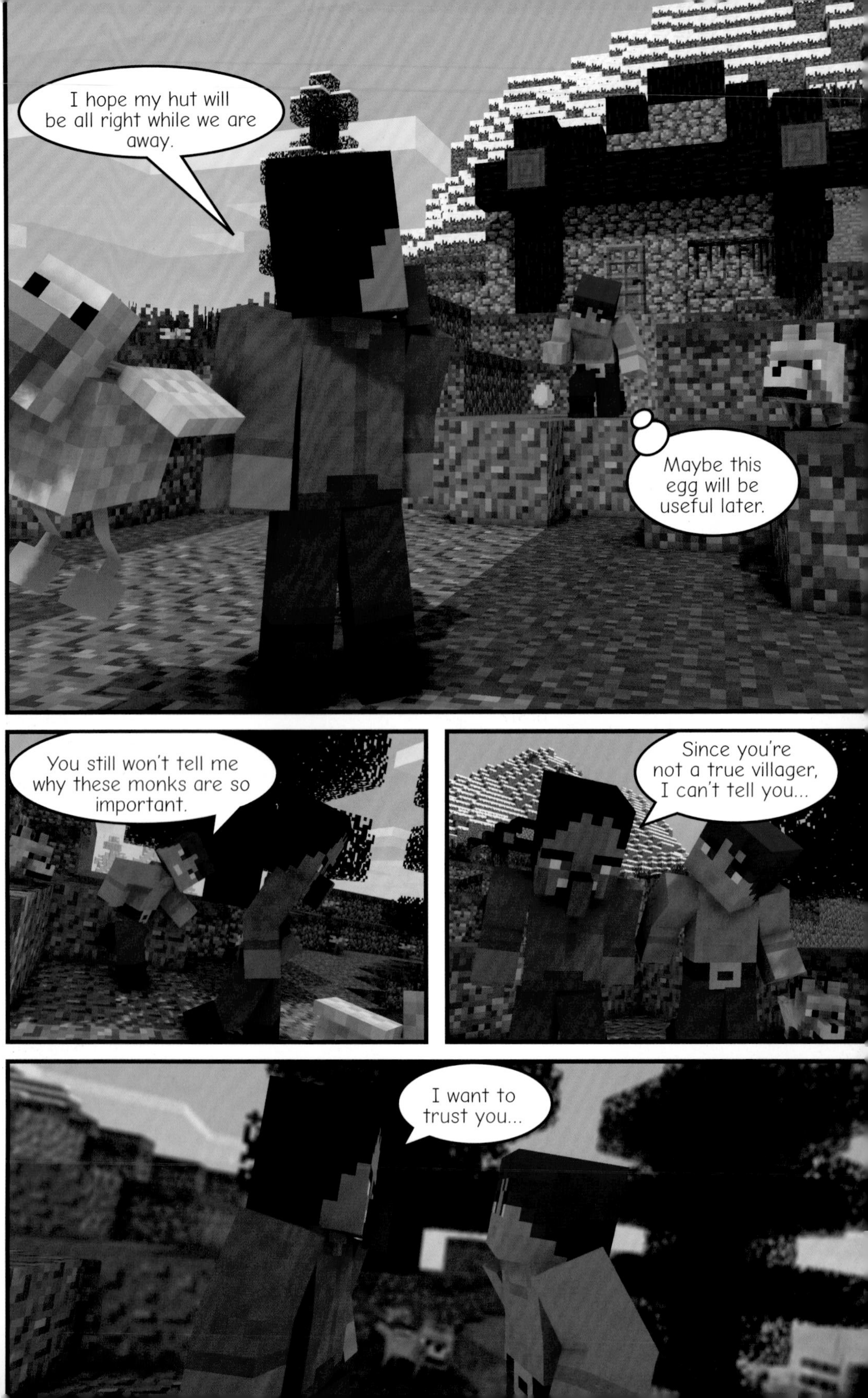
I hope my hut will be all right while we are away.
Maybe this egg will be useful later.
You still won't tell me why these monks are so important.
Since you're not a true villager, I can't tell you...
I want to trust you...

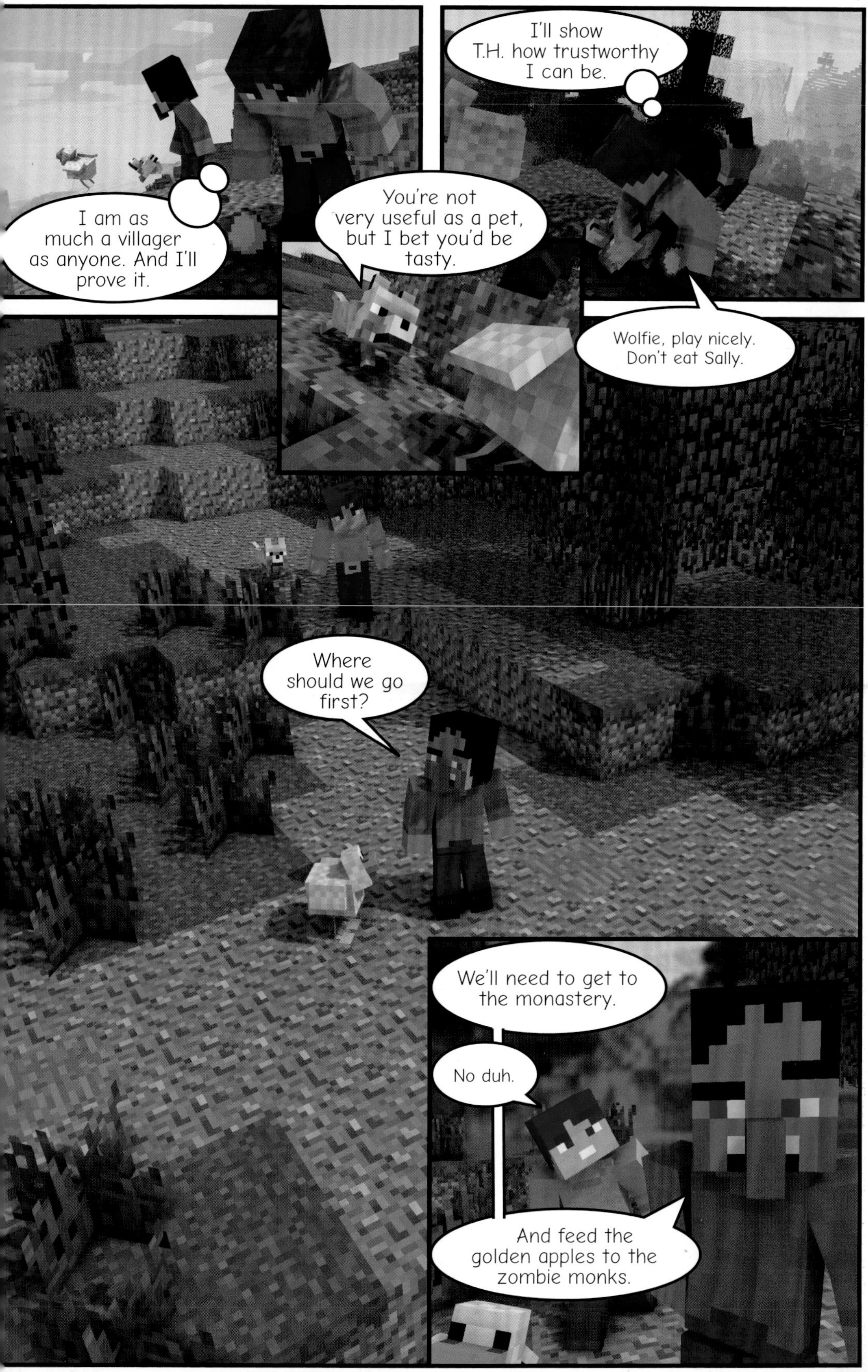
I am as much a villager as anyone. And I'll prove it.
I'll show T.H. how trustworthy I can be.
You're not very useful as a pet, but I bet you'd be tasty.
Wolfie, play nicely. Don't eat Sally.
Where should we go first?
We'll need to get to the monastery.
No duh.
And feed the golden apples to the zombie monks.

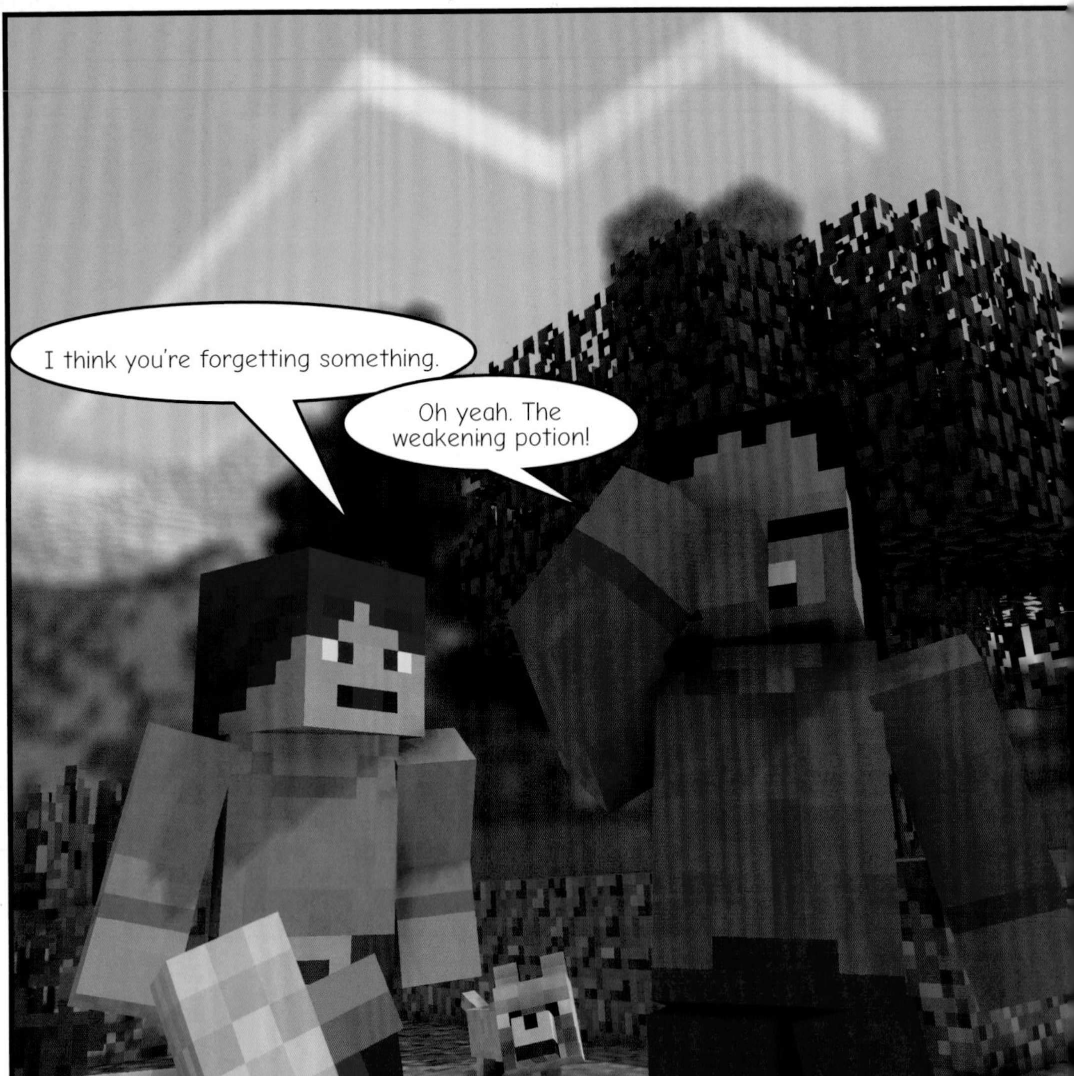
I think you're forgetting something.
Oh yeah. The weakening potion!

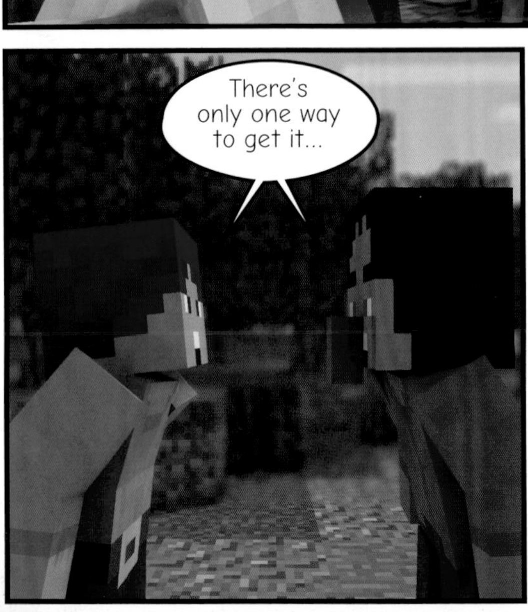
There's only one way to get it...

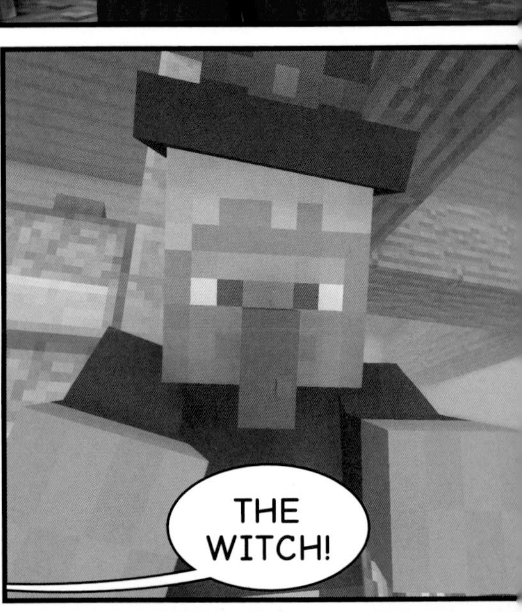
THE WITCH!

CHAPTER 2

THE WITCH

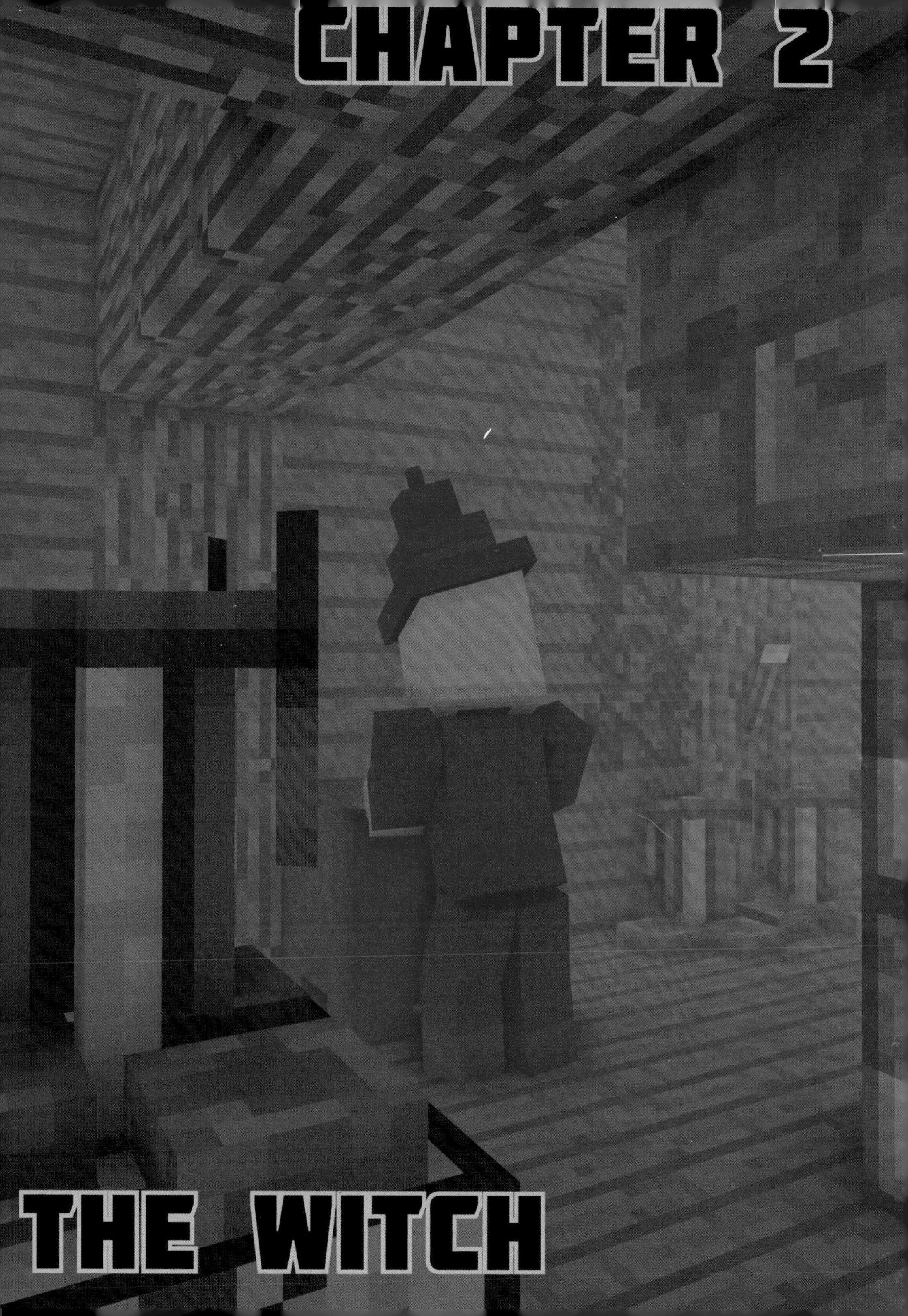

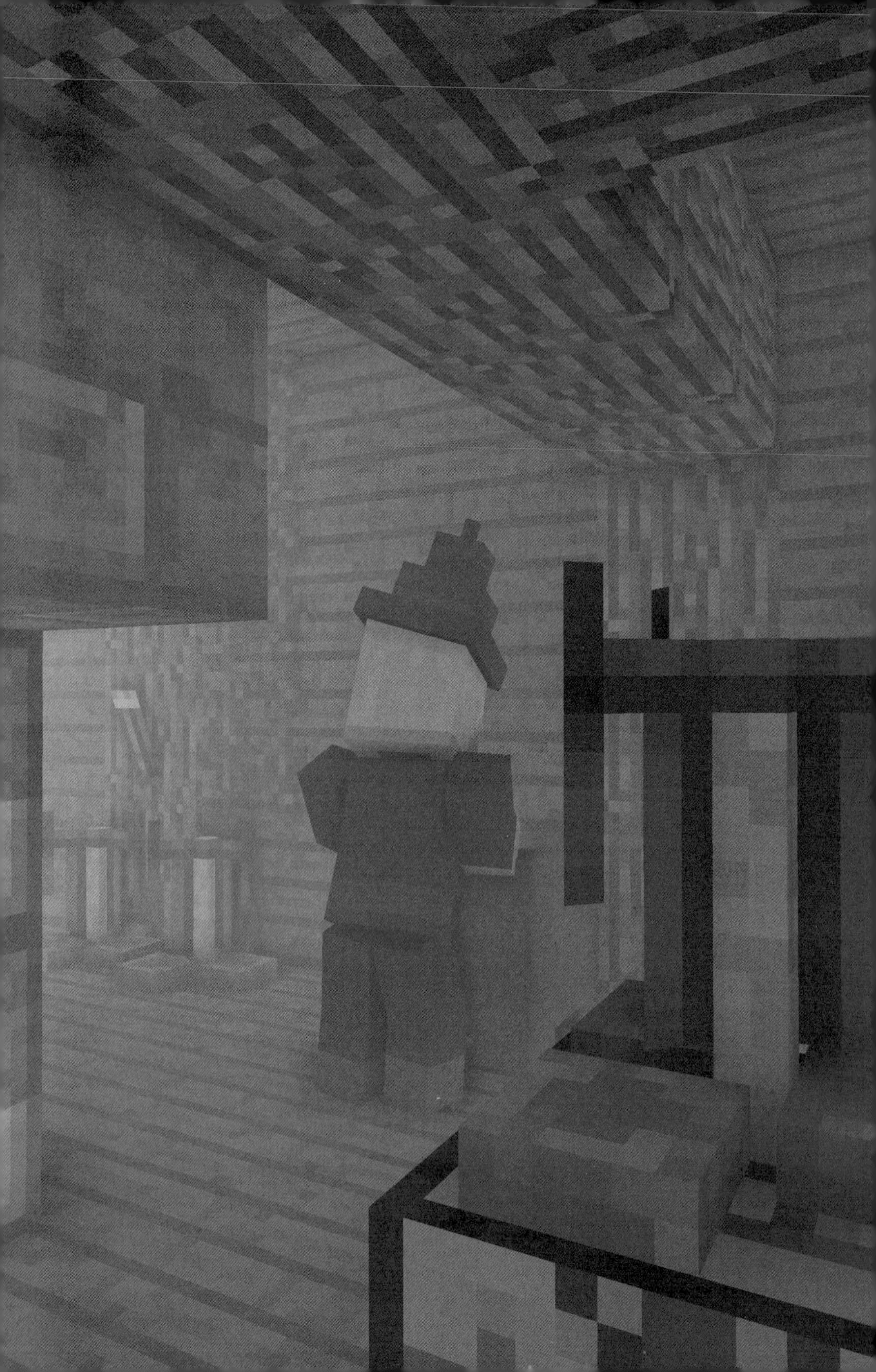

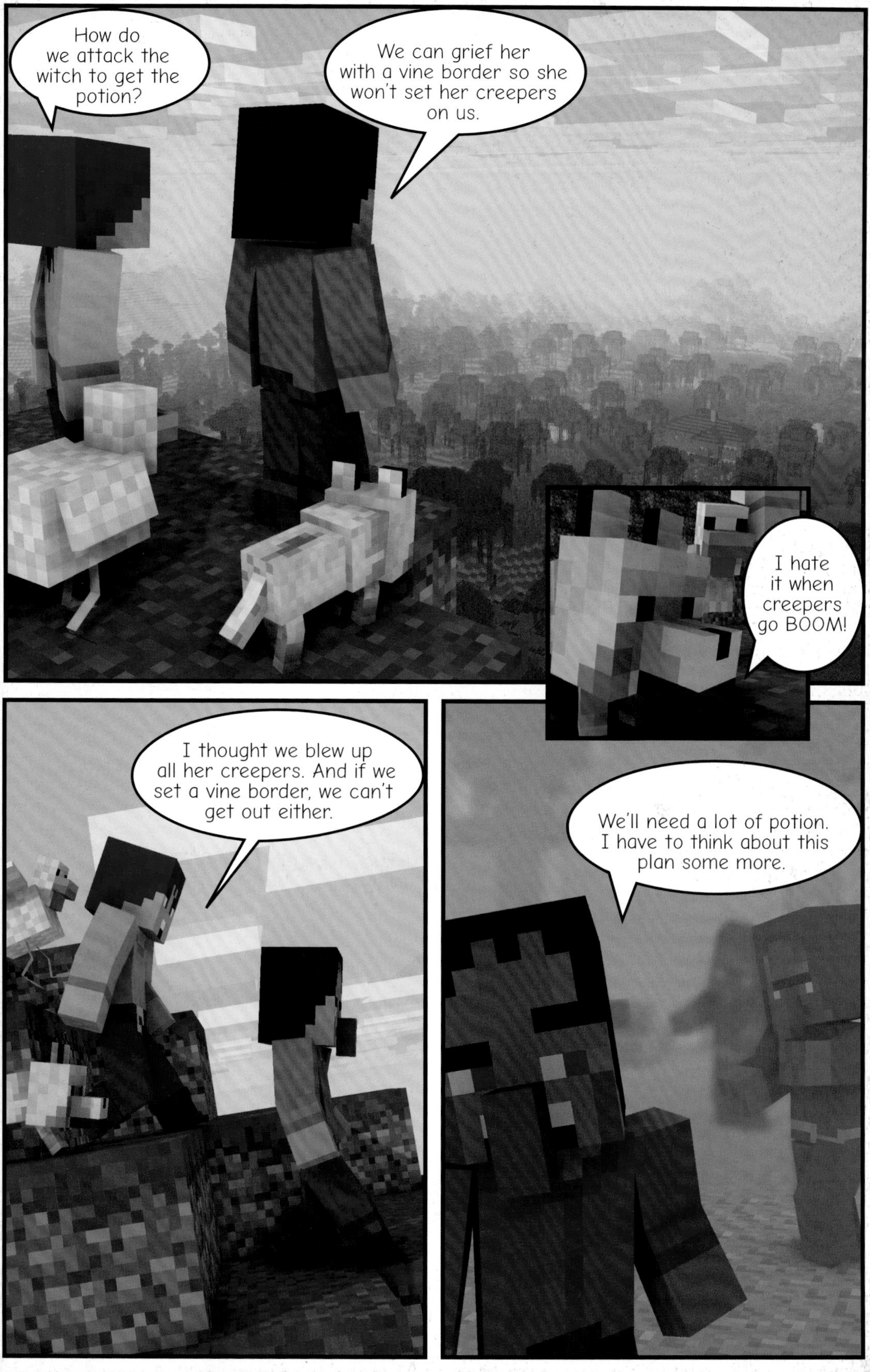
How do we attack the witch to get the potion?
We can grief her with a vine border so she won't set her creepers on us.
I hate it when creepers go BOOM!
I thought we blew up all her creepers. And if we set a vine border, we can't get out either.
We'll need a lot of potion. I have to think about this plan some more.

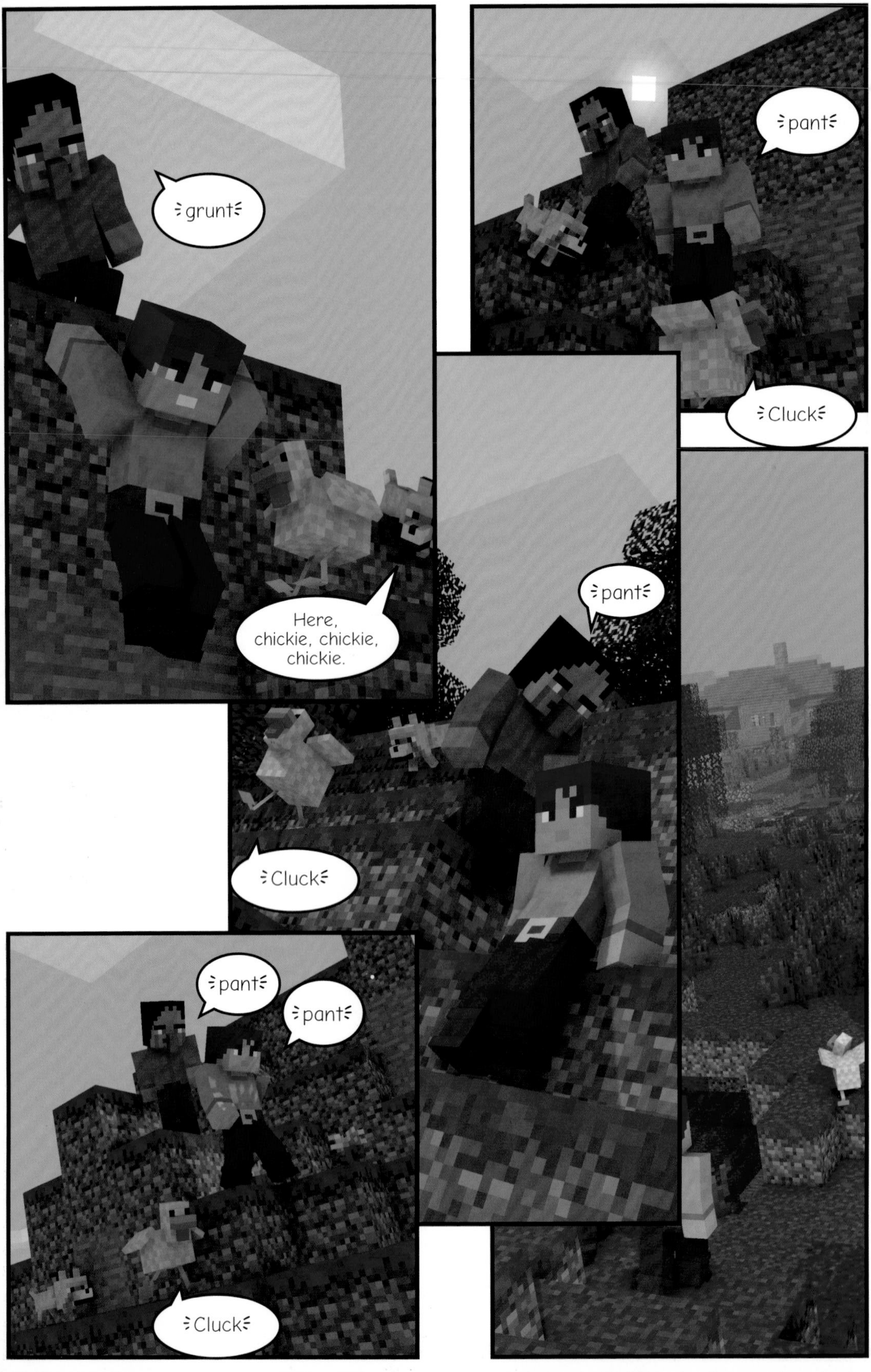
grunt
Here, chickie, chickie, chickie.
pant
Cluck
pant
Cluck
pant
pant
Cluck

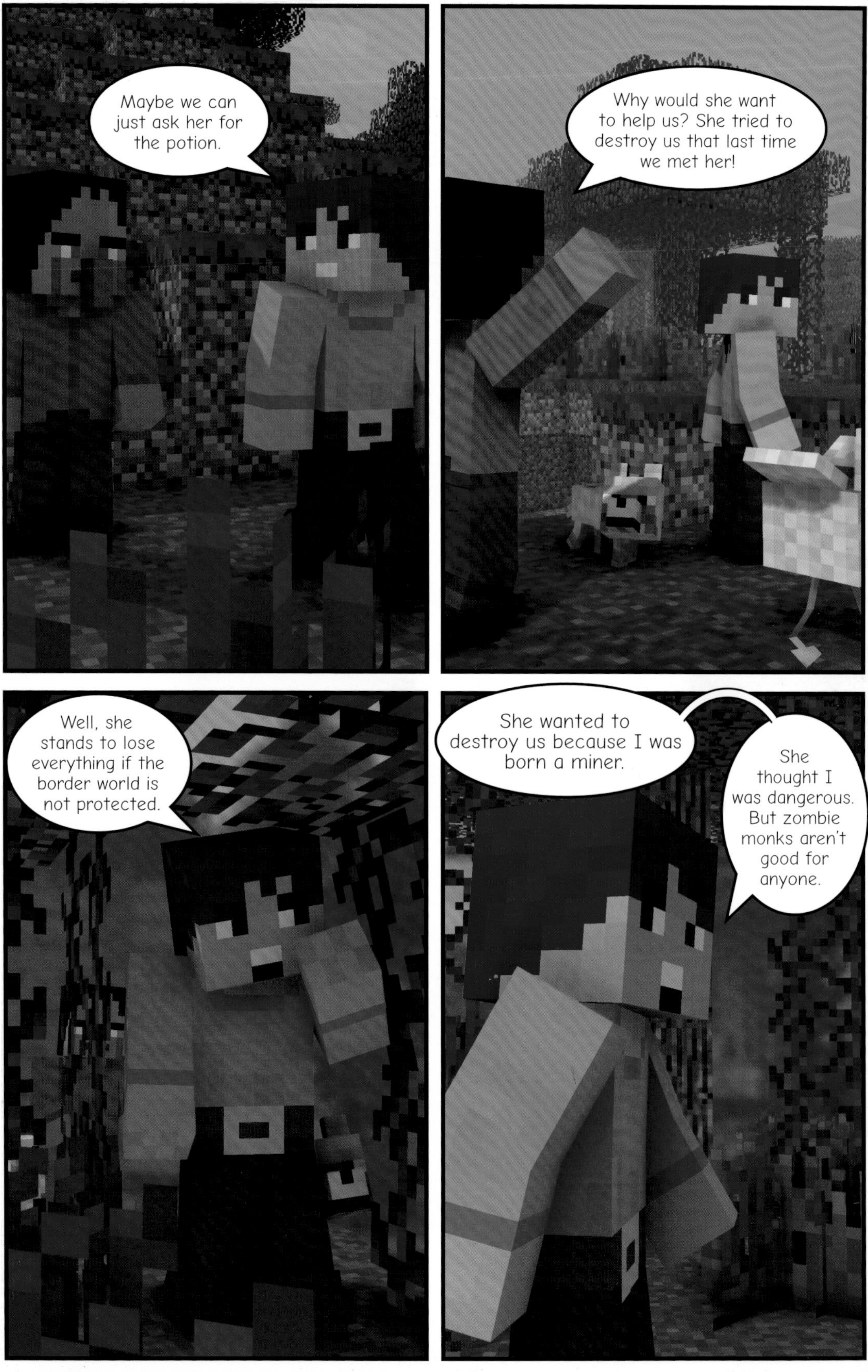
Maybe we can just ask her for the potion.
Why would she want to help us? She tried to destroy us that last time we met her!
Well, she stands to lose everything if the border world is not protected.
She wanted to destroy us because I was born a miner.
She thought I was dangerous. But zombie monks aren't good for anyone.

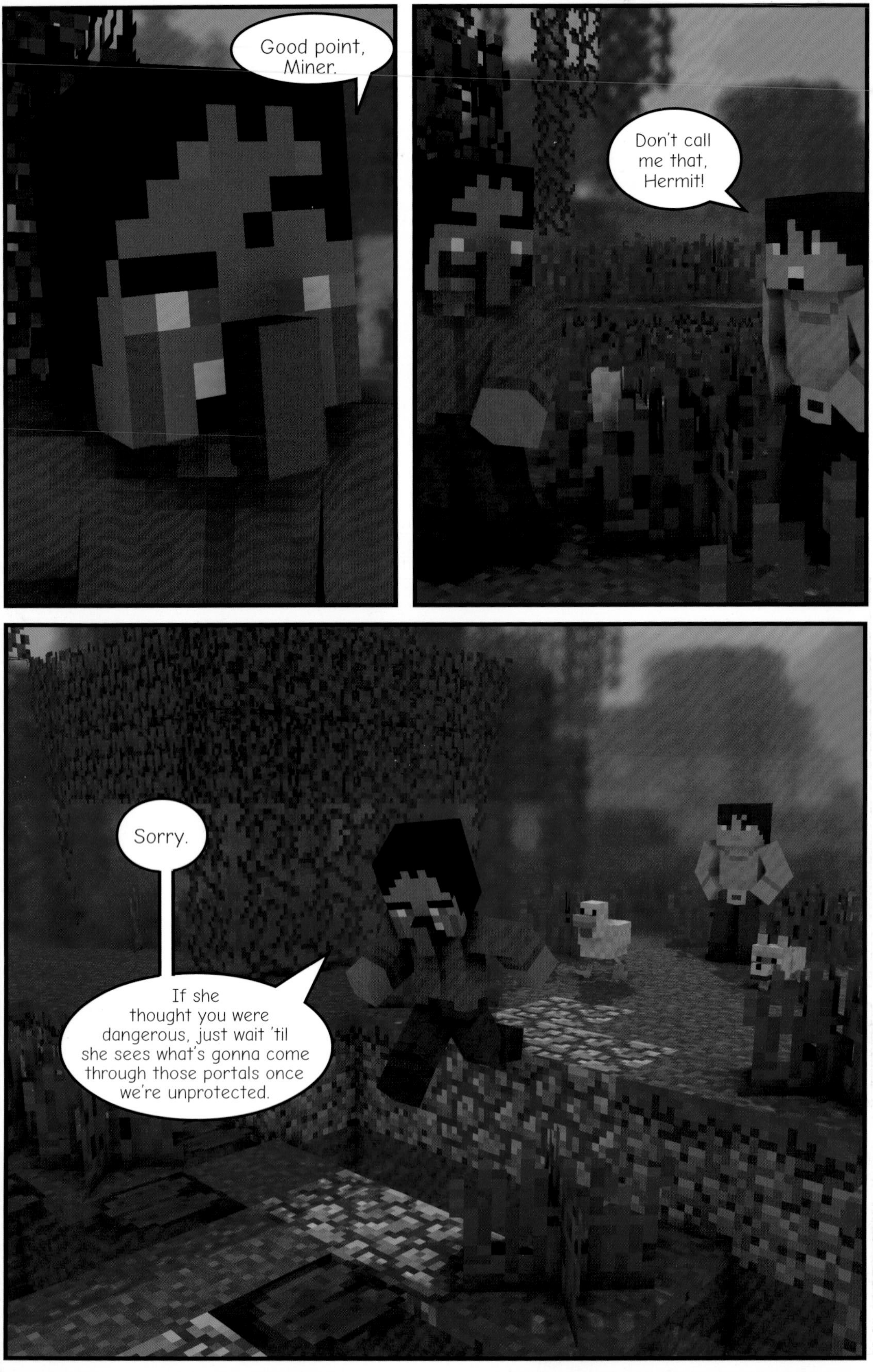
Good point, Miner.
Don't call me that, Hermit!
Sorry.
If she thought you were dangerous, just wait 'til she sees what's gonna come through those portals once we're unprotected.

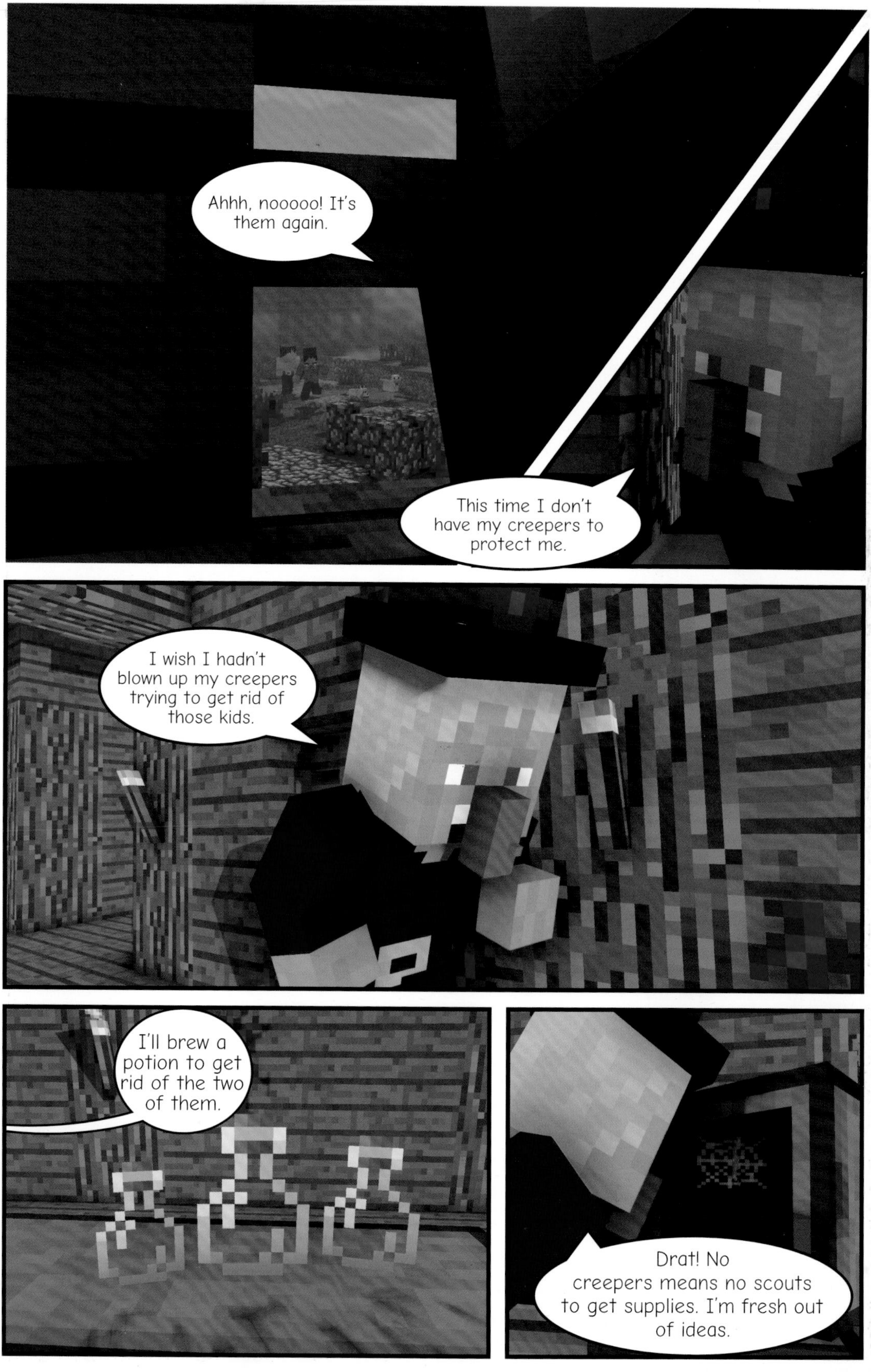
Ahhh, nooooo! It's them again.
This time I don't have my creepers to protect me.
I wish I hadn't blown up my creepers trying to get rid of those kids.
I'll brew a potion to get rid of the two of them.
Drat! No creepers means no scouts to get supplies. I'm fresh out of ideas.

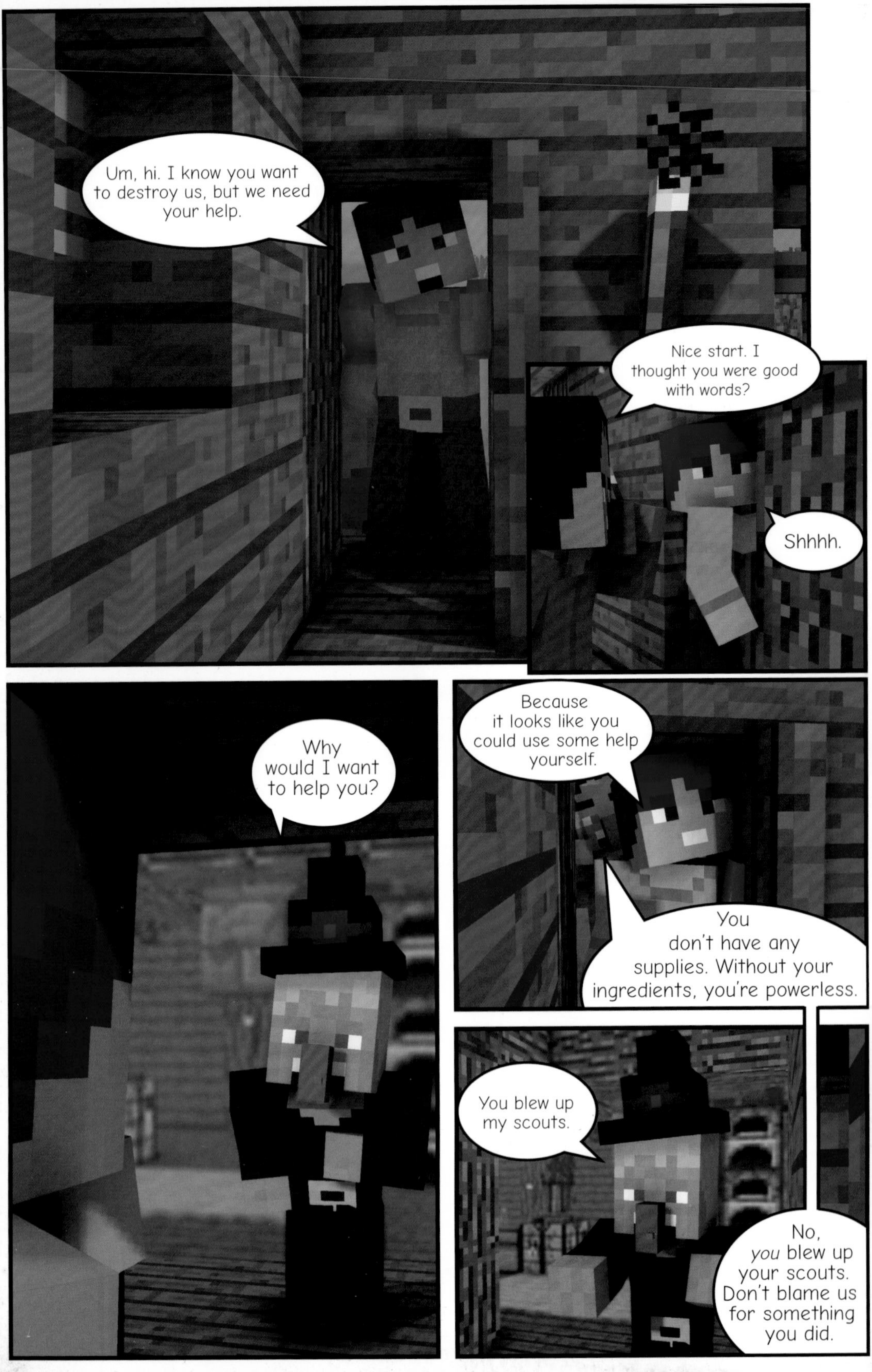
Um, hi. I know you want to destroy us, but we need your help.
Nice start. I thought you were good with words?
Shhhh.
Why would I want to help you?
Because it looks like you could use some help yourself.
You don't have any supplies. Without your ingredients, you're powerless.
You blew up my scouts.
No, *you* blew up your scouts. Don't blame us for something you did.

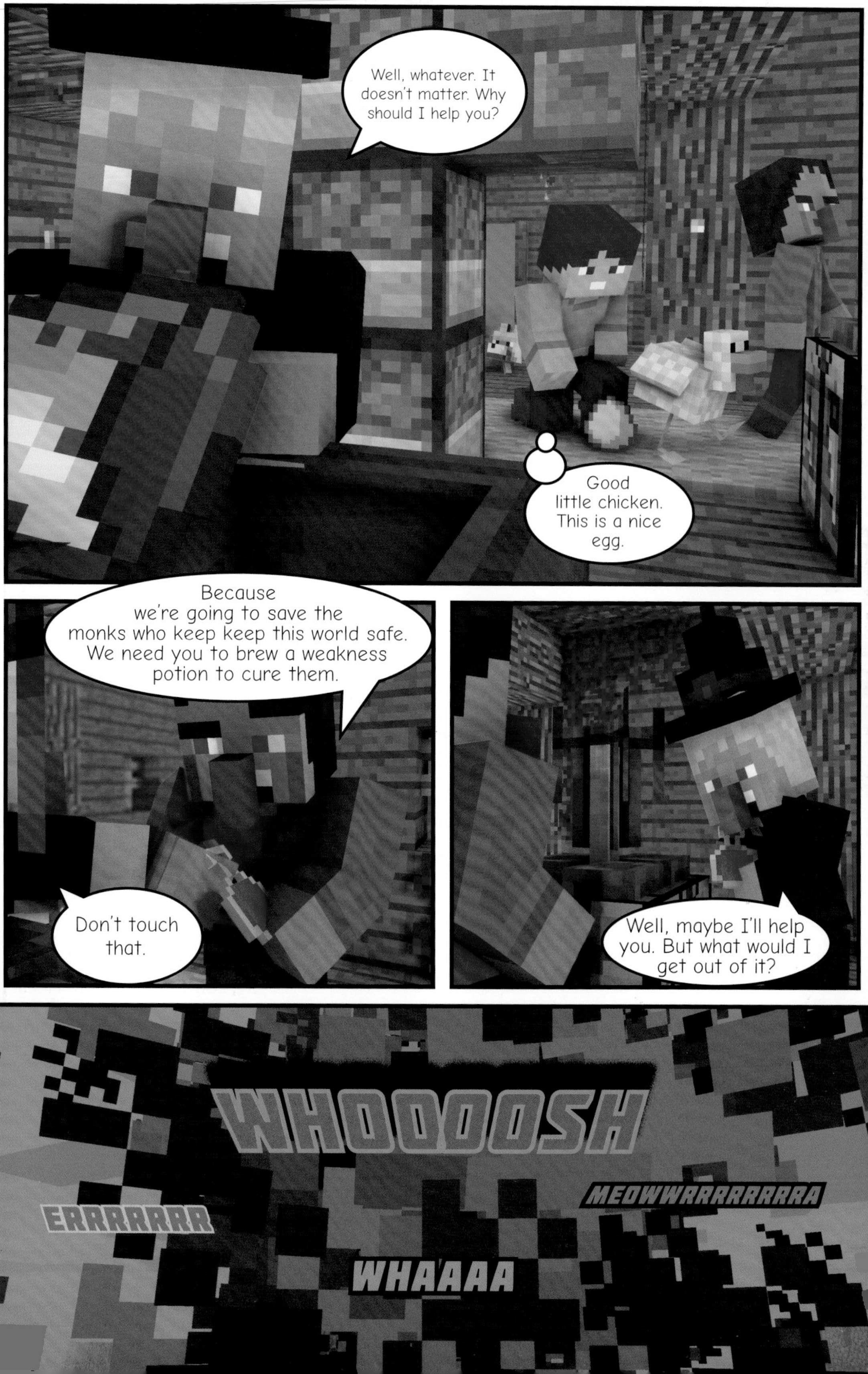
Well, whatever. It doesn't matter. Why should I help you?
Good little chicken. This is a nice egg.
Because we're going to save the monks who keep keep this world safe. We need you to brew a weakness potion to cure them.
Don't touch that.
Well, maybe I'll help you. But what would I get out of it?
WHOOOOSH
MEOWWRRRRRRRRA
ERRRRRRR
WHAAAA

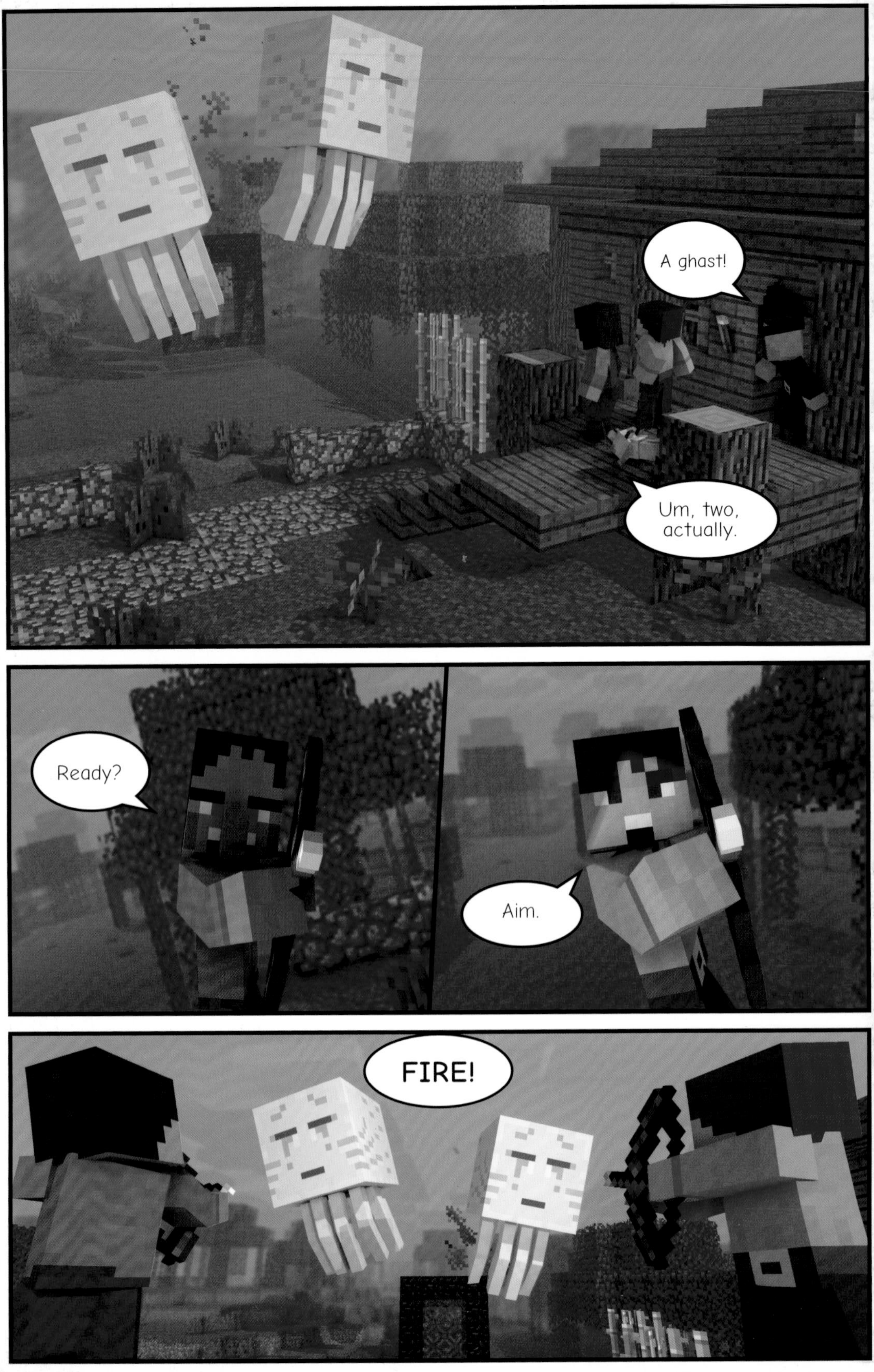
A ghast!
Um, two, actually.
Ready?
Aim.
FIRE!

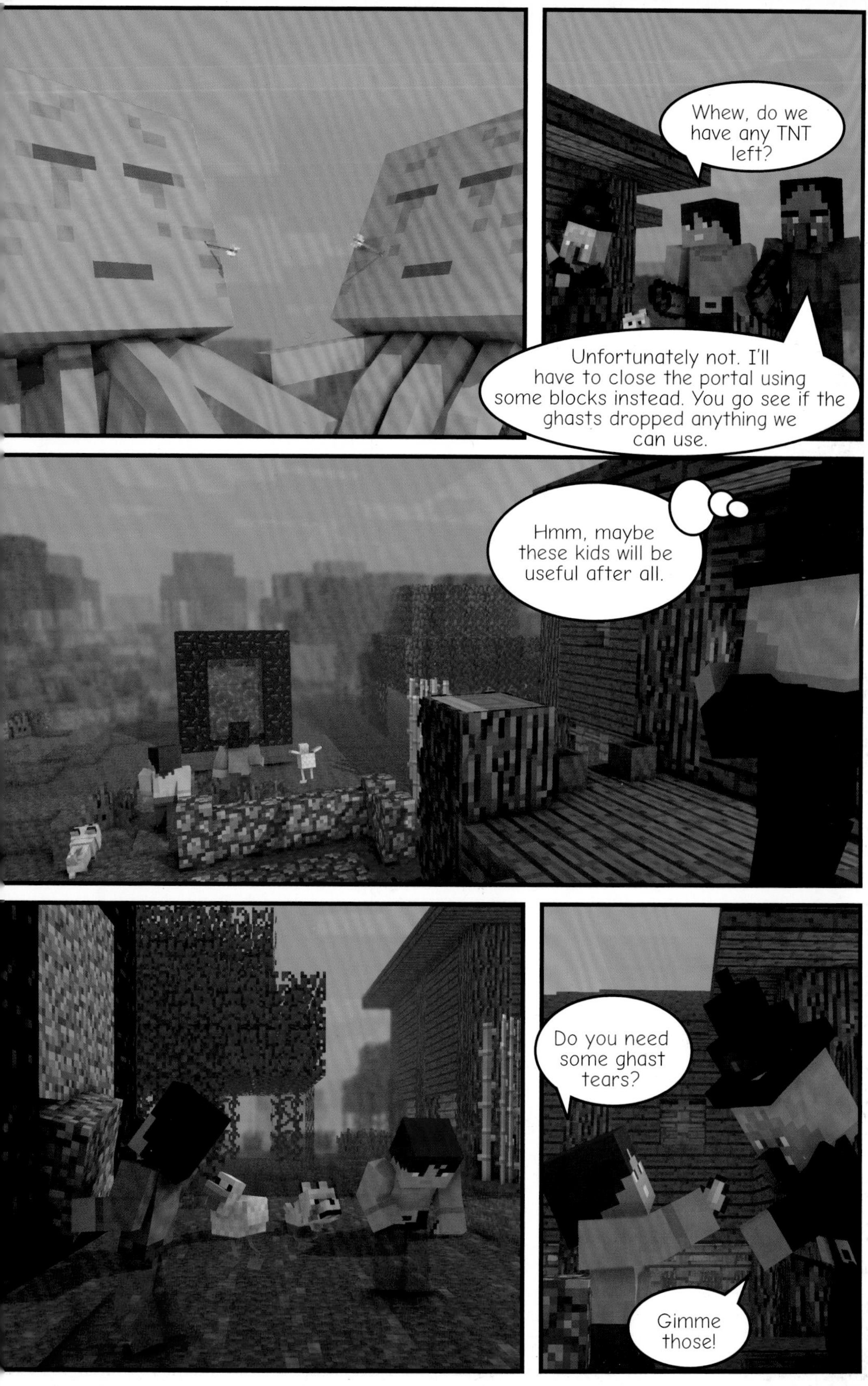

Whew, do we have any TNT left?
Unfortunately not. I'll have to close the portal using some blocks instead. You go see if the ghasts dropped anything we can use.
Hmm, maybe these kids will be useful after all.
Do you need some ghast tears?
Gimme those!

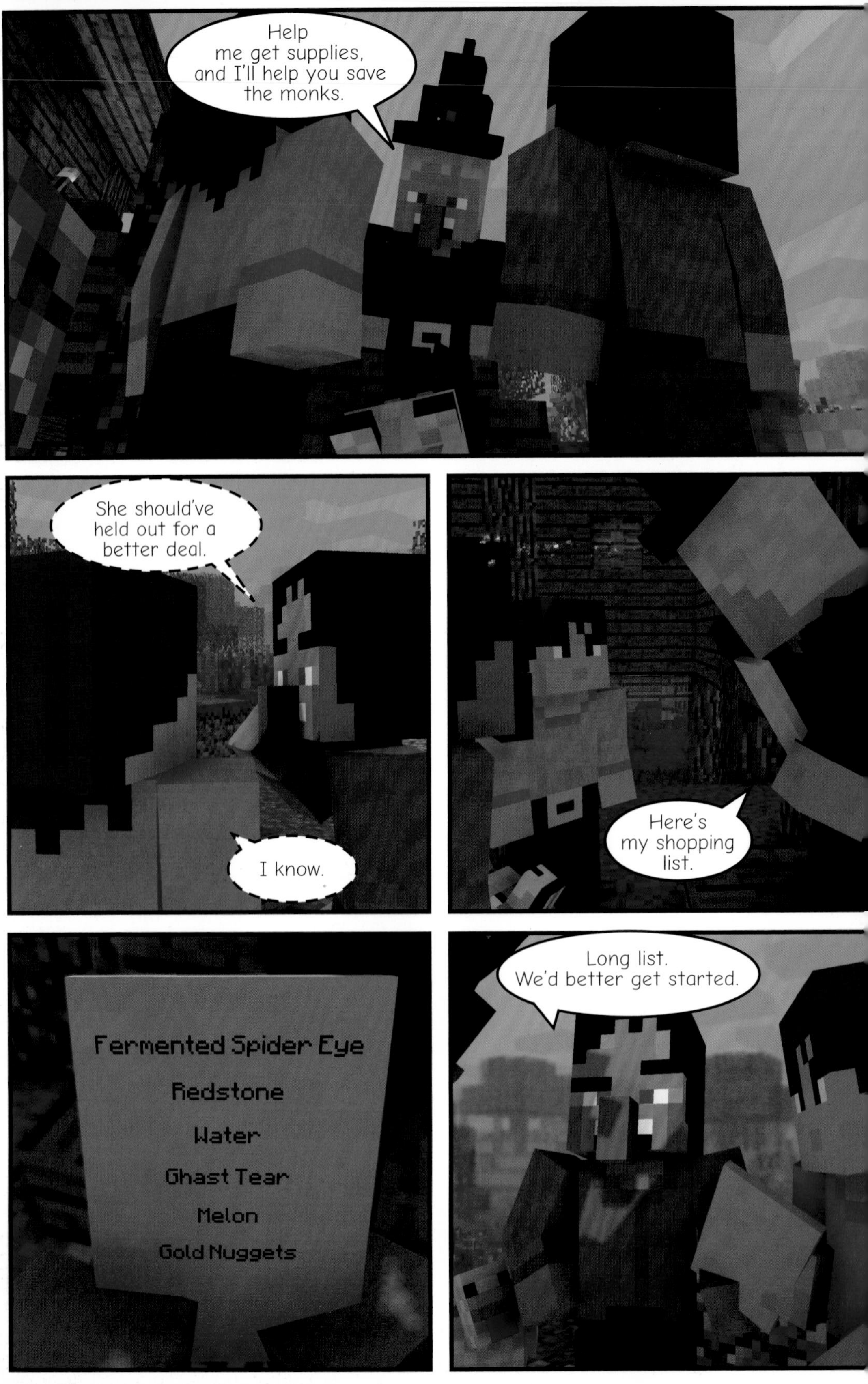
Help me get supplies, and I'll help you save the monks.
She should've held out for a better deal.
I know.
Here's my shopping list.
Fermented Spider Eye
Redstone
Water
Ghast Tear
Melon
Gold Nuggets
Long list. We'd better get started.

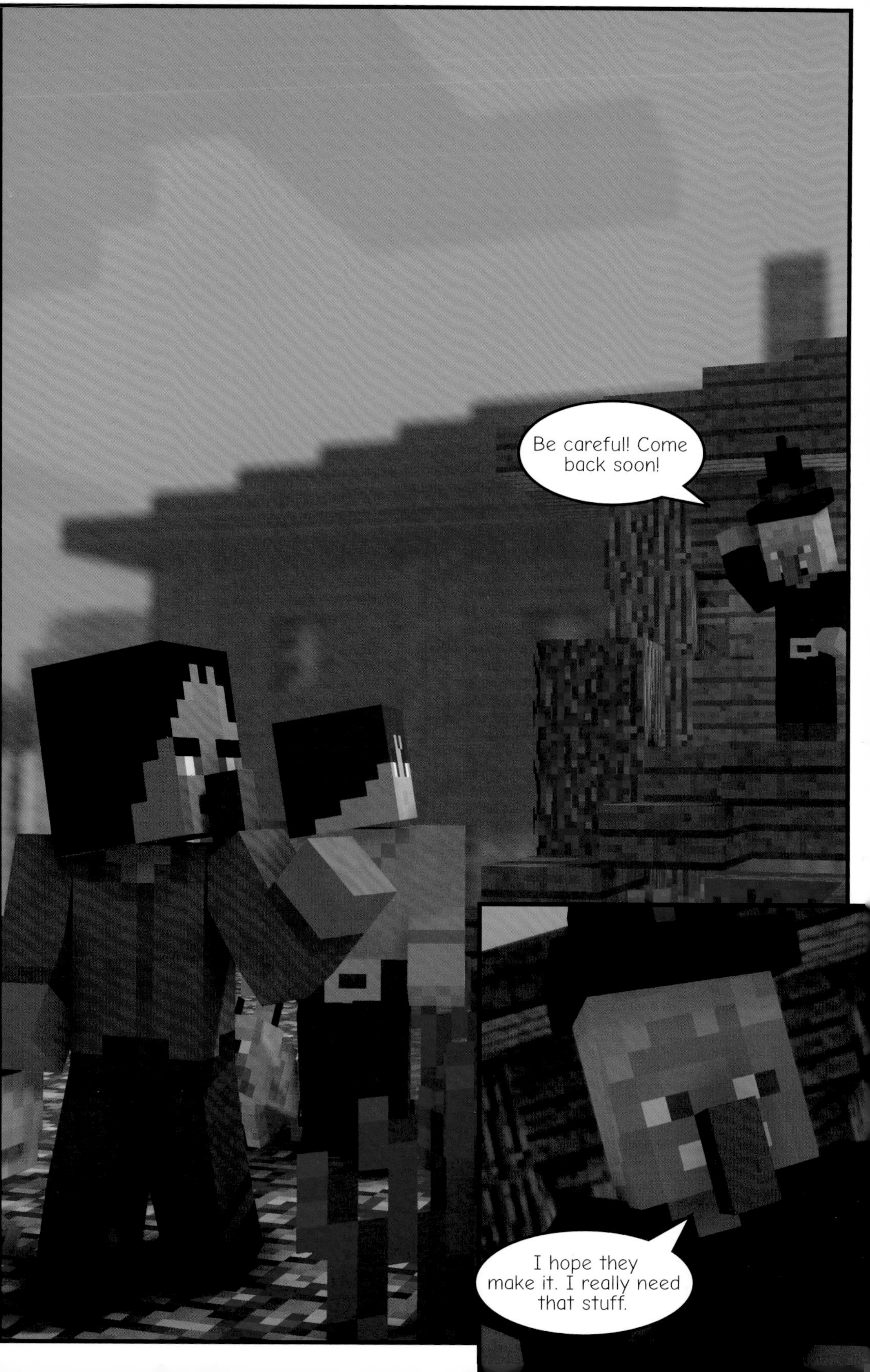
Be careful! Come back soon!
I hope they make it. I really need that stuff.

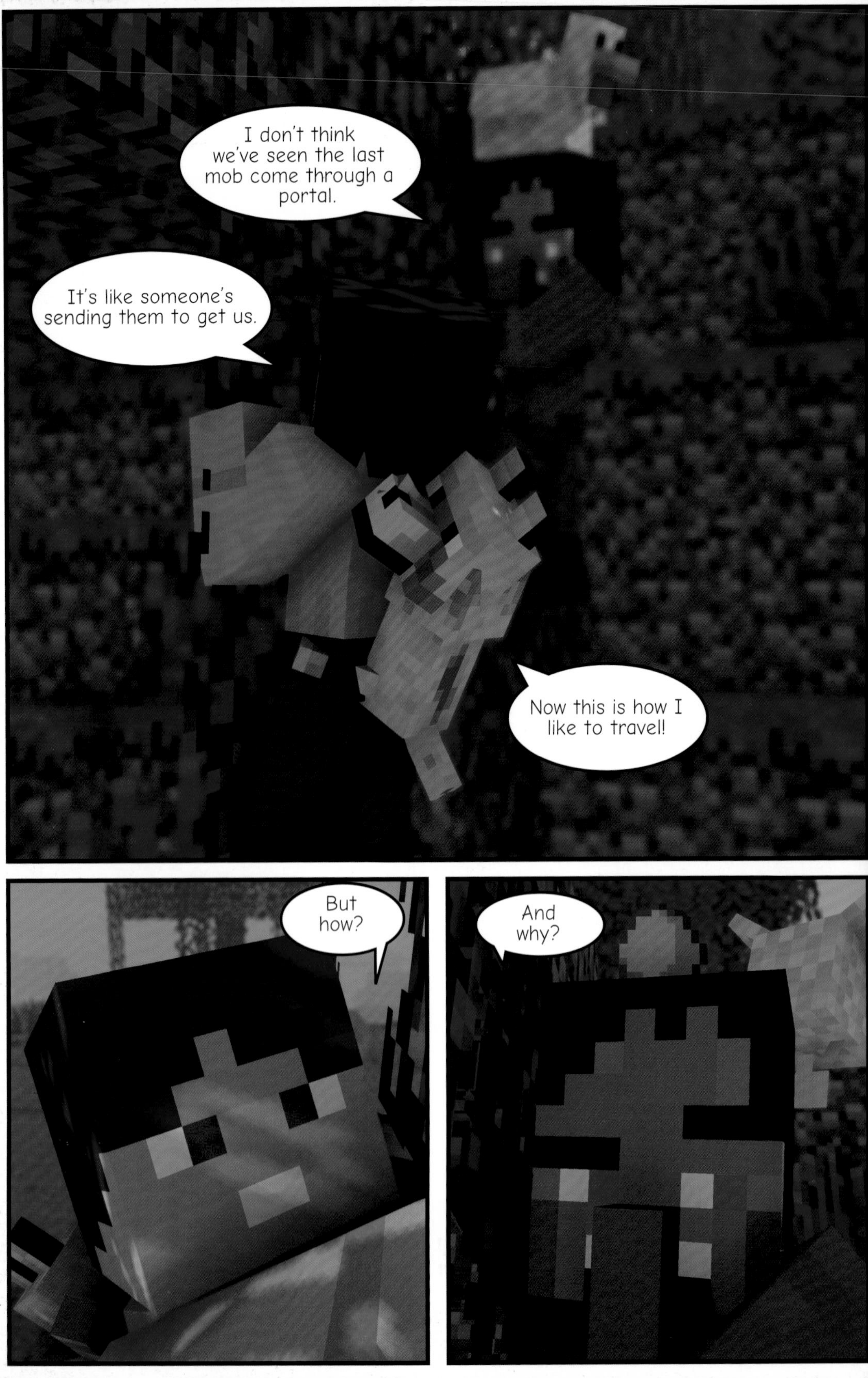
I don't think we've seen the last mob come through a portal.
It's like someone's sending them to get us.
Now this is how I like to travel!
But how?
And why?

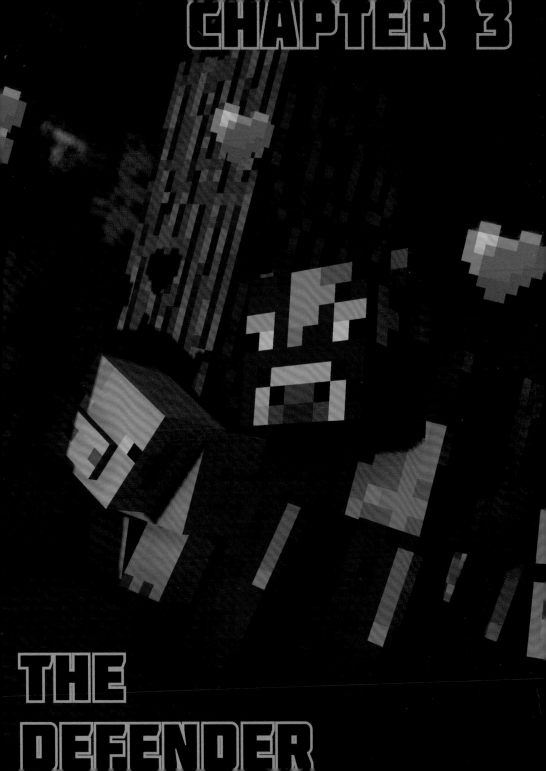

CHAPTER 3

THE
DEFENDER

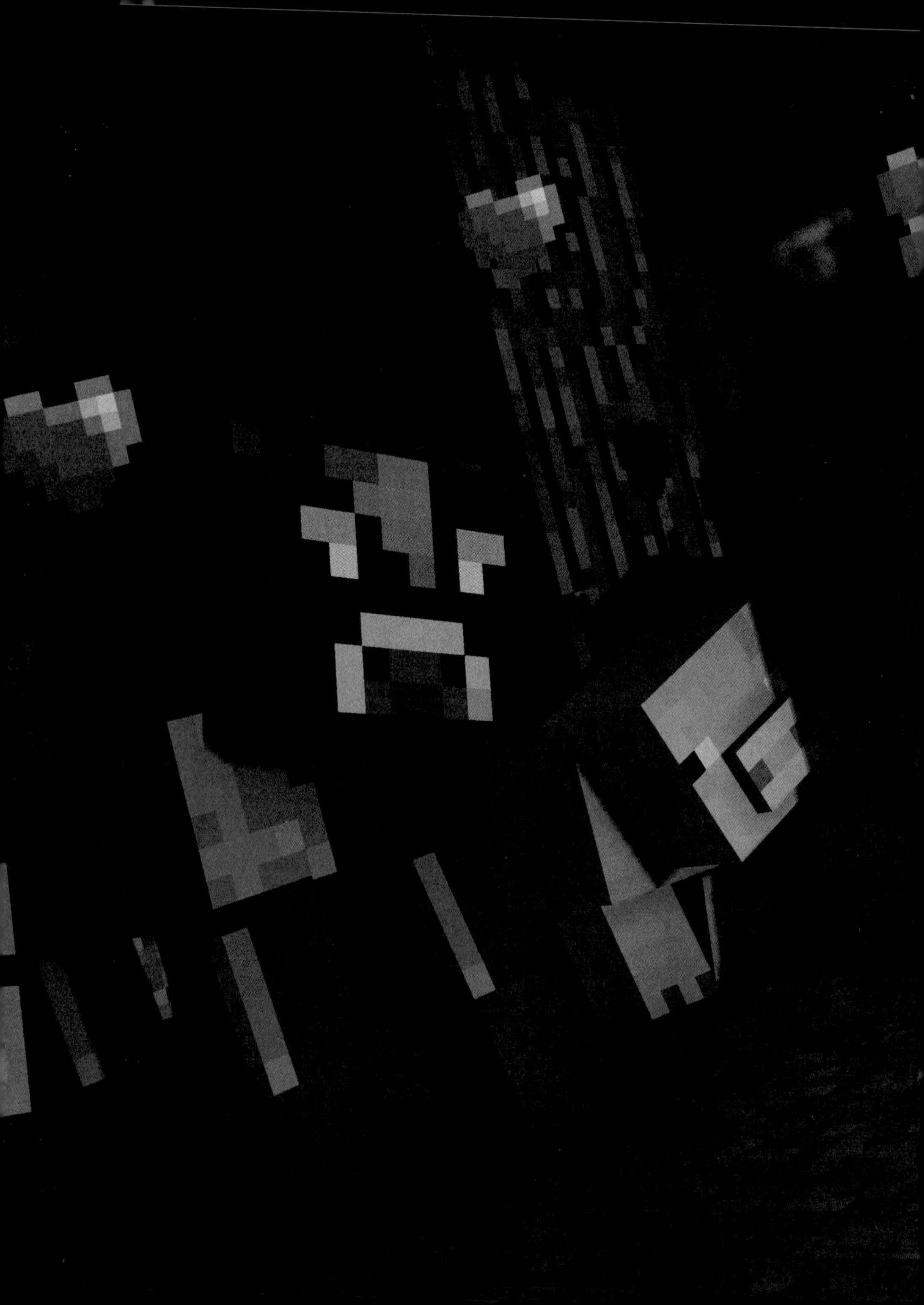

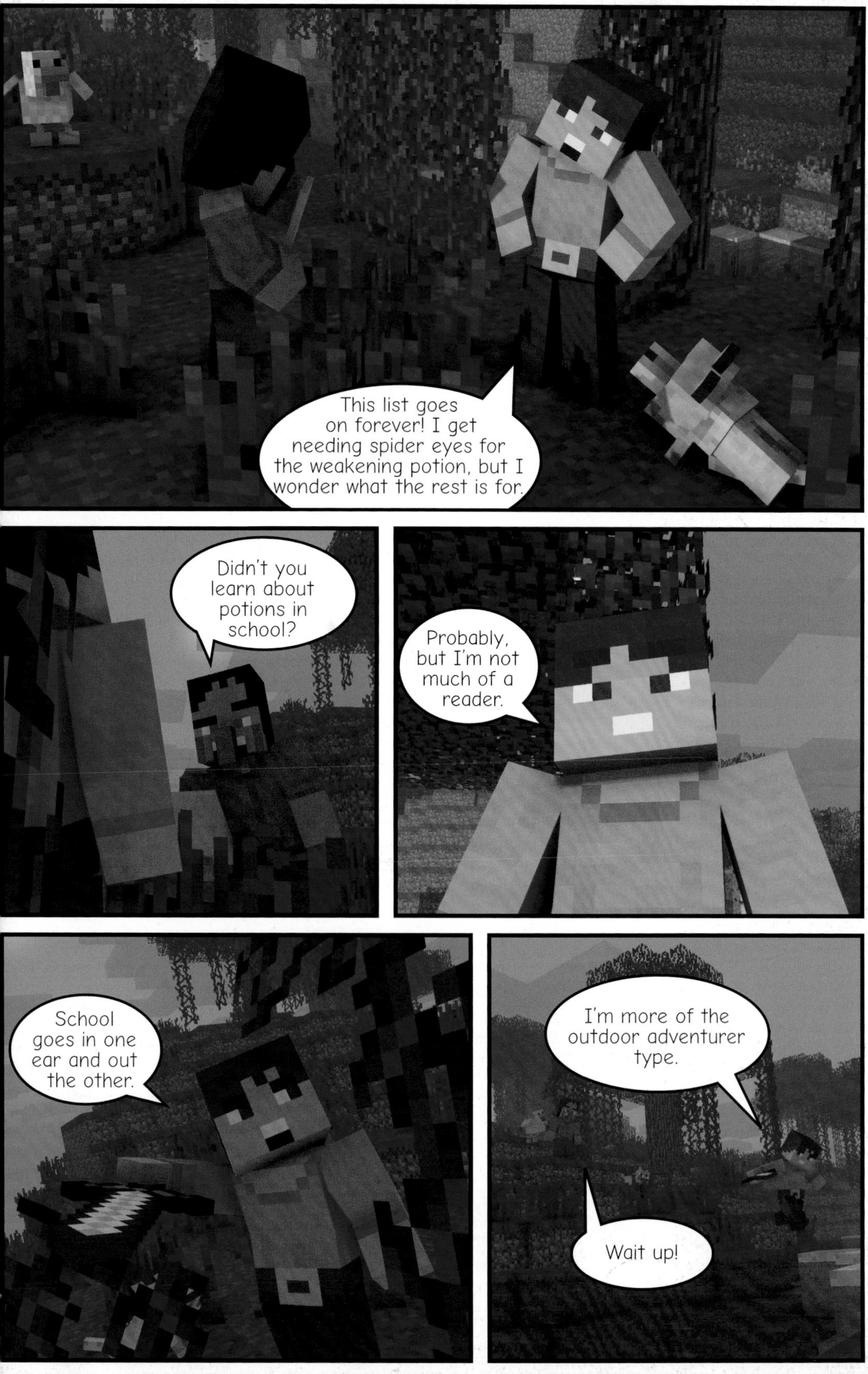
This list goes on forever! I get needing spider eyes for the weakening potion, but I wonder what the rest is for.
Didn't you learn about potions in school?
Probably, but I'm not much of a reader.
School goes in one ear and out the other.
I'm more of the outdoor adventurer type.
Wait up!

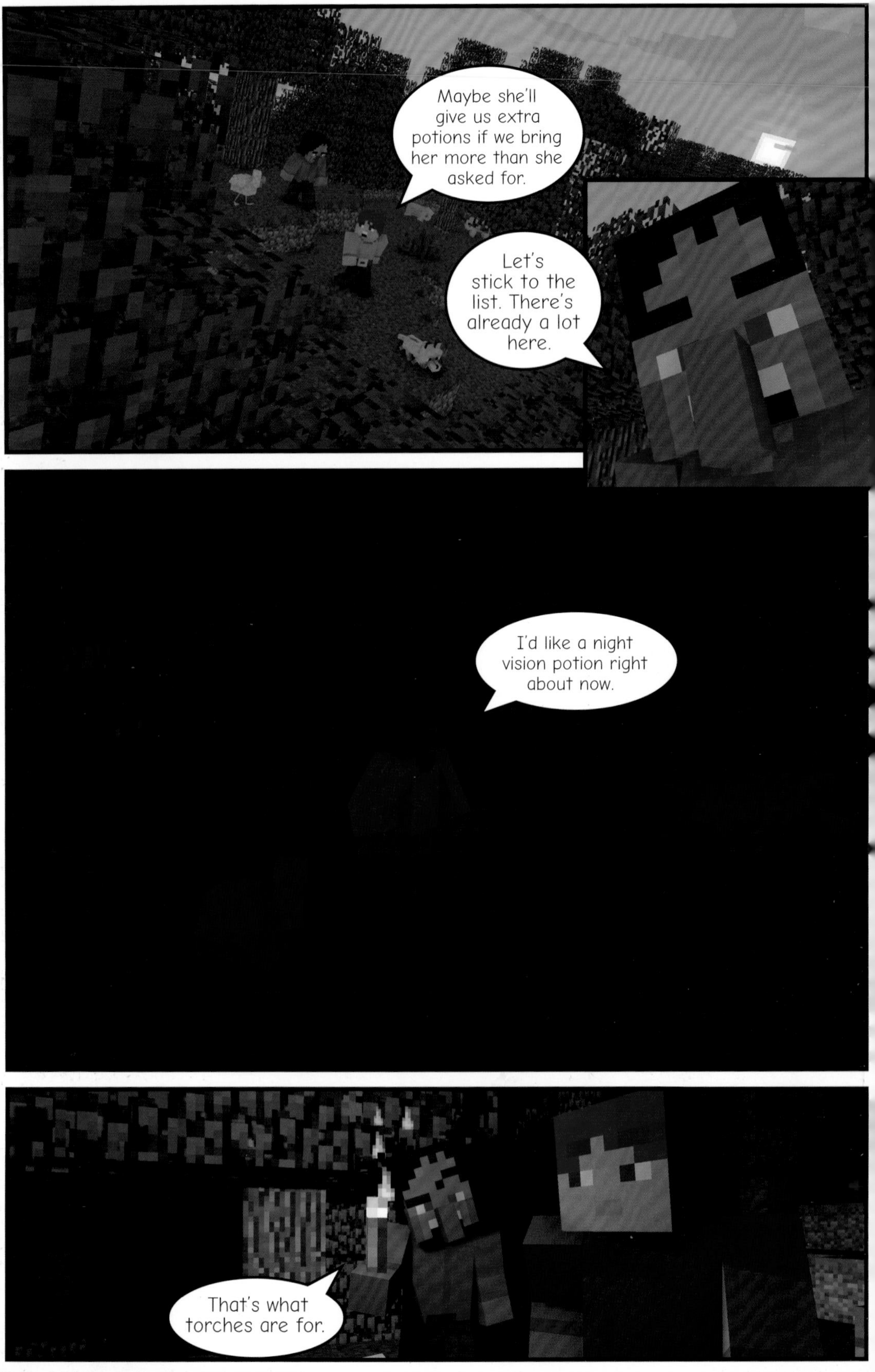
Maybe she'll give us extra potions if we bring her more than she asked for.
Let's stick to the list. There's already a lot here.
I'd like a night vision potion right about now.
That's what torches are for.

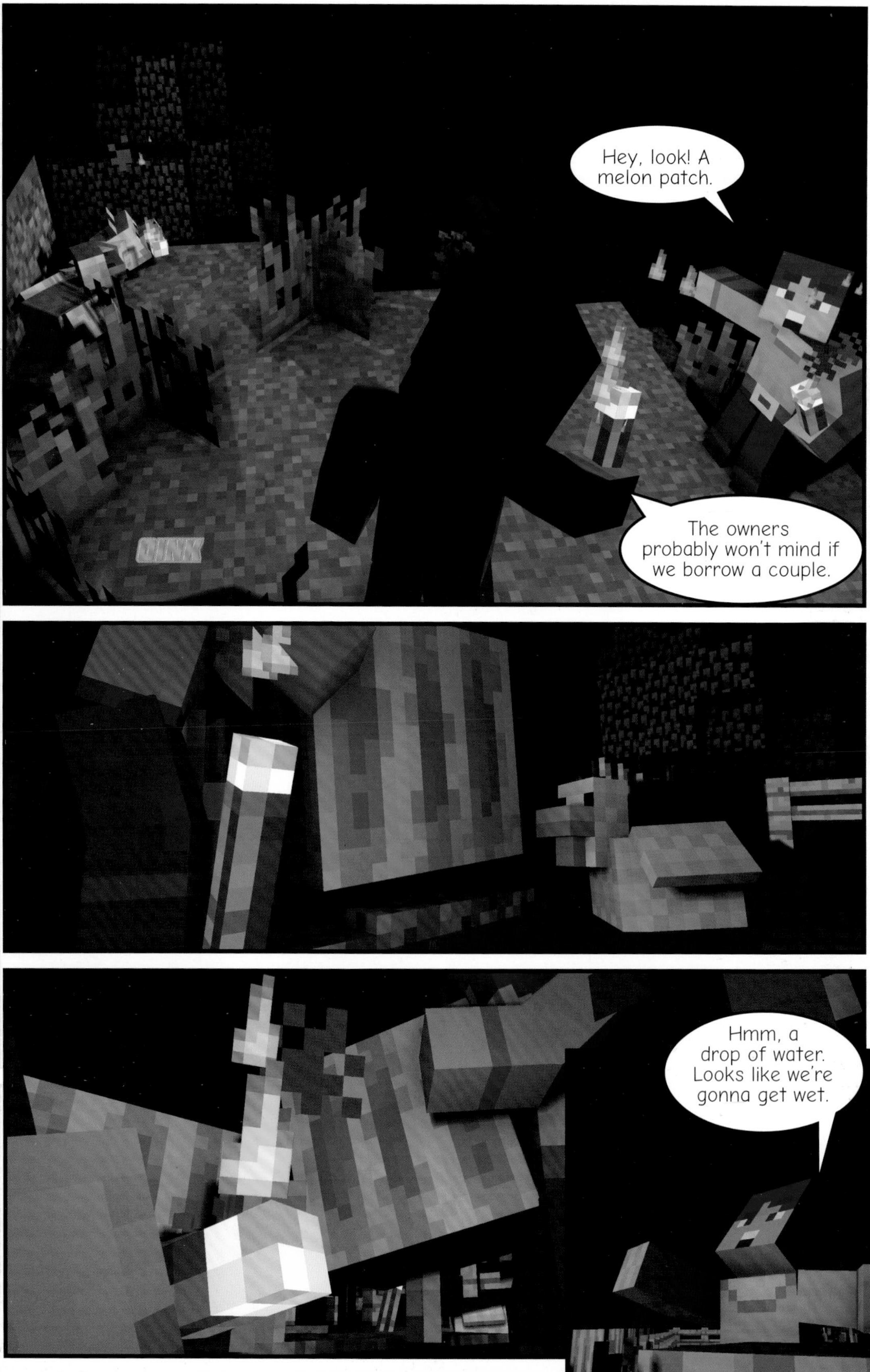
Hey, look! A melon patch.
OINK
The owners probably won't mind if we borrow a couple.
Hmm, a drop of water. Looks like we're gonna get wet.

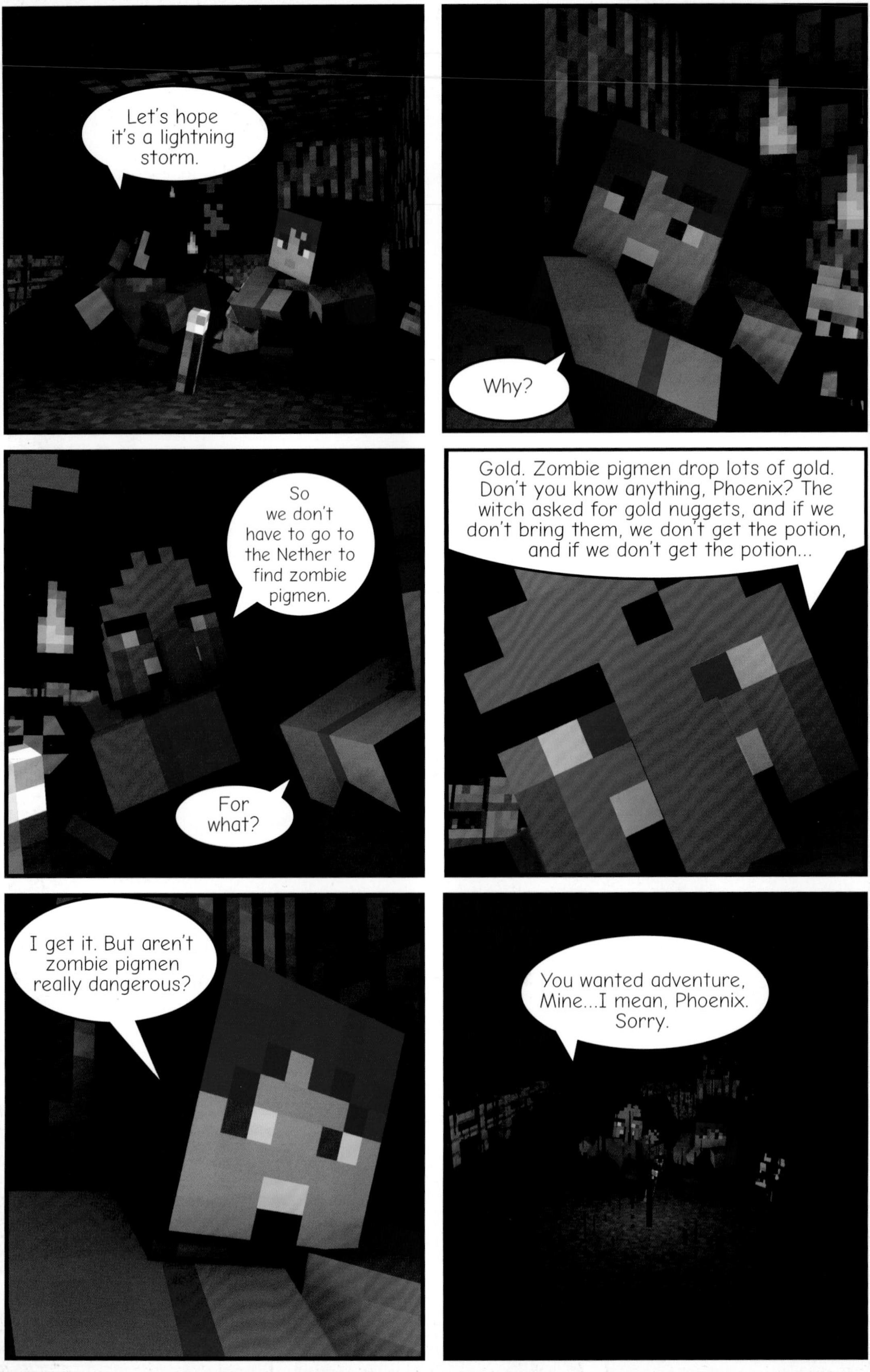
Let's hope it's a lightning storm.
Why?
So we don't have to go to the Nether to find zombie pigmen.
For what?
Gold. Zombie pigmen drop lots of gold. Don't you know anything, Phoenix? The witch asked for gold nuggets, and if we don't bring them, we don't get the potion, and if we don't get the potion...
I get it. But aren't zombie pigmen really dangerous?
You wanted adventure, Mine...I mean, Phoenix. Sorry.

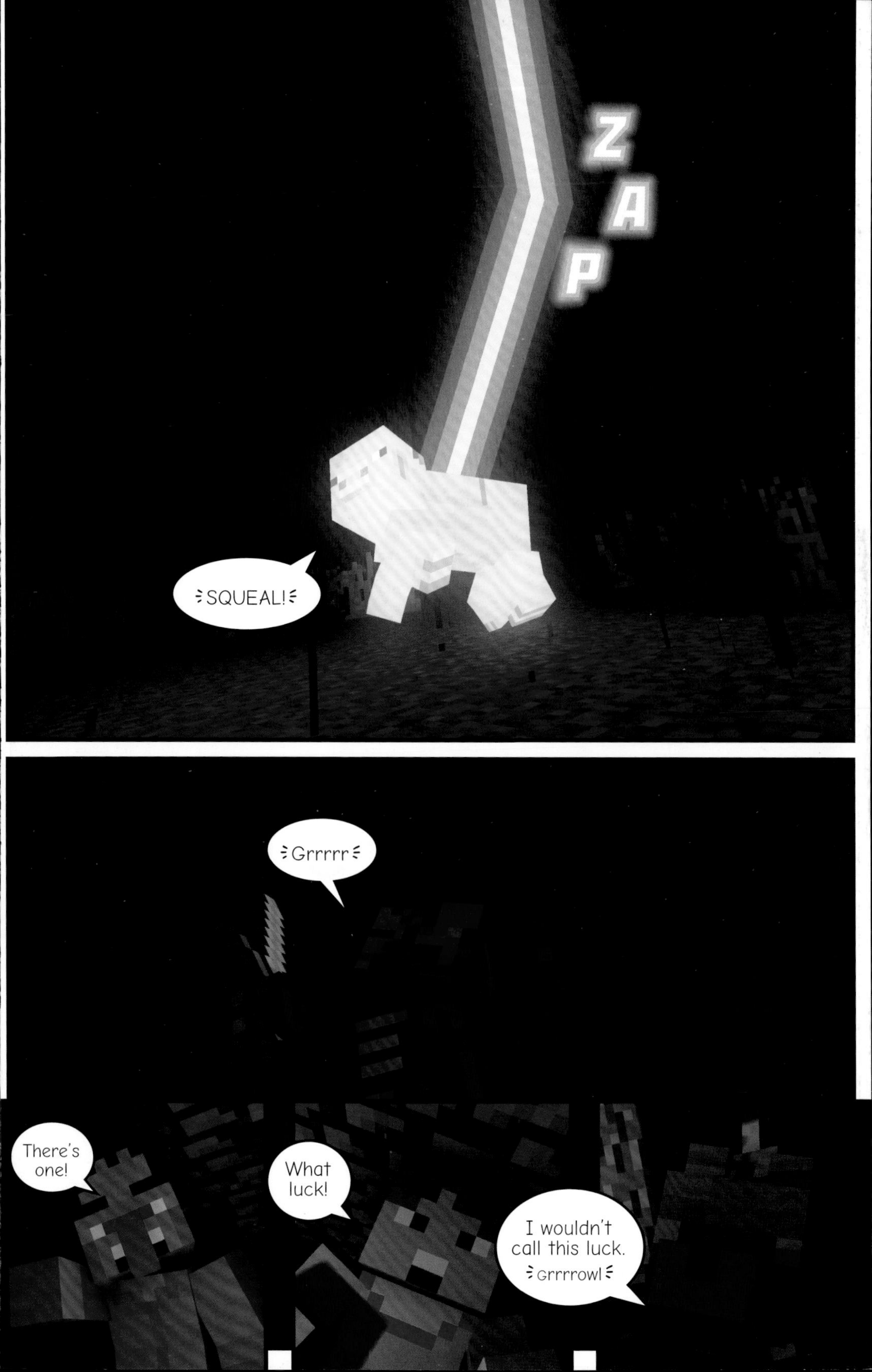
ZAP
SQUEAL!
Grrrrr
There's one!
What luck!
I wouldn't call this luck.
Grrrrowl!

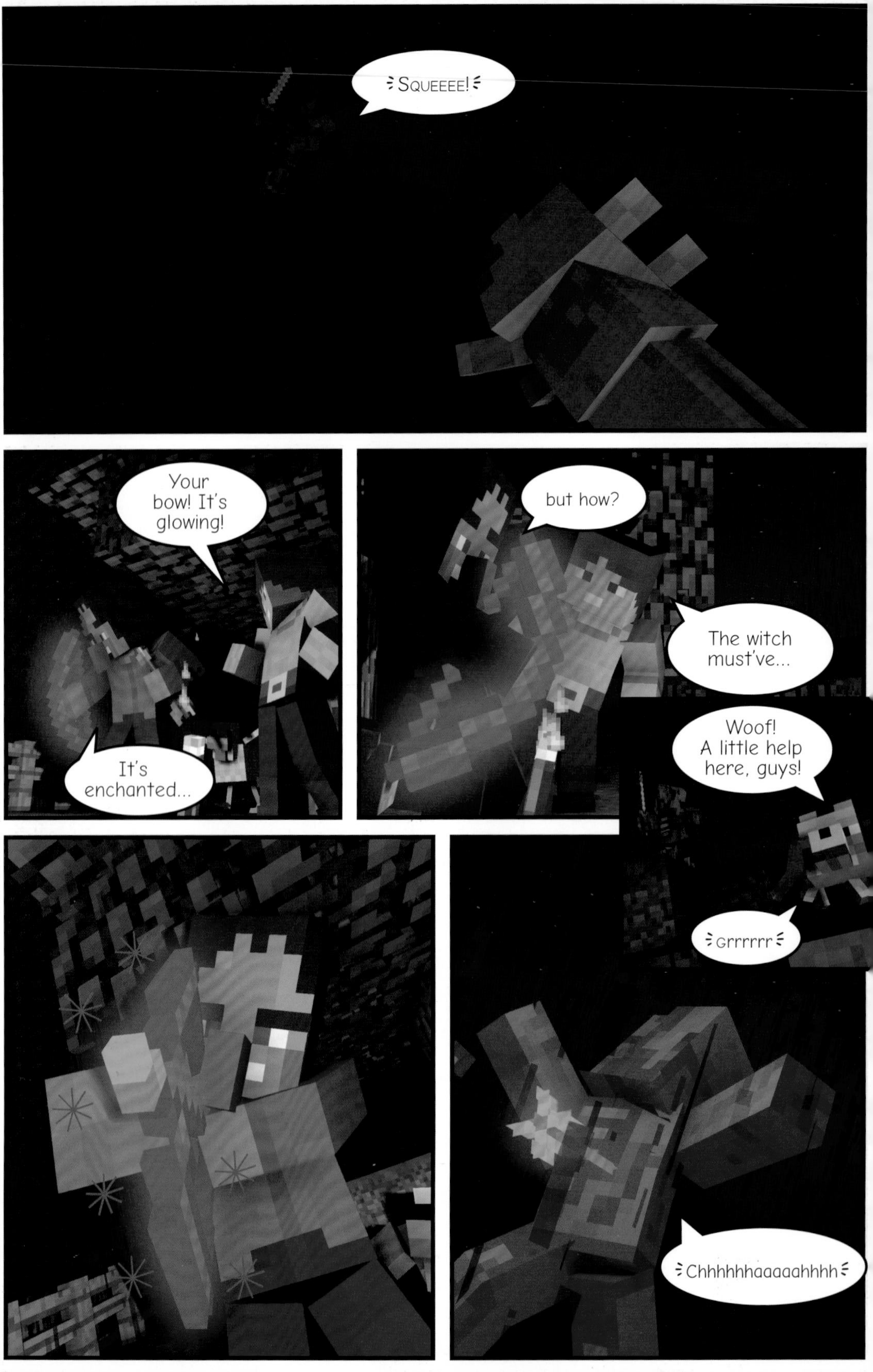
SQUEEEE!
Your bow! It's glowing!
It's enchanted...
but how?
The witch must've...
Woof! A little help here, guys!
Grrrrrr
Chhhhhhaaaaahhhh

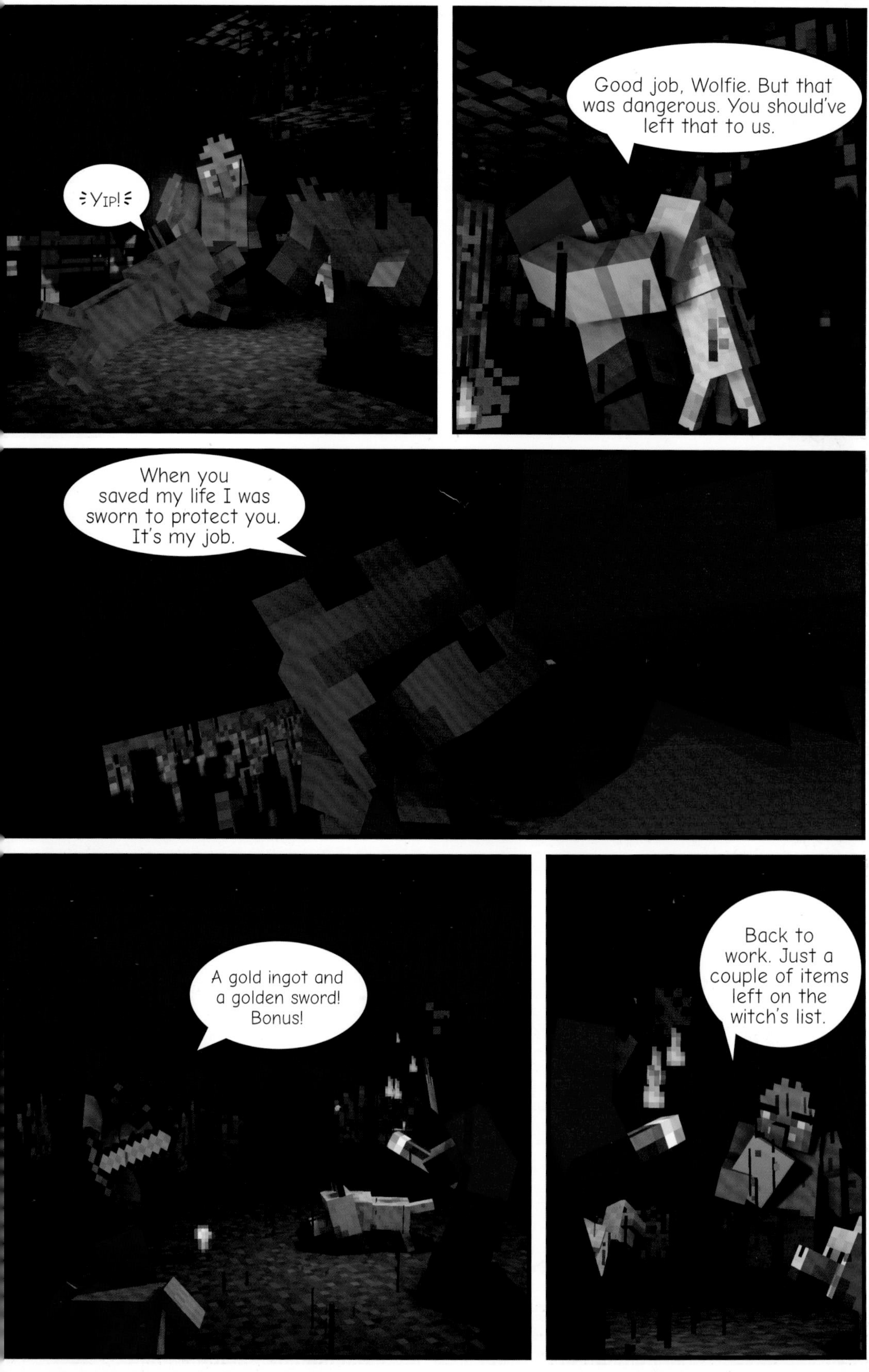
YIP!
Good job, Wolfie. But that was dangerous. You should've left that to us.
When you saved my life I was sworn to protect you. It's my job.
A gold ingot and a golden sword! Bonus!
Back to work. Just a couple of items left on the witch's list.

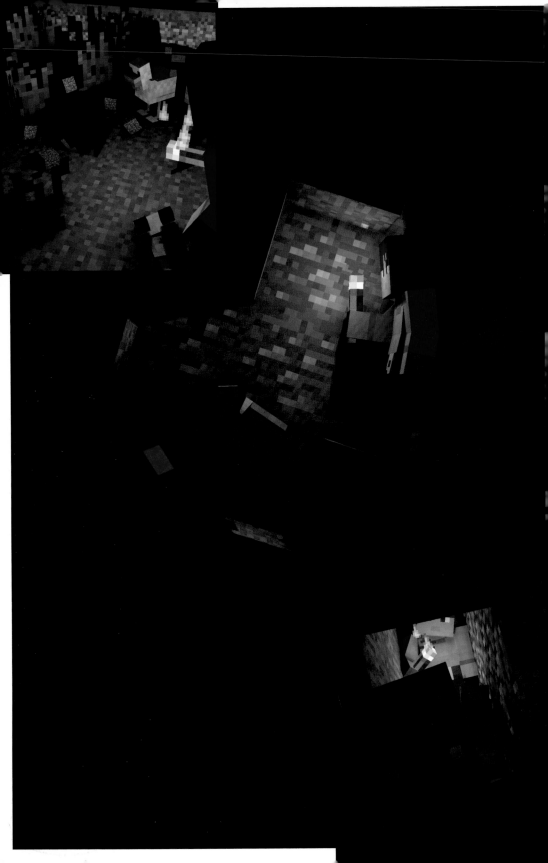

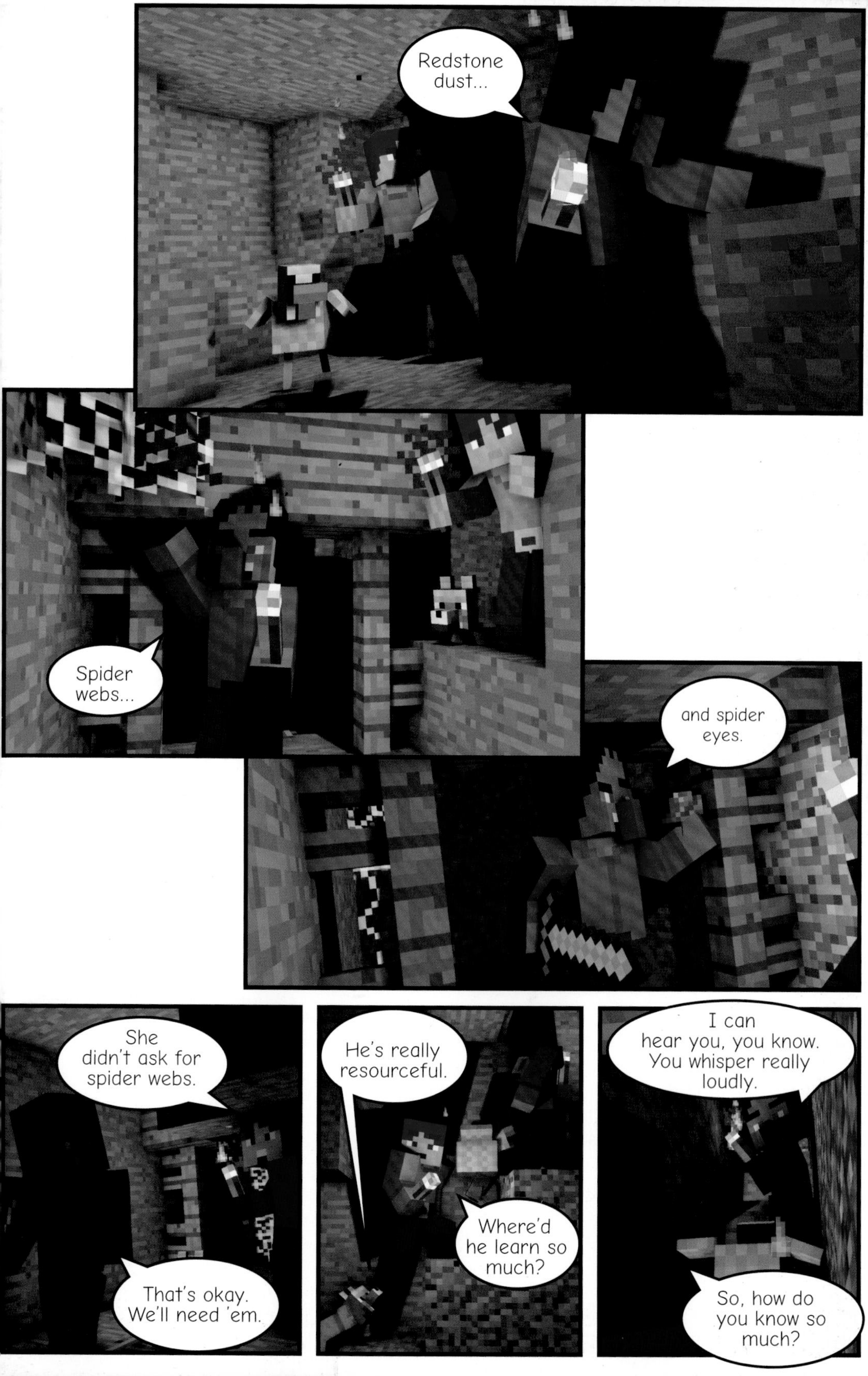
Redstone dust...
Spider webs...
and spider eyes.
She didn't ask for spider webs.
That's okay. We'll need 'em.
He's really resourceful.
Where'd he learn so much?
I can hear you, you know. You whisper really loudly.
So, how do you know so much?

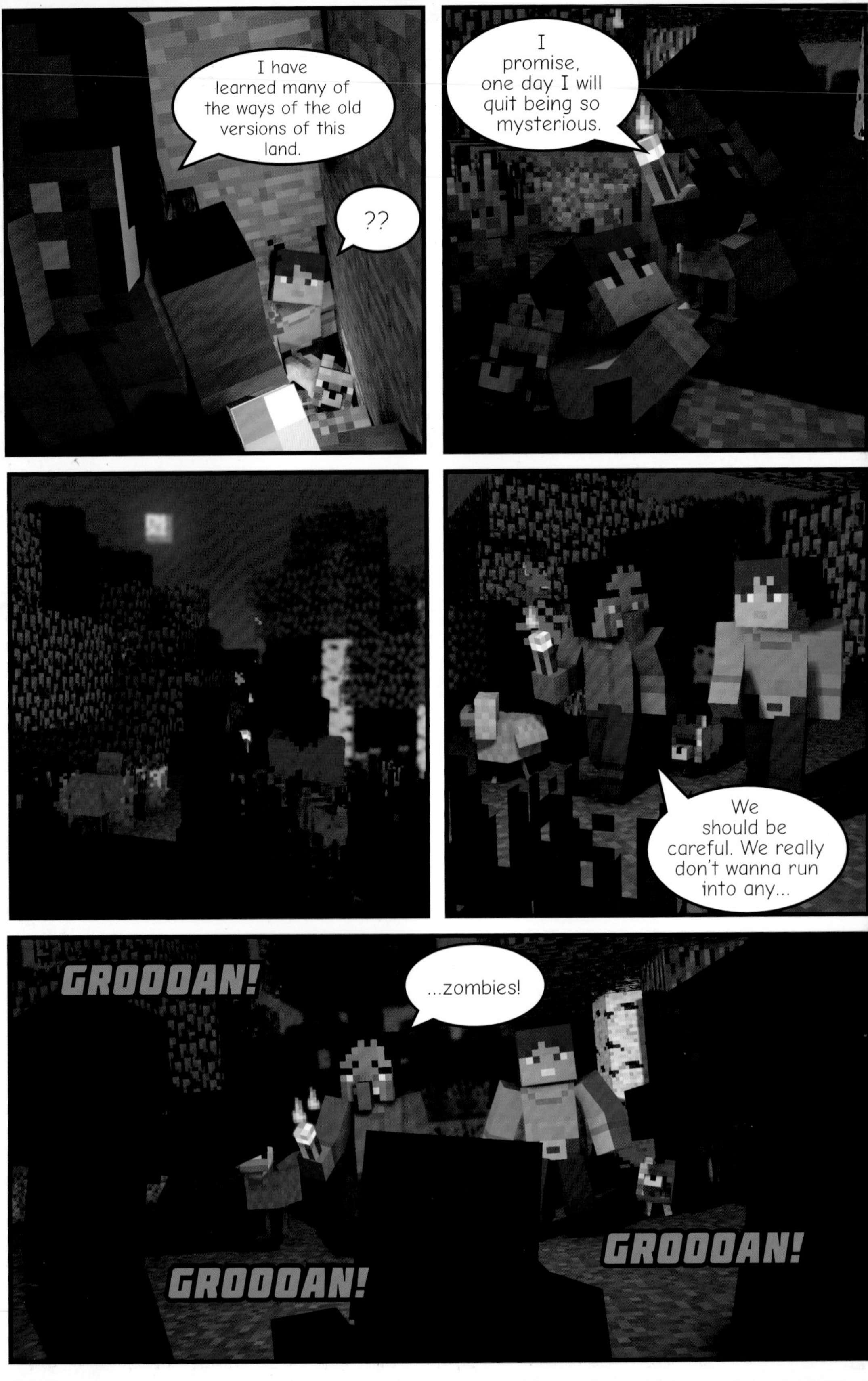
I have learned many of the ways of the old versions of this land.
??
I promise, one day I will quit being so mysterious.
We should be careful. We really don't wanna run into any...
GROOOAN!
...zombies!
GROOOAN!
GROOOAN!

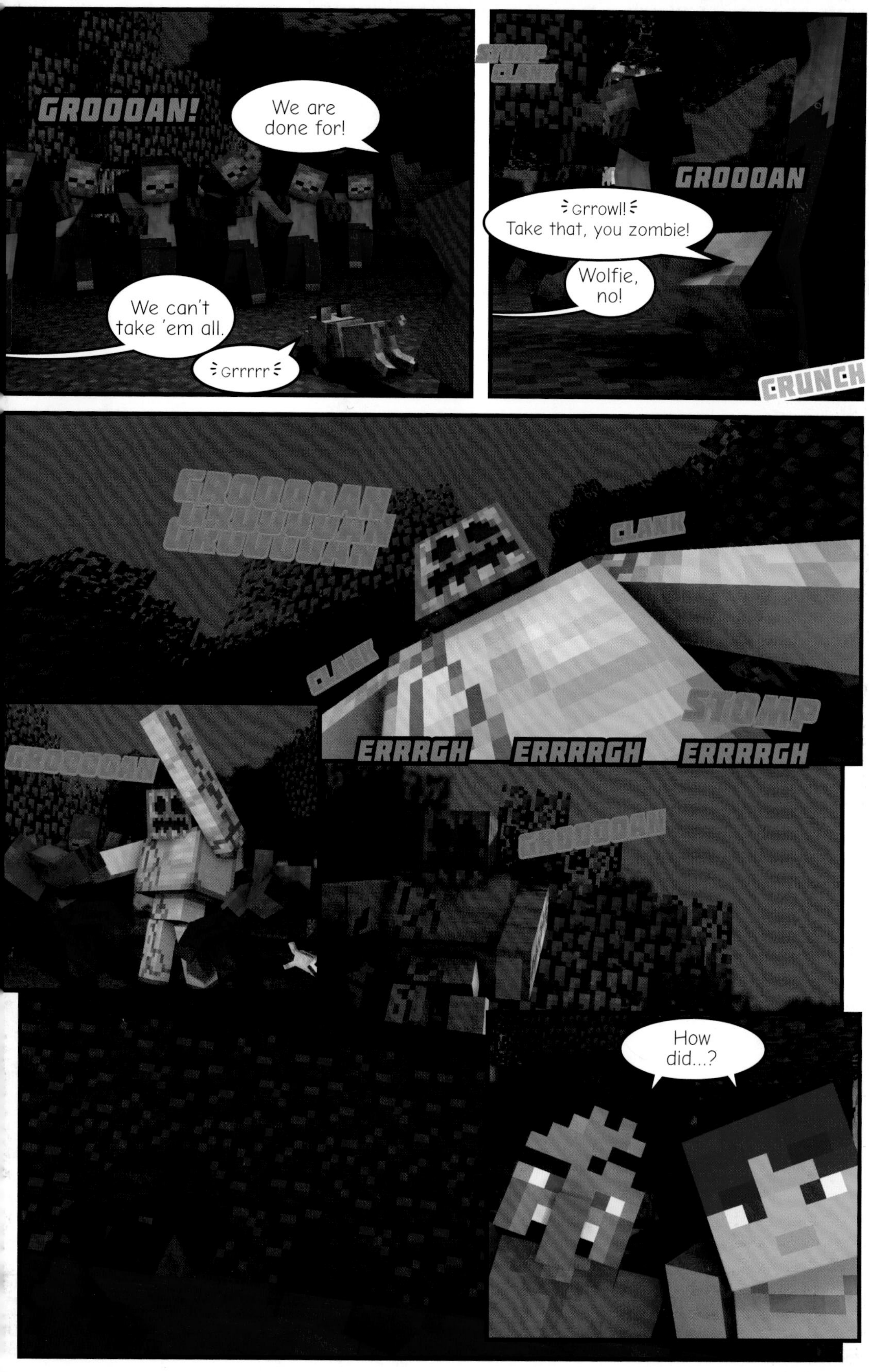
GROOOAN!
We are done for!
We can't take 'em all.
Grrrrr
STOMP
CLANK
GROOOAN
Grrowl!
Take that, you zombie!
Wolfie, no!
CRUNCH
CLANK
CLANK
STOMP
ERRRGH
ERRRRGH
ERRRRGH
GROOOAN
How did...?

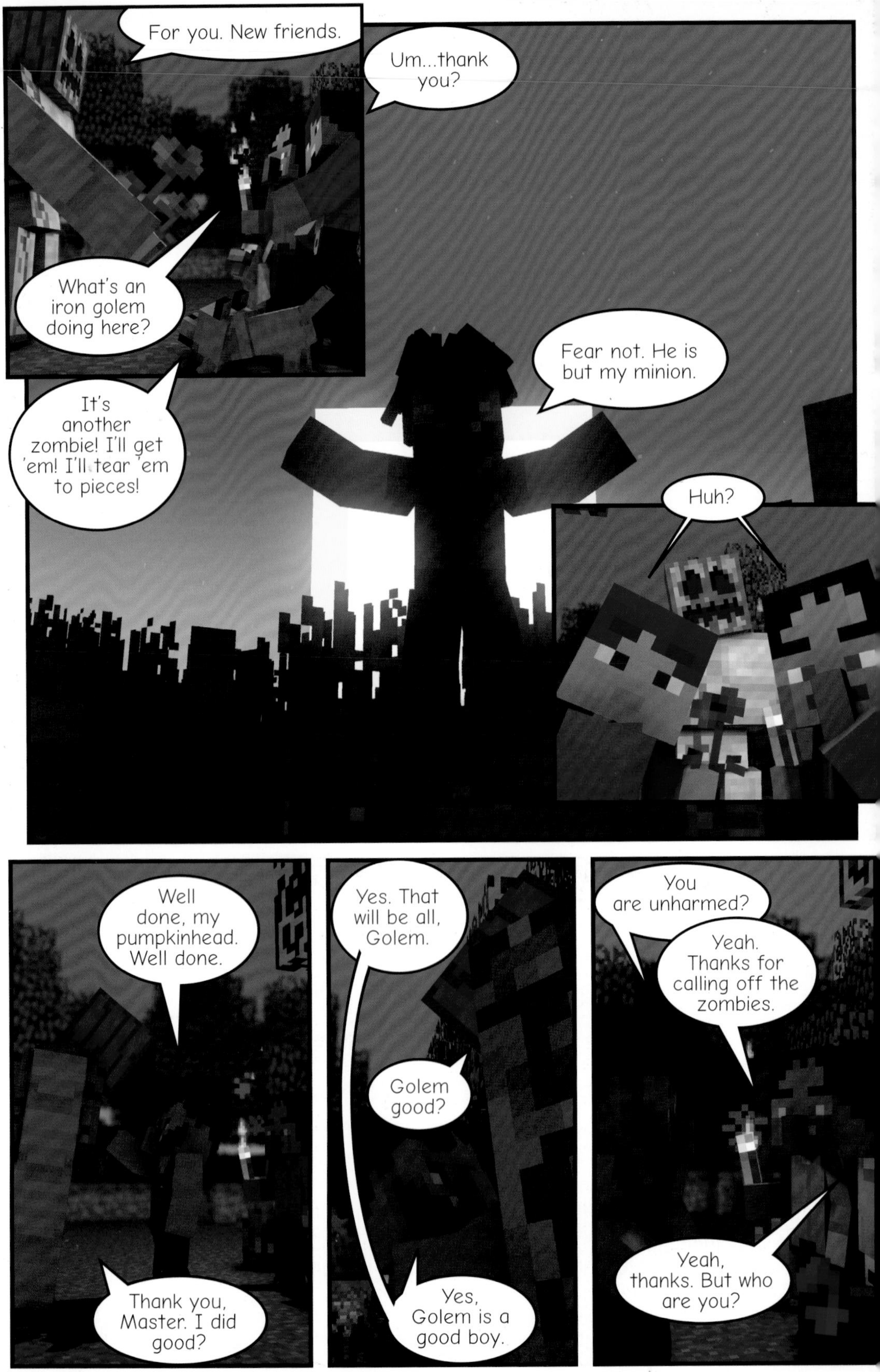
For you. New friends.
Um...thank you?
What's an iron golem doing here?
It's another zombie! I'll get 'em! I'll tear 'em to pieces!
Fear not. He is but my minion.
Huh?
Well done, my pumpkinhead. Well done.
Thank you, Master. I did good?
Yes. That will be all, Golem.
Golem good?
Yes, Golem is a good boy.
You are unharmed?
Yeah. Thanks for calling off the zombies.
Yeah, thanks. But who are you?

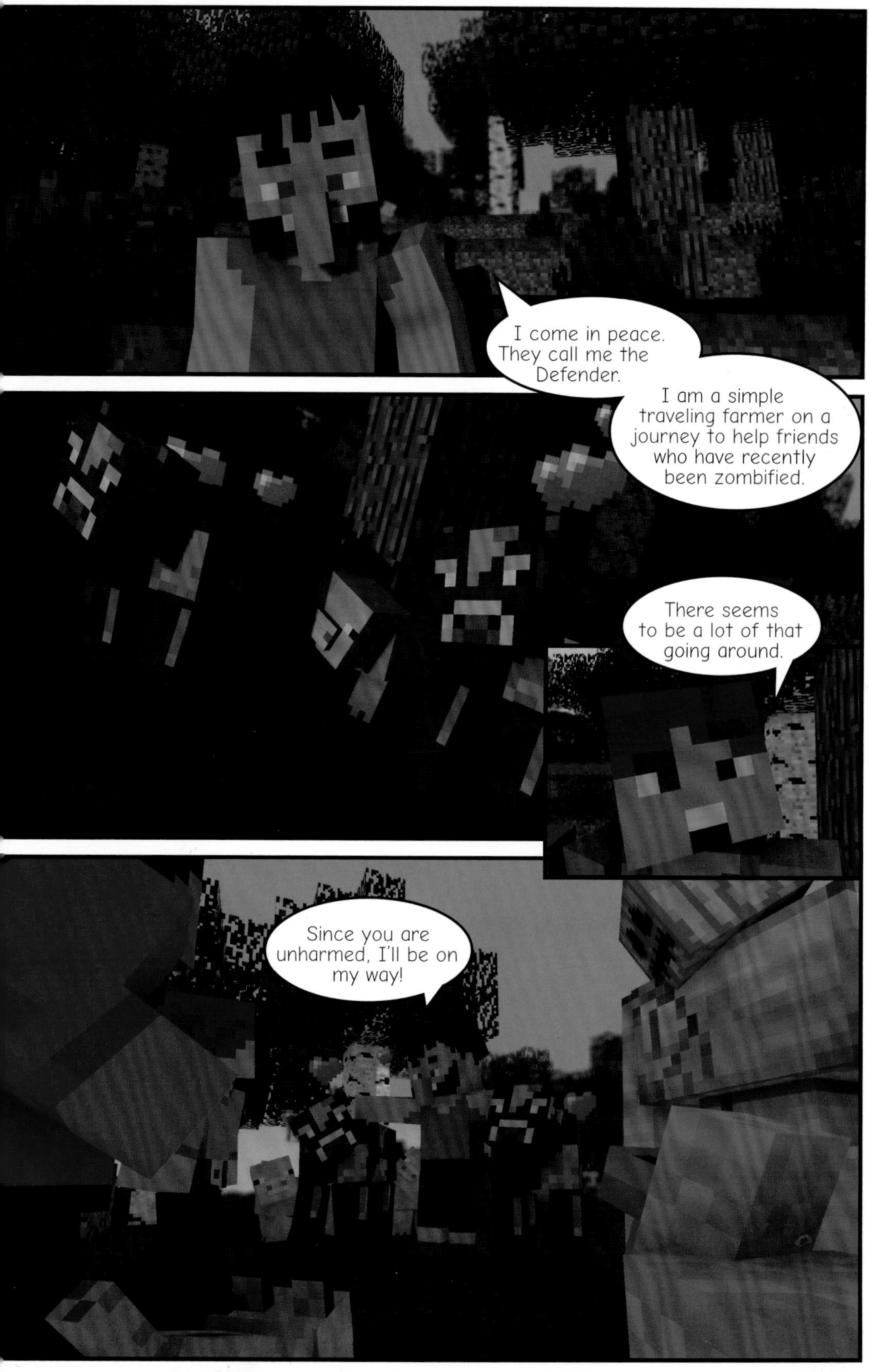
I come in peace. They call me the Defender.
I am a simple traveling farmer on a journey to help friends who have recently been zombified.
There seems to be a lot of that going around.
Since you are unharmed, I'll be on my way!

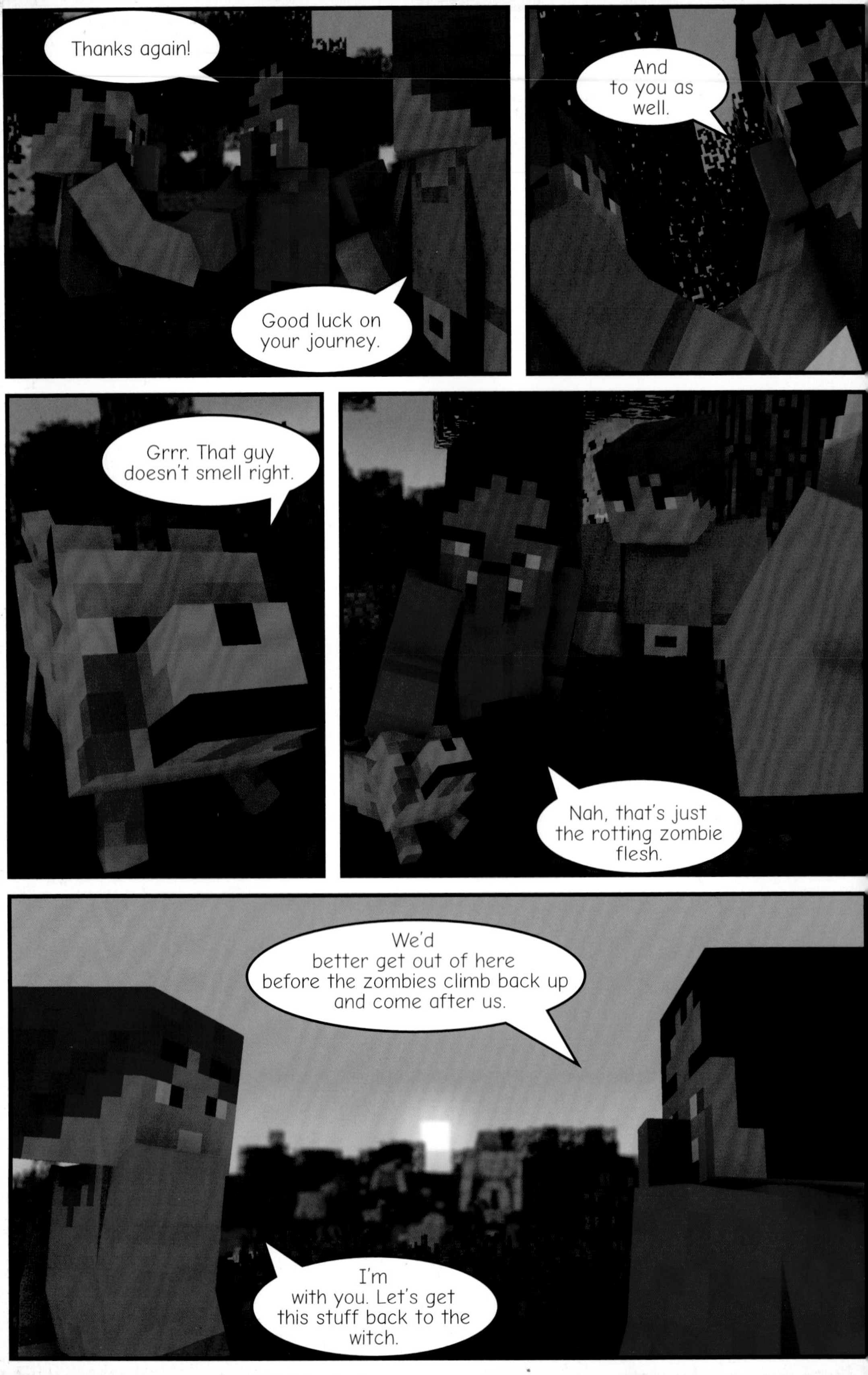
Thanks again!
Good luck on your journey.
And to you as well.
Grrr. That guy doesn't smell right.
Nah, that's just the rotting zombie flesh.
We'd better get out of here before the zombies climb back up and come after us.
I'm with you. Let's get this stuff back to the witch.

CHAPTER 4

SHELTER

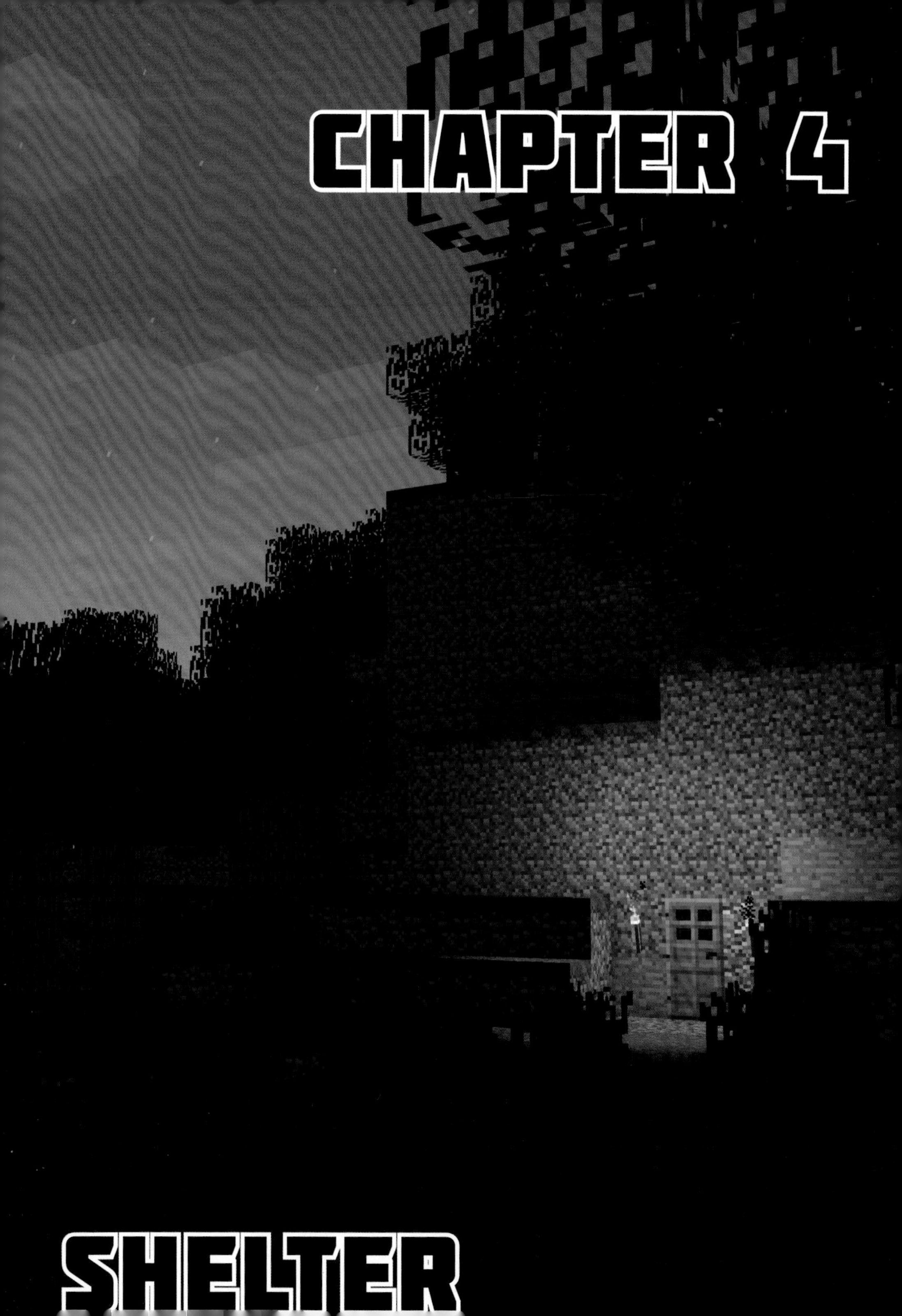

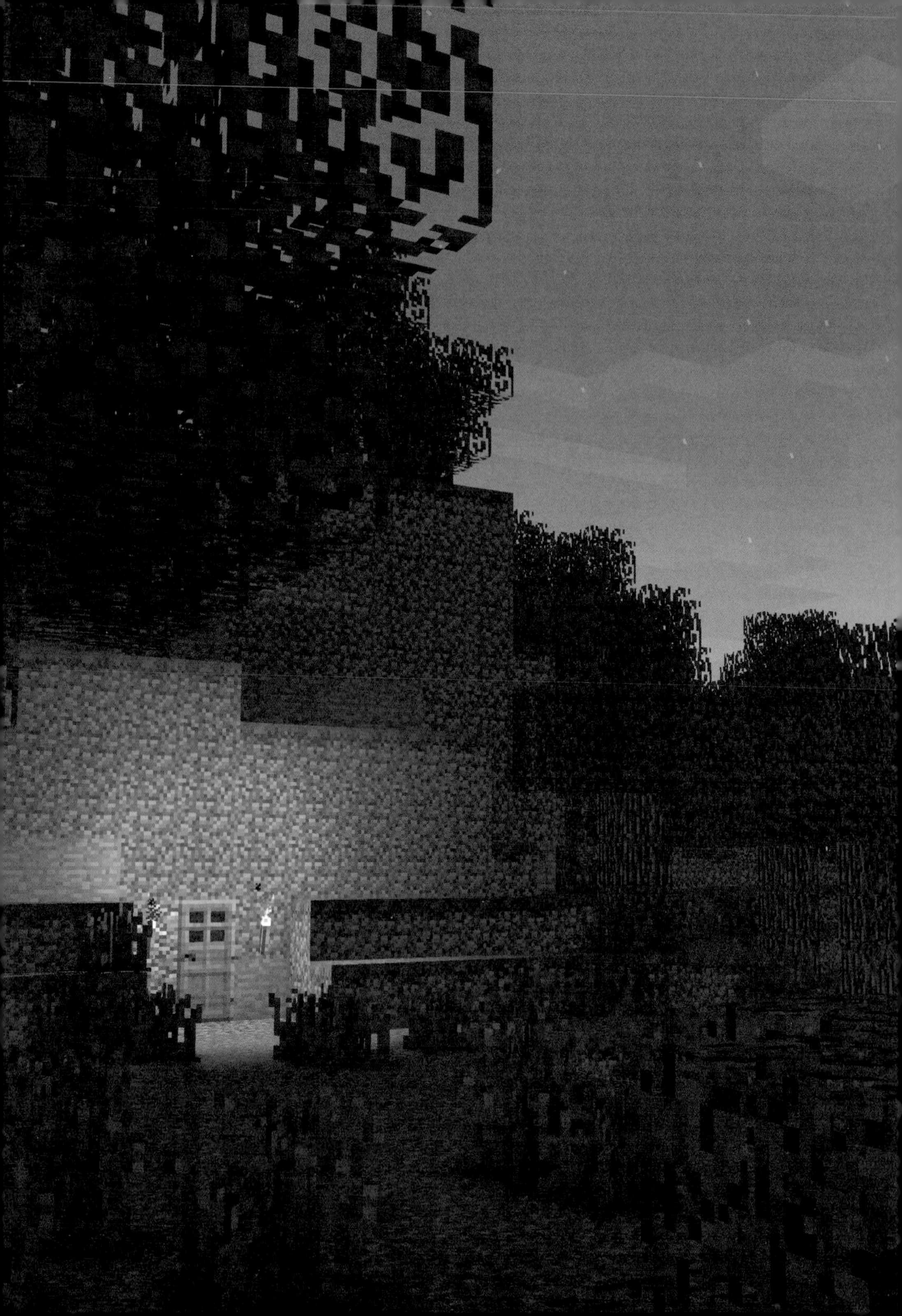

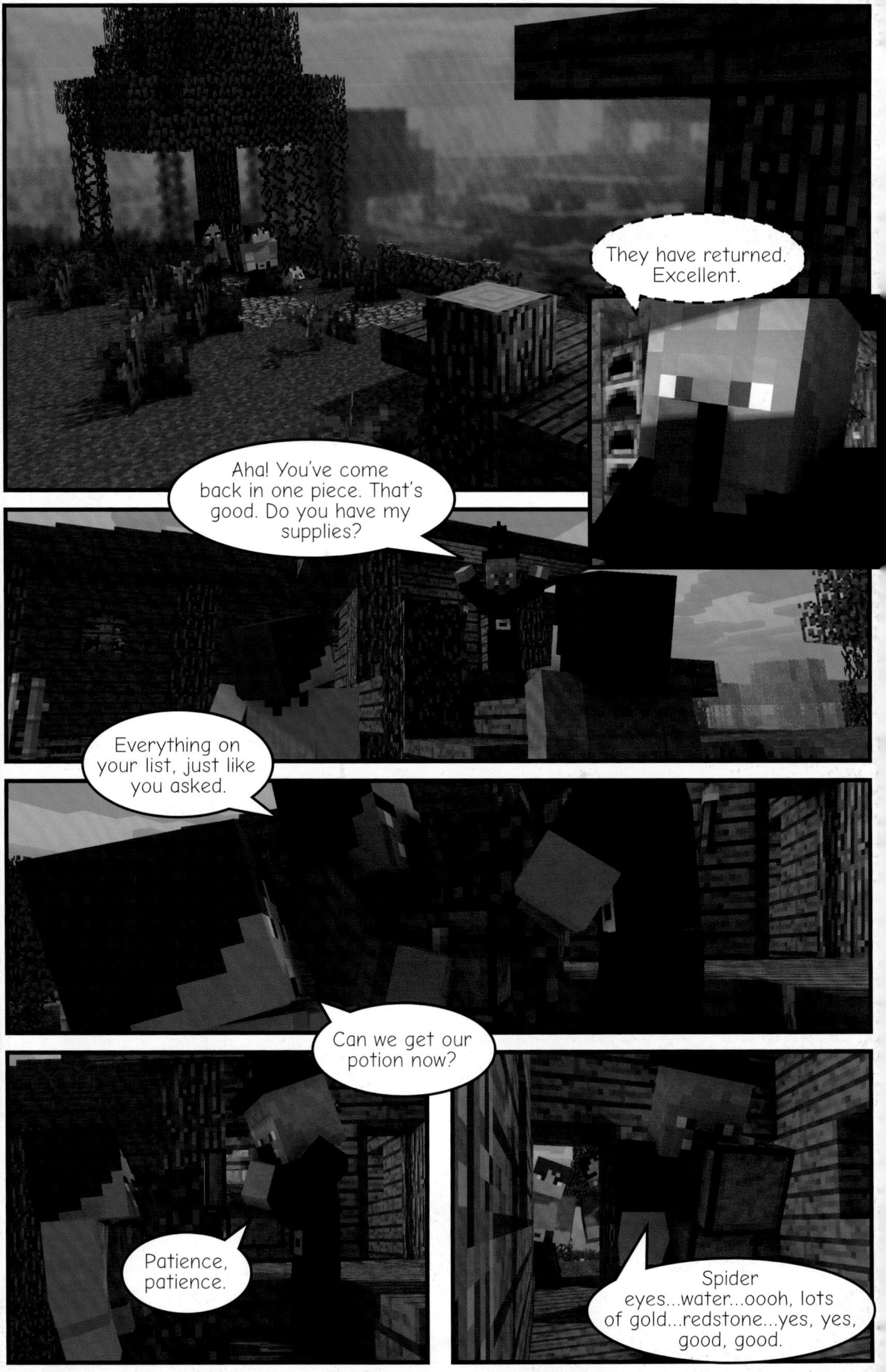
They have returned. Excellent.
Aha! You've come back in one piece. That's good. Do you have my supplies?
Everything on your list, just like you asked.
Can we get our potion now?
Patience, patience.
Spider eyes...water...oooh, lots of gold...redstone...yes, yes, good, good.

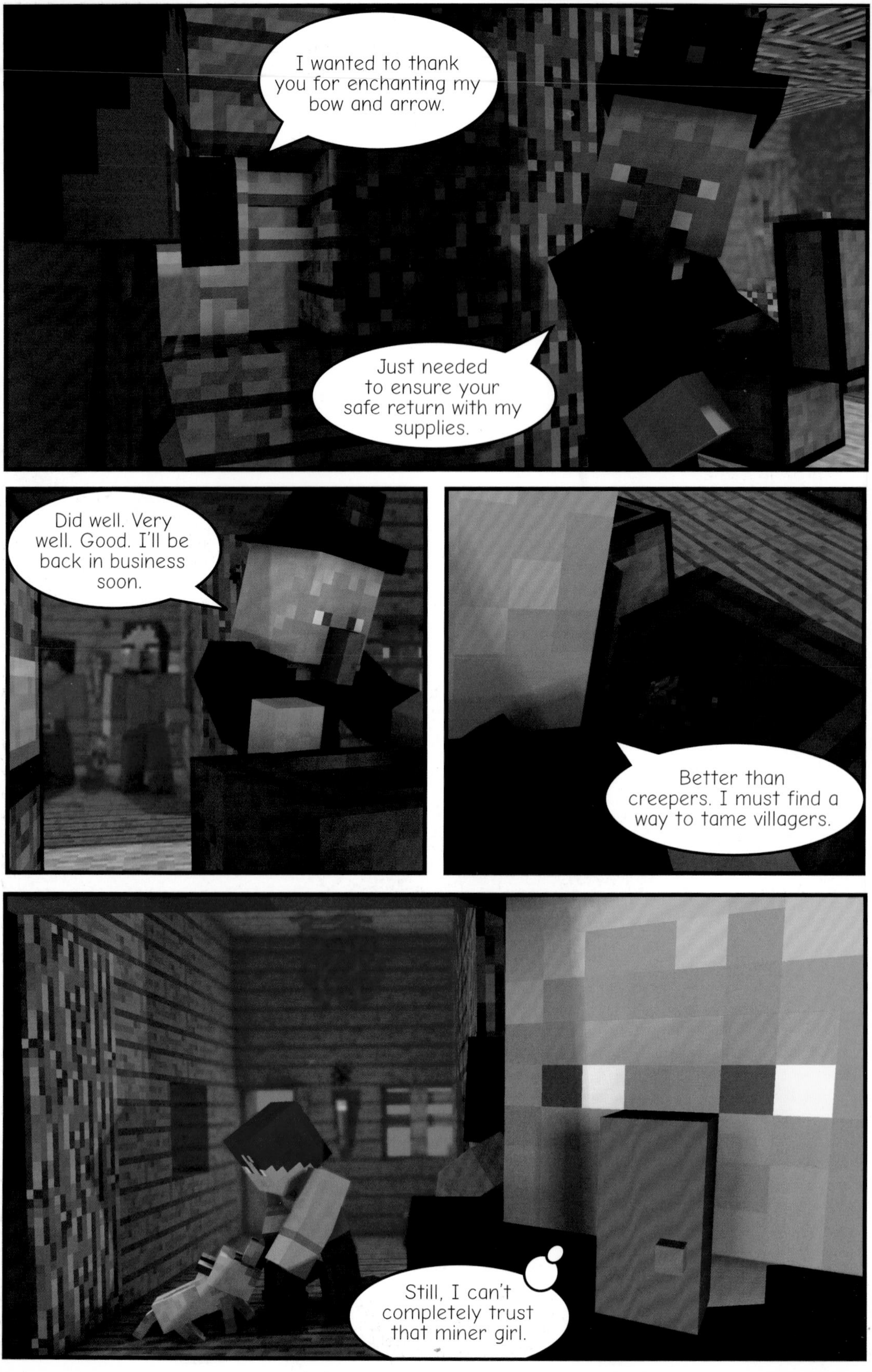
I wanted to thank you for enchanting my bow and arrow.
Just needed to ensure your safe return with my supplies.
Did well. Very well. Good. I'll be back in business soon.
Better than creepers. I must find a way to tame villagers.
Still, I can't completely trust that miner girl.

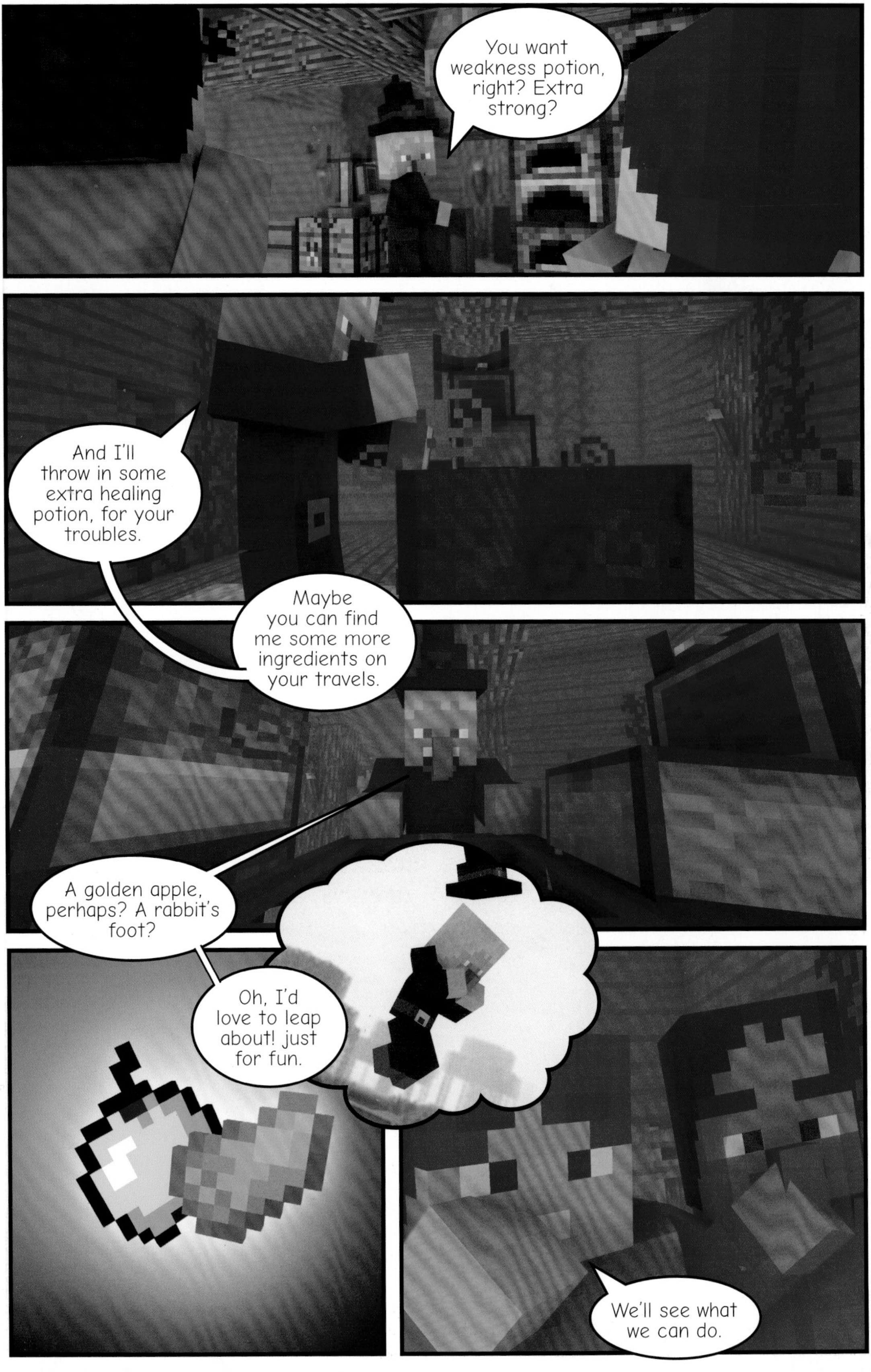
You want weakness potion, right? Extra strong?
And I'll throw in some extra healing potion, for your troubles.
Maybe you can find me some more ingredients on your travels.
A golden apple, perhaps? A rabbit's foot?
Oh, I'd love to leap about! just for fun.
We'll see what we can do.

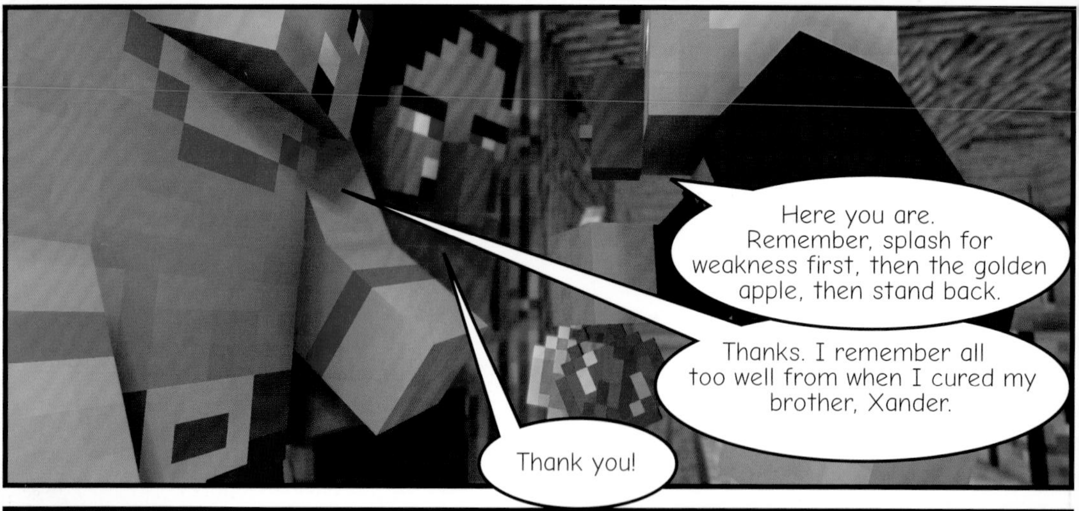
Here you are. Remember, splash for weakness first, then the golden apple, then stand back.
Thanks. I remember all too well from when I cured my brother, Xander.
Thank you!

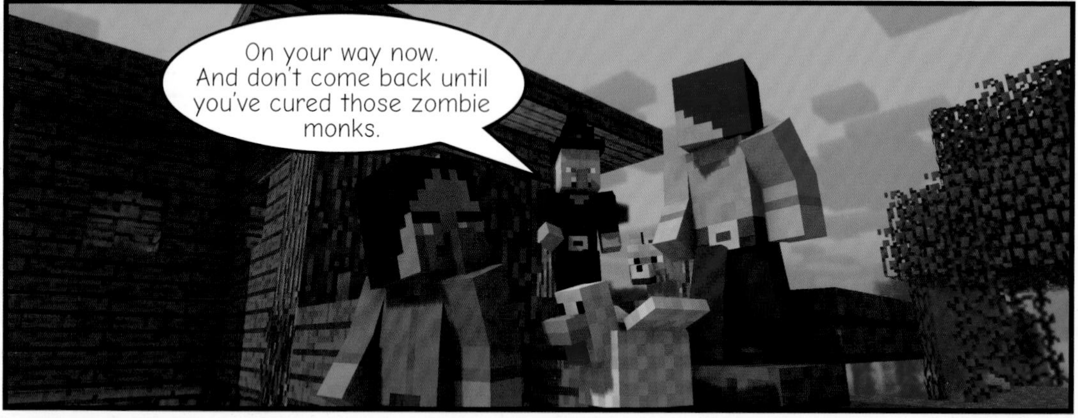
On your way now. And don't come back until you've cured those zombie monks.

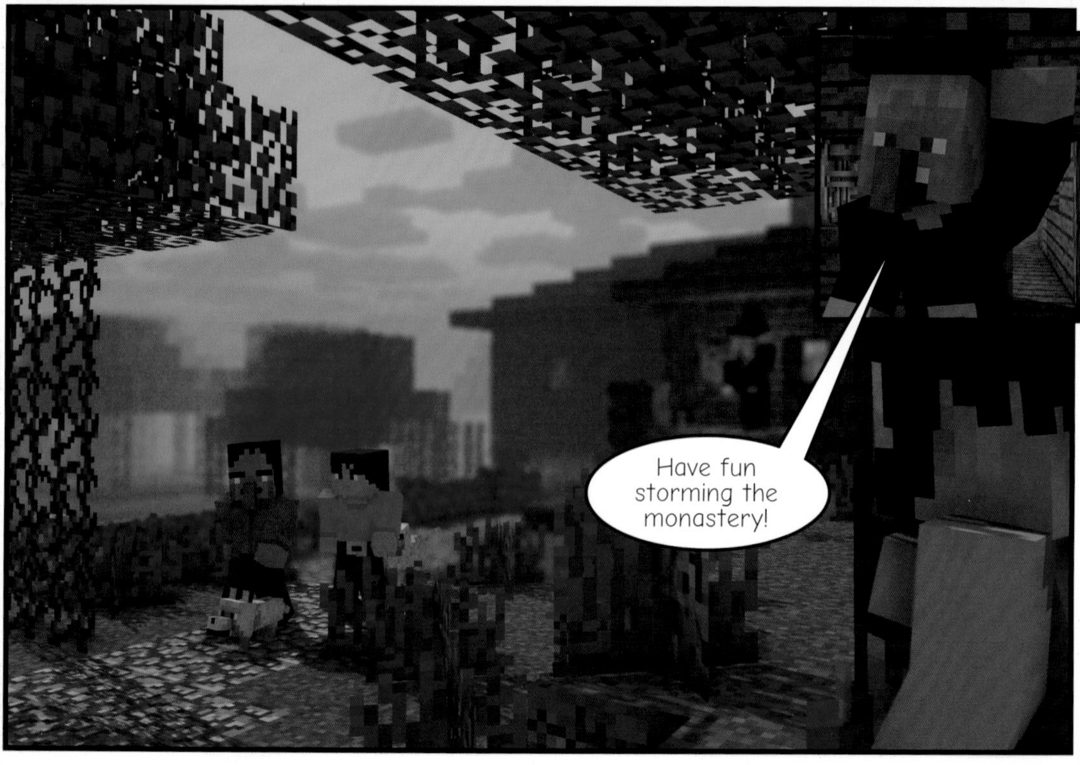
Have fun storming the monastery!

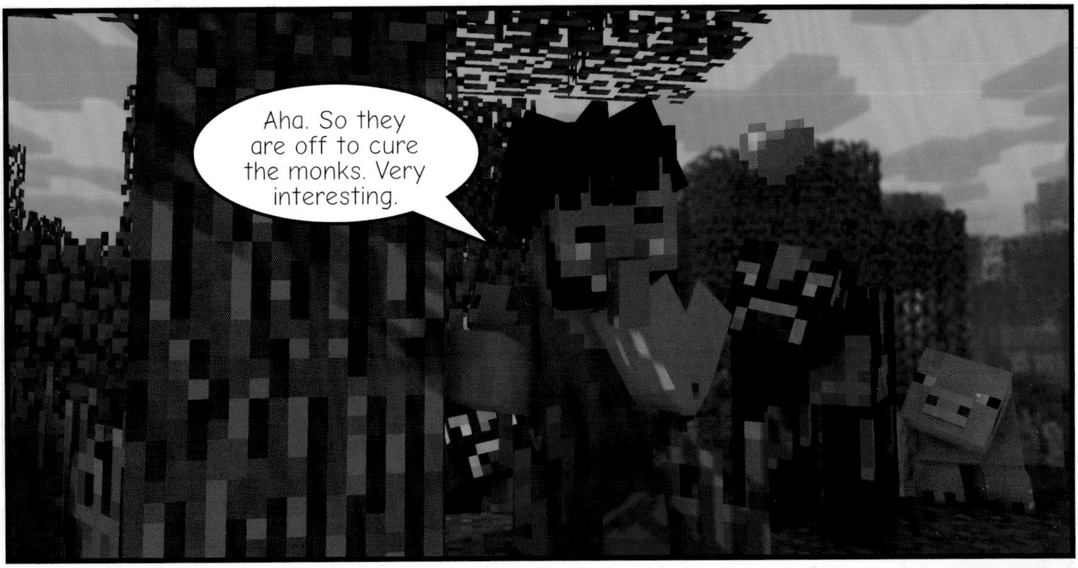
Aha. So they are off to cure the monks. Very interesting.

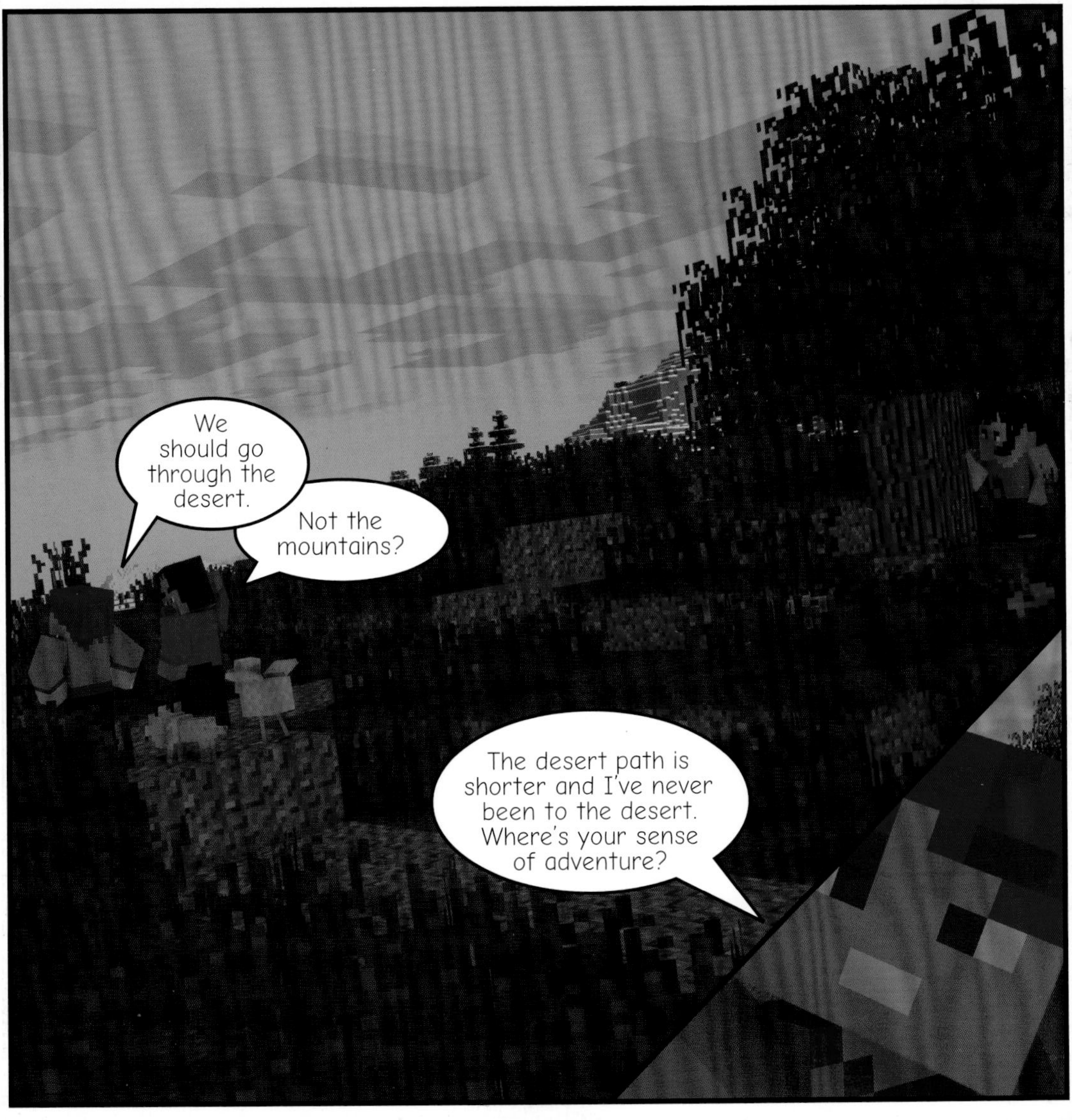
We should go through the desert.
Not the mountains?
The desert path is shorter and I've never been to the desert. Where's your sense of adventure?

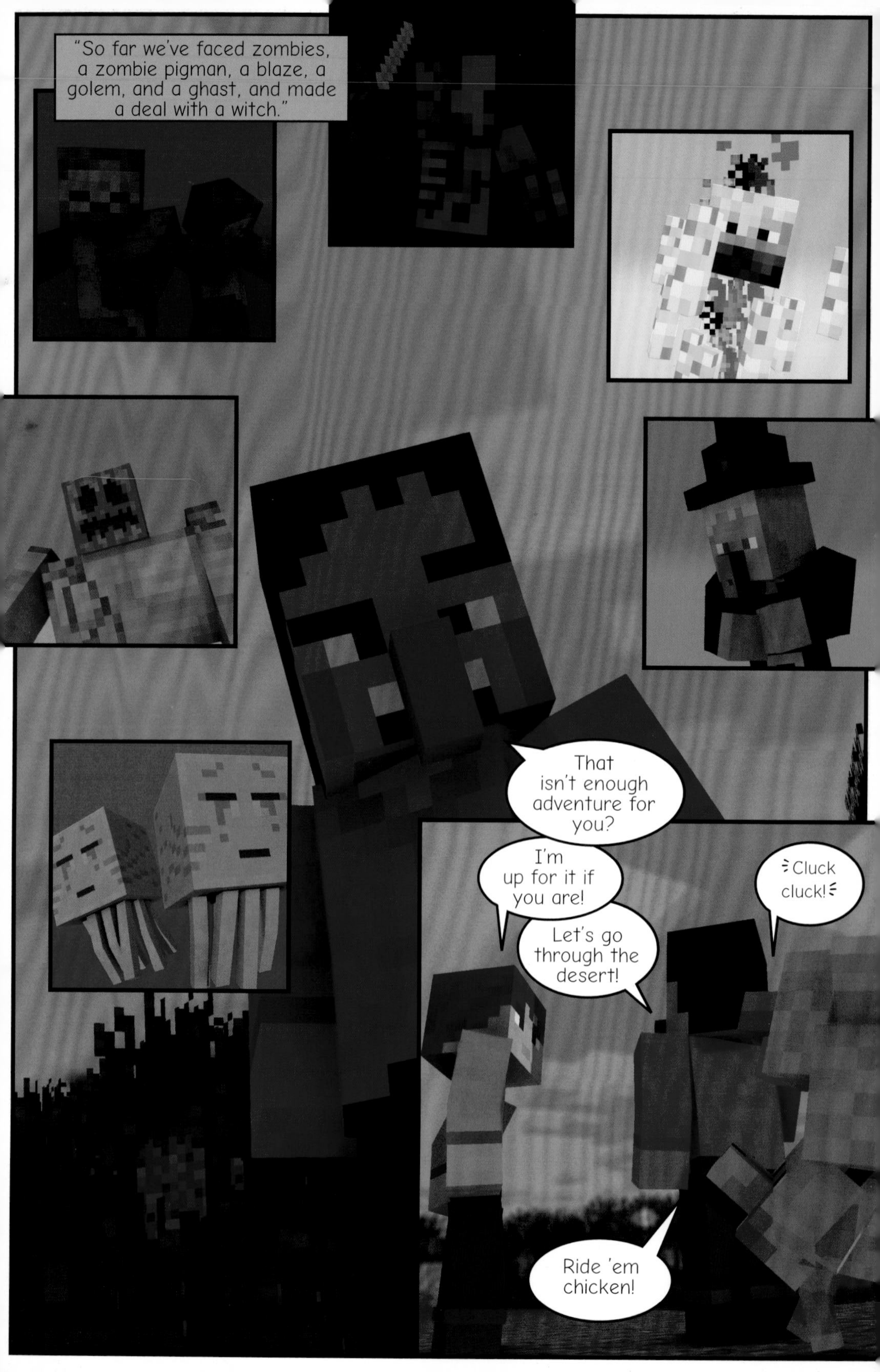
"So far we've faced zombies, a zombie pigman, a blaze, a golem, and a ghast, and made a deal with a witch."
That isn't enough adventure for you?
I'm up for it if you are!
Let's go through the desert!
Cluck cluck!
Ride 'em chicken!

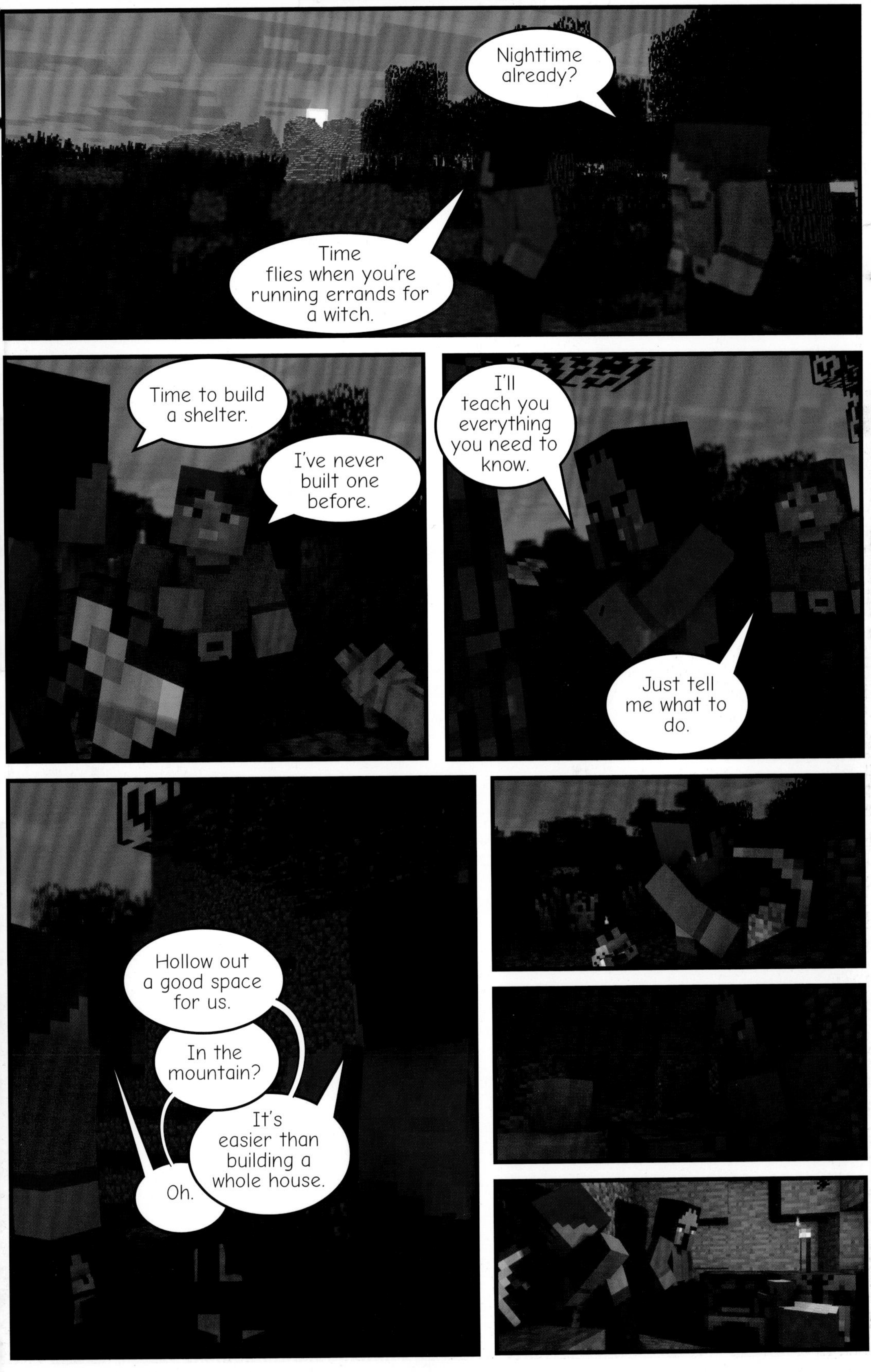
Nighttime already?
Time flies when you're running errands for a witch.
Time to build a shelter.
I've never built one before.
I'll teach you everything you need to know.
Just tell me what to do.
Hollow out a good space for us.
In the mountain?
It's easier than building a whole house.
Oh.

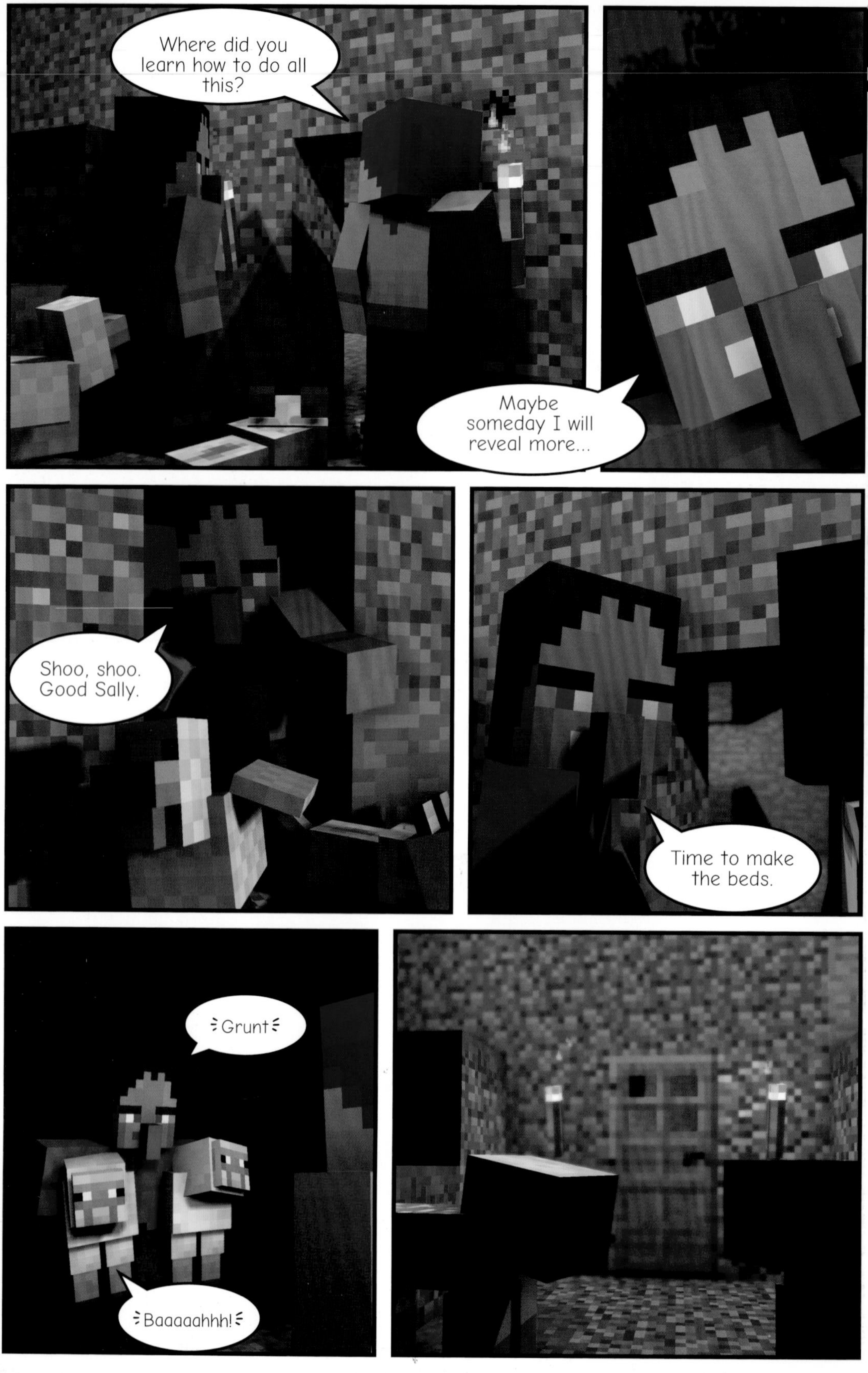
Where did you learn how to do all this?
Maybe someday I will reveal more...
Shoo, shoo. Good Sally.
Time to make the beds.
Grunt
Baaaaahhh!

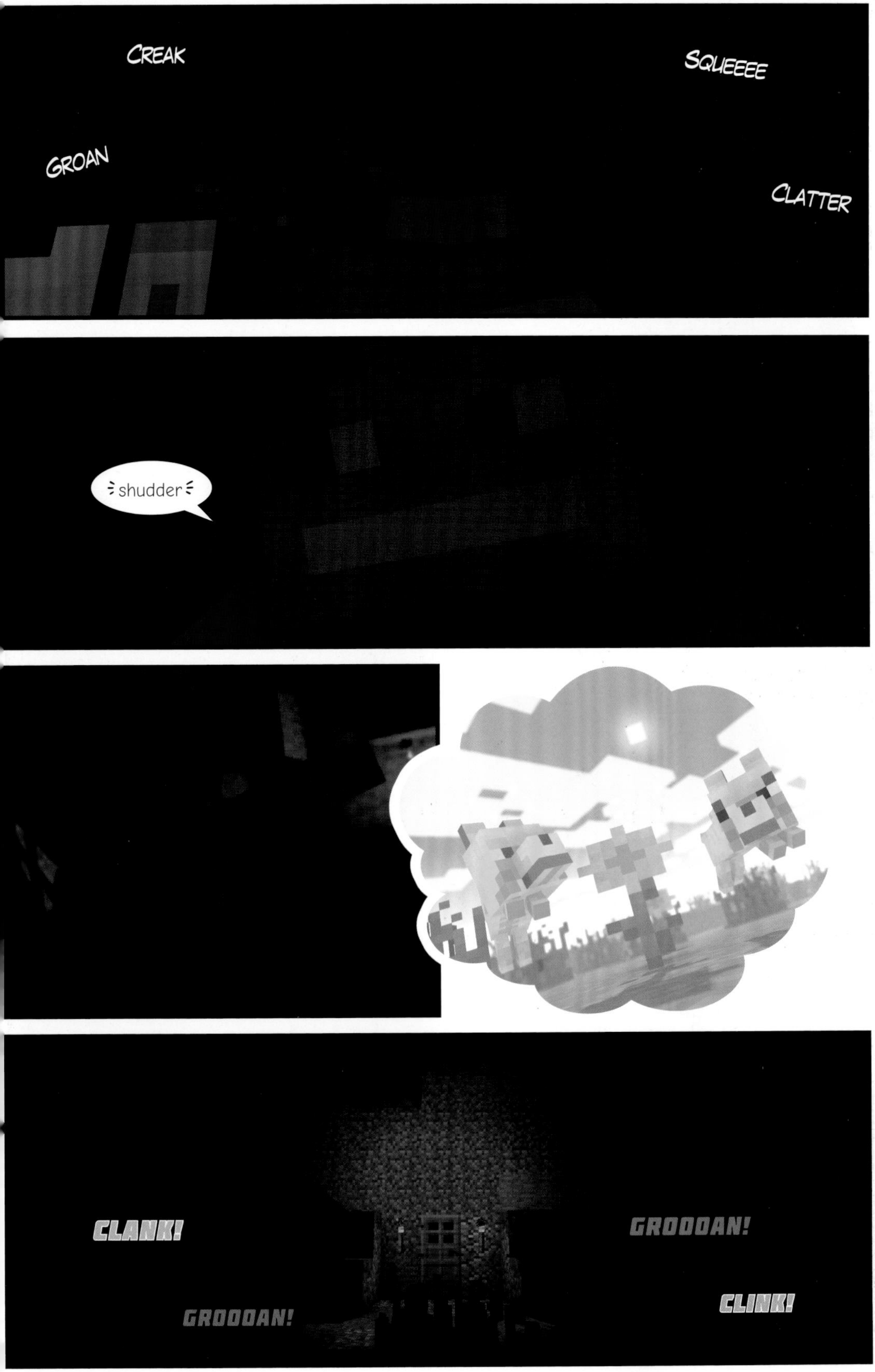
CREAK
SQUEEEE
GROAN
CLATTER
shudder
CLANK!
GROOOAN!
GROOOAN!
CLINK!

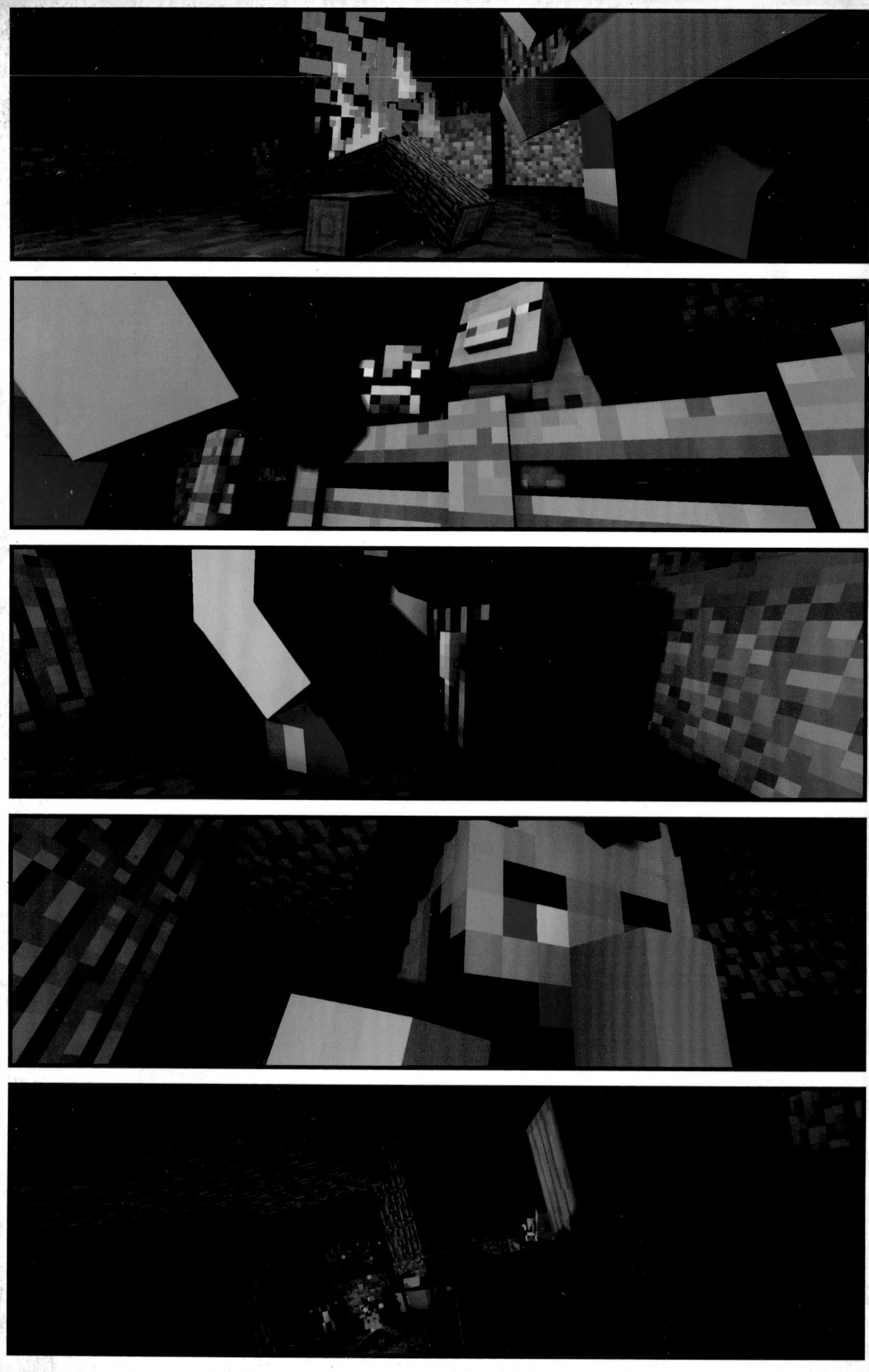

CHAPTER 5

THE TEMPLE

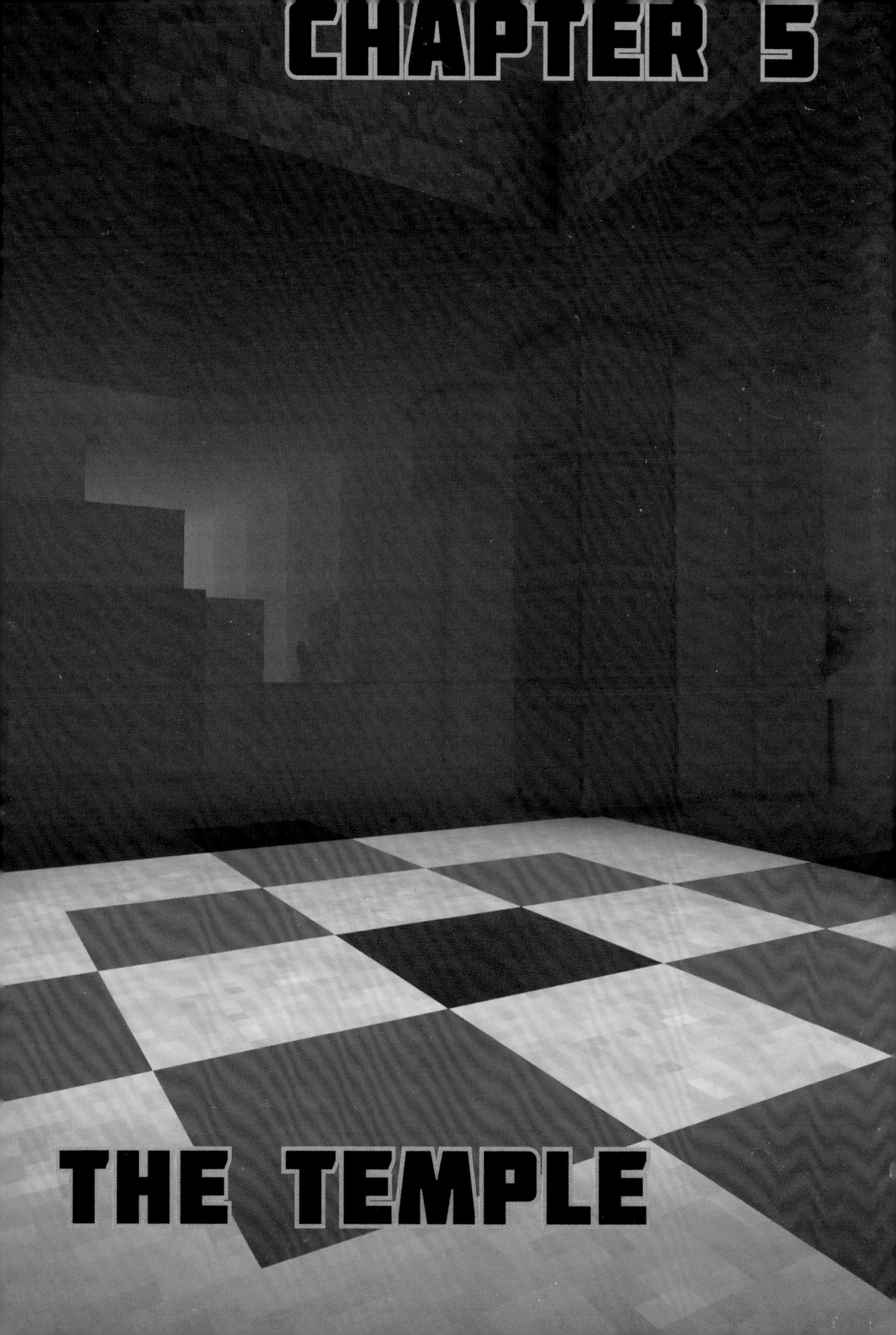

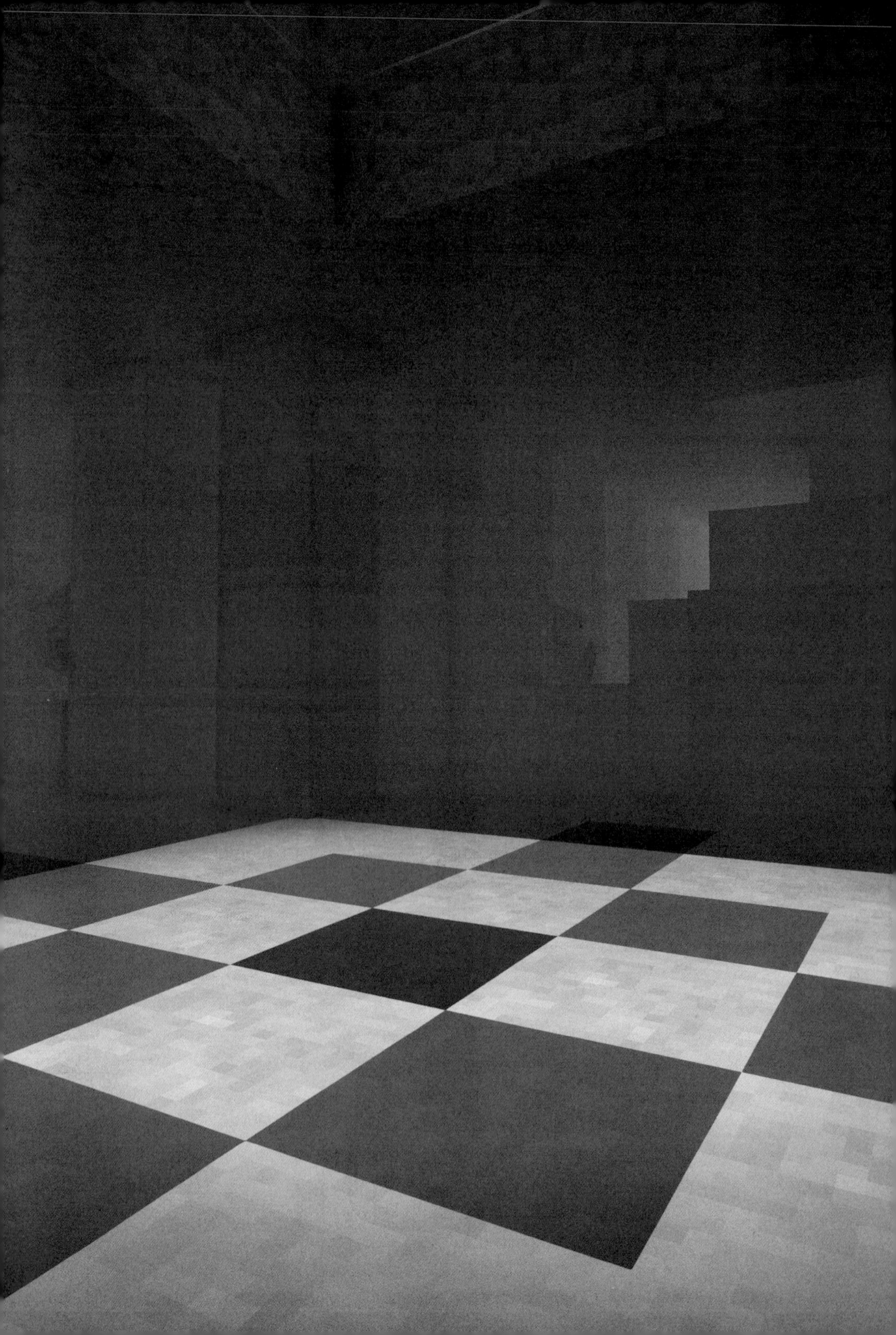

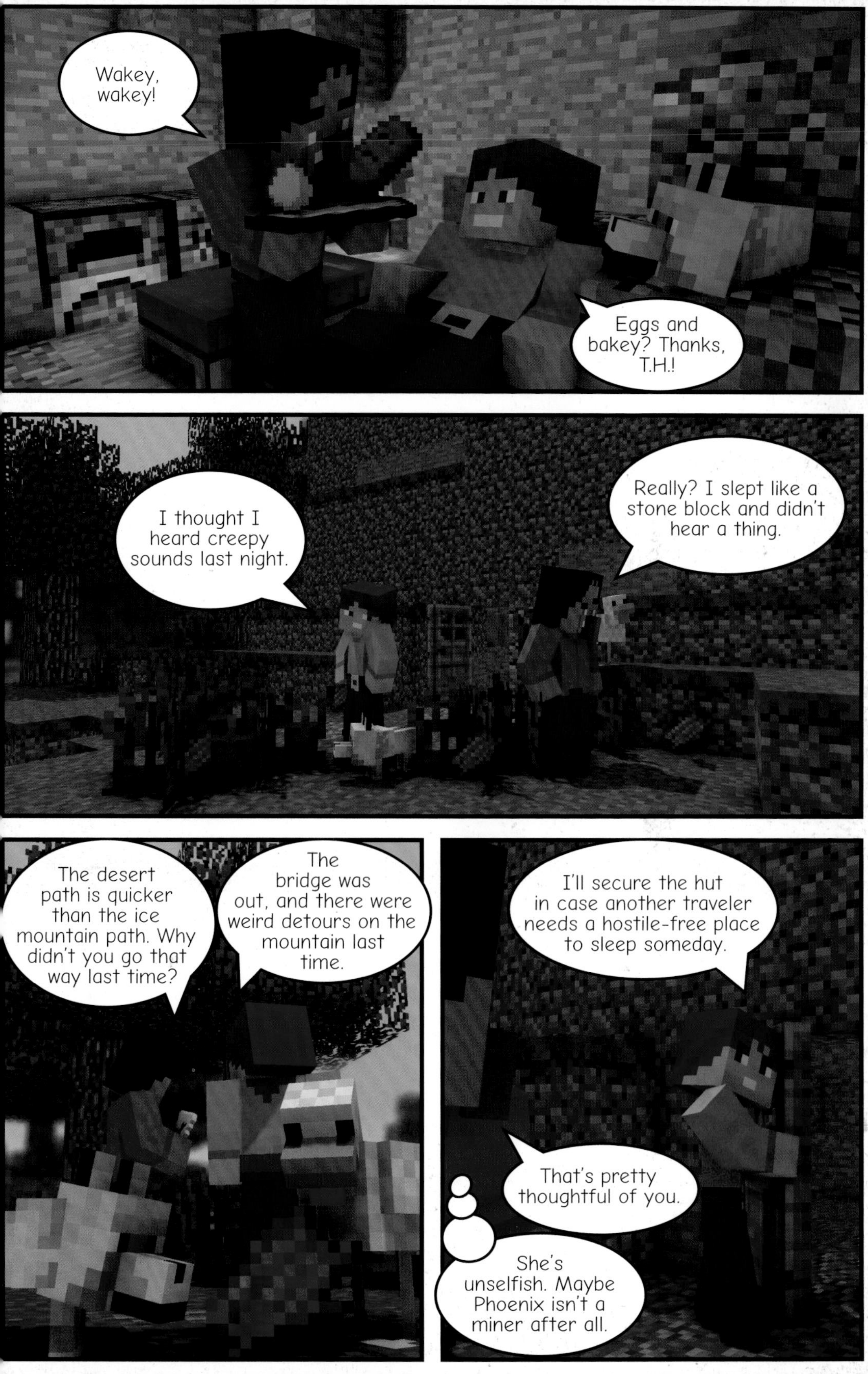
Wakey, wakey!
Eggs and bakey? Thanks, T.H.!
I thought I heard creepy sounds last night.
Really? I slept like a stone block and didn't hear a thing.
The desert path is quicker than the ice mountain path. Why didn't you go that way last time?
The bridge was out, and there were weird detours on the mountain last time.
I'll secure the hut in case another traveler needs a hostile-free place to sleep someday.
That's pretty thoughtful of you.
She's unselfish. Maybe Phoenix isn't a miner after all.

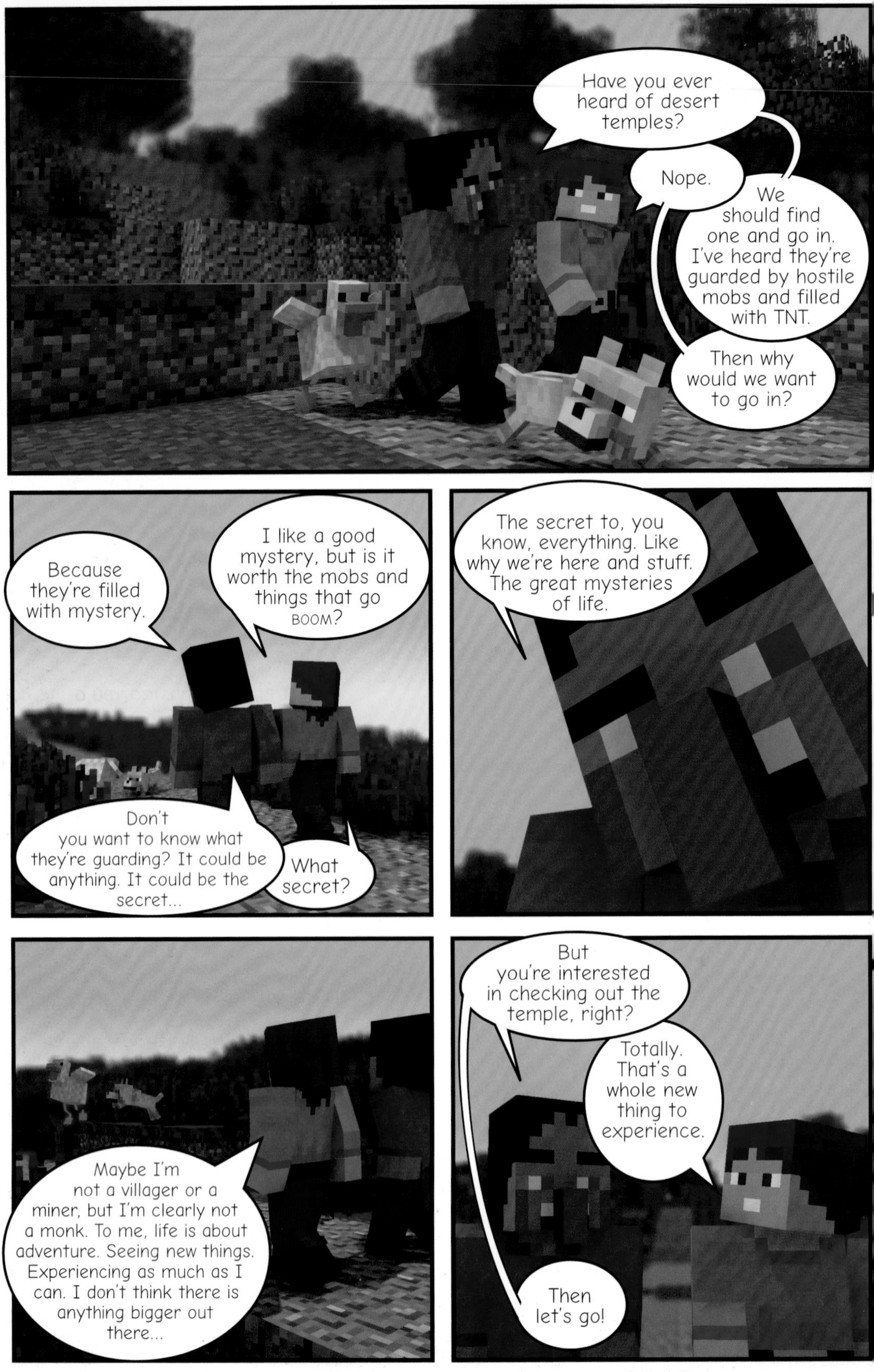
Have you ever heard of desert temples?
Nope.
We should find one and go in. I've heard they're guarded by hostile mobs and filled with TNT.
Then why would we want to go in?
Because they're filled with mystery.
I like a good mystery, but is it worth the mobs and things that go BOOM?
Don't you want to know what they're guarding? It could be anything. It could be the secret...
What secret?
The secret to, you know, everything. Like why we're here and stuff. The great mysteries of life.
Maybe I'm not a villager or a miner, but I'm clearly not a monk. To me, life is about adventure. Seeing new things. Experiencing as much as I can. I don't think there is anything bigger out there...
But you're interested in checking out the temple, right?
Totally. That's a whole new thing to experience.
Then let's go!

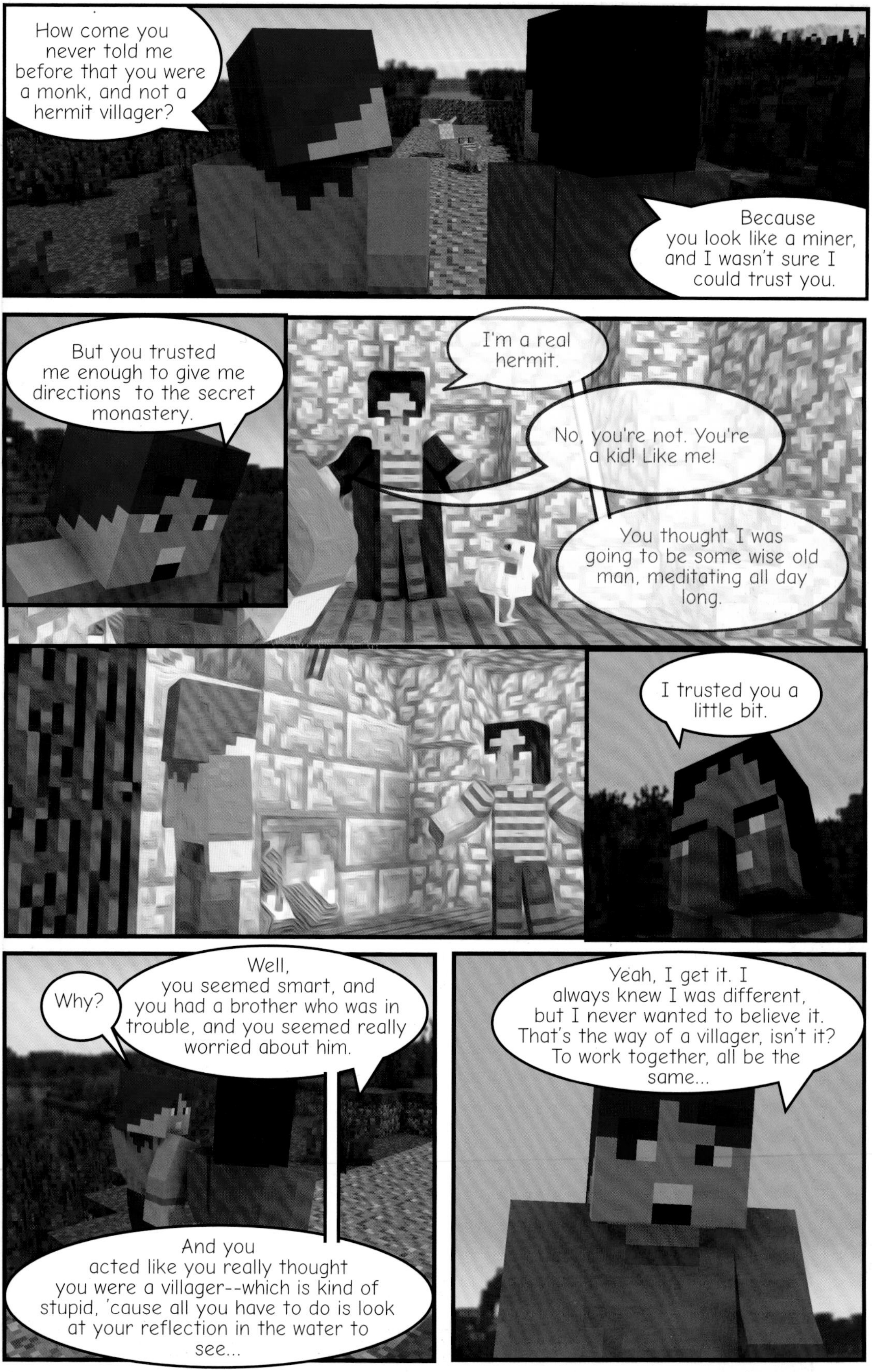
How come you never told me before that you were a monk, and not a hermit villager?
Because you look like a miner, and I wasn't sure I could trust you.
But you trusted me enough to give me directions to the secret monastery.
I'm a real hermit.
No, you're not. You're a kid! Like me!
You thought I was going to be some wise old man, meditating all day long.
I trusted you a little bit.
Why?
Well, you seemed smart, and you had a brother who was in trouble, and you seemed really worried about him.
And you acted like you really thought you were a villager--which is kind of stupid, 'cause all you have to do is look at your reflection in the water to see...
Yeah, I get it. I always knew I was different, but I never wanted to believe it. That's the way of a villager, isn't it? To work together, all be the same...

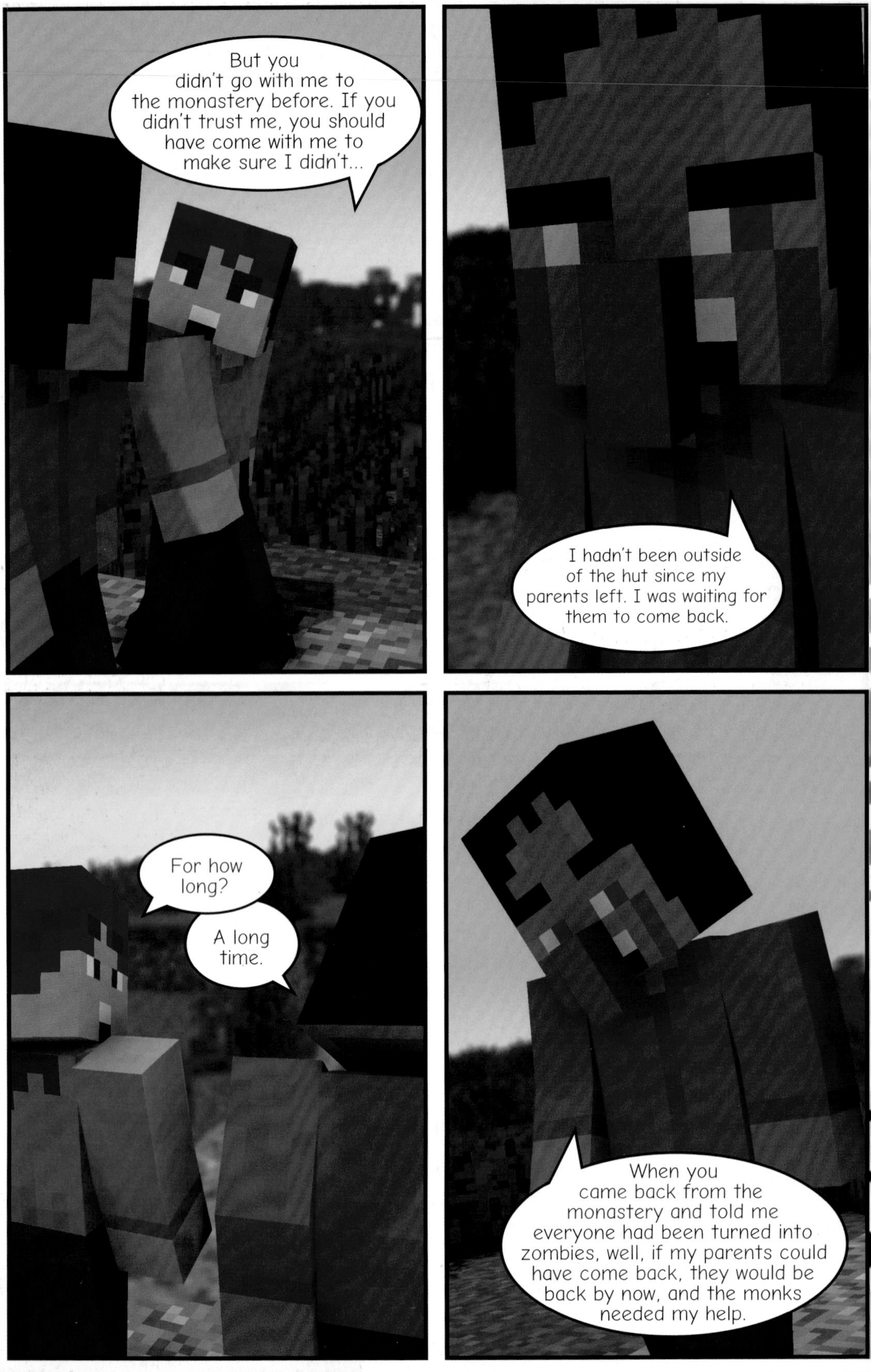
But you didn't go with me to the monastery before. If you didn't trust me, you should have come with me to make sure I didn't...
I hadn't been outside of the hut since my parents left. I was waiting for them to come back.
For how long?
A long time.
When you came back from the monastery and told me everyone had been turned into zombies, well, if my parents could have come back, they would be back by now, and the monks needed my help.

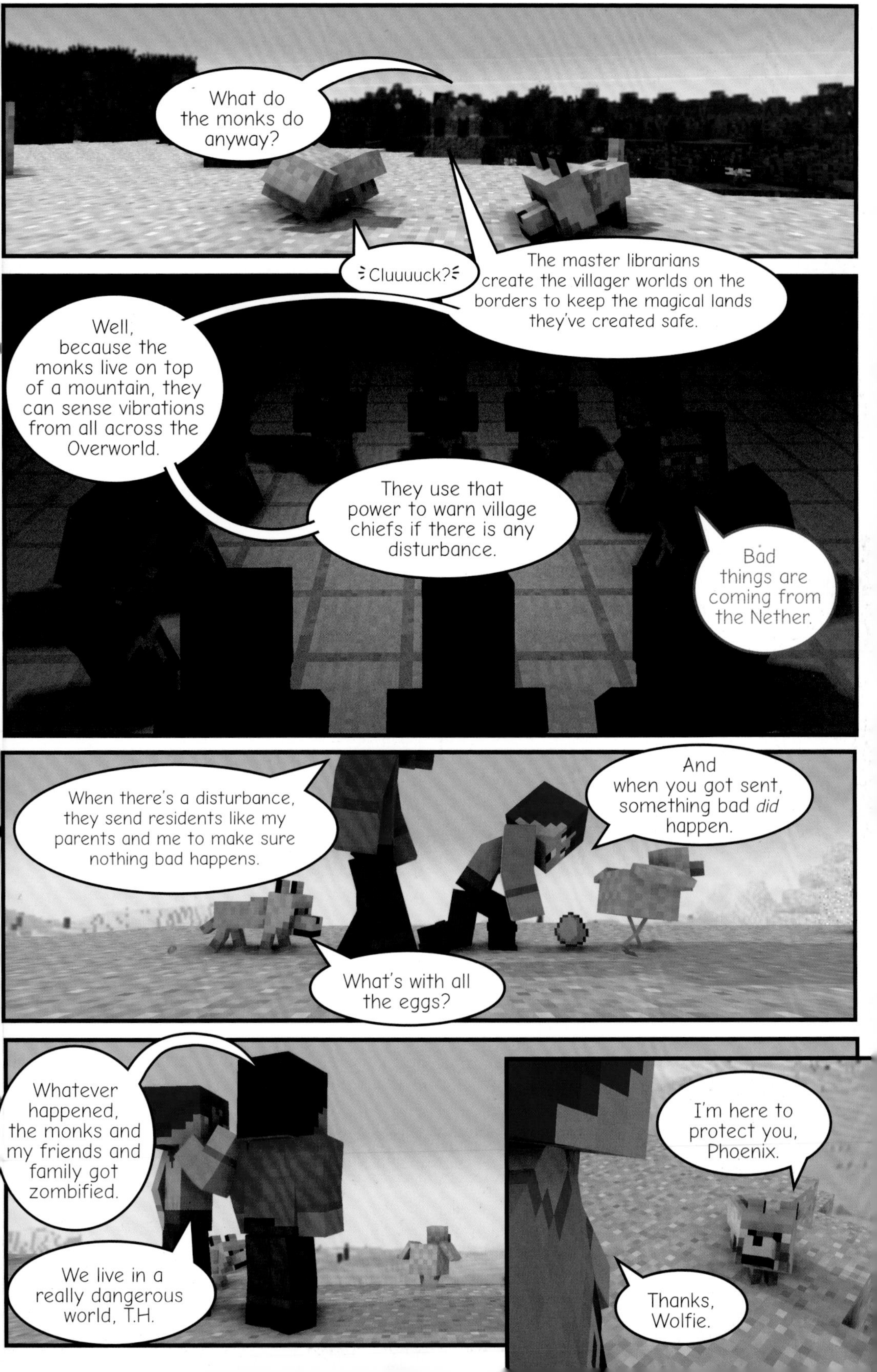
What do the monks do anyway?
Cluuuuck?
The master librarians create the villager worlds on the borders to keep the magical lands they've created safe.
Well, because the monks live on top of a mountain, they can sense vibrations from all across the Overworld.
They use that power to warn village chiefs if there is any disturbance.
Bad things are coming from the Nether.
When there's a disturbance, they send residents like my parents and me to make sure nothing bad happens.
And when you got sent, something bad *did* happen.
What's with all the eggs?
Whatever happened, the monks and my friends and family got zombified.
We live in a really dangerous world, T.H.
I'm here to protect you, Phoenix.
Thanks, Wolfie.

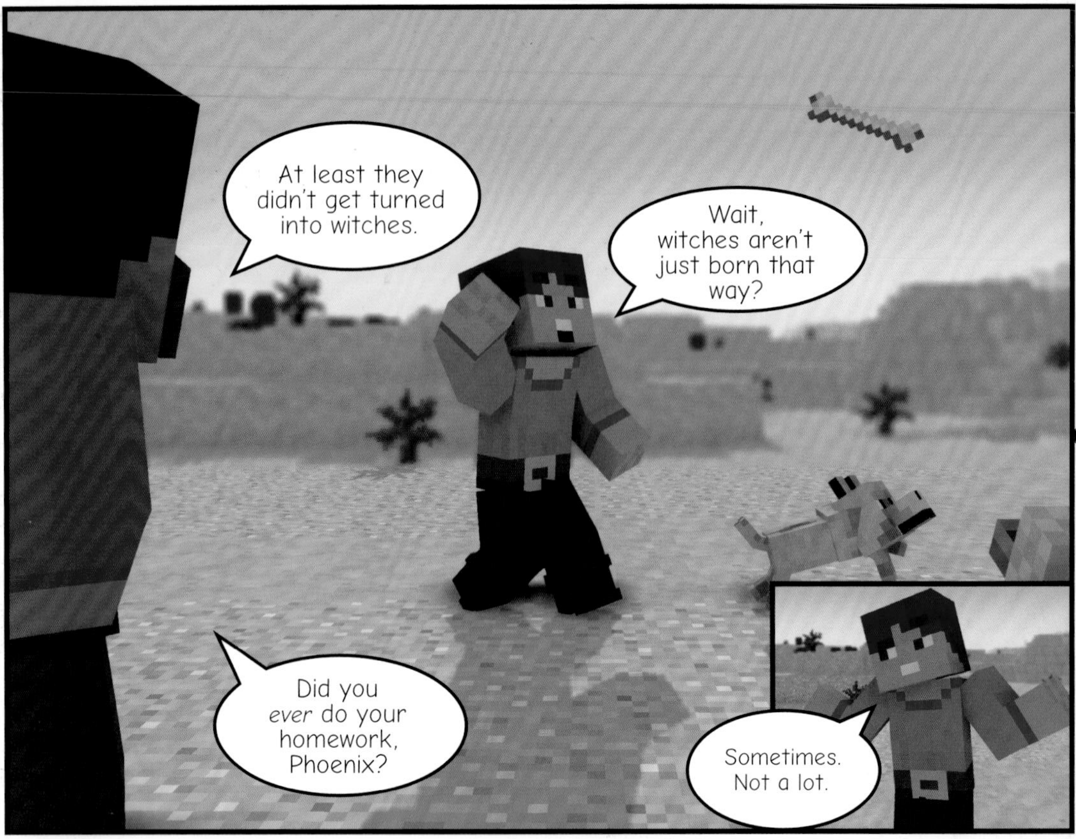
At least they didn't get turned into witches.
Wait, witches aren't just born that way?
Did you *ever* do your homework, Phoenix?
Sometimes. Not a lot.

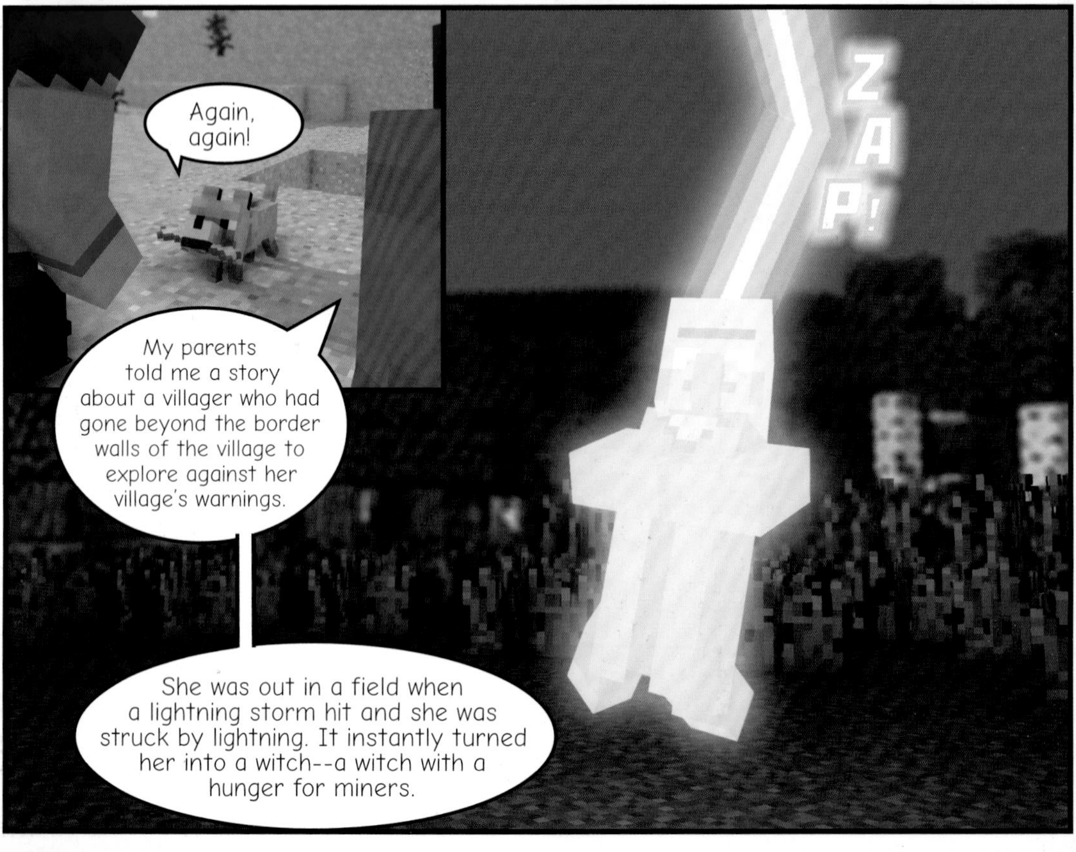
Again, again!
My parents told me a story about a villager who had gone beyond the border walls of the village to explore against her village's warnings.
She was out in a field when a lightning storm hit and she was struck by lightning. It instantly turned her into a witch--a witch with a hunger for miners.
ZAP!

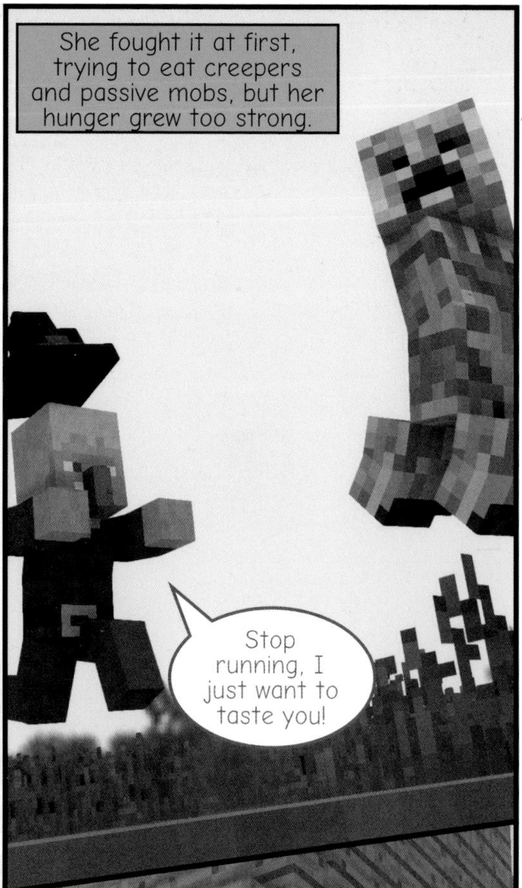
She fought it at first, trying to eat creepers and passive mobs, but her hunger grew too strong.
Stop running, I just want to taste you!

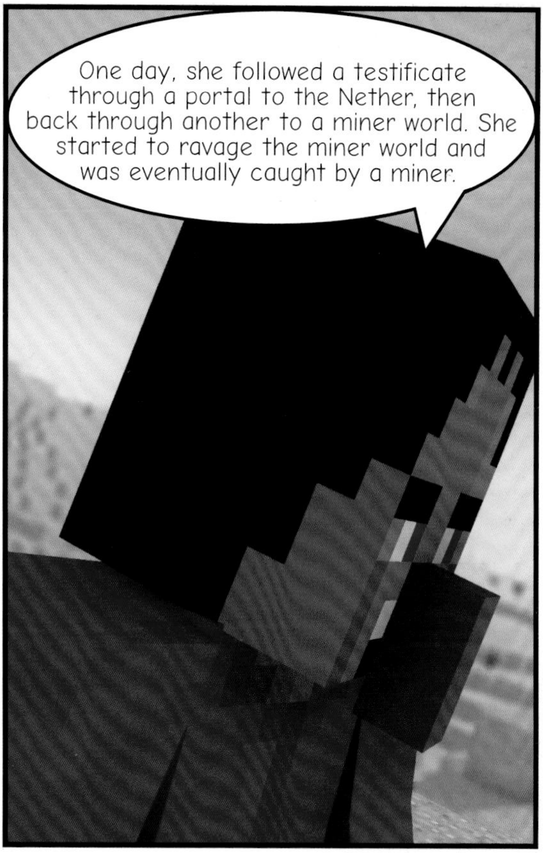
One day, she followed a testificate through a portal to the Nether, then back through another to a miner world. She started to ravage the miner world and was eventually caught by a miner.

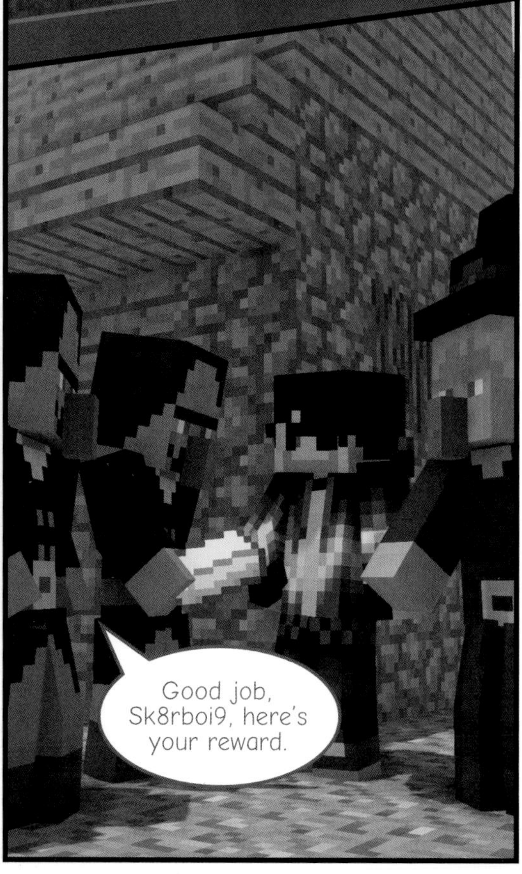
Good job, Sk8rboi9, here's your reward.

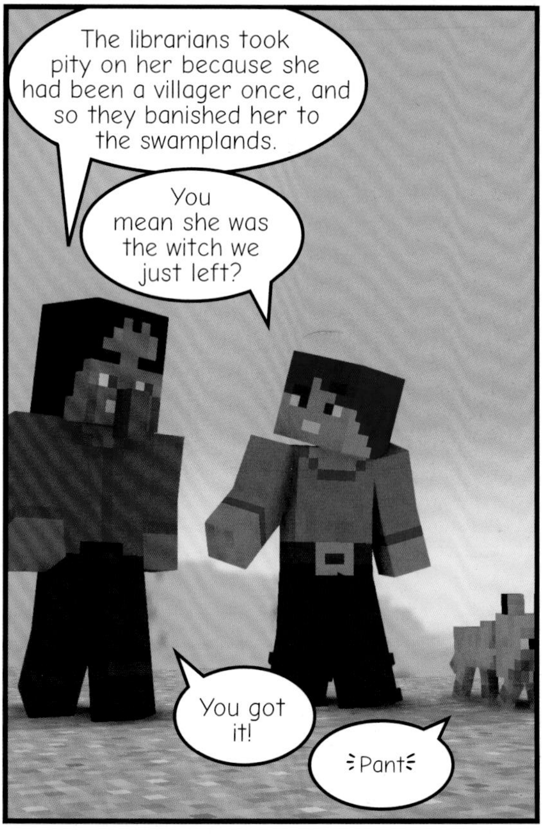
The librarians took pity on her because she had been a villager once, and so they banished her to the swamplands.
You mean she was the witch we just left?
You got it!
Pant

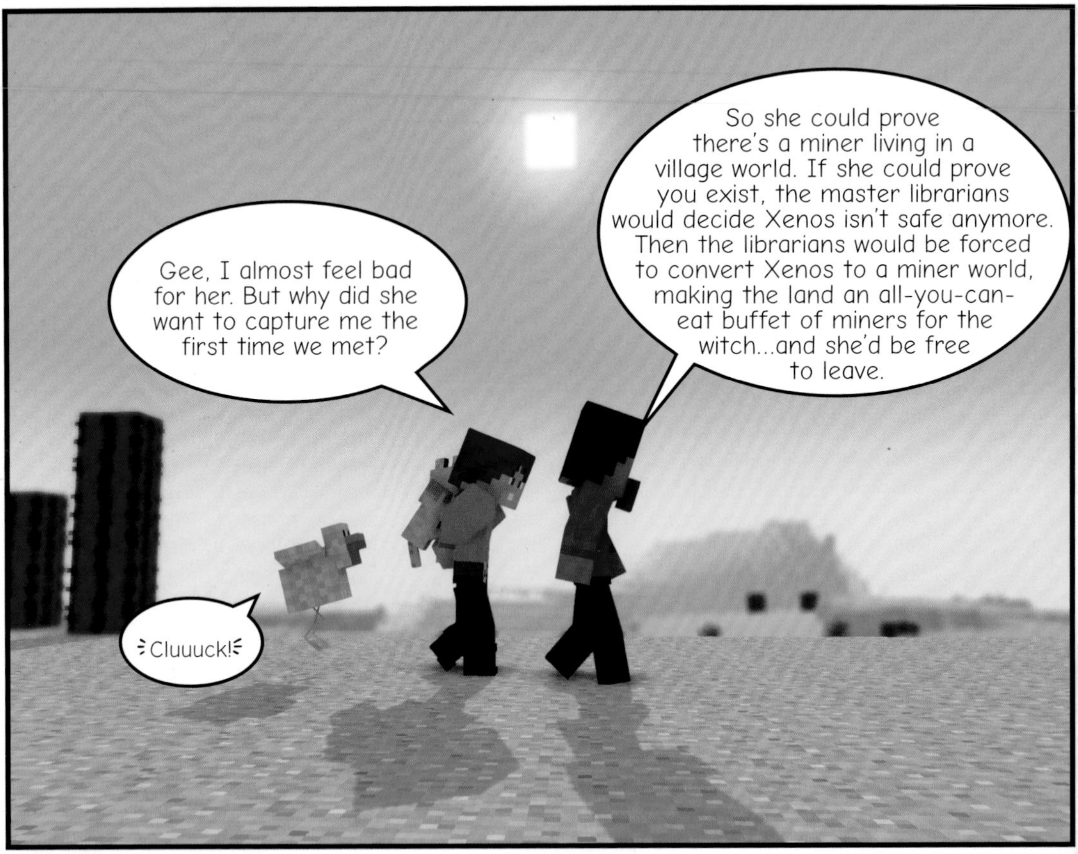
Gee, I almost feel bad for her. But why did she want to capture me the first time we met?
So she could prove there's a miner living in a village world. If she could prove you exist, the master librarians would decide Xenos isn't safe anymore. Then the librarians would be forced to convert Xenos to a miner world, making the land an all-you-can-eat buffet of miners for the witch...and she'd be free to leave.
Cluuuck!

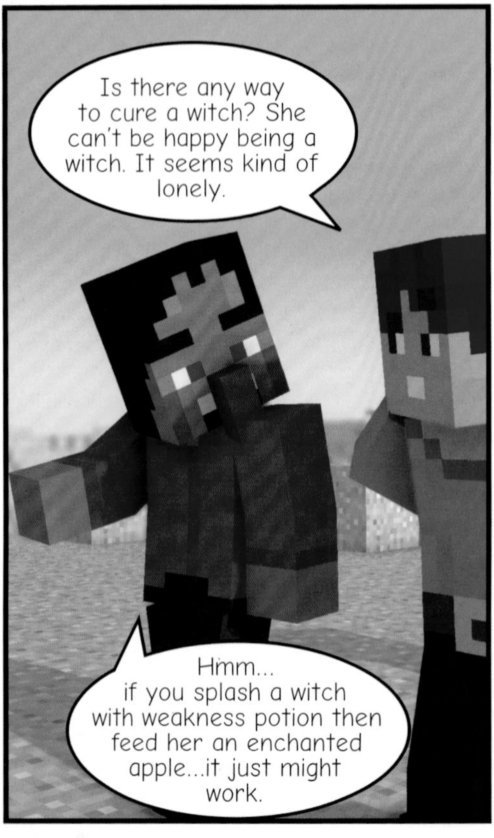
Is there any way to cure a witch? She can't be happy being a witch. It seems kind of lonely.
Hmm... if you splash a witch with weakness potion then feed her an enchanted apple...it just might work.

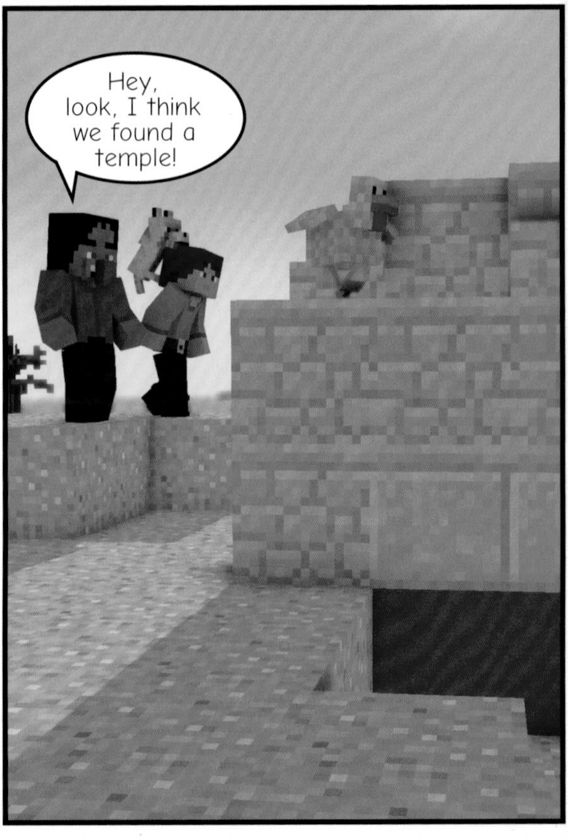
Hey, look, I think we found a temple!

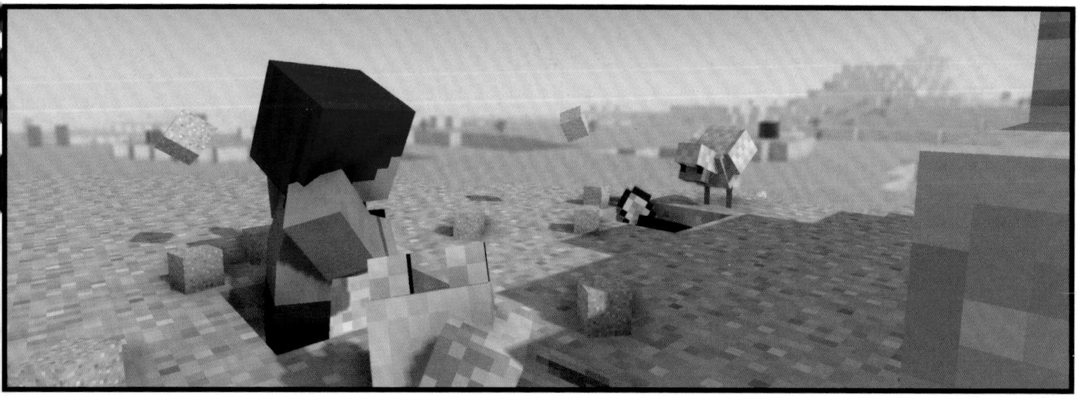

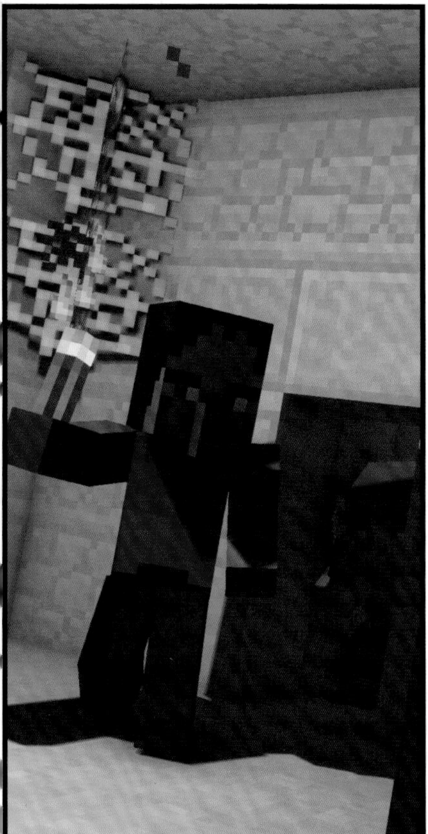

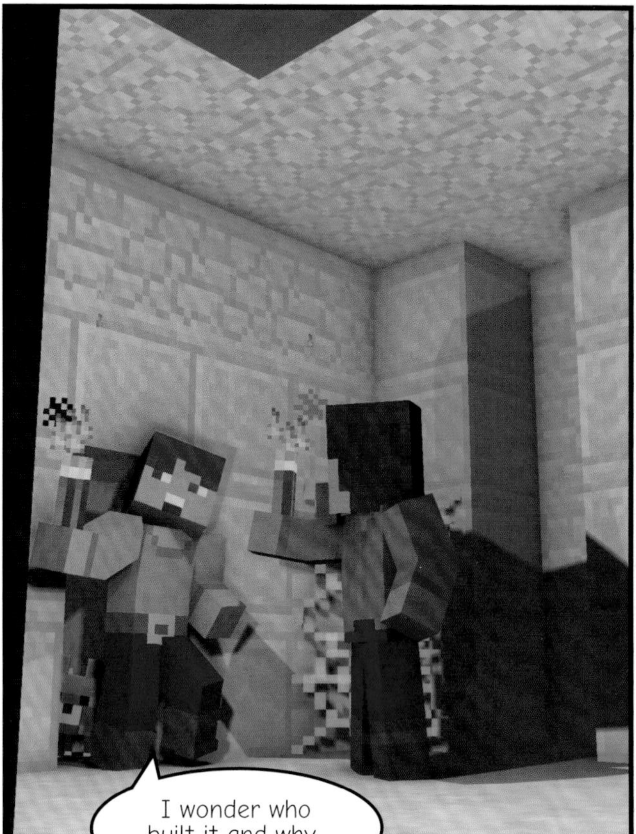
I wonder who built it and why.

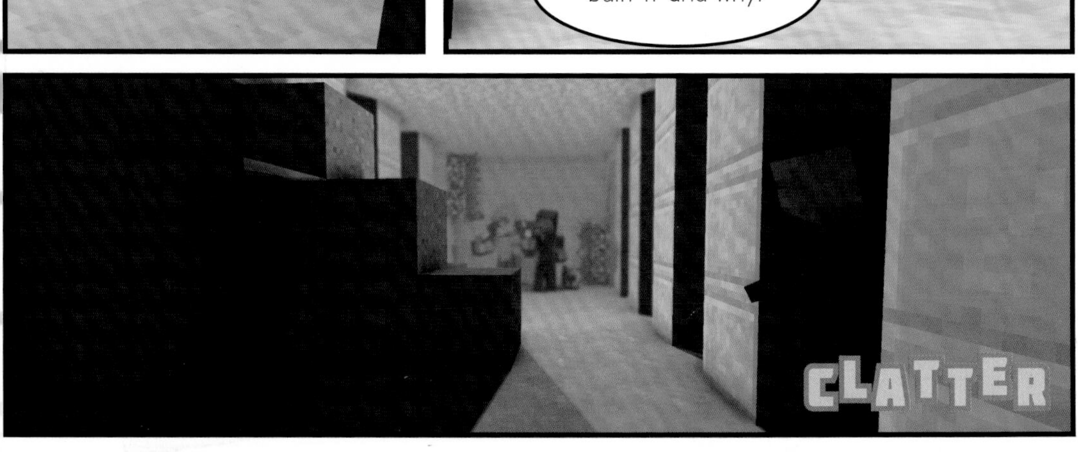
CLATTER

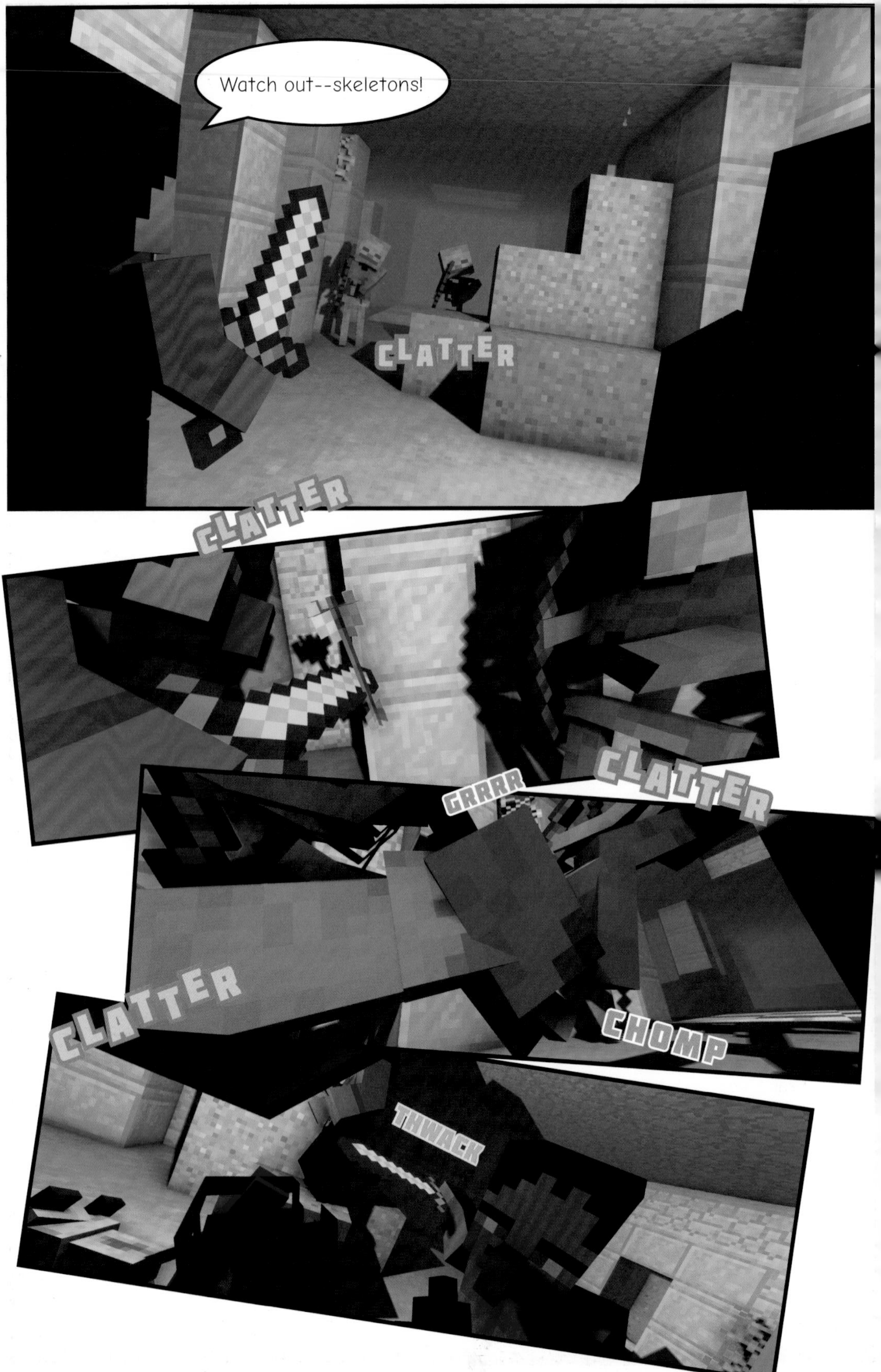
Watch out--skeletons!
CLATTER
CLATTER
GRRRR
CLATTER
CLATTER
CHOMP
THWACK

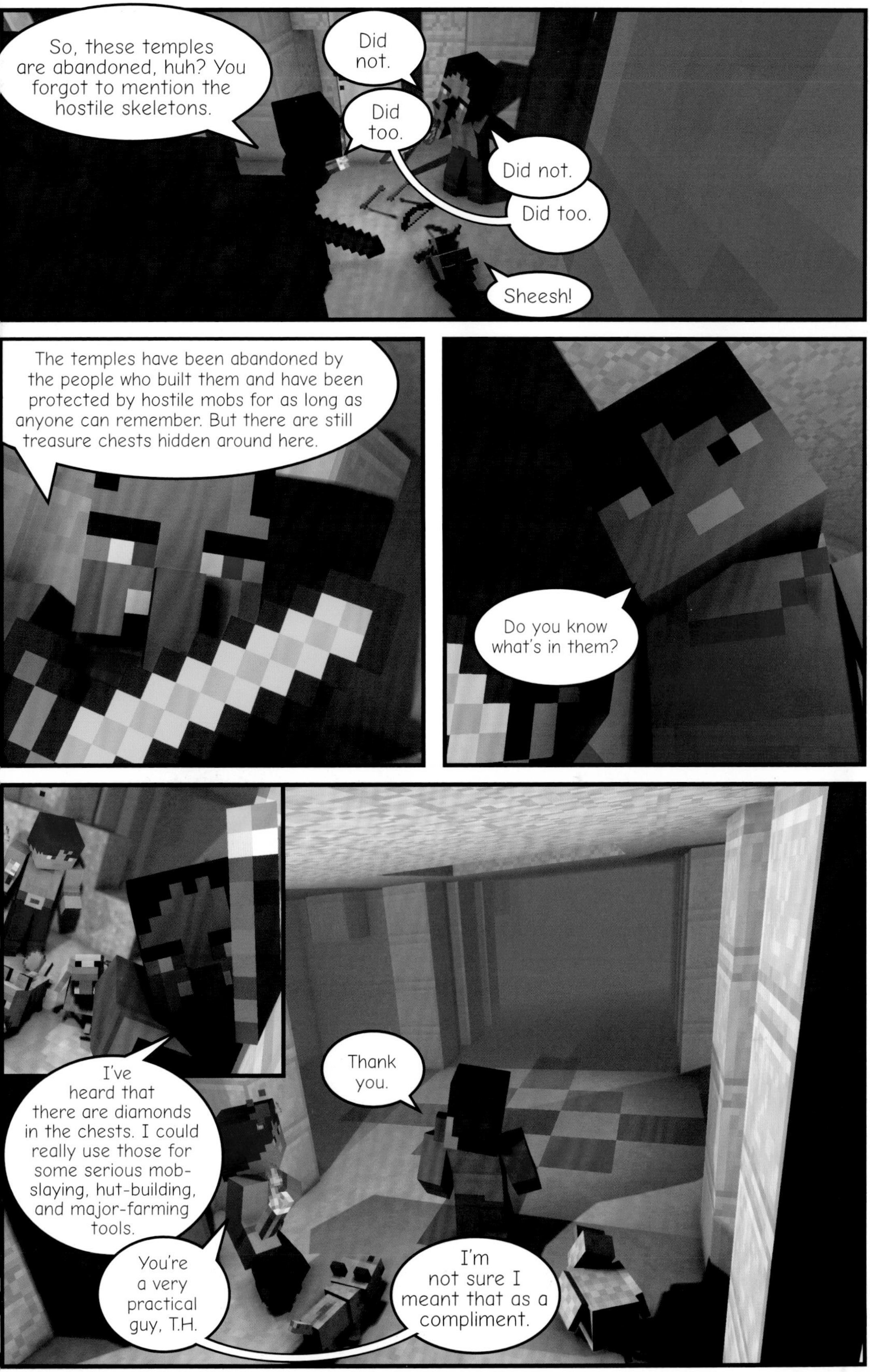
So, these temples are abandoned, huh? You forgot to mention the hostile skeletons.
Did not.
Did too.
Did not.
Did too.
Sheesh!
The temples have been abandoned by the people who built them and have been protected by hostile mobs for as long as anyone can remember. But there are still treasure chests hidden around here.
Do you know what's in them?
I've heard that there are diamonds in the chests. I could really use those for some serious mob-slaying, hut-building, and major-farming tools.
Thank you.
You're a very practical guy, T.H.
I'm not sure I meant that as a compliment.

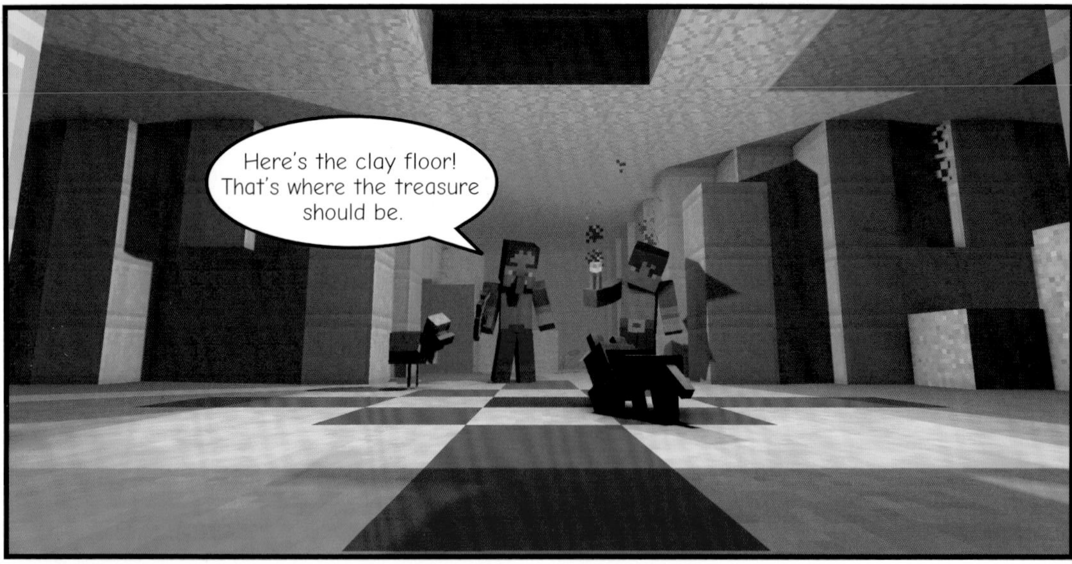
Here's the clay floor! That's where the treasure should be.

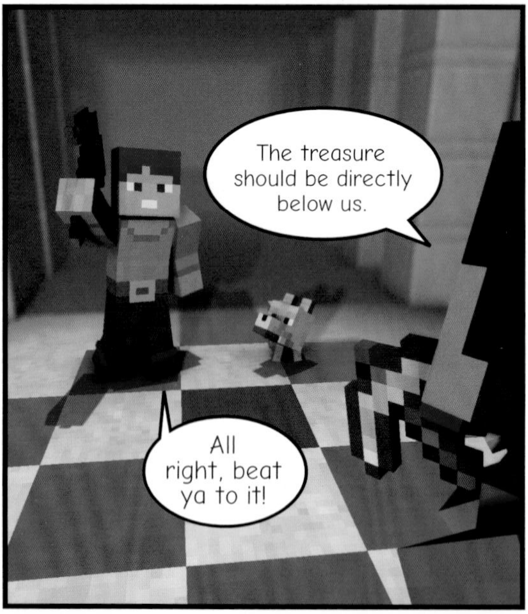
The treasure should be directly below us.
All right, beat ya to it!

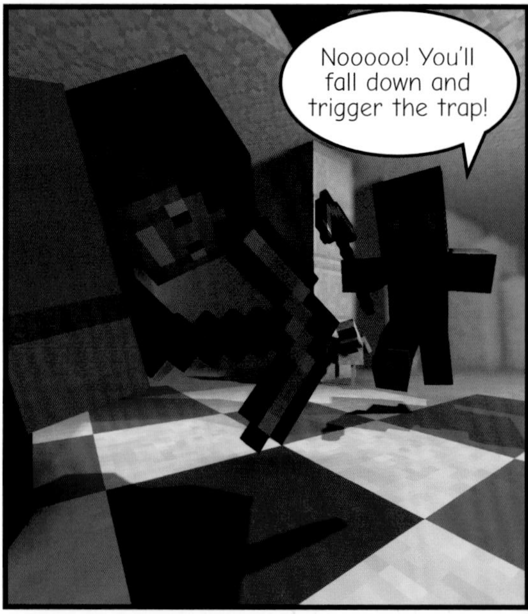
Nooooo! You'll fall down and trigger the trap!

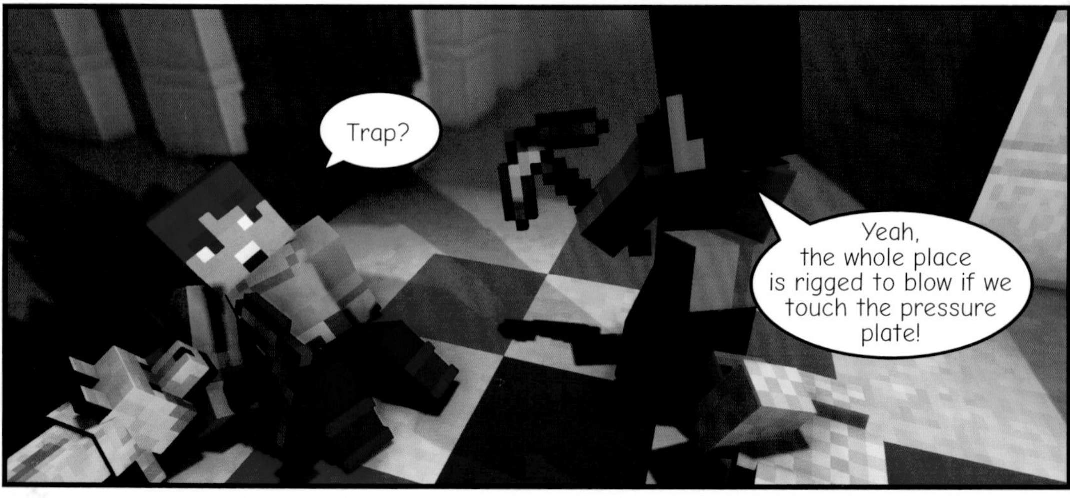
Trap?
Yeah, the whole place is rigged to blow if we touch the pressure plate!

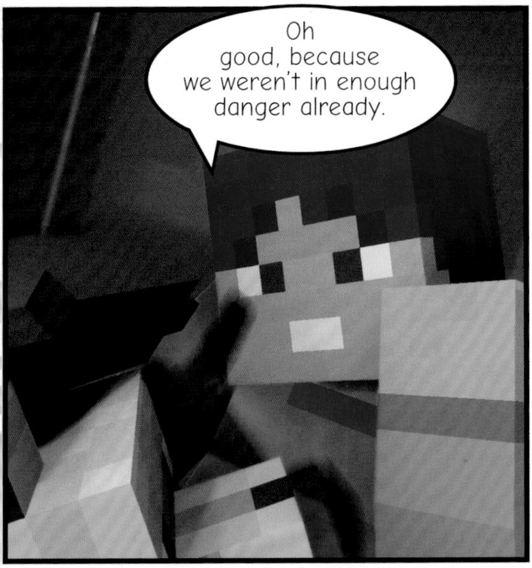
Oh good, because we weren't in enough danger already.

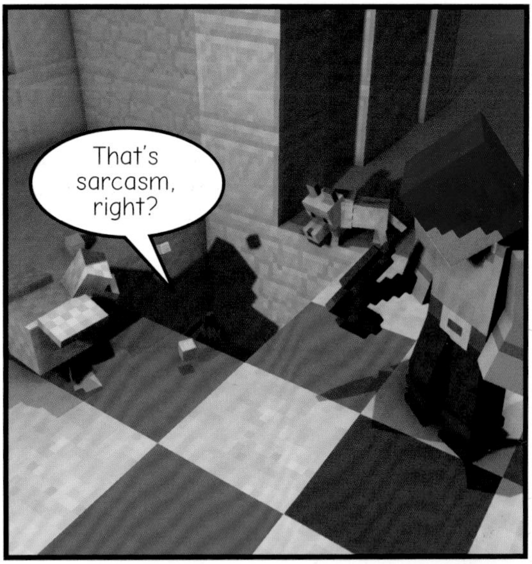
That's sarcasm, right?

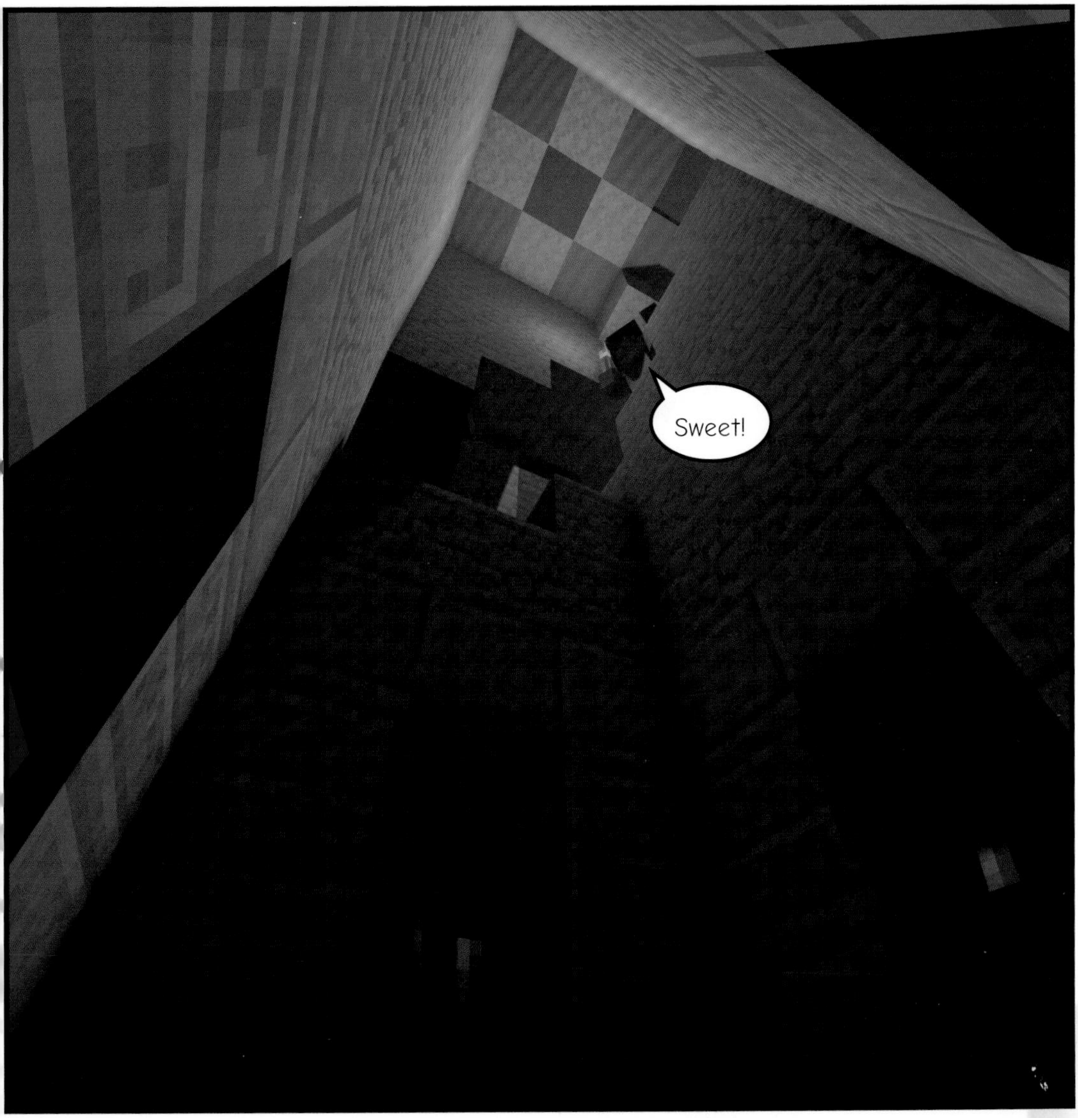
Sweet!

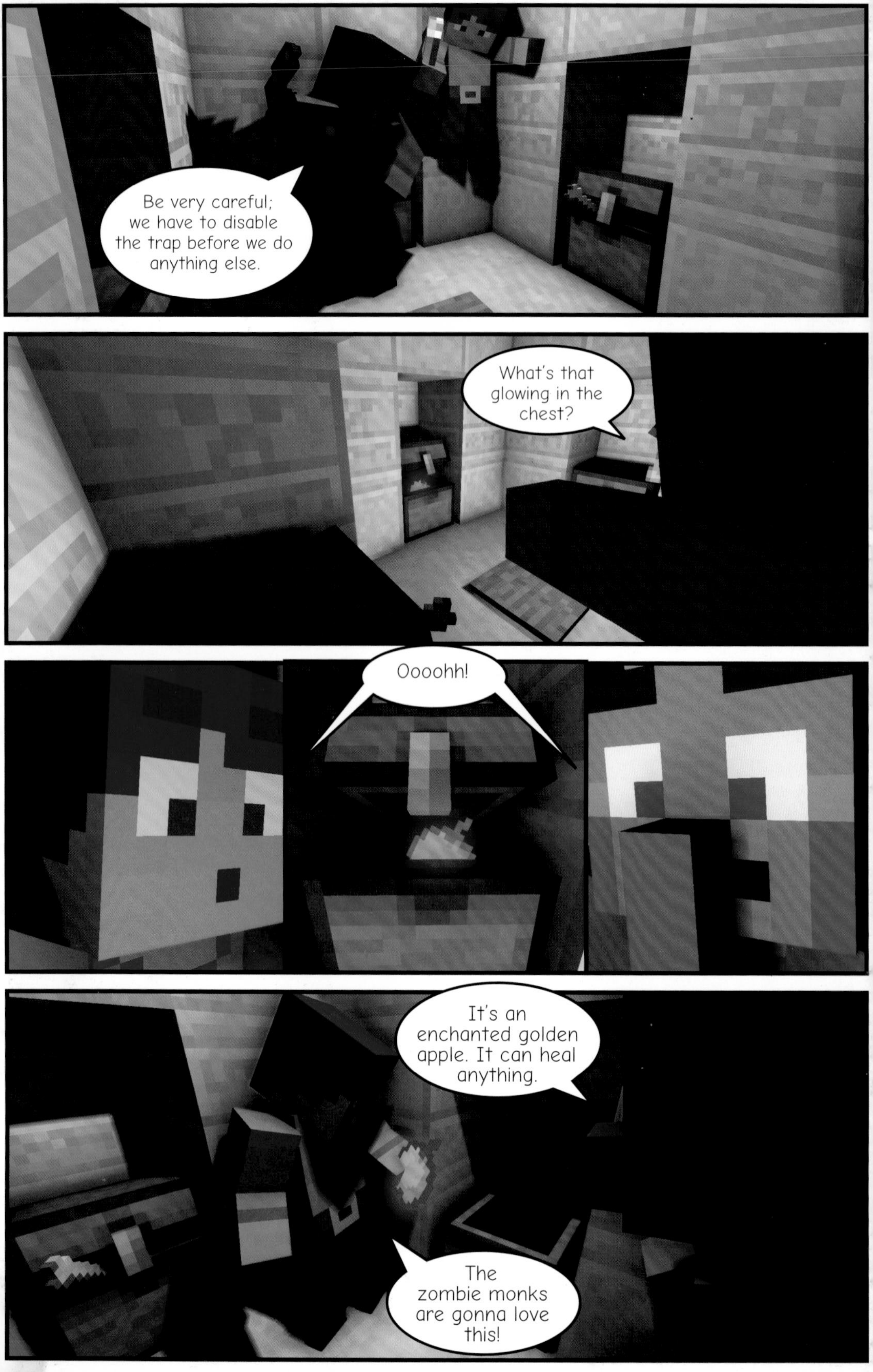
Be very careful; we have to disable the trap before we do anything else.
What's that glowing in the chest?
Oooohh!
It's an enchanted golden apple. It can heal anything.
The zombie monks are gonna love this!

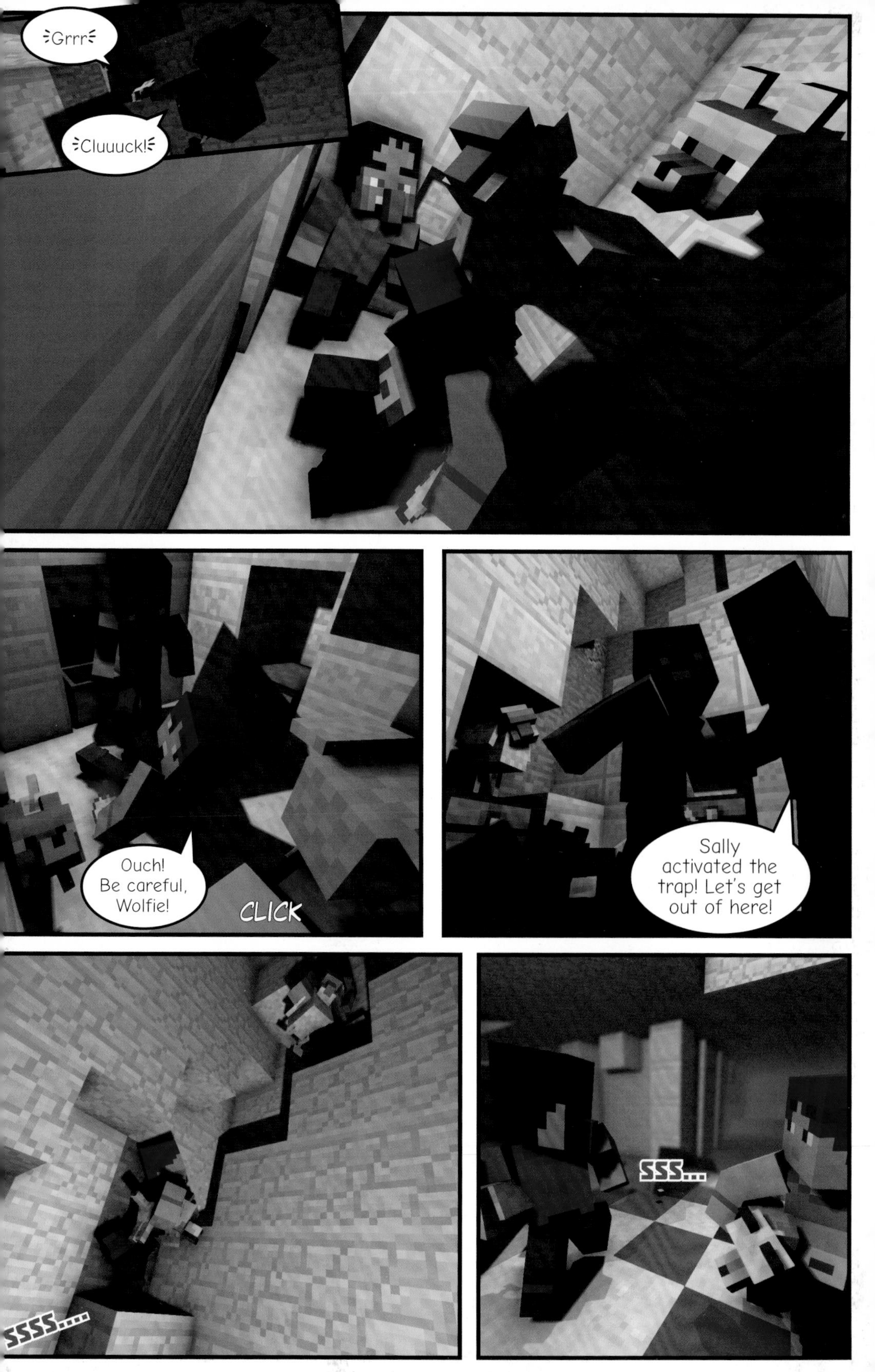

Grrr
Cluuuck!
Ouch! Be careful, Wolfie!
CLICK
Sally activated the trap! Let's get out of here!
SSSS....
SSS...

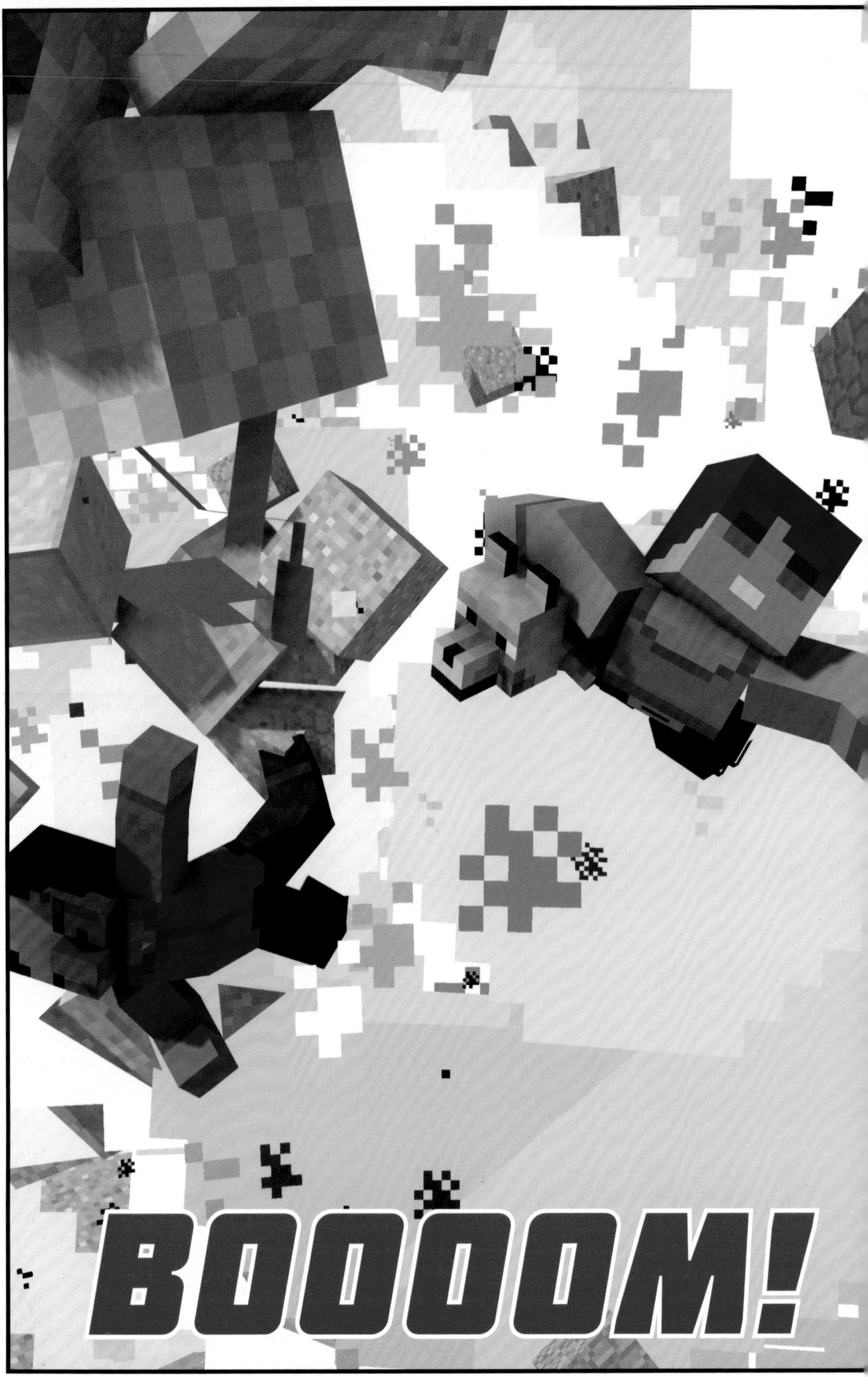
BOOOOM!

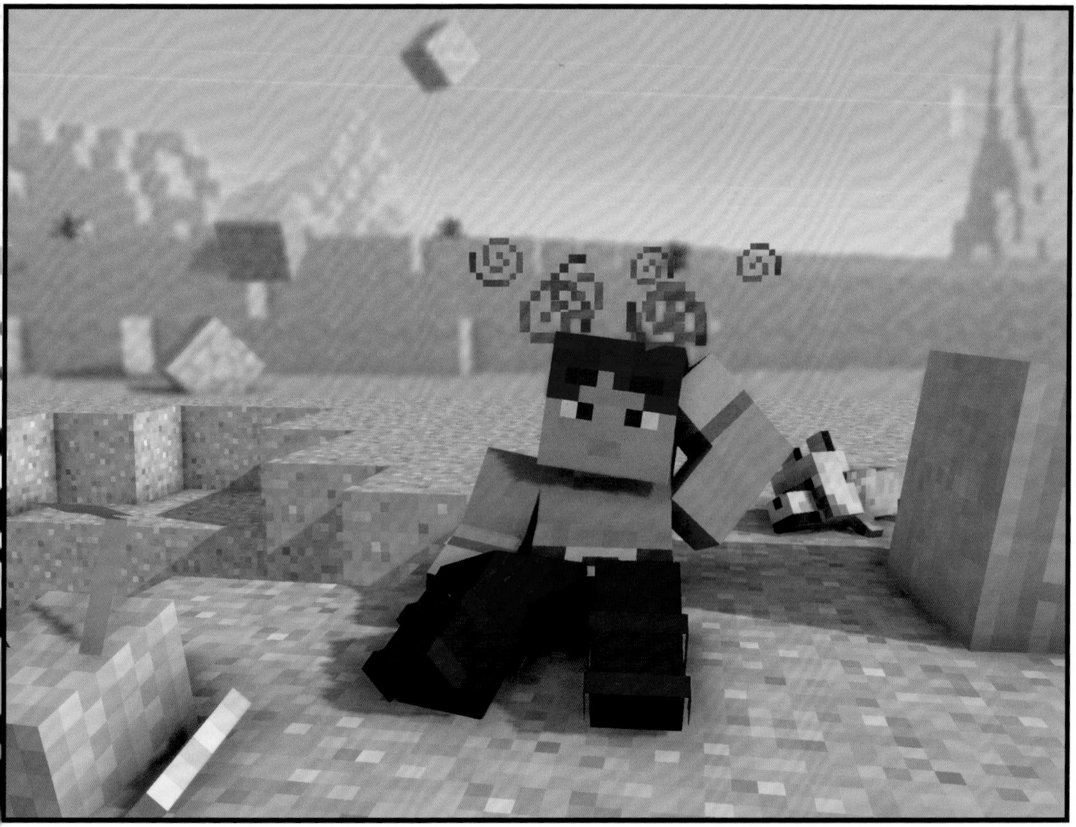

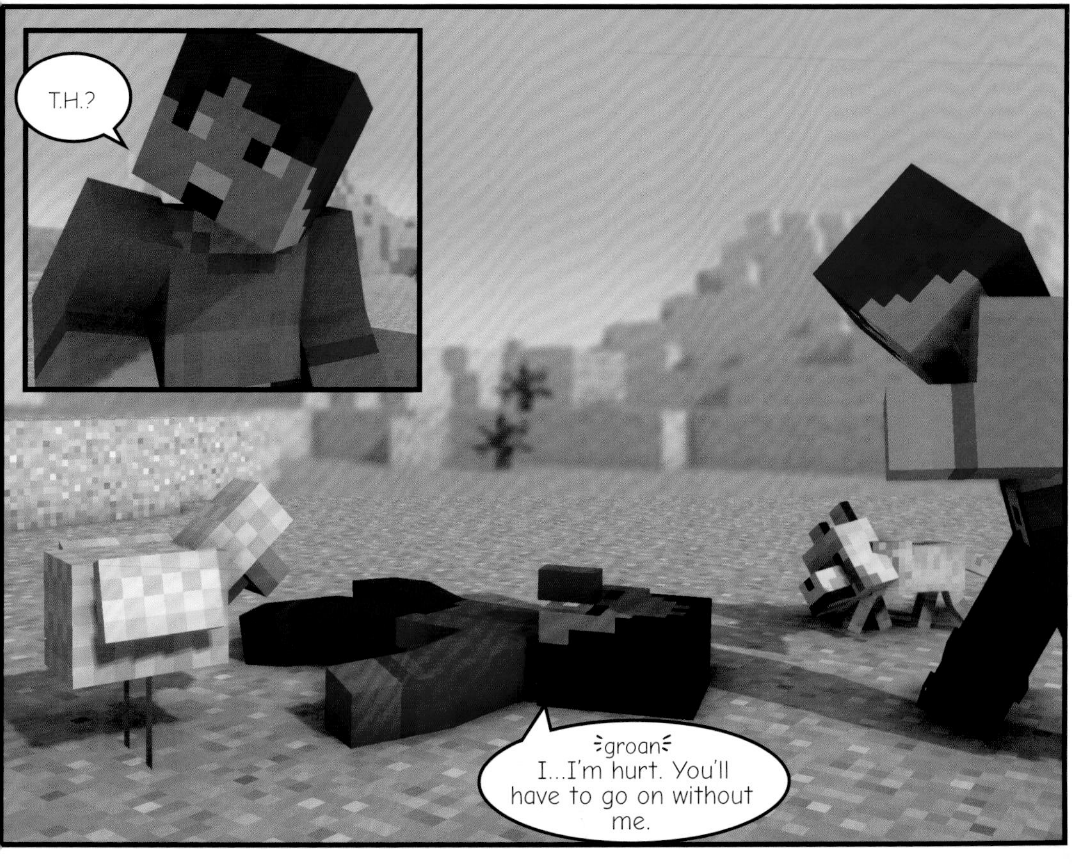
T.H.?
groan
I...I'm hurt. You'll have to go on without me.

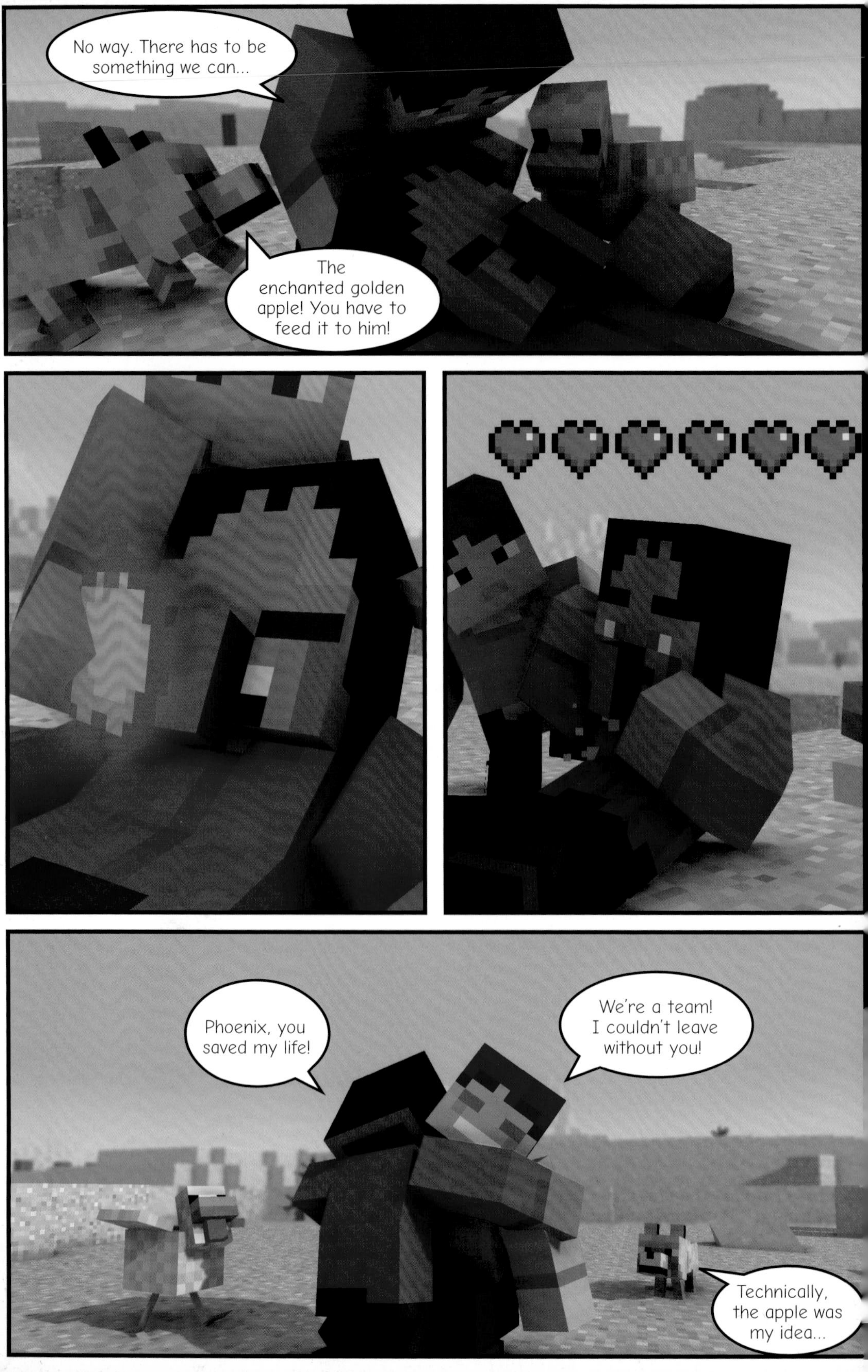
No way. There has to be something we can...
The enchanted golden apple! You have to feed it to him!
Phoenix, you saved my life!
We're a team! I couldn't leave without you!
Technically, the apple was my idea...

CHAPTER 6

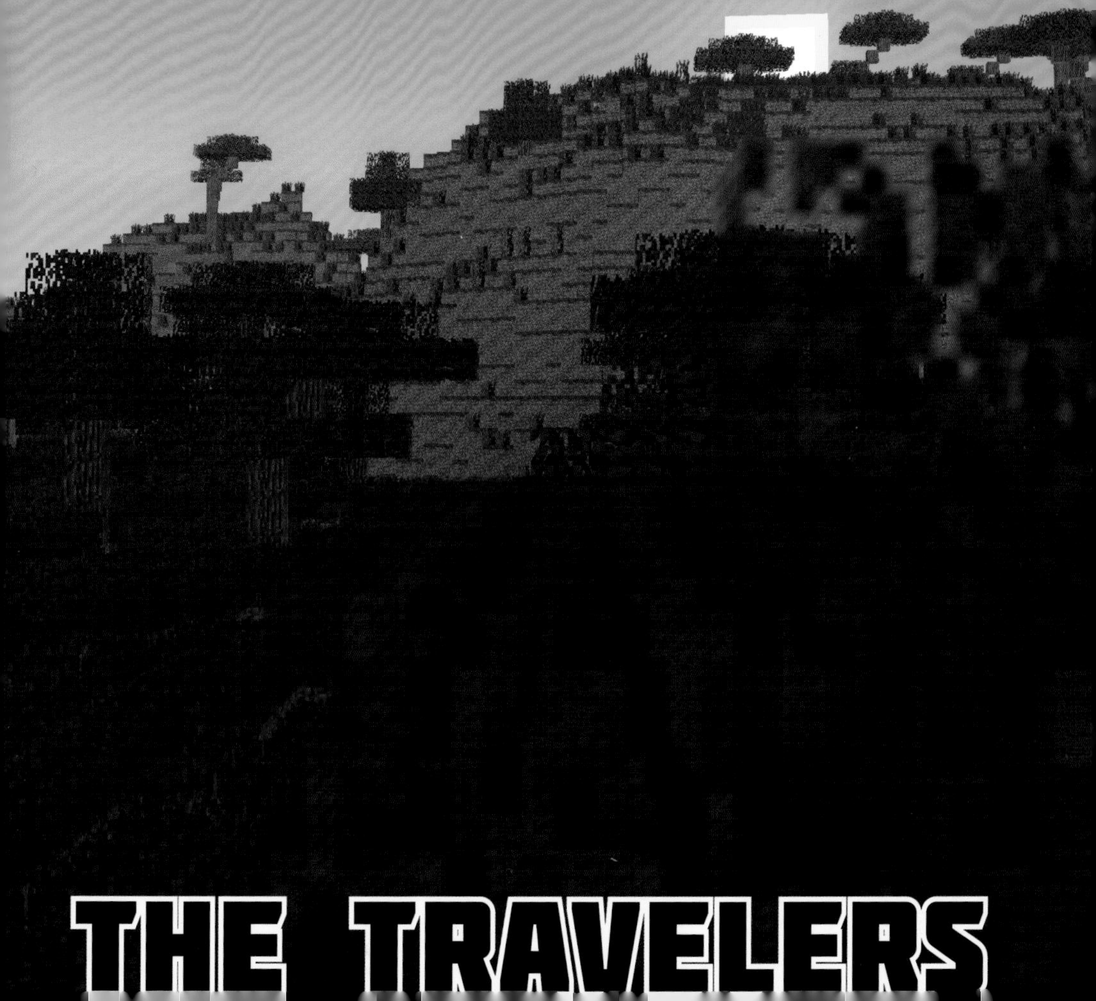

THE TRAVELERS

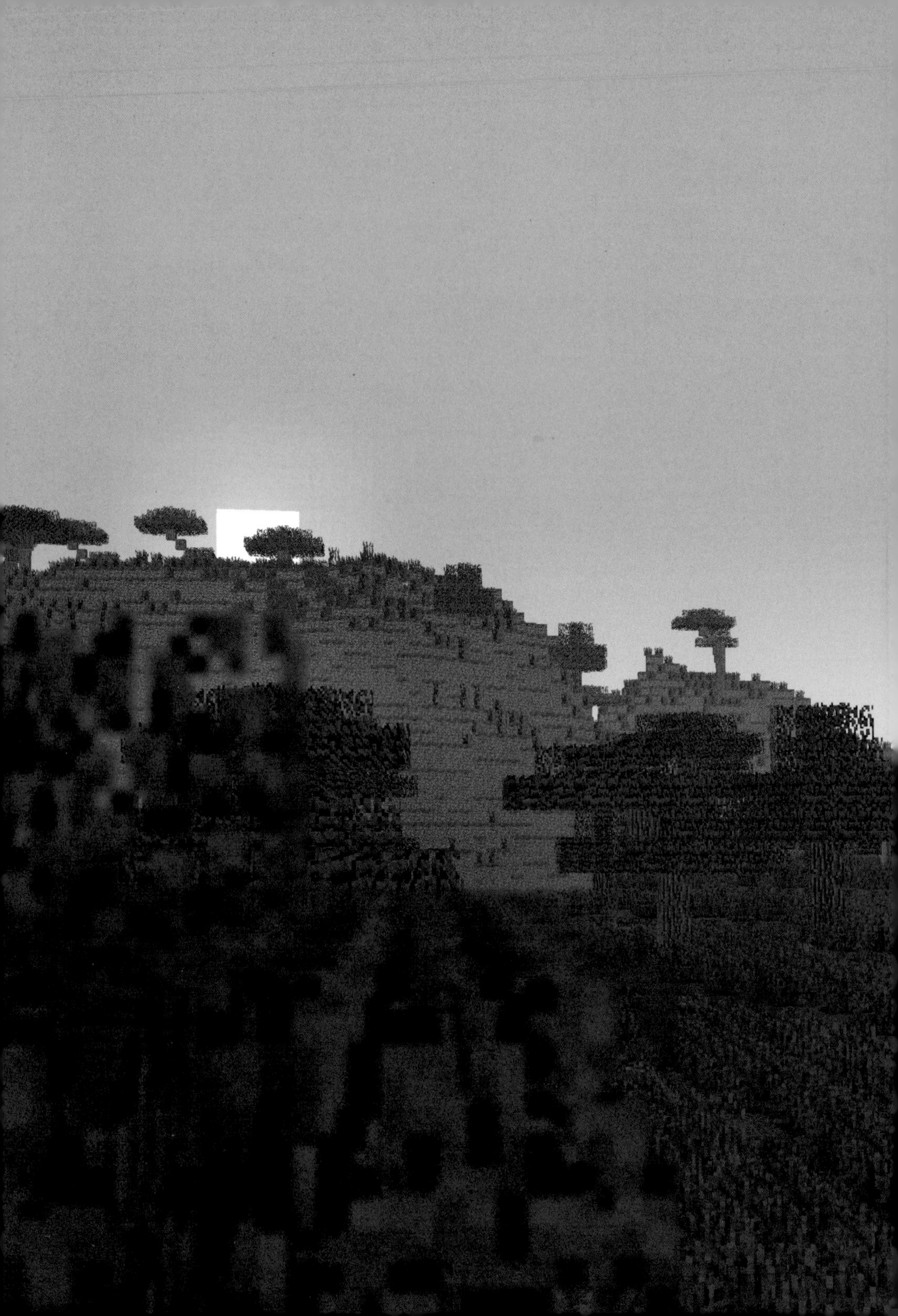

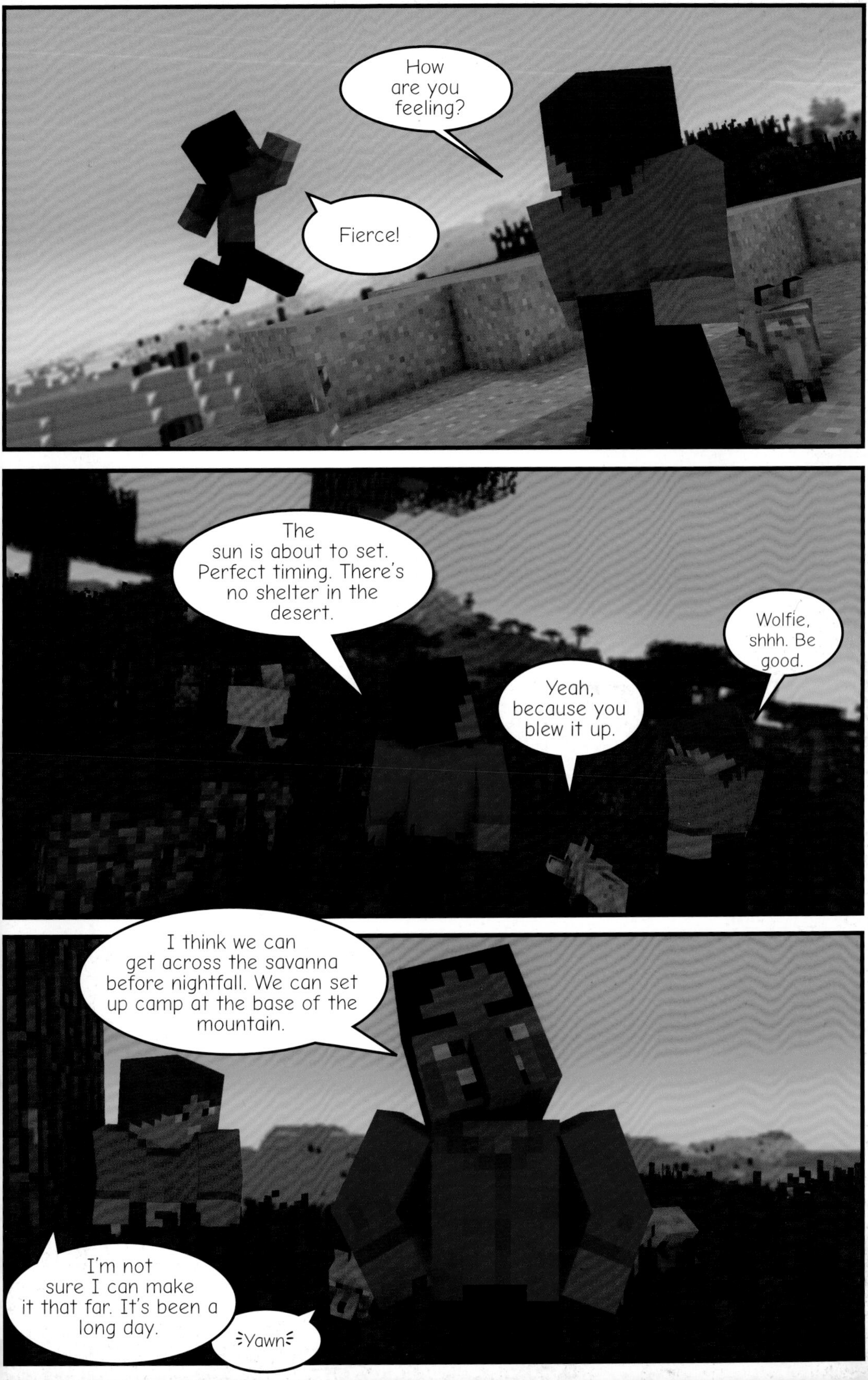
How are you feeling?
Fierce!
The sun is about to set. Perfect timing. There's no shelter in the desert.
Yeah, because you blew it up.
Wolfie, shhh. Be good.
I think we can get across the savanna before nightfall. We can set up camp at the base of the mountain.
I'm not sure I can make it that far. It's been a long day.
Yawn

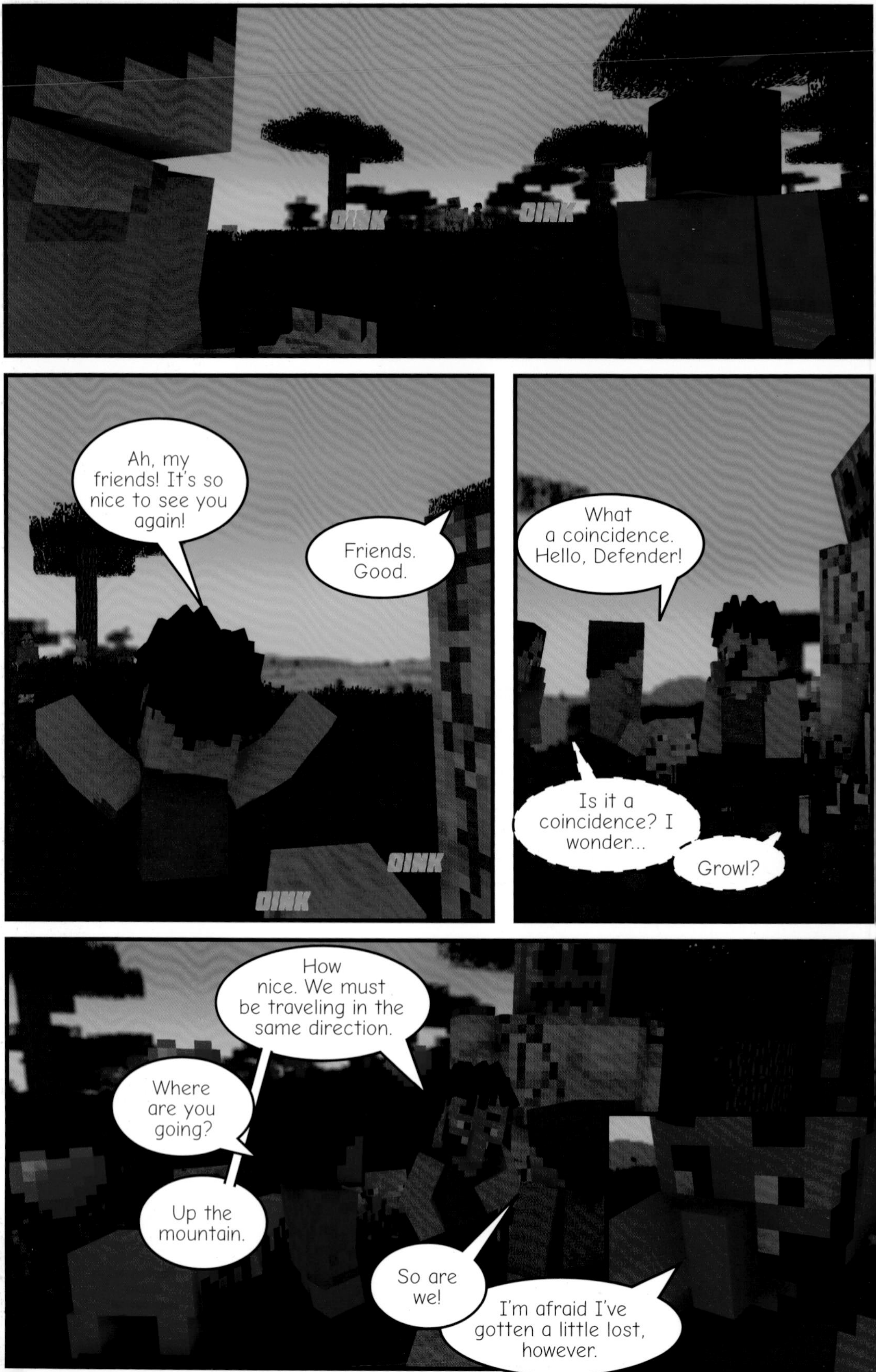
OINK
OINK
Ah, my friends! It's so nice to see you again!
Friends. Good.
OINK
OINK
What a coincidence. Hello, Defender!
Is it a coincidence? I wonder...
Growl?
How nice. We must be traveling in the same direction.
Where are you going?
Up the mountain.
So are we!
I'm afraid I've gotten a little lost, however.

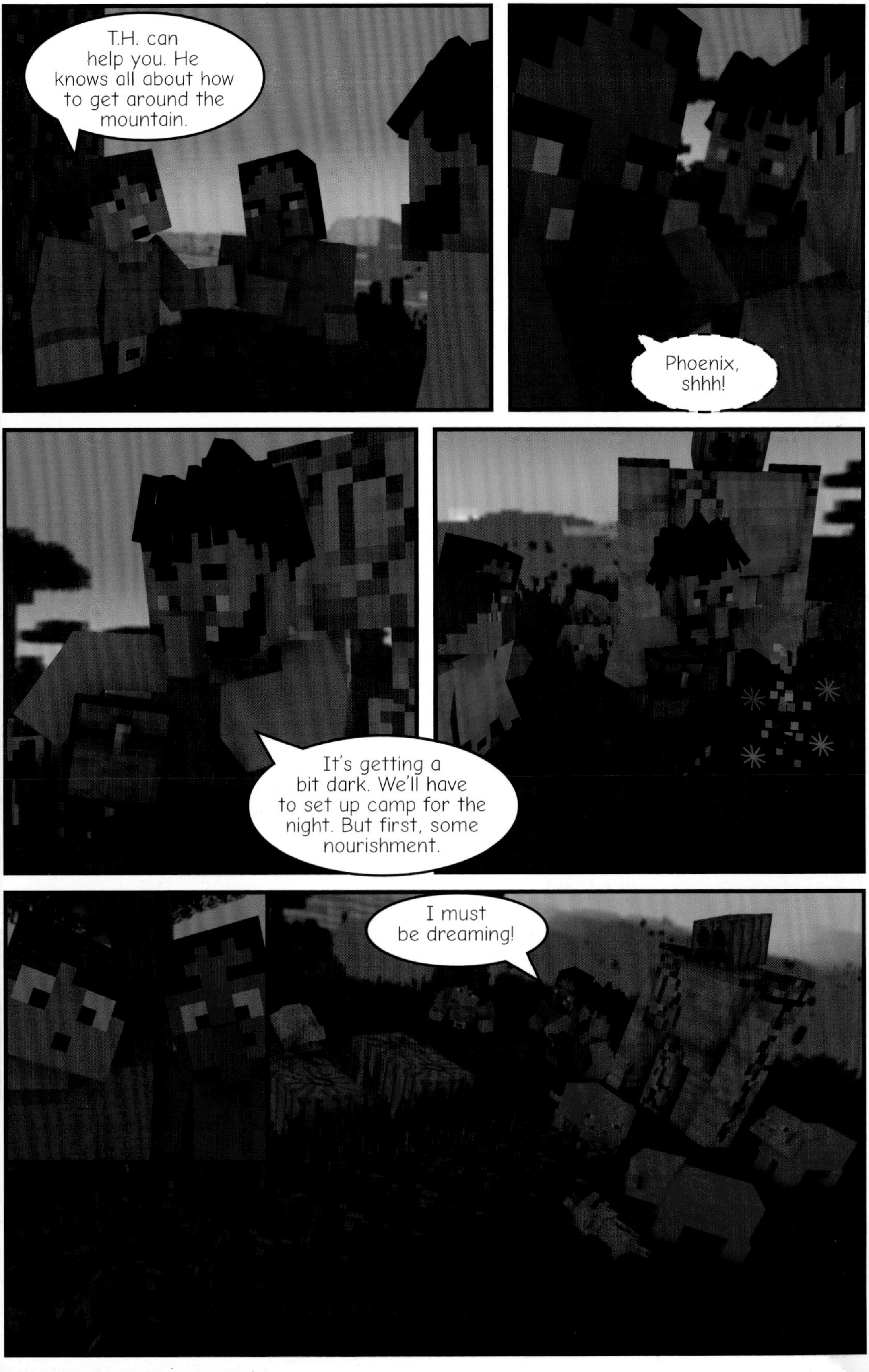
T.H. can help you. He knows all about how to get around the mountain.
Phoenix, shhh!
It's getting a bit dark. We'll have to set up camp for the night. But first, some nourishment.
I must be dreaming!

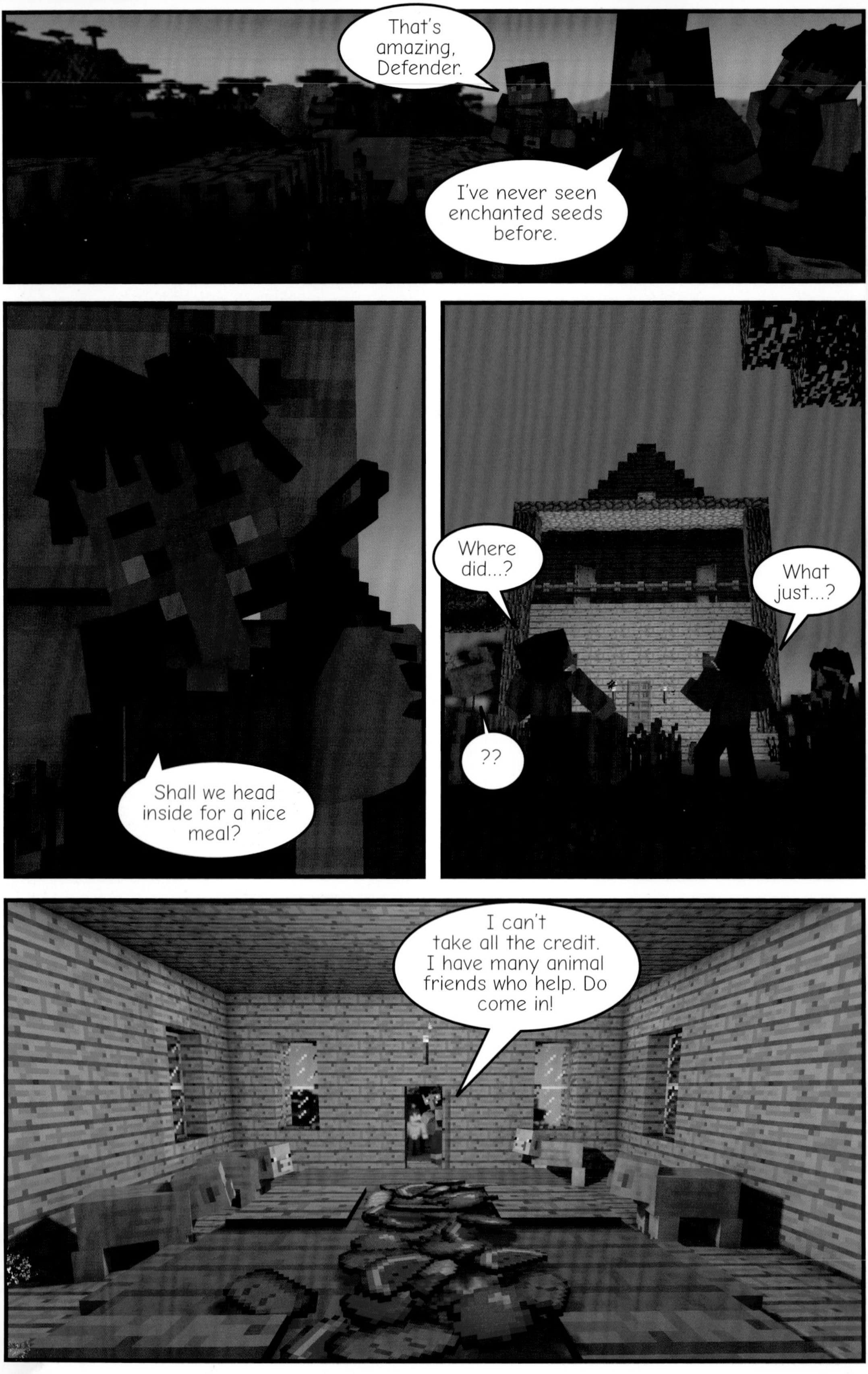

That's amazing, Defender.
I've never seen enchanted seeds before.
Shall we head inside for a nice meal?
Where did...?
What just...?
??
I can't take all the credit. I have many animal friends who help. Do come in!

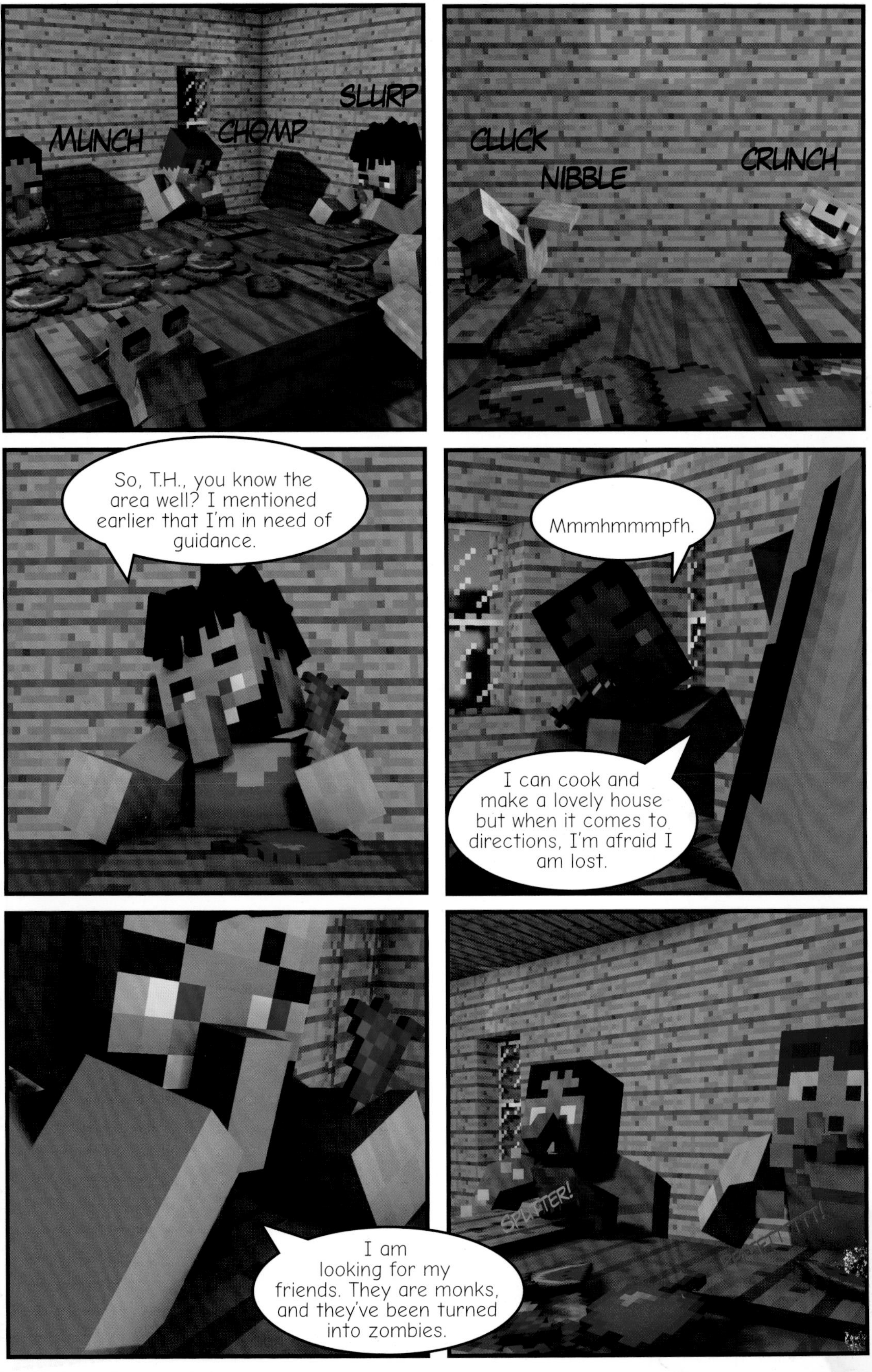
MUNCH
CHOMP
SLURP
CLUCK
NIBBLE
CRUNCH
So, T.H., you know the area well? I mentioned earlier that I'm in need of guidance.
Mmmhmmmpfh.
I can cook and make a lovely house but when it comes to directions, I'm afraid I am lost.
I am looking for my friends. They are monks, and they've been turned into zombies.
SPLATTER!

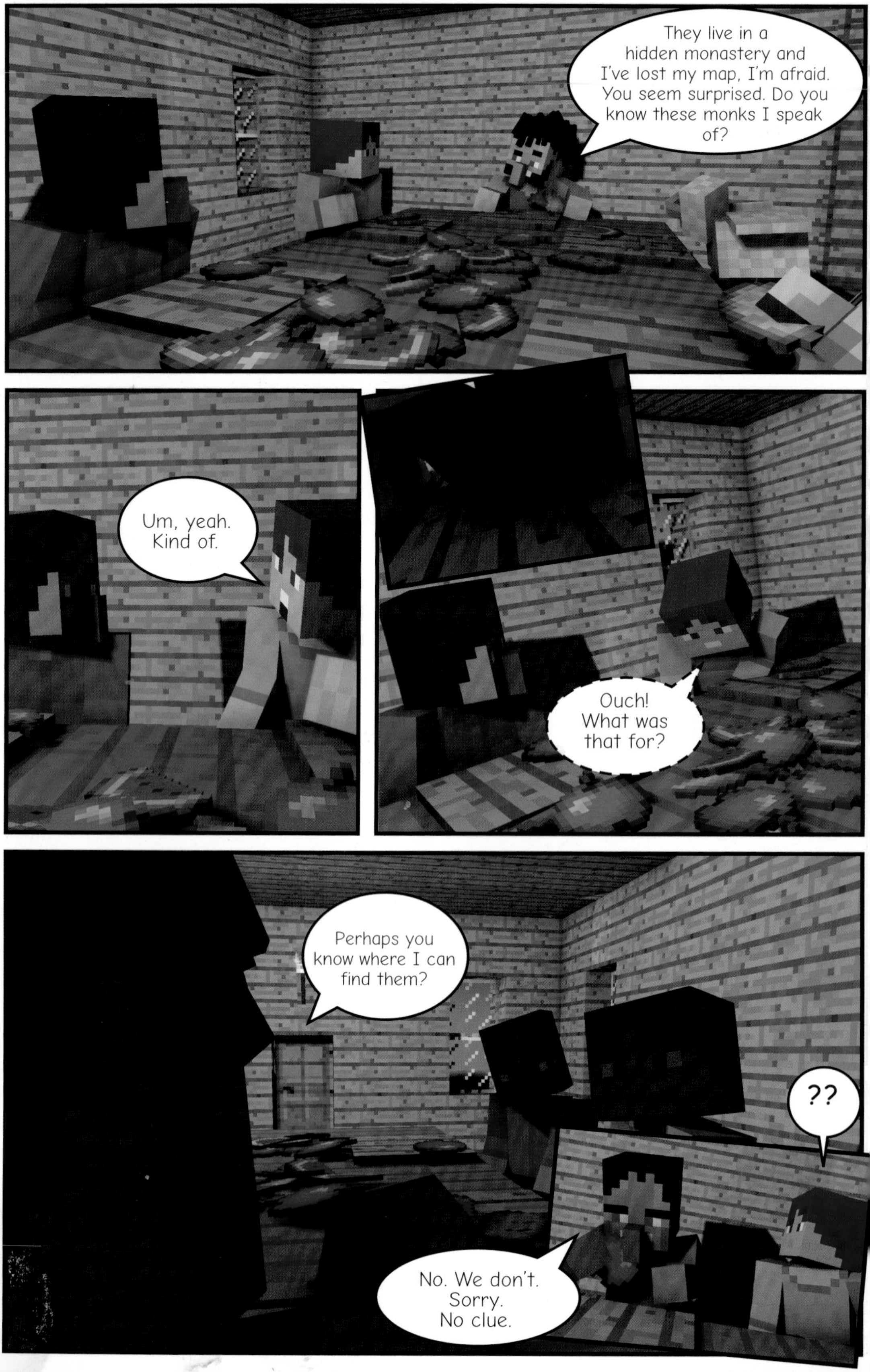
They live in a hidden monastery and I've lost my map, I'm afraid. You seem surprised. Do you know these monks I speak of?
Um, yeah. Kind of.
Ouch! What was that for?
Perhaps you know where I can find them?
??
No. We don't. Sorry. No clue.

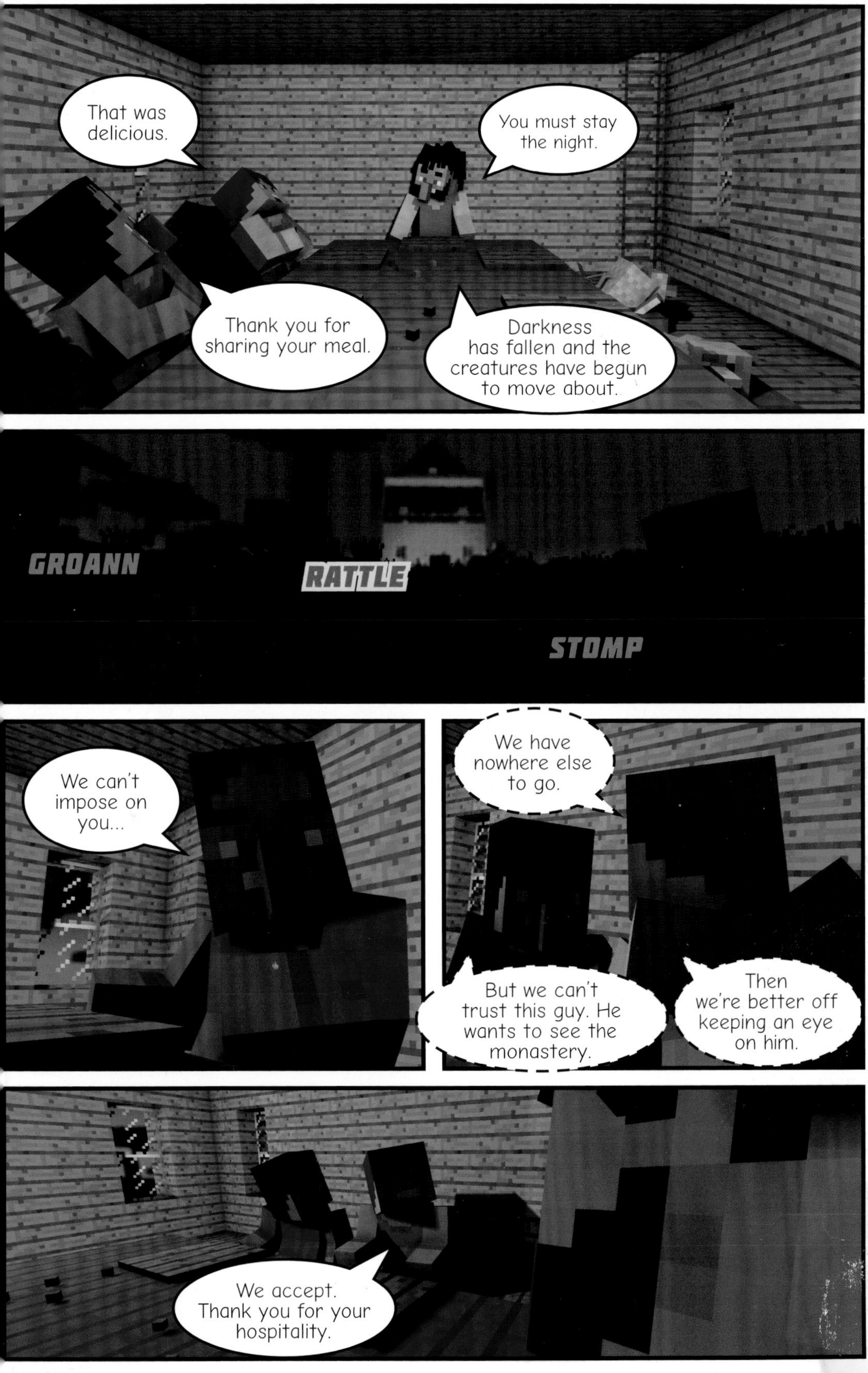
That was delicious.
You must stay the night.
Thank you for sharing your meal.
Darkness has fallen and the creatures have begun to move about.
GROANN
RATTLE
STOMP
We can't impose on you...
We have nowhere else to go.
But we can't trust this guy. He wants to see the monastery.
Then we're better off keeping an eye on him.
We accept. Thank you for your hospitality.

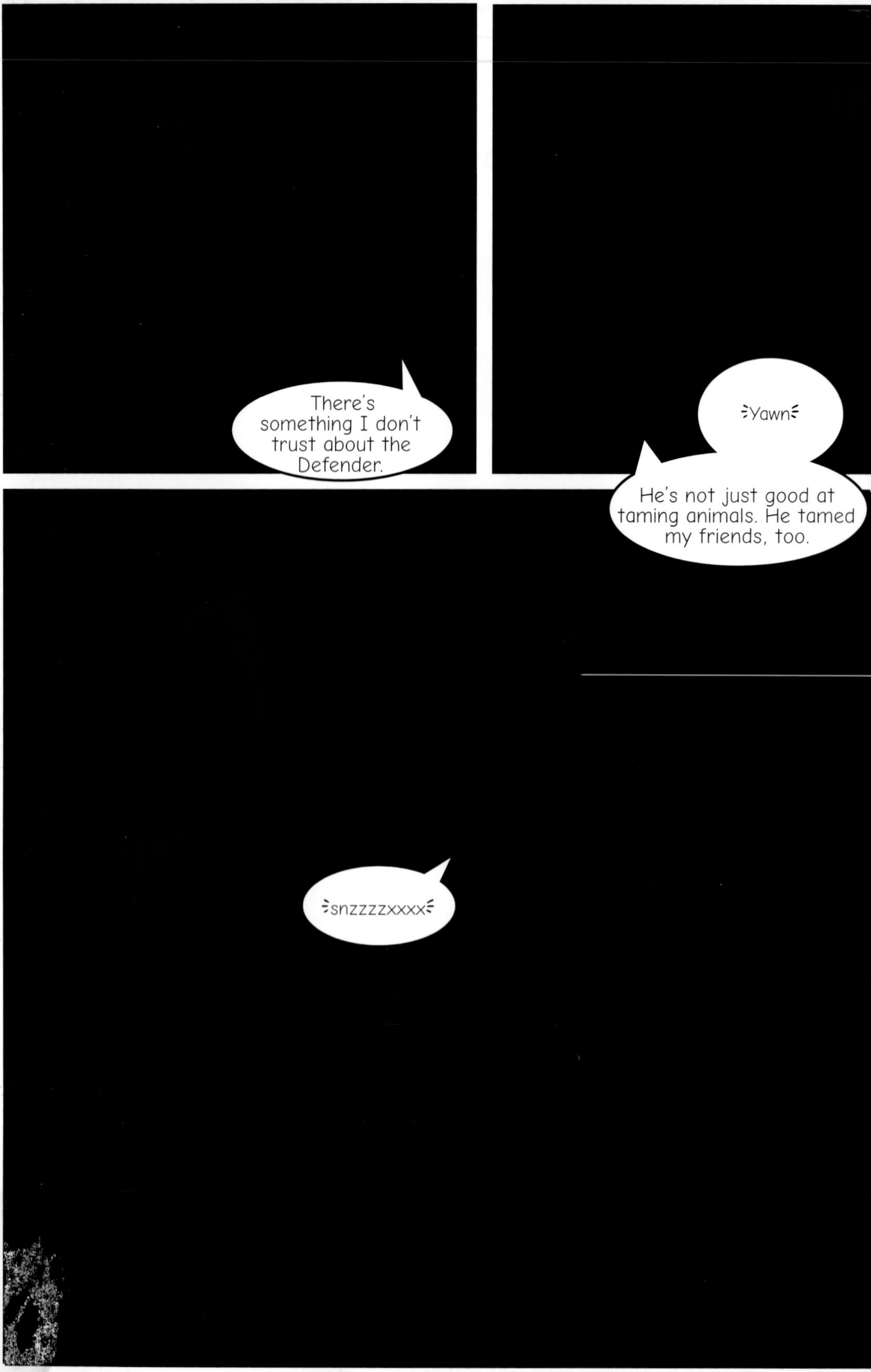
There's something I don't trust about the Defender.
Yawn
He's not just good at taming animals. He tamed my friends, too.
snzzzzxxxx

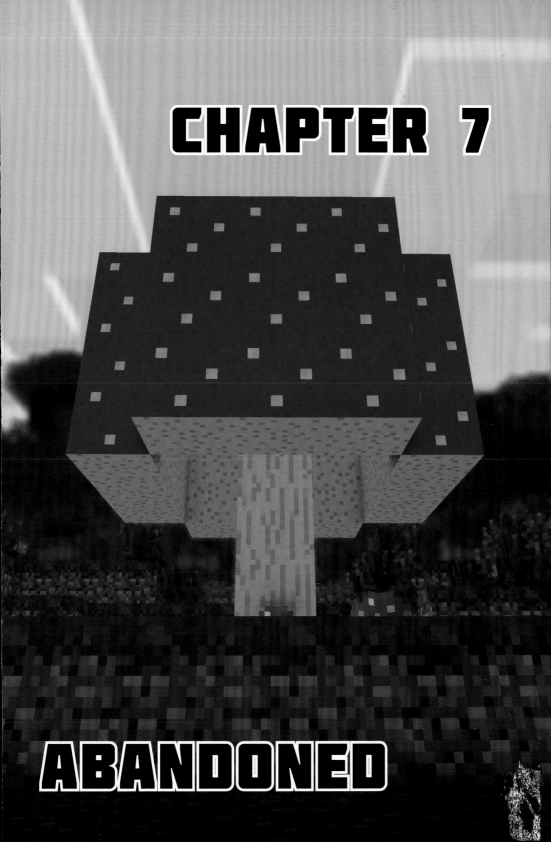

CHAPTER 7

ABANDONED

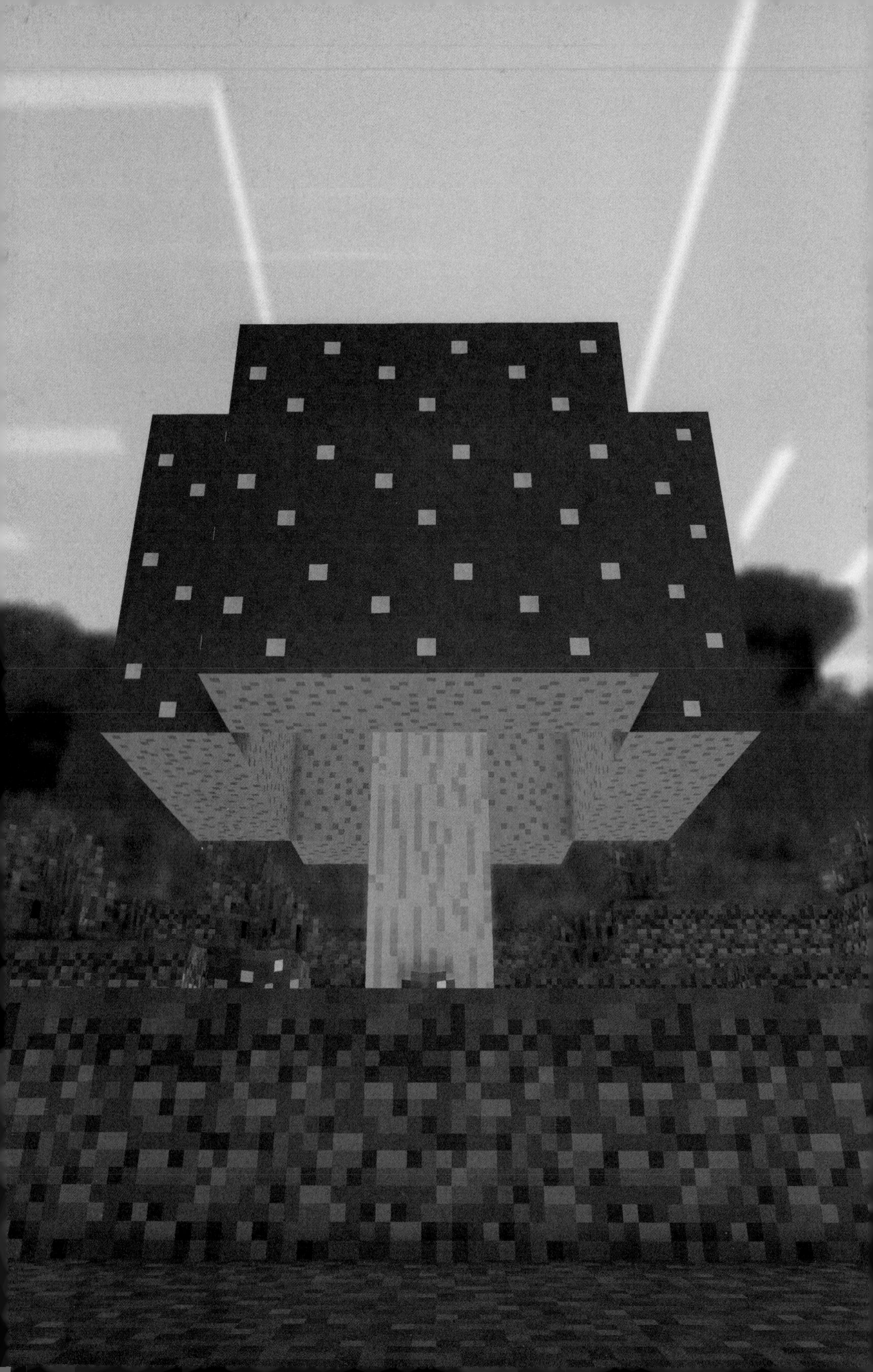

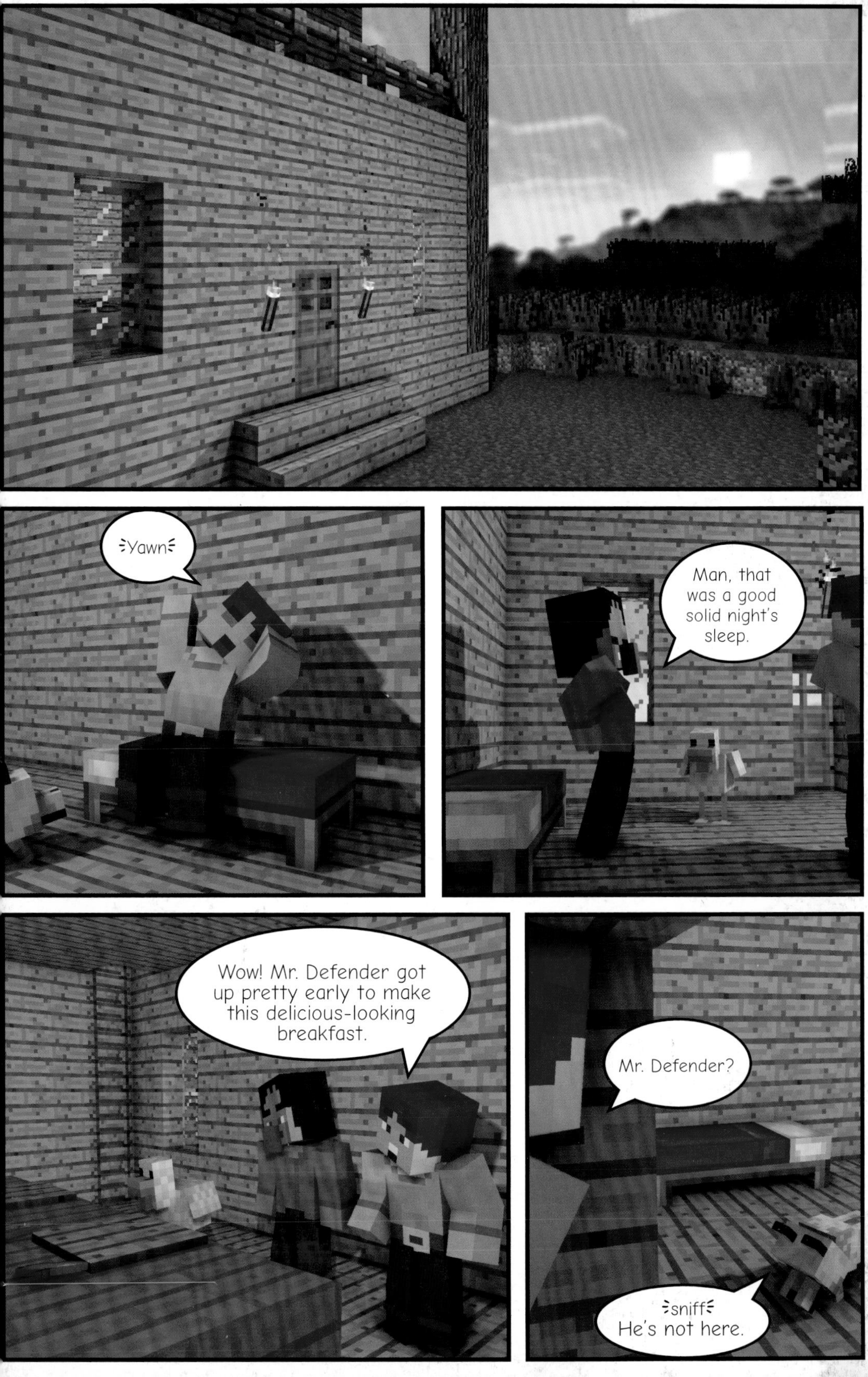
Yawn
Man, that was a good solid night's sleep.
Wow! Mr. Defender got up pretty early to make this delicious-looking breakfast.
Mr. Defender?
sniff
He's not here.

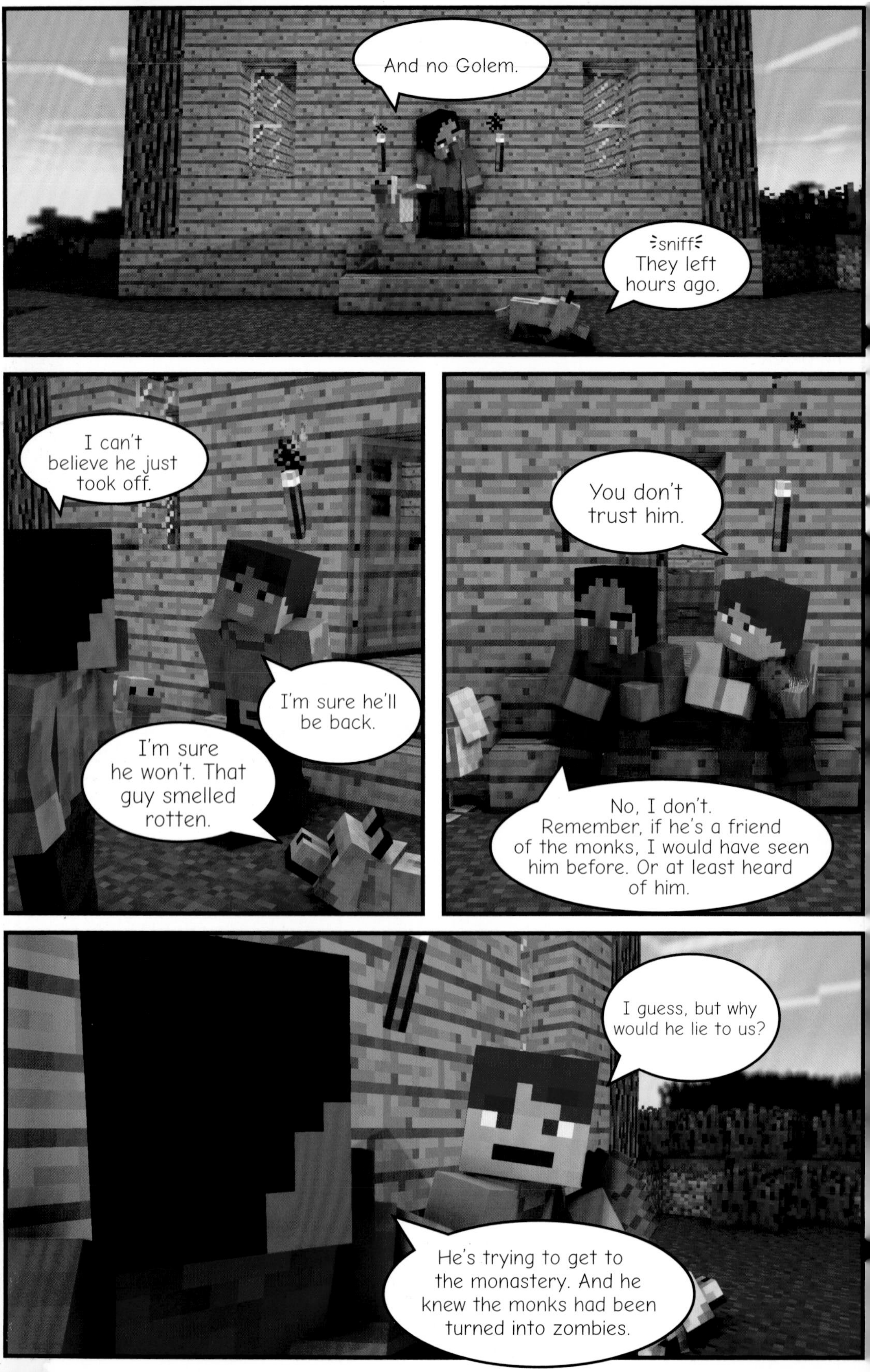
And no Golem.
sniff They left hours ago.
I can't believe he just took off.
I'm sure he'll be back.
I'm sure he won't. That guy smelled rotten.
You don't trust him.
No, I don't. Remember, if he's a friend of the monks, I would have seen him before. Or at least heard of him.
I guess, but why would he lie to us?
He's trying to get to the monastery. And he knew the monks had been turned into zombies.

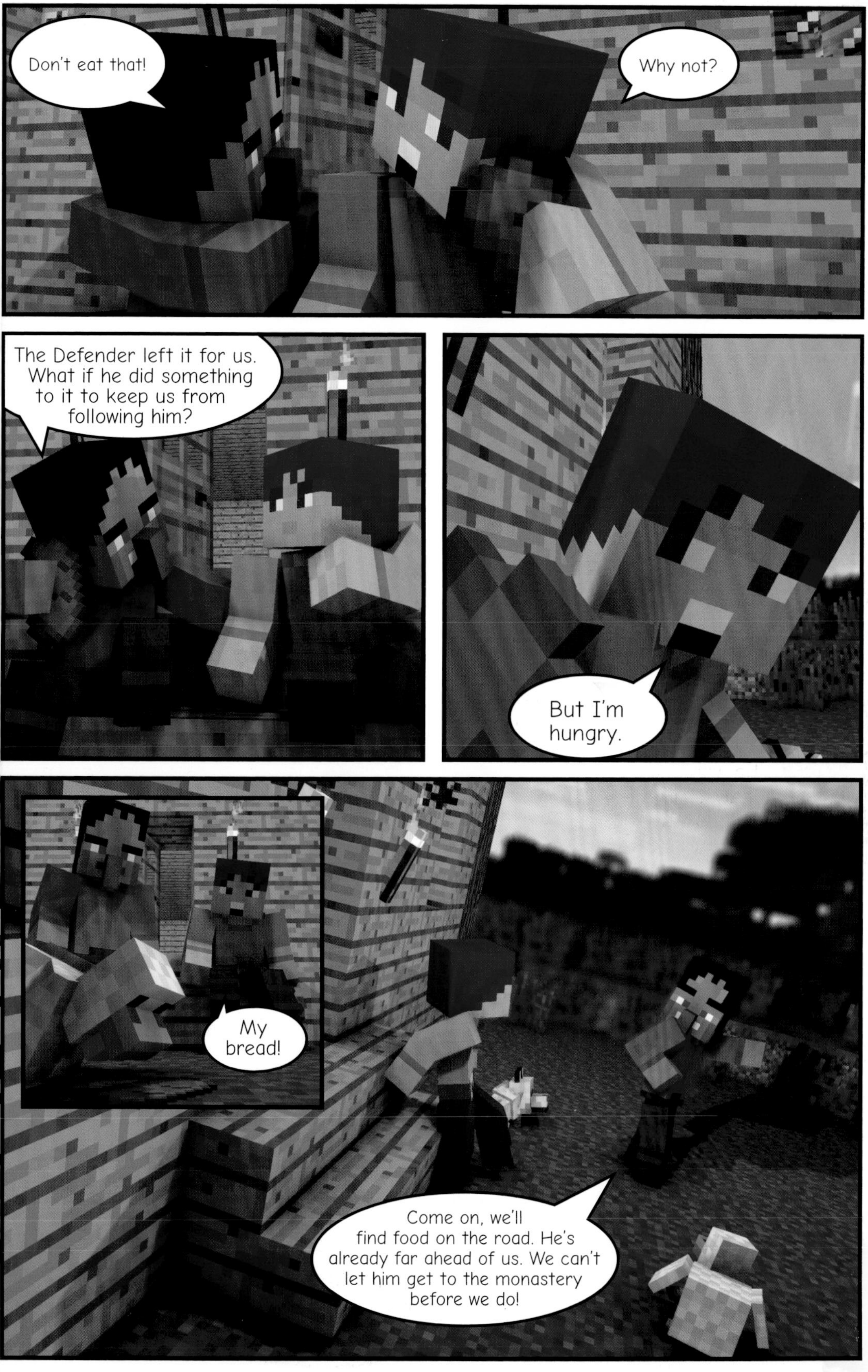
Don't eat that!
Why not?
The Defender left it for us. What if he did something to it to keep us from following him?
But I'm hungry.
My bread!
Come on, we'll find food on the road. He's already far ahead of us. We can't let him get to the monastery before we do!

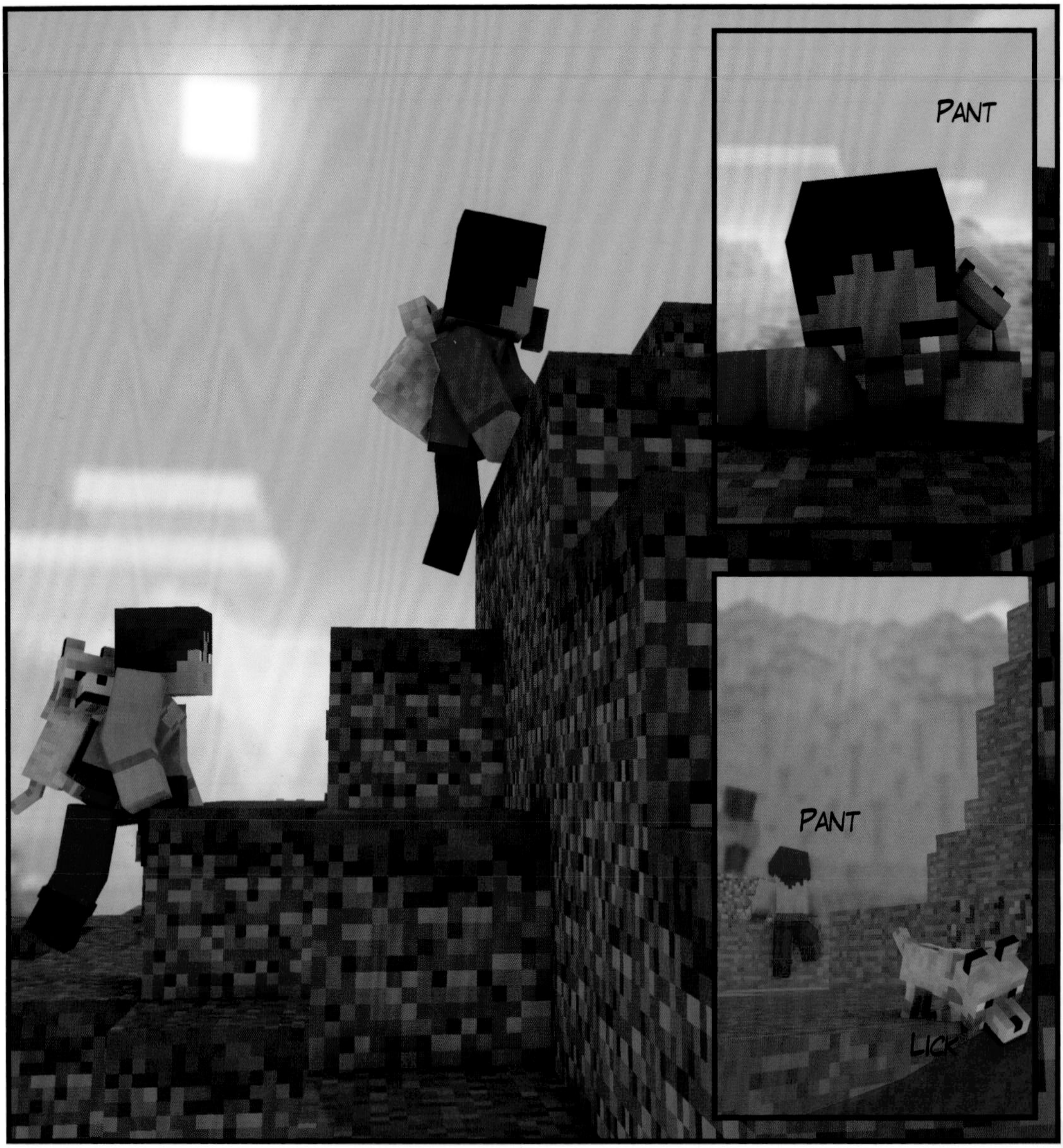
PANT
PANT
LICK

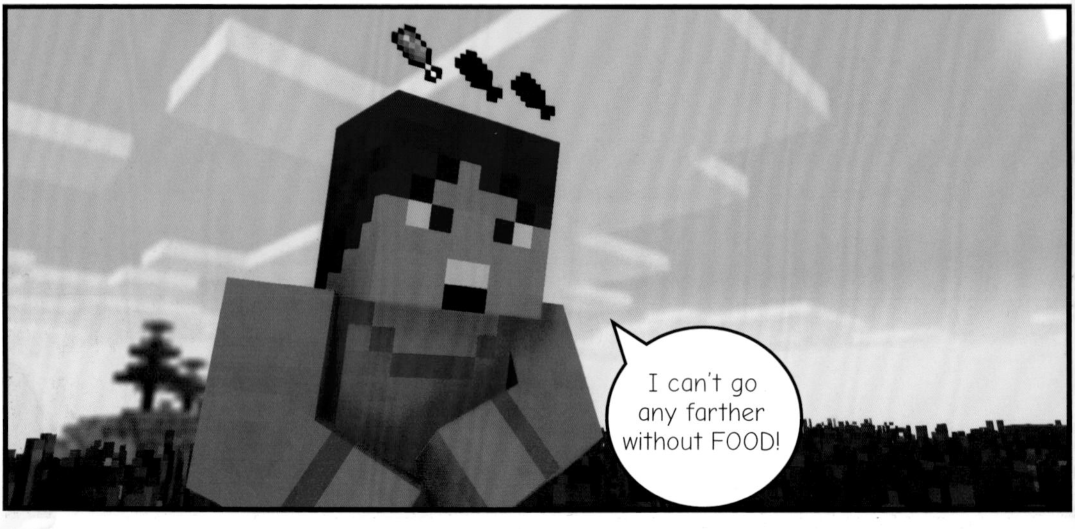
I can't go any farther without FOOD!

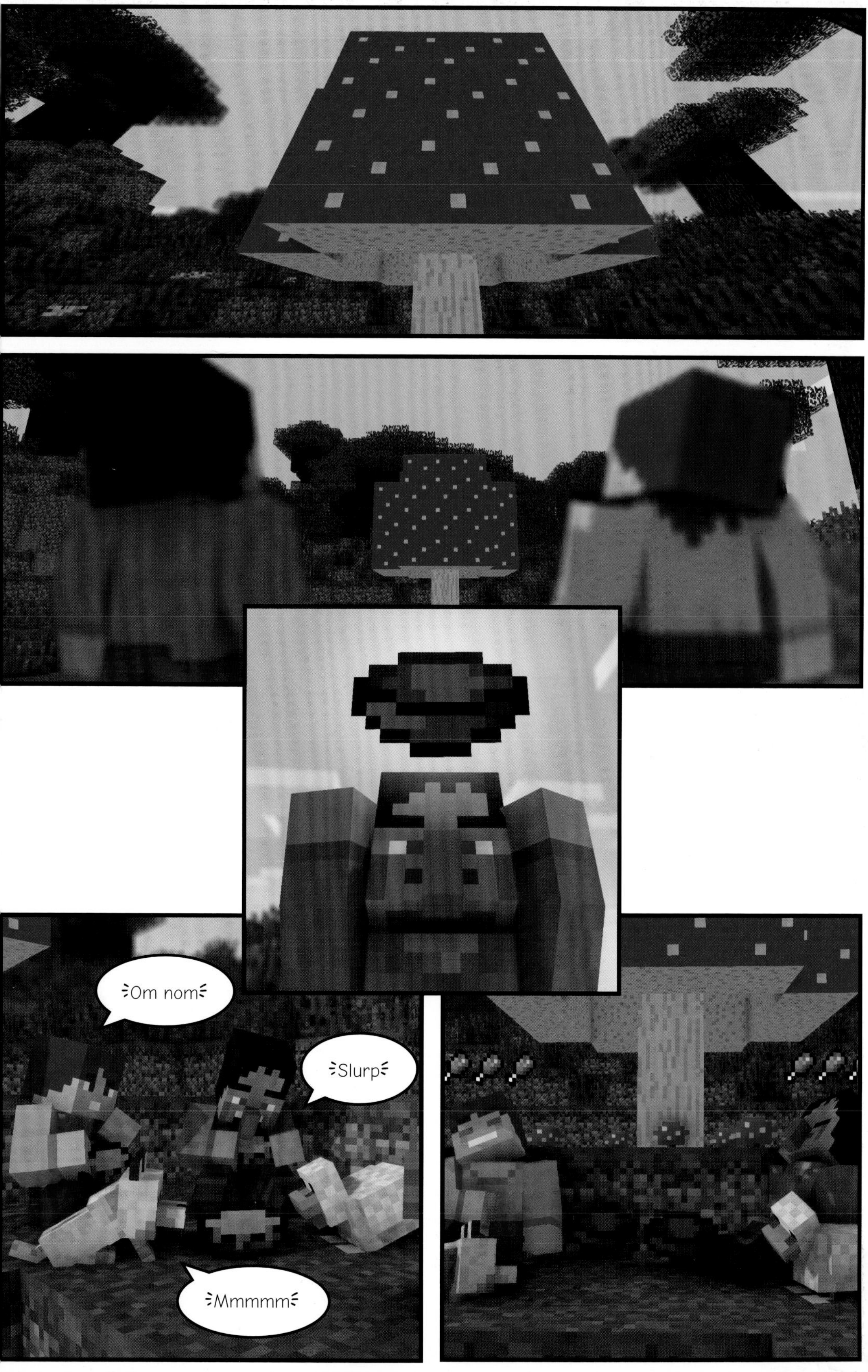
Om nom
Slurp
Mmmmm

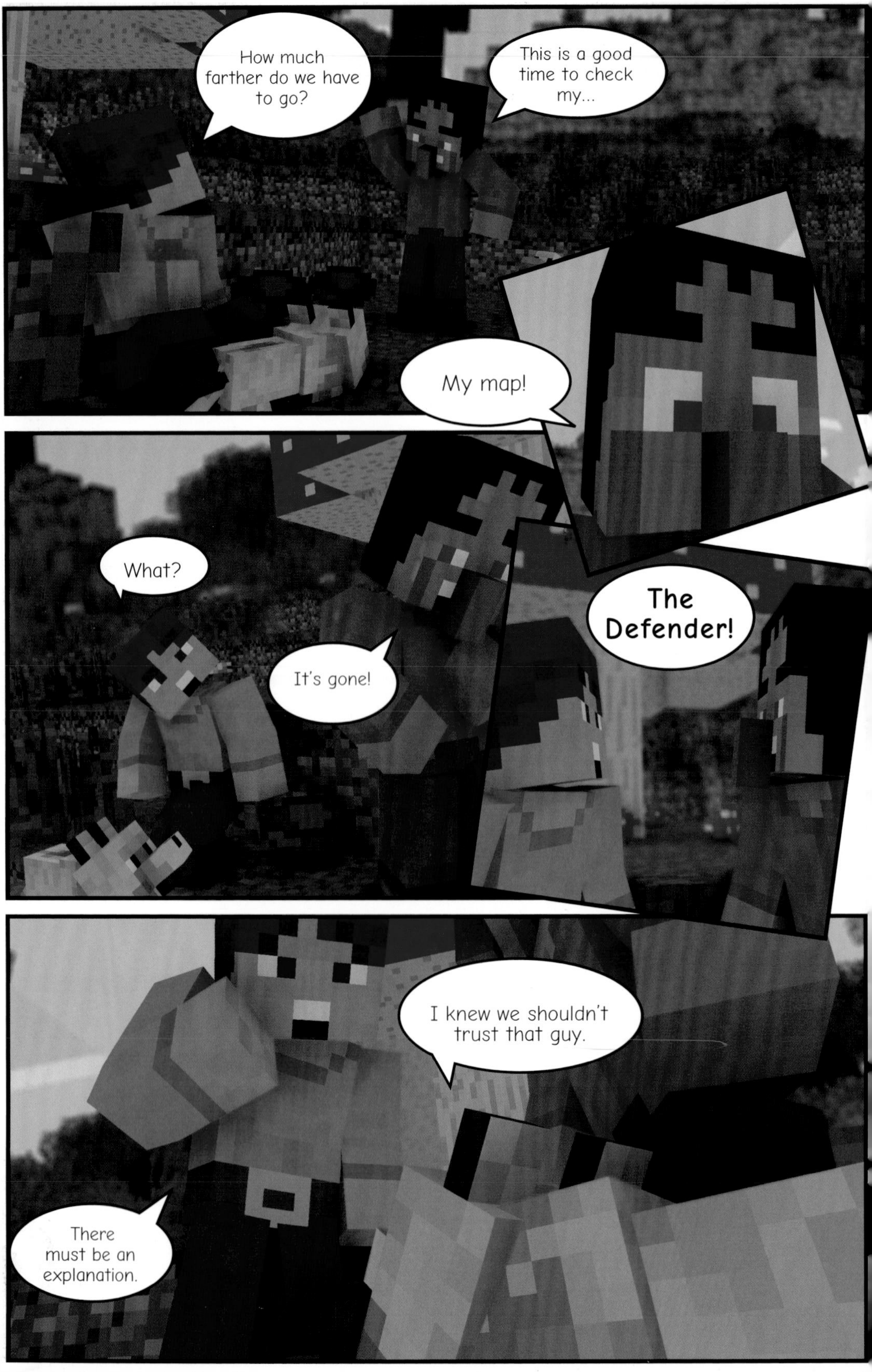
How much farther do we have to go?
This is a good time to check my...
My map!
What?
It's gone!
The Defender!
I knew we shouldn't trust that guy.
There must be an explanation.

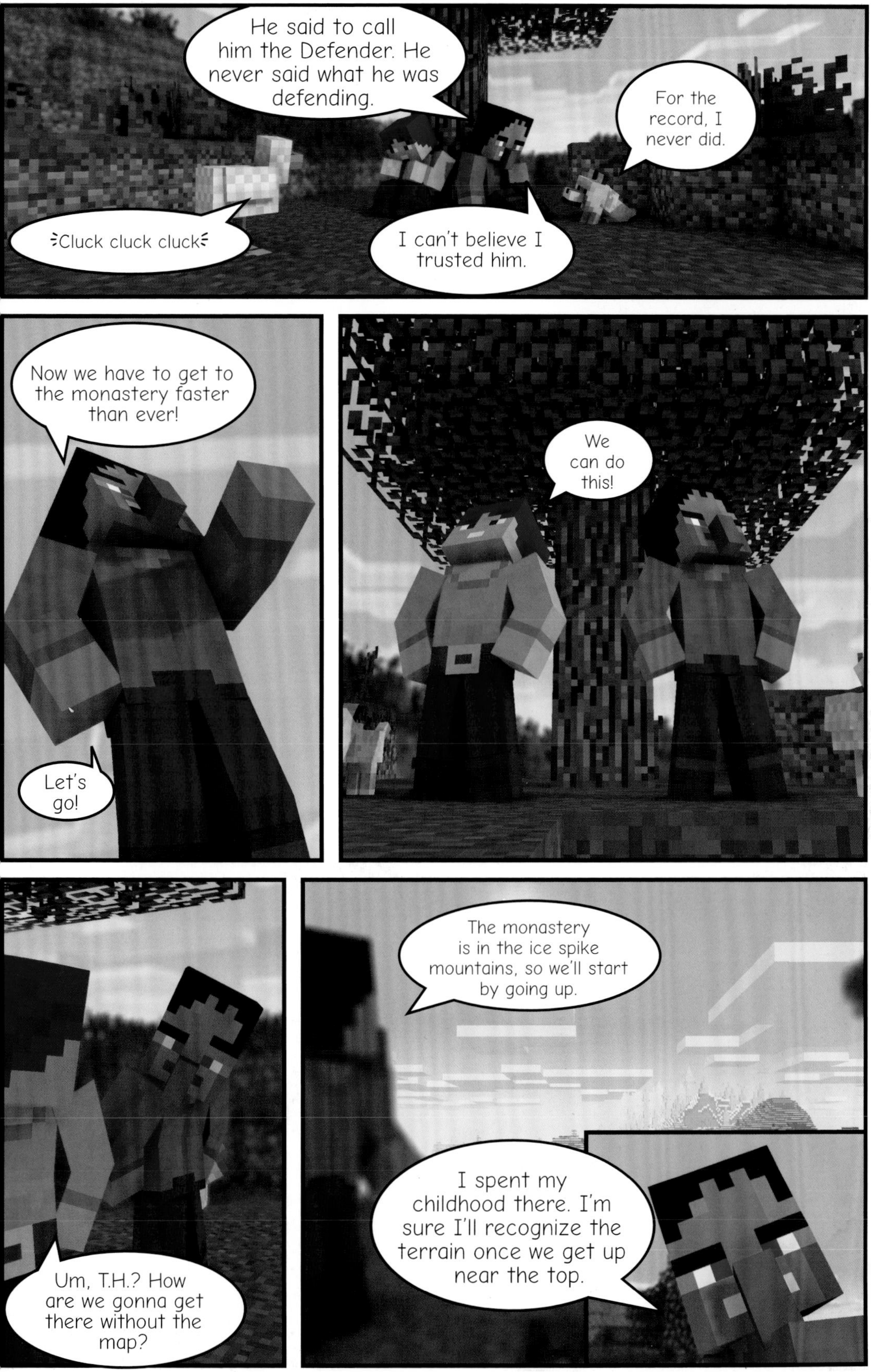
He said to call him the Defender. He never said what he was defending.
For the record, I never did.
Cluck cluck cluck
I can't believe I trusted him.
Now we have to get to the monastery faster than ever!
Let's go!
We can do this!
Um, T.H.? How are we gonna get there without the map?
The monastery is in the ice spike mountains, so we'll start by going up.
I spent my childhood there. I'm sure I'll recognize the terrain once we get up near the top.

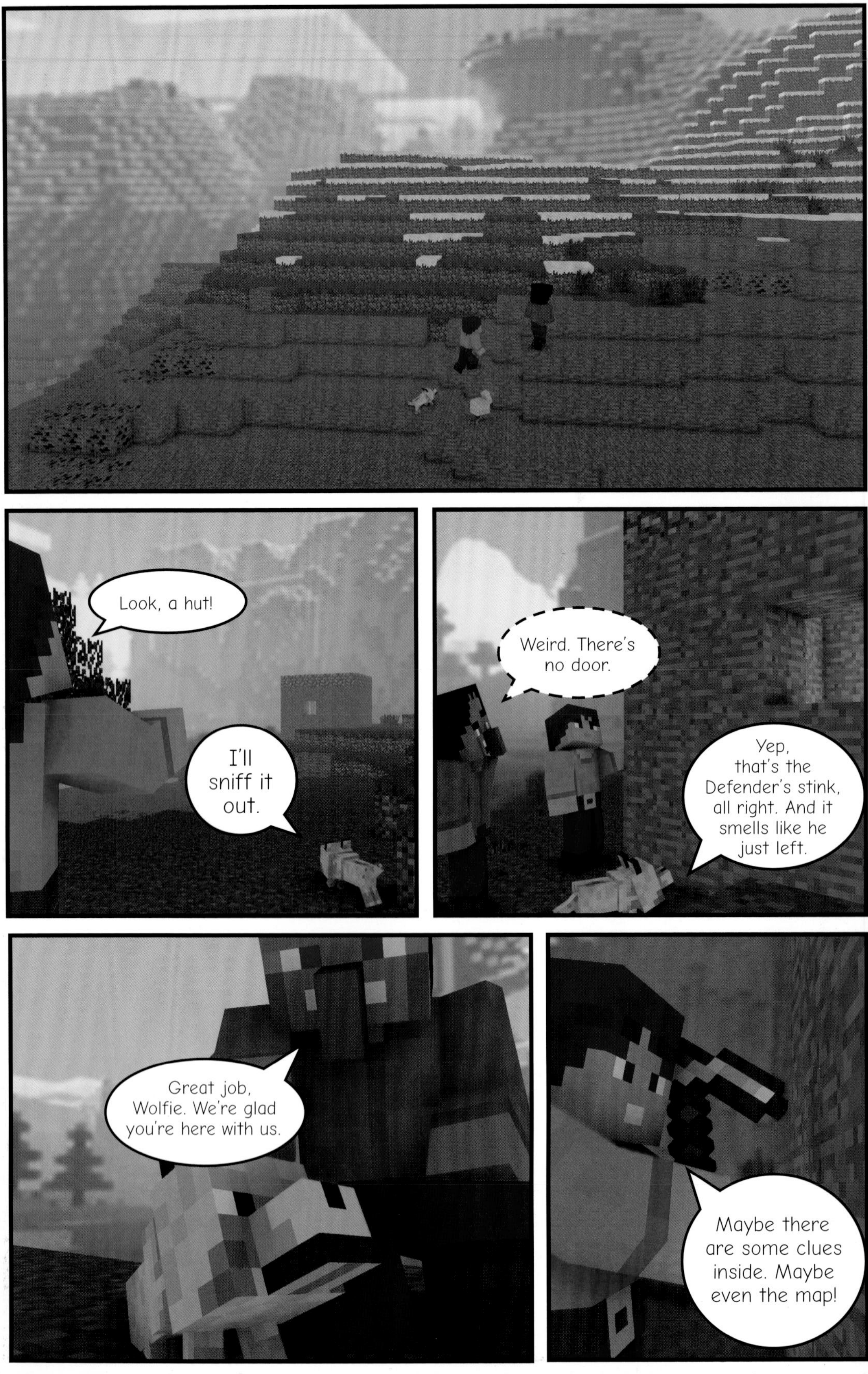
Look, a hut!
I'll sniff it out.
Weird. There's no door.
Yep, that's the Defender's stink, all right. And it smells like he just left.
Great job, Wolfie. We're glad you're here with us.
Maybe there are some clues inside. Maybe even the map!

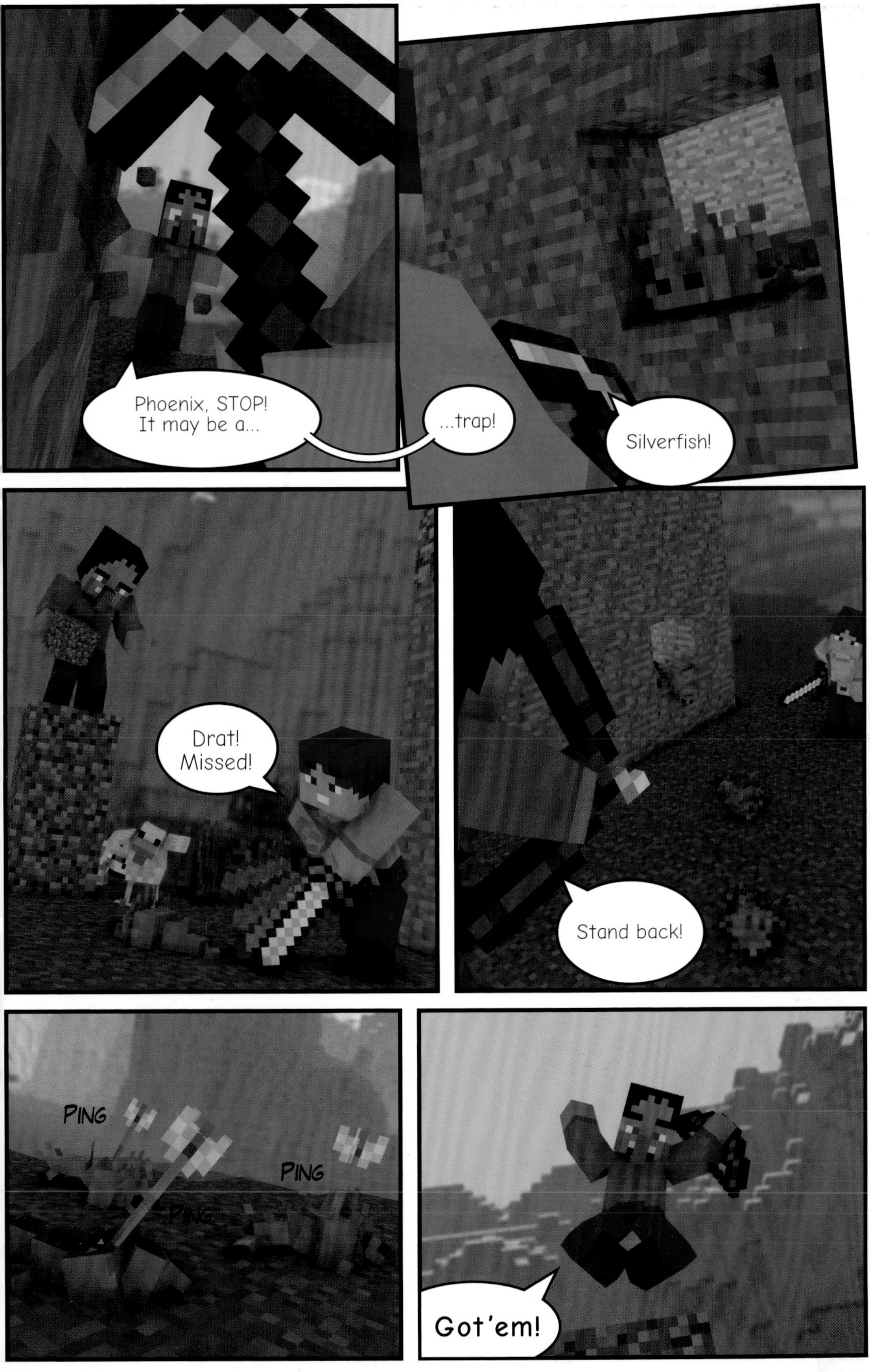

Phoenix, STOP! It may be a...
...trap!
Silverfish!
Drat! Missed!
Stand back!
PING
PING
PING
Got'em!

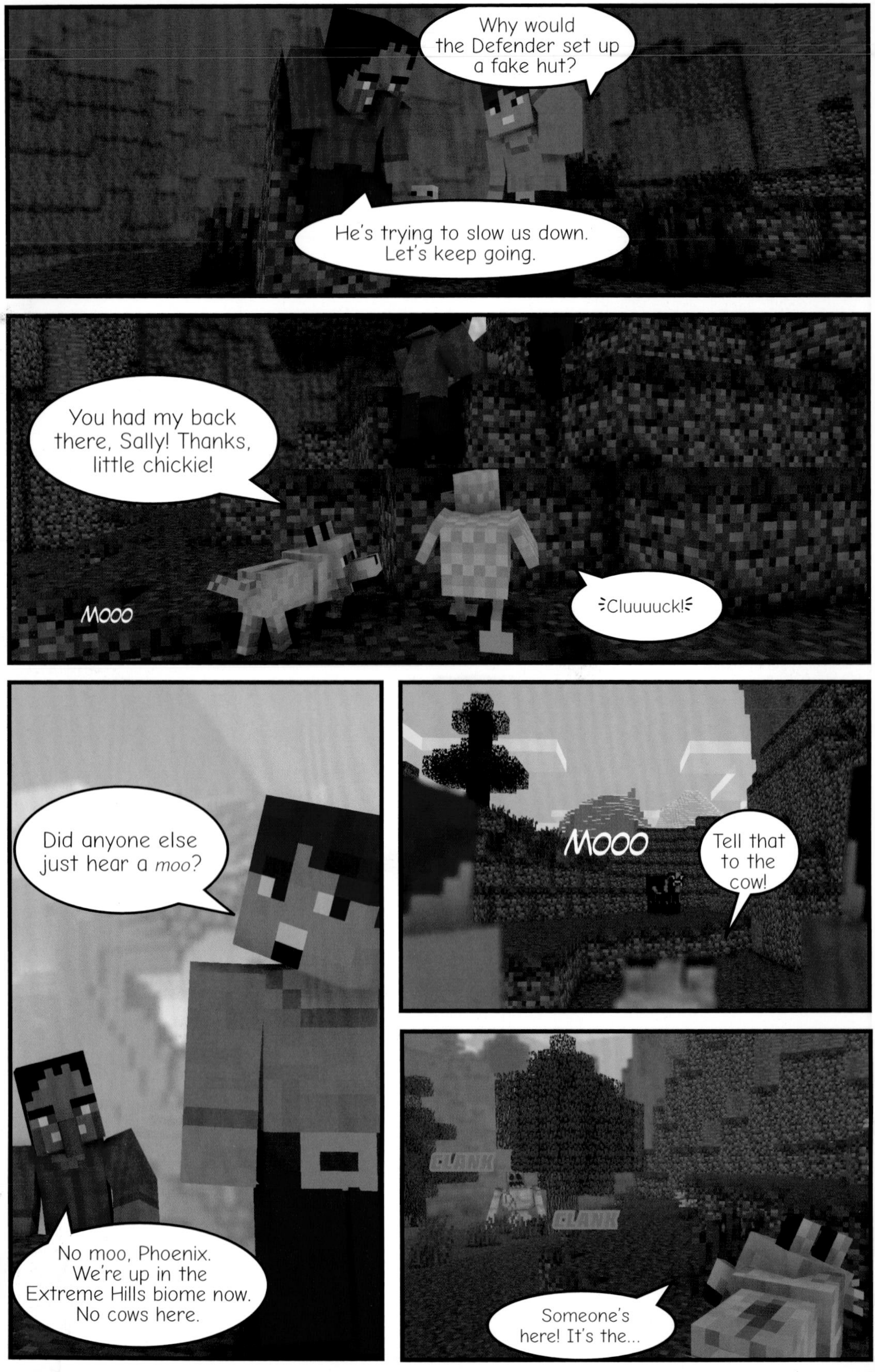
Why would the Defender set up a fake hut?
He's trying to slow us down. Let's keep going.
You had my back there, Sally! Thanks, little chickie!
MOOO
Cluuuuck!
Did anyone else just hear a *moo*?
No moo, Phoenix. We're up in the Extreme Hills biome now. No cows here.
MOOO
Tell that to the cow!
CLANK
CLANK
Someone's here! It's the...

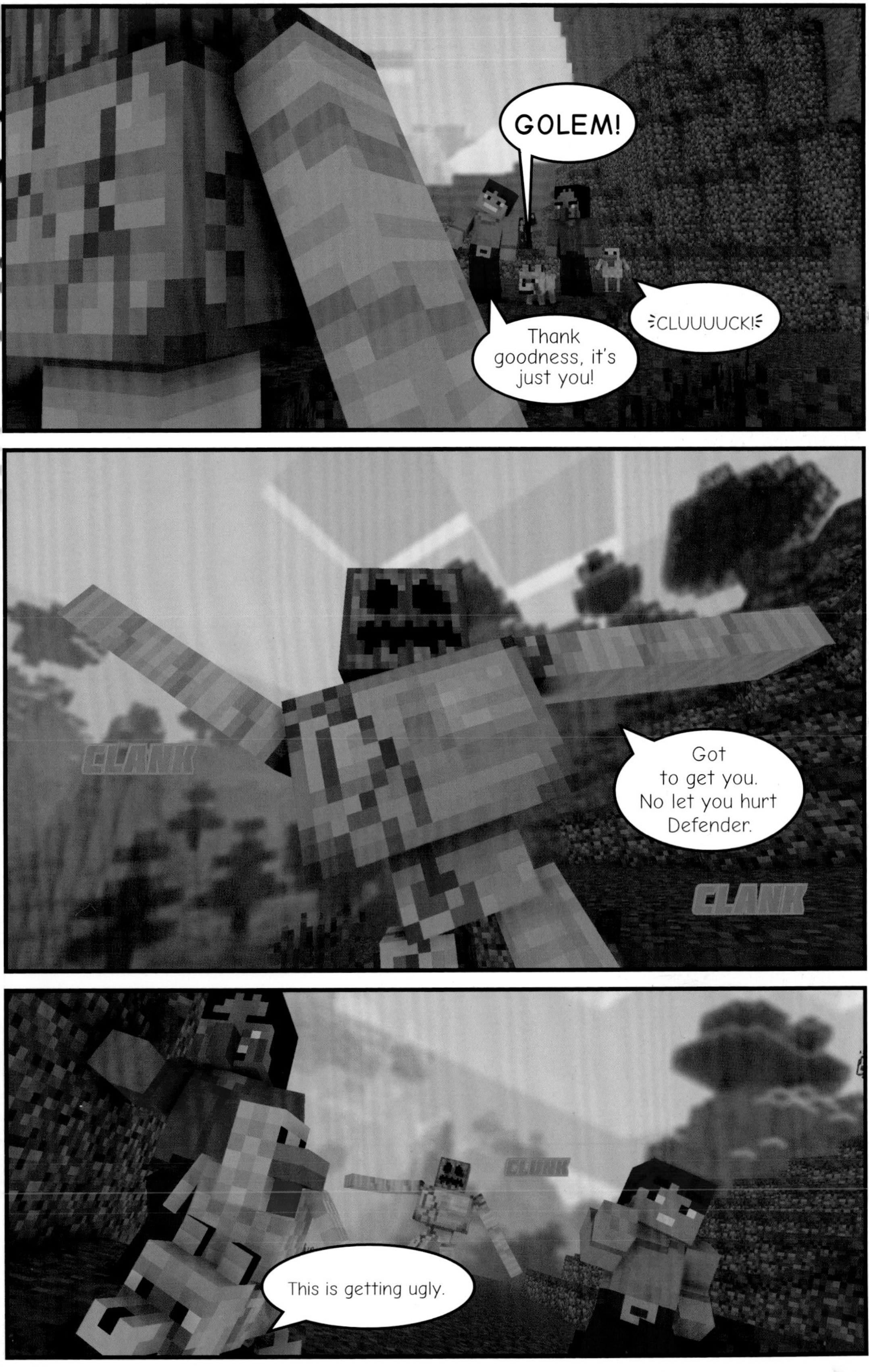
GOLEM!
Thank goodness, it's just you!
CLUUUUCK!
CLANK
Got to get you. No let you hurt Defender.
CLANK
CLUNK
This is getting ugly.

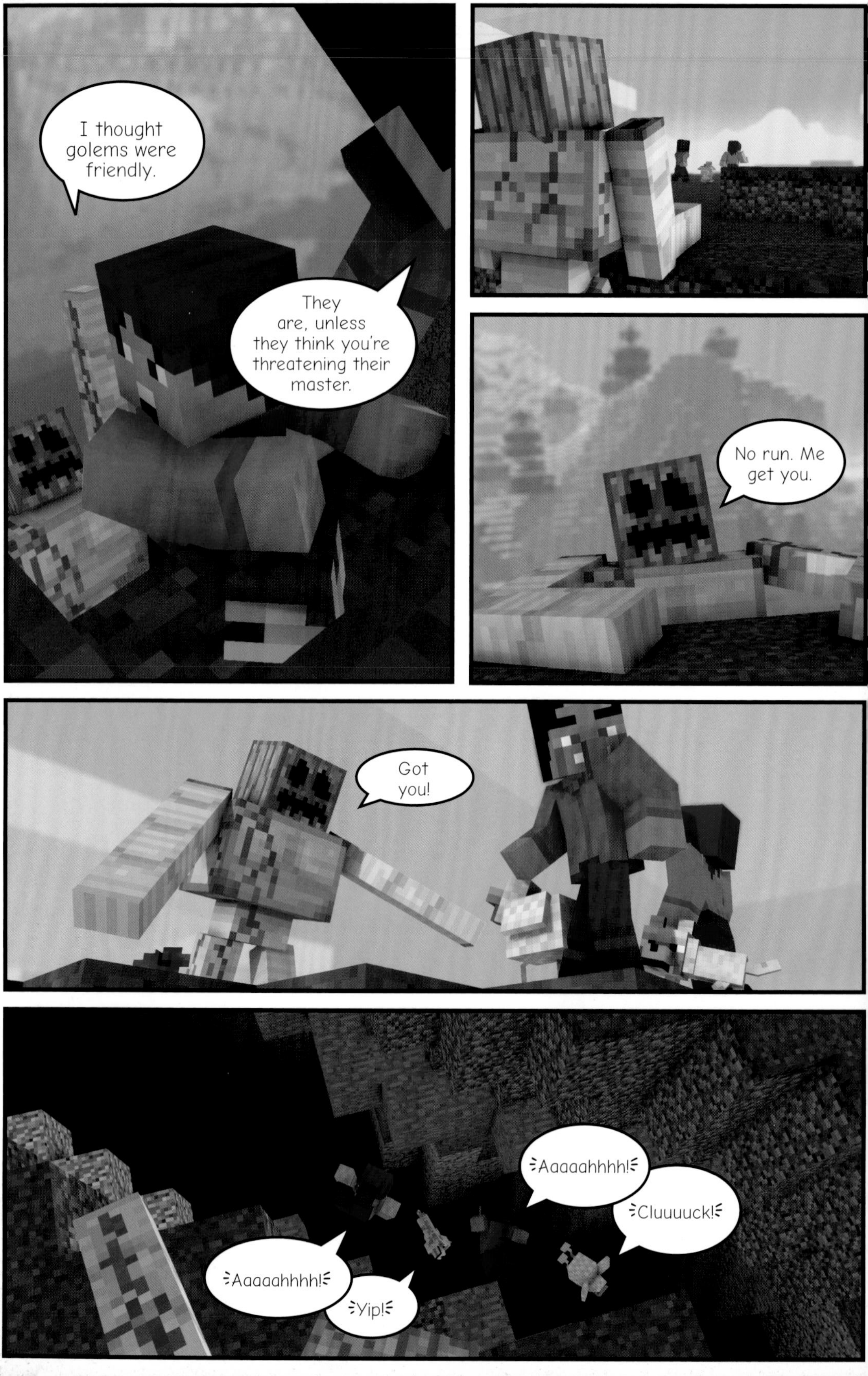
I thought golems were friendly.
They are, unless they think you're threatening their master.
No run. Me get you.
Got you!
Aaaaahhhh!
Cluuuuck!
Aaaaahhhh!
Yip!

CHAPTER 8

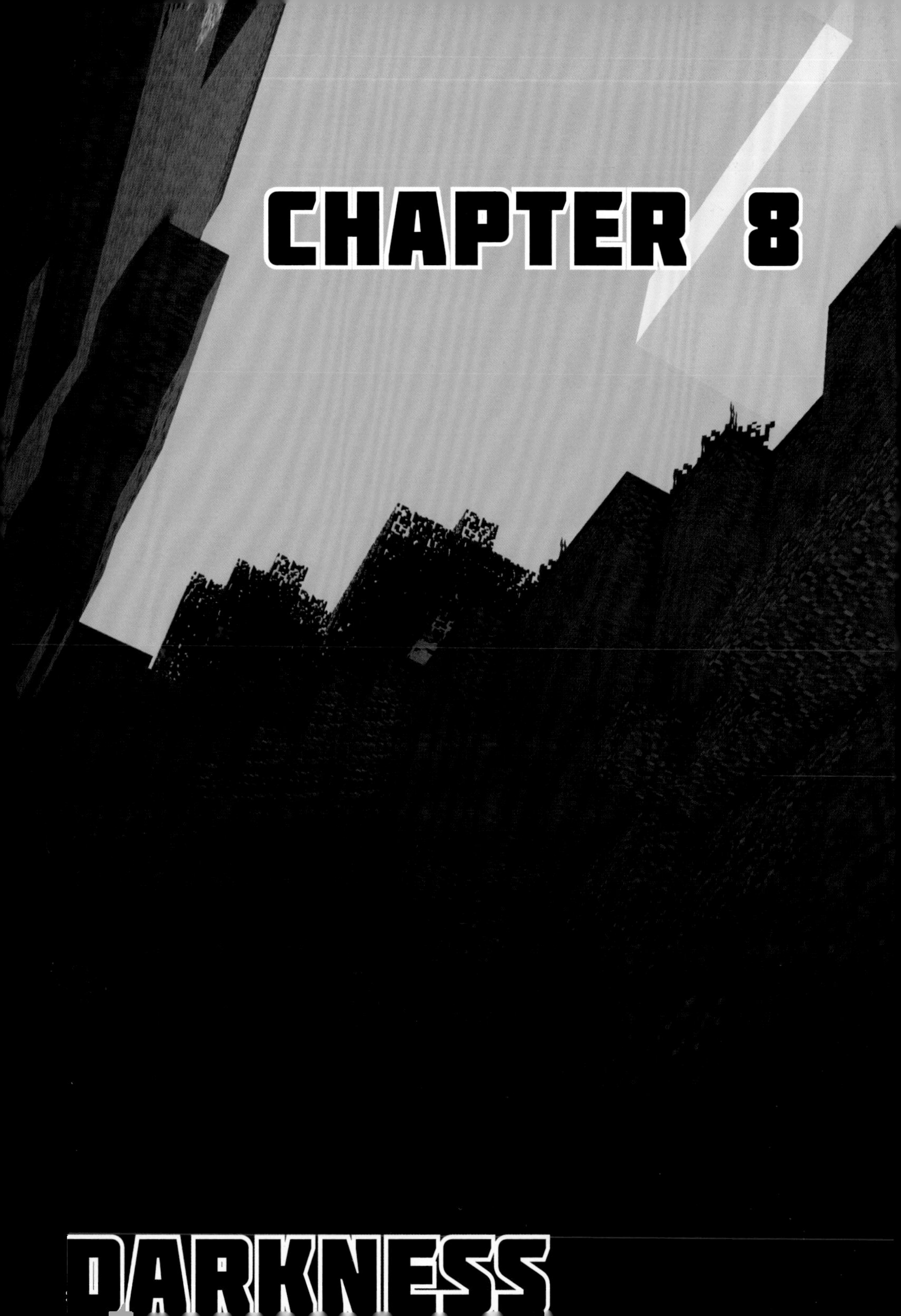

DARKNESS

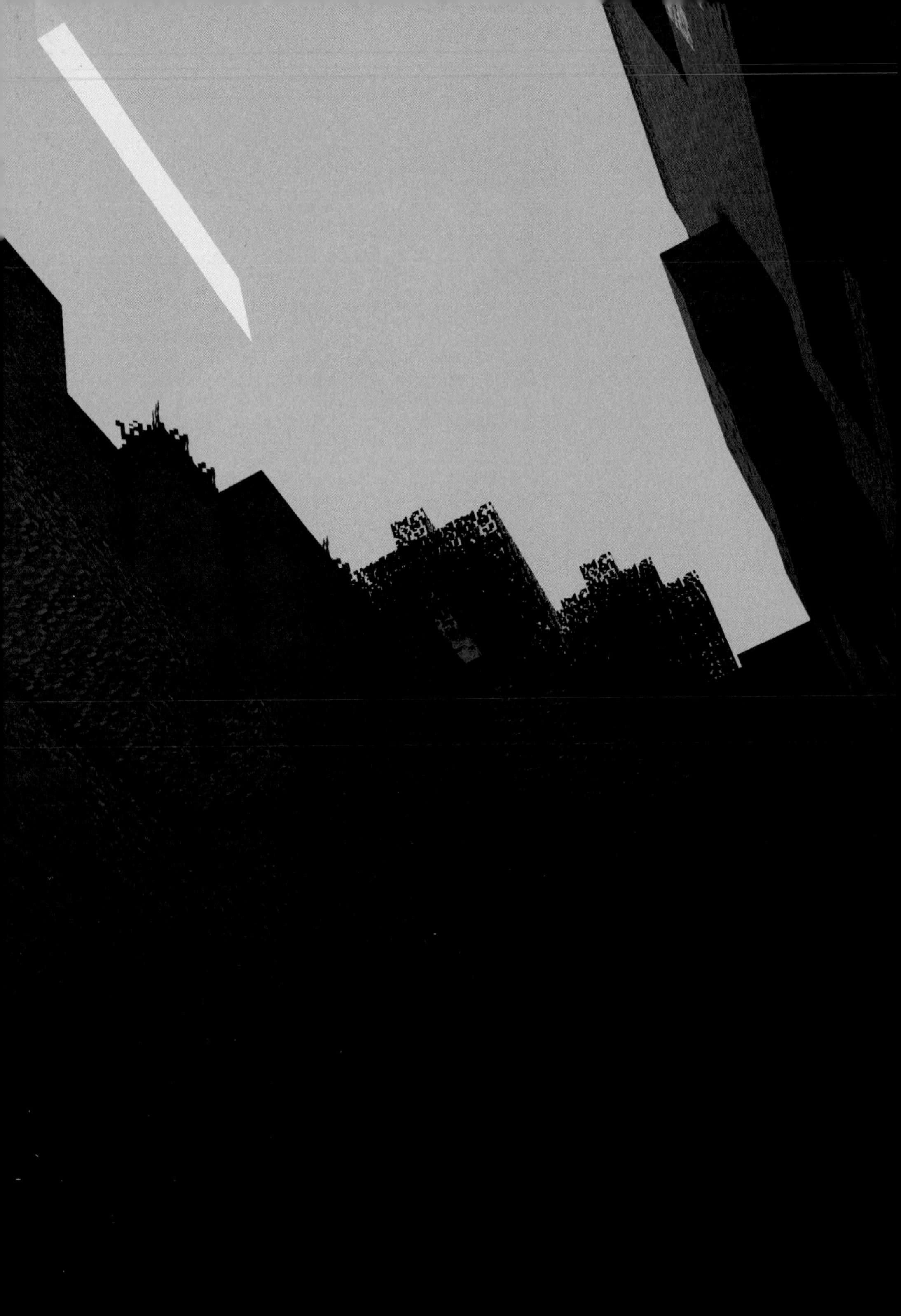

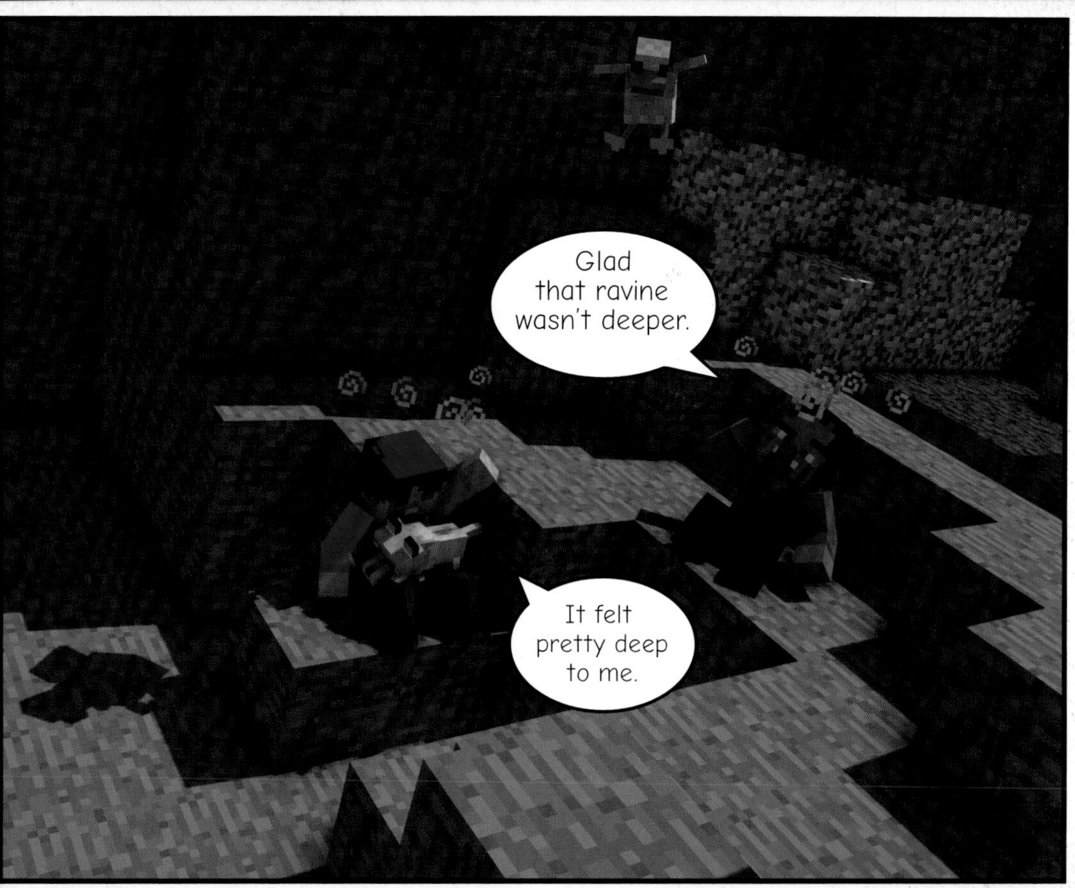
Glad that ravine wasn't deeper.
It felt pretty deep to me.

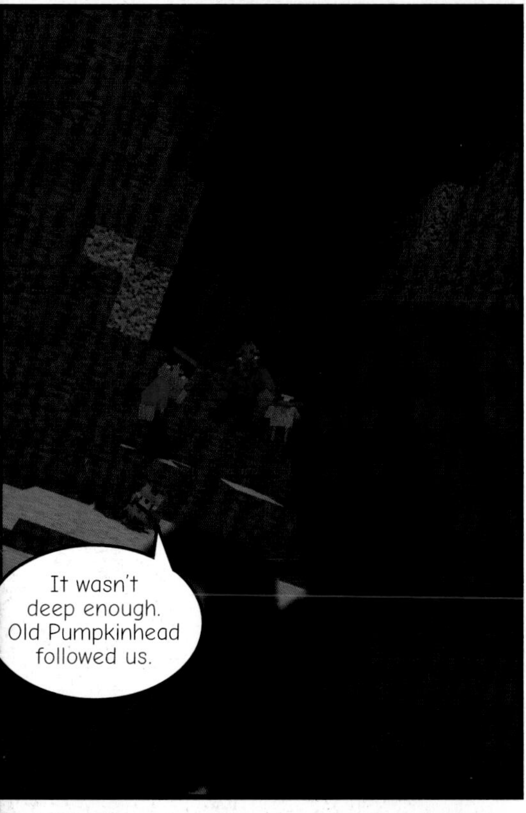
It wasn't deep enough. Old Pumpkinhead followed us.

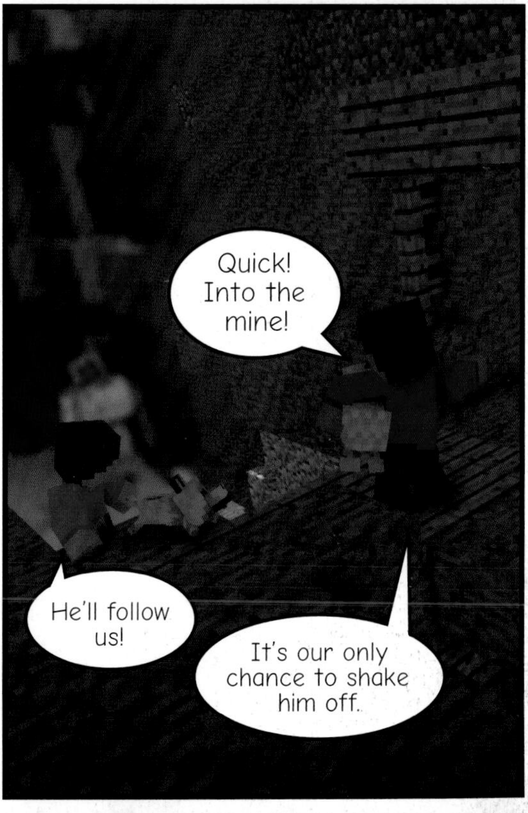
Quick! Into the mine!
He'll follow us!
It's our only chance to shake him off.

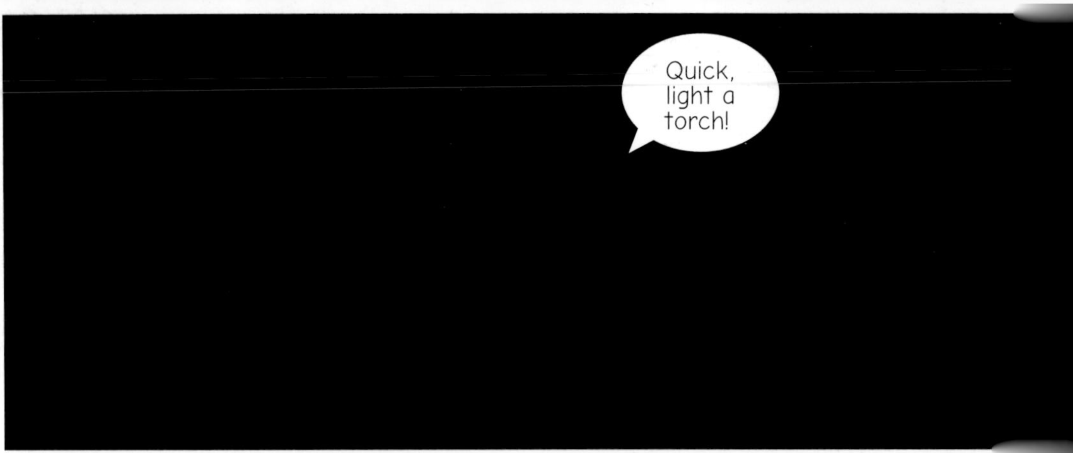
Quick, light a torch!

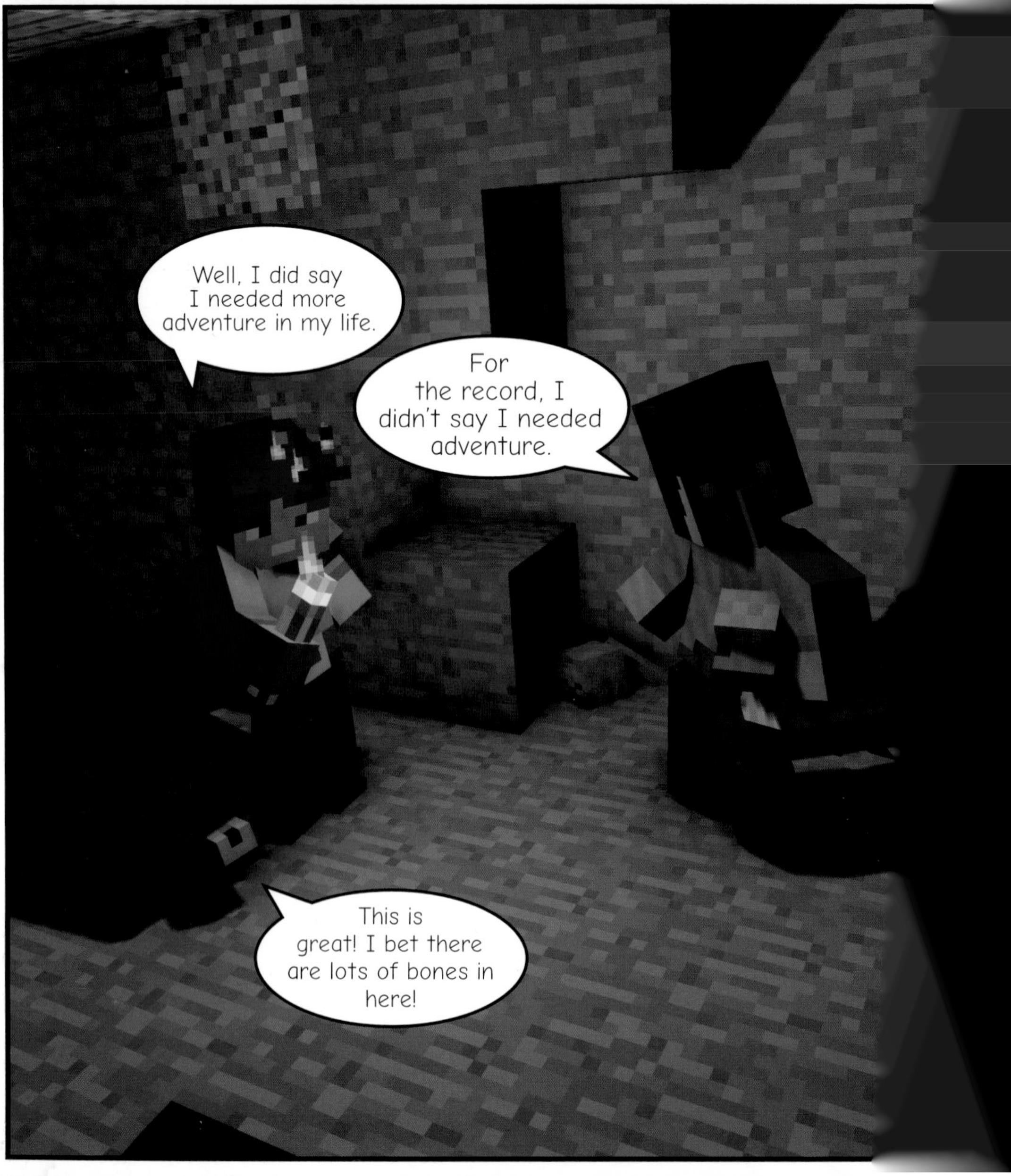
Well, I did say I needed more adventure in my life.
For the record, I didn't say I needed adventure.
This is great! I bet there are lots of bones in here!

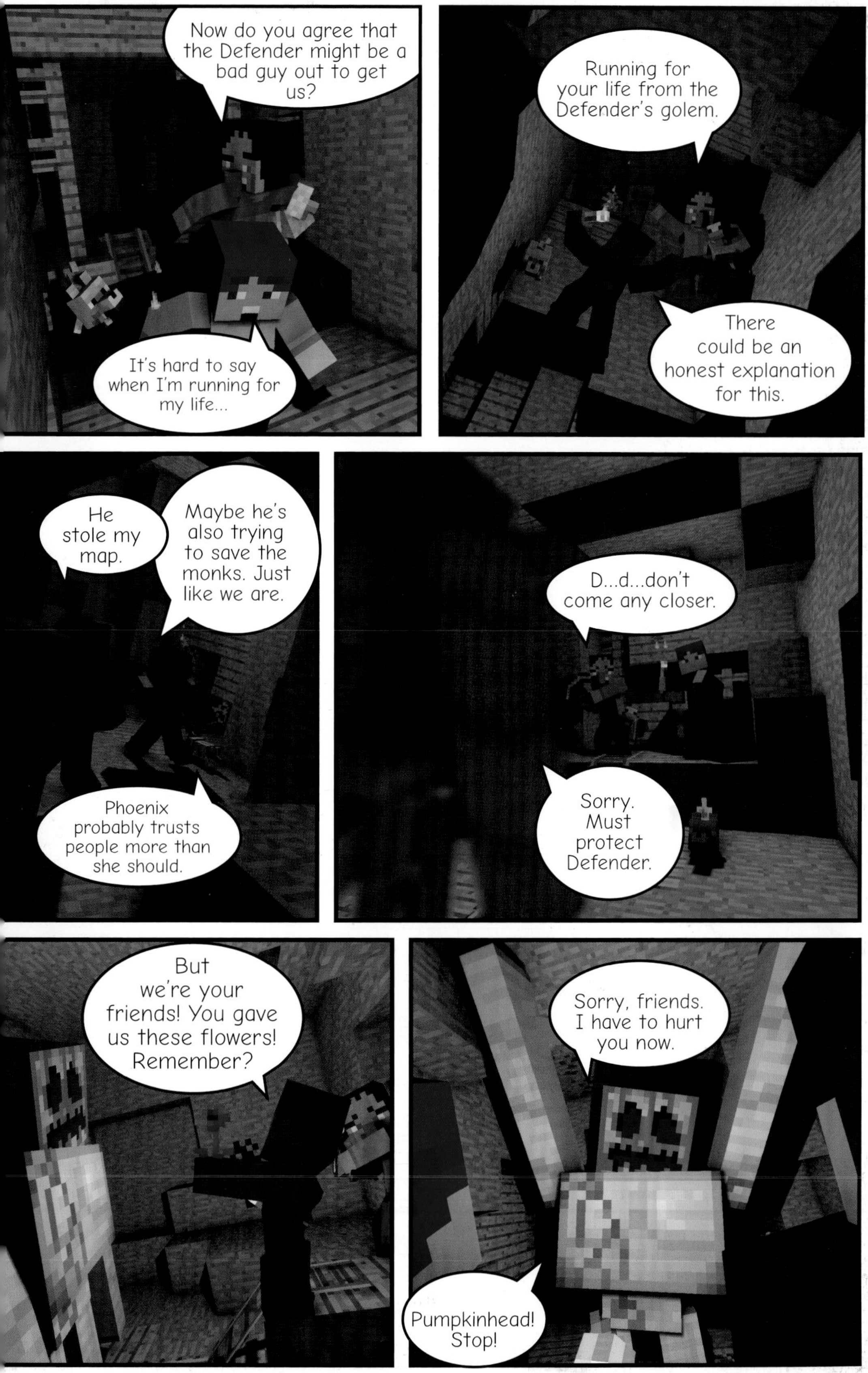
Now do you agree that the Defender might be a bad guy out to get us?
It's hard to say when I'm running for my life...
Running for your life from the Defender's golem.
There could be an honest explanation for this.
He stole my map.
Maybe he's also trying to save the monks. Just like we are.
Phoenix probably trusts people more than she should.
D...d...don't come any closer.
Sorry. Must protect Defender.
But we're your friends! You gave us these flowers! Remember?
Sorry, friends. I have to hurt you now.
Pumpkinhead! Stop!

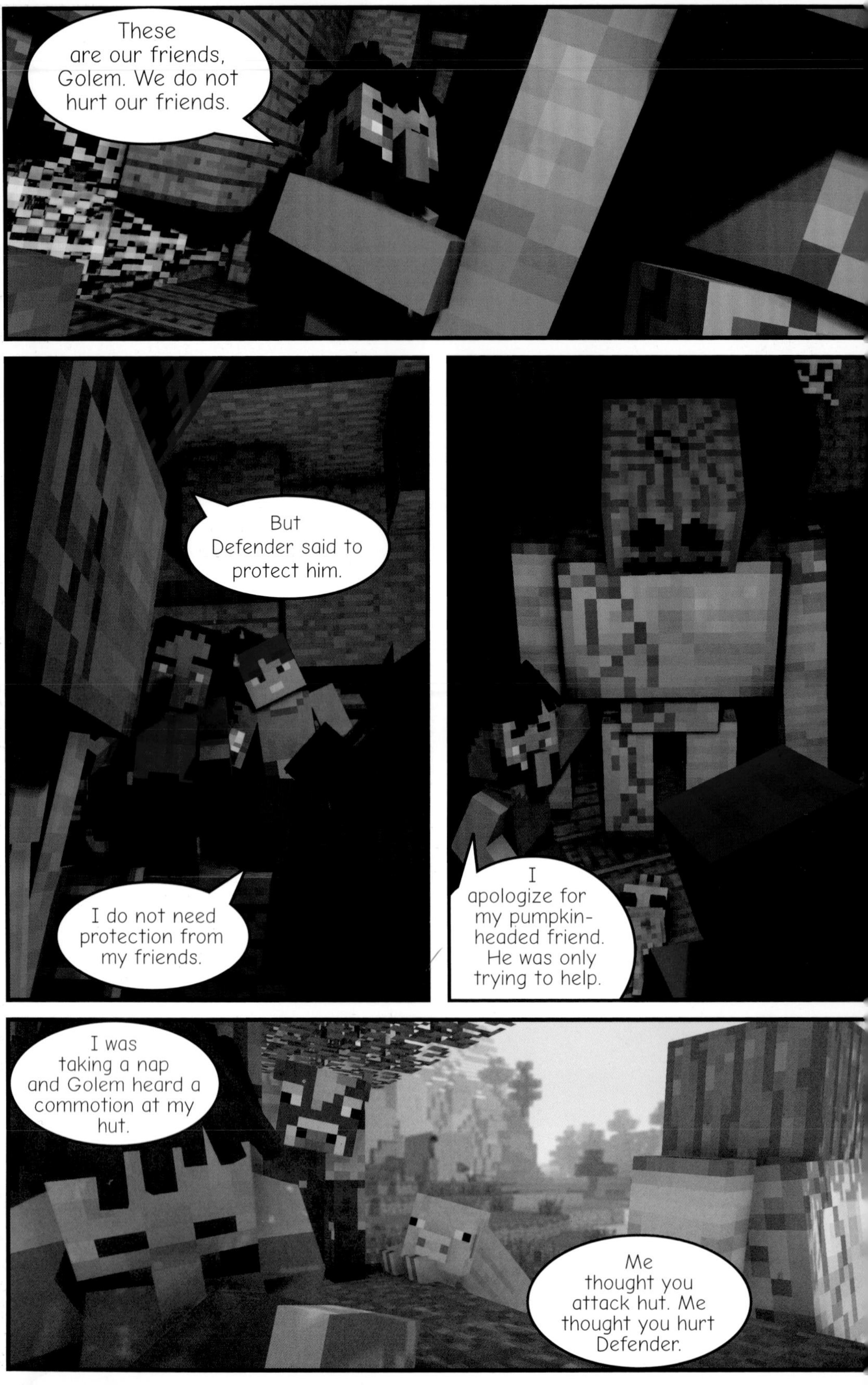
These are our friends, Golem. We do not hurt our friends.
But Defender said to protect him.
I do not need protection from my friends.
I apologize for my pumpkin-headed friend. He was only trying to help.
I was taking a nap and Golem heard a commotion at my hut.
Me thought you attack hut. Me thought you hurt Defender.

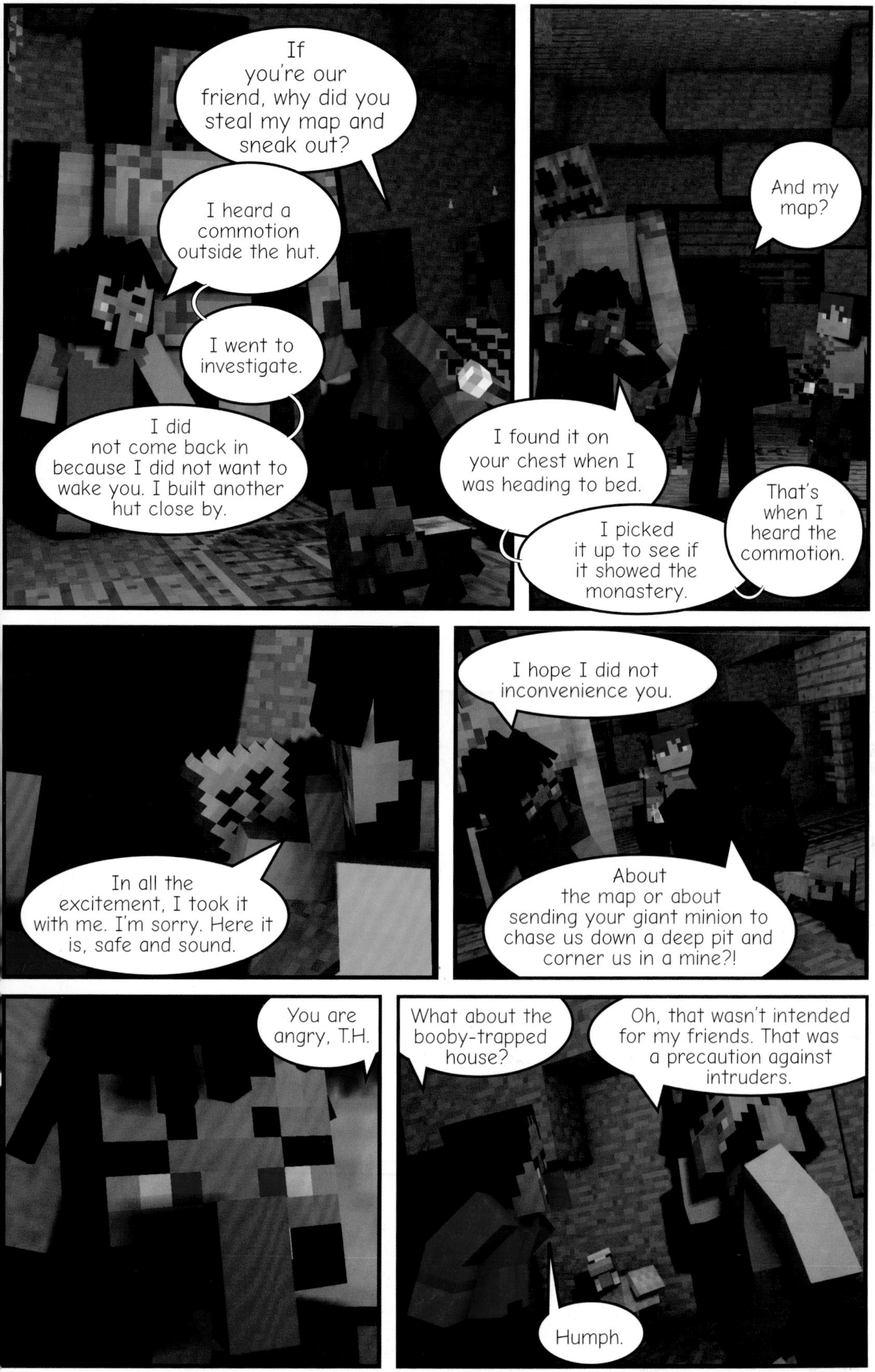
If you're our friend, why did you steal my map and sneak out?
I heard a commotion outside the hut.
I went to investigate.
I did not come back in because I did not want to wake you. I built another hut close by.
And my map?
I found it on your chest when I was heading to bed.
I picked it up to see if it showed the monastery.
That's when I heard the commotion.
In all the excitement, I took it with me. I'm sorry. Here it is, safe and sound.
I hope I did not inconvenience you.
About the map or about sending your giant minion to chase us down a deep pit and corner us in a mine?!
You are angry, T.H.
What about the booby-trapped house?
Oh, that wasn't intended for my friends. That was a precaution against intruders.
Humph.

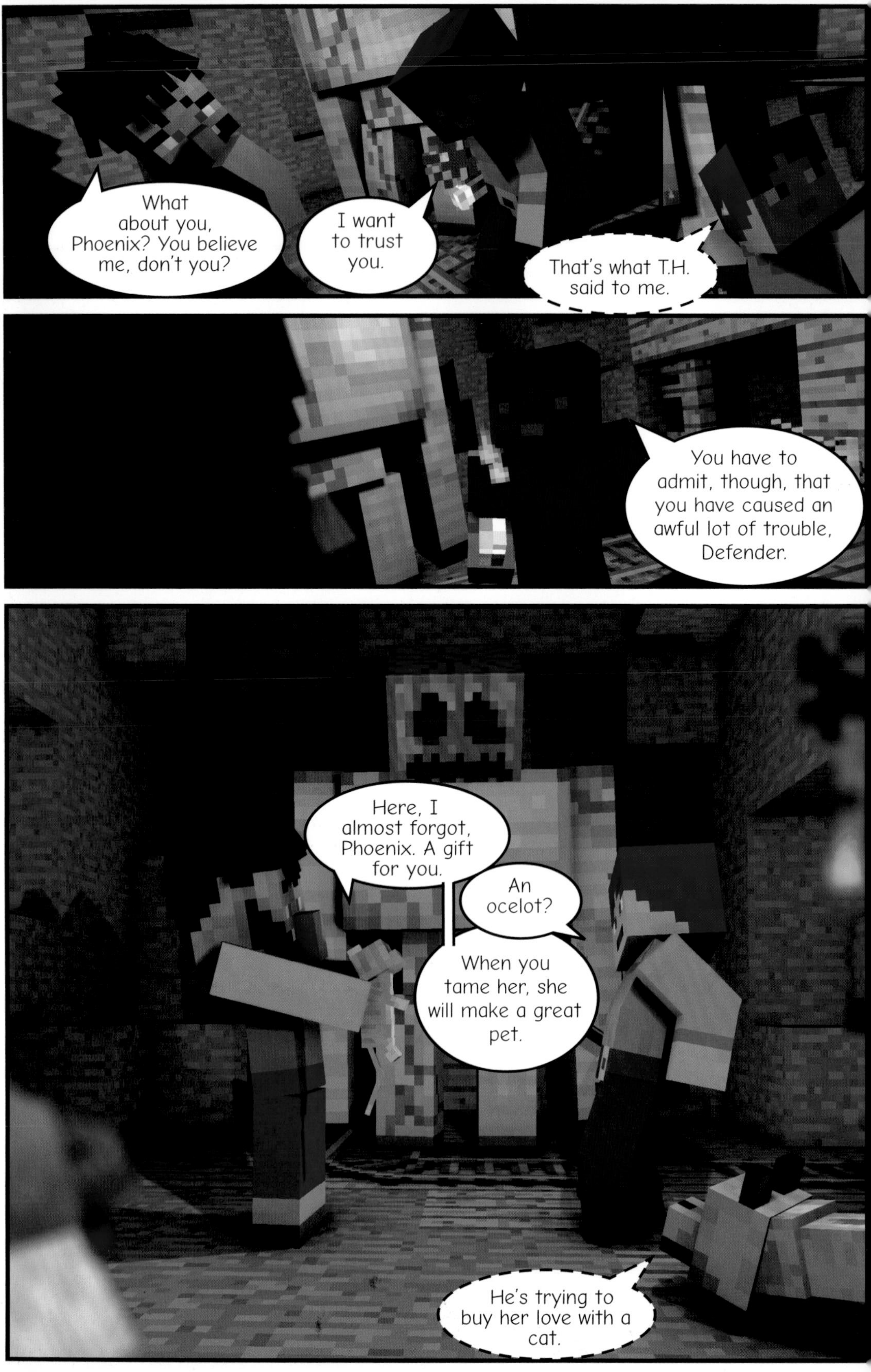
What about you, Phoenix? You believe me, don't you?
I want to trust you.
That's what T.H. said to me.
You have to admit, though, that you have caused an awful lot of trouble, Defender.
Here, I almost forgot, Phoenix. A gift for you.
An ocelot?
When you tame her, she will make a great pet.
He's trying to buy her love with a cat.

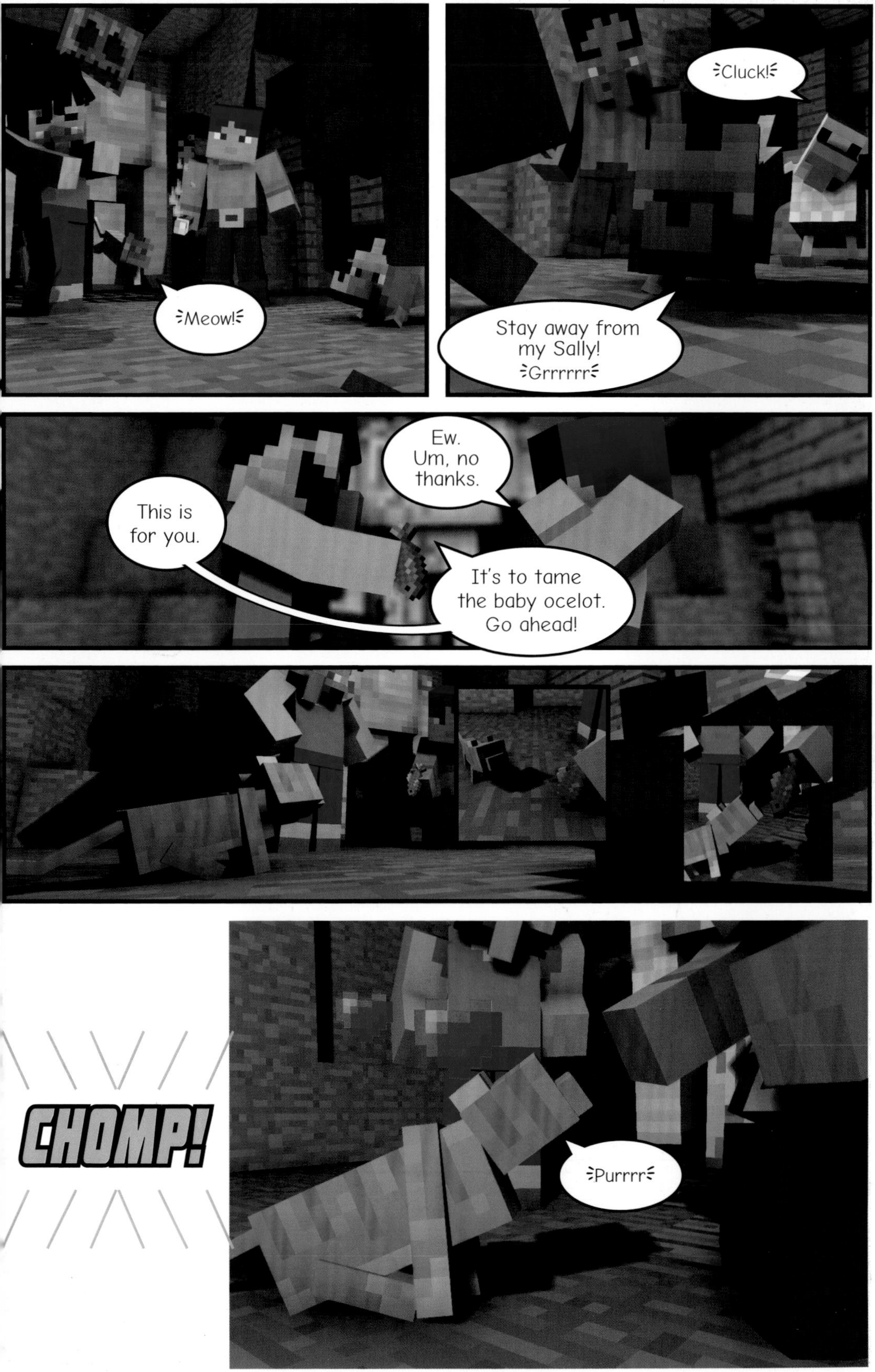
Meow!
Cluck!
Stay away from my Sally! Grrrrrr
This is for you.
Ew. Um, no thanks.
It's to tame the baby ocelot. Go ahead!
CHOMP!
Purrrr

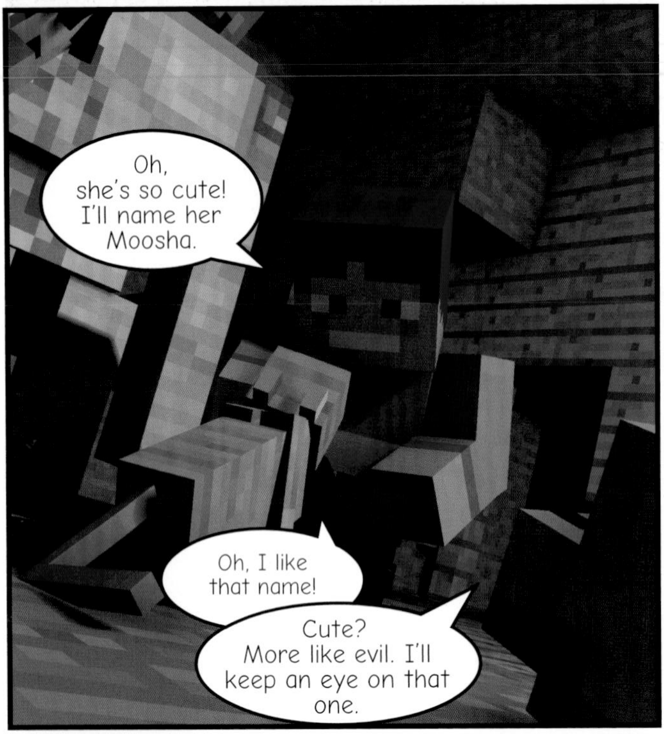
Oh, she's so cute! I'll name her Moosha.
Oh, I like that name!
Cute? More like evil. I'll keep an eye on that one.

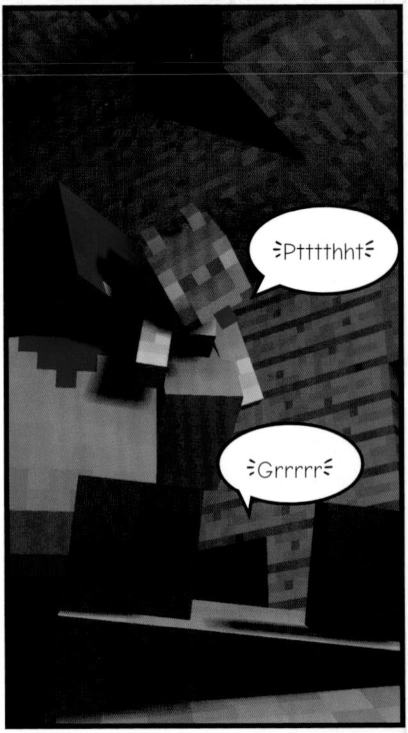
Pttttthht
Grrrrr

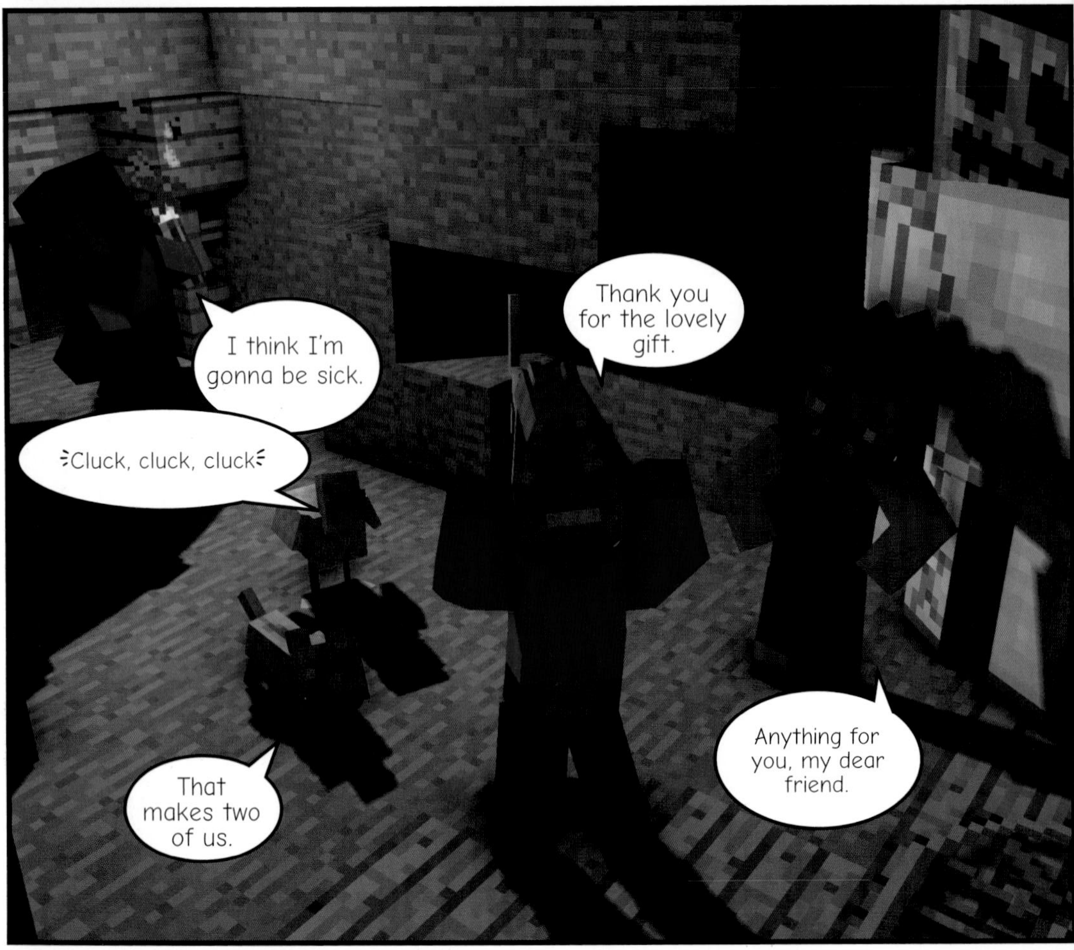
I think I'm gonna be sick.
Thank you for the lovely gift.
Cluck, cluck, cluck
That makes two of us.
Anything for you, my dear friend.

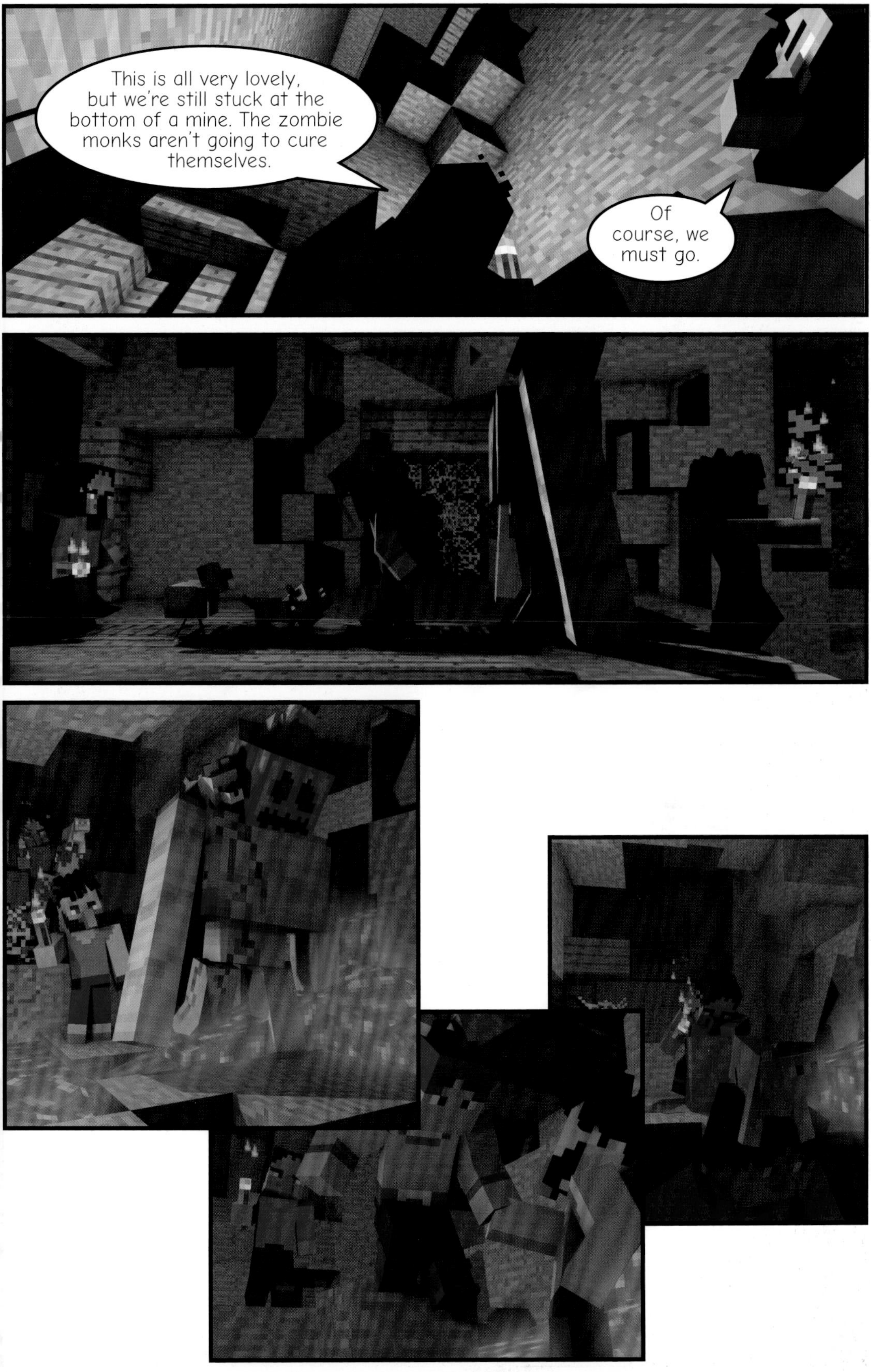
This is all very lovely, but we're still stuck at the bottom of a mine. The zombie monks aren't going to cure themselves.
Of course, we must go.

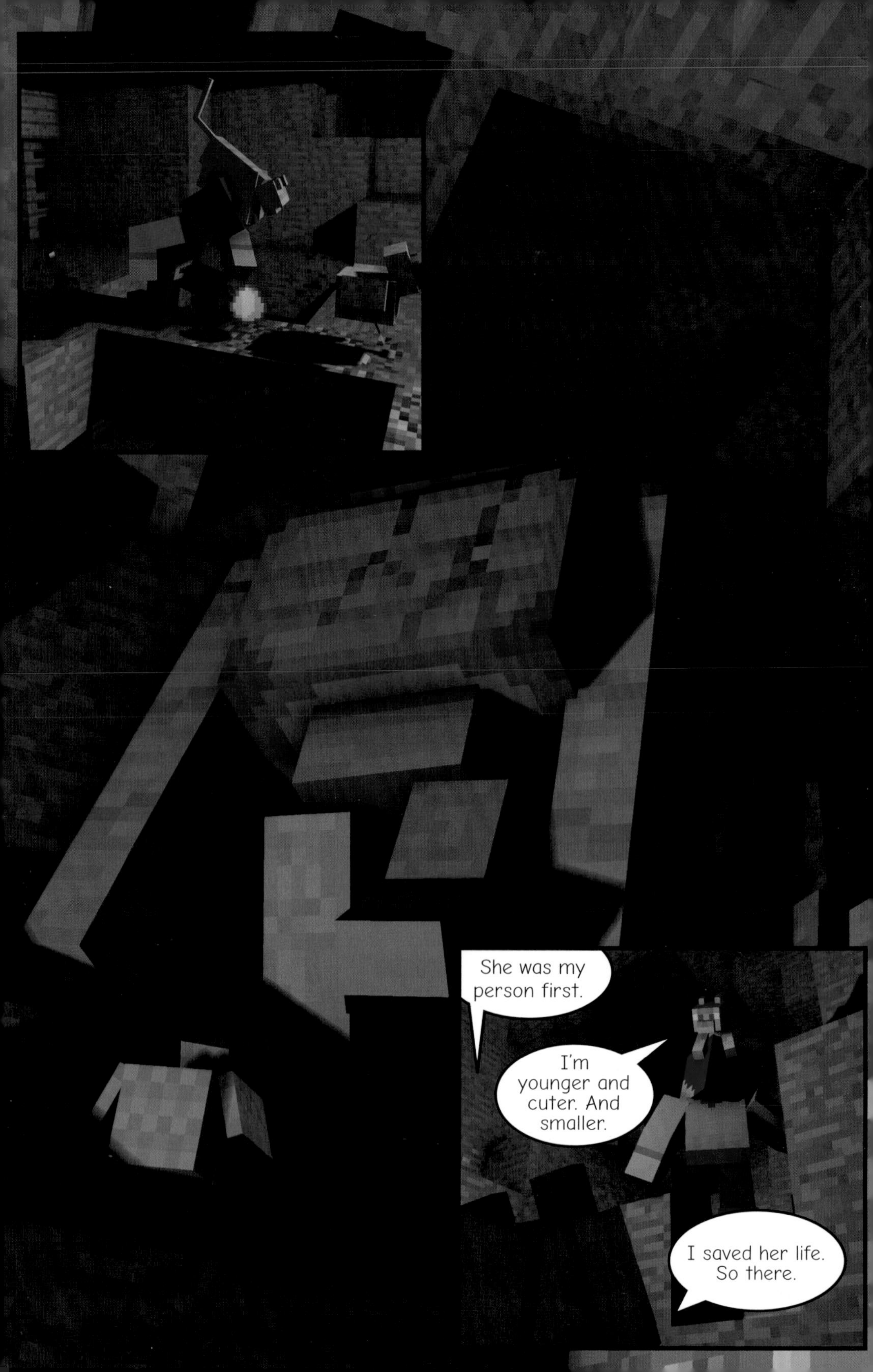
She was my person first.
I'm younger and cuter. And smaller.
I saved her life. So there.

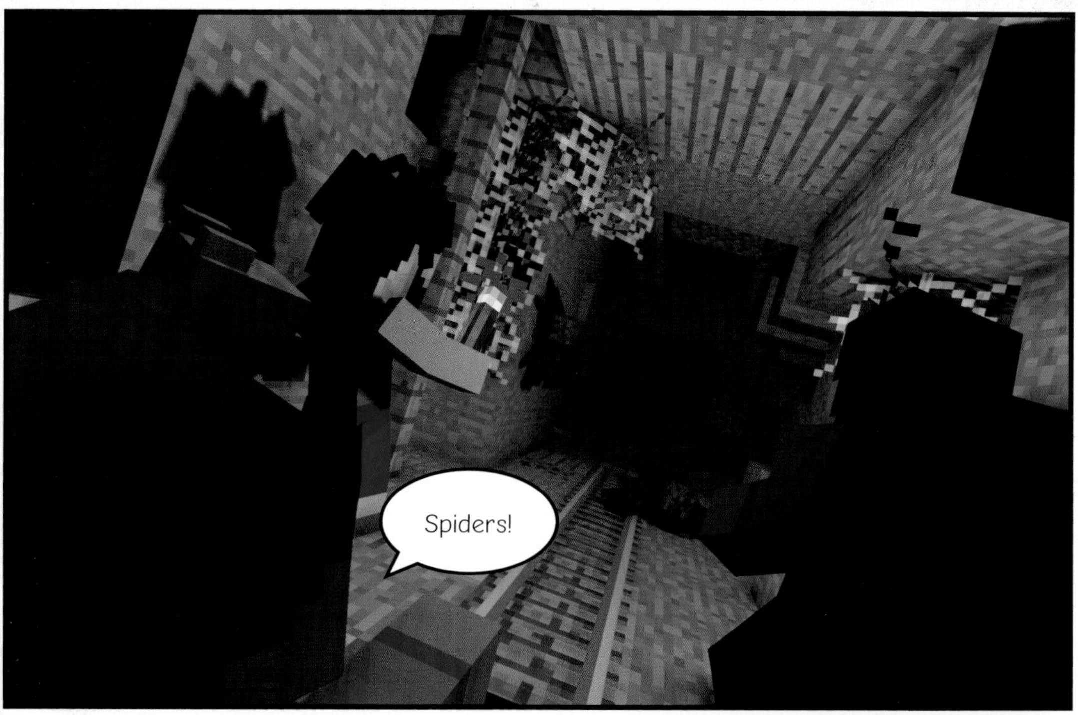
Spiders!

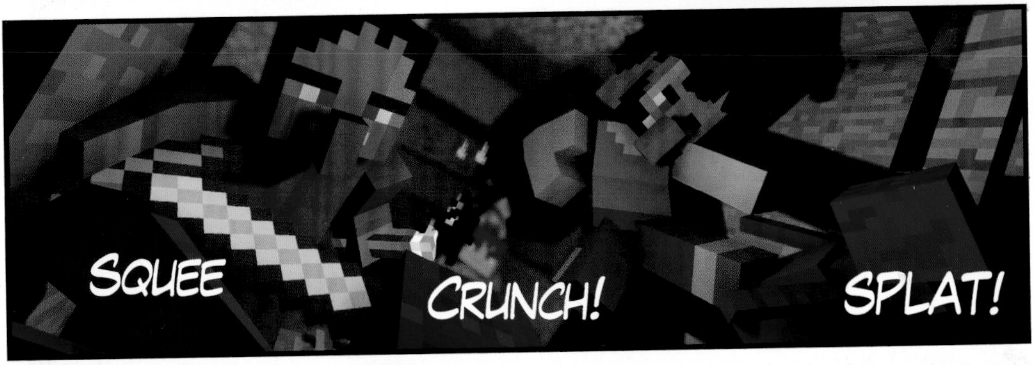
SQUEE
CRUNCH!
SPLAT!

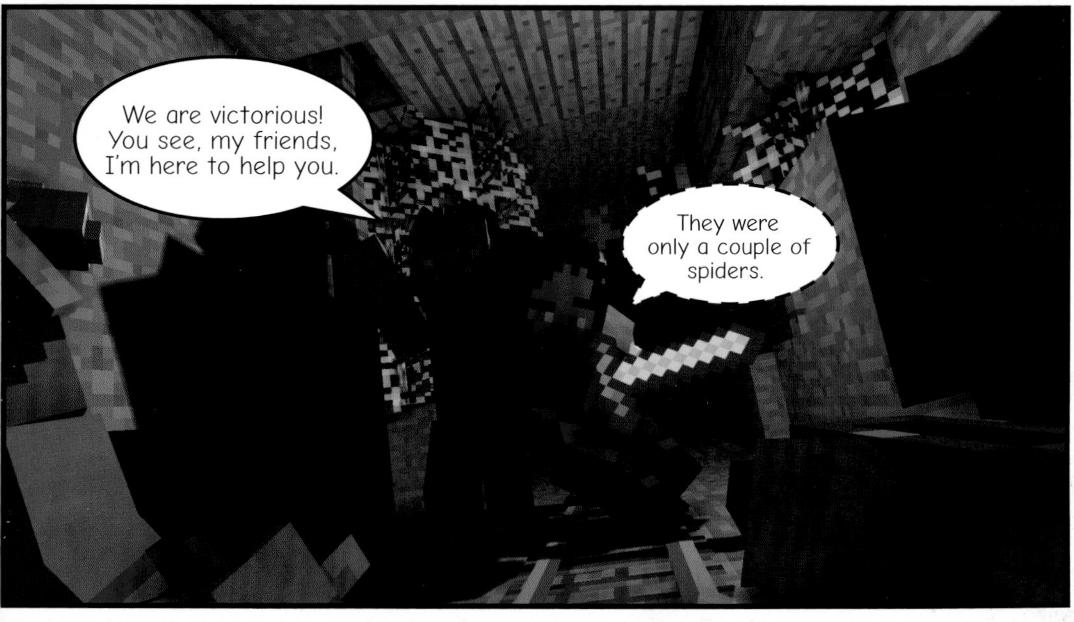
We are victorious! You see, my friends, I'm here to help you.
They were only a couple of spiders.

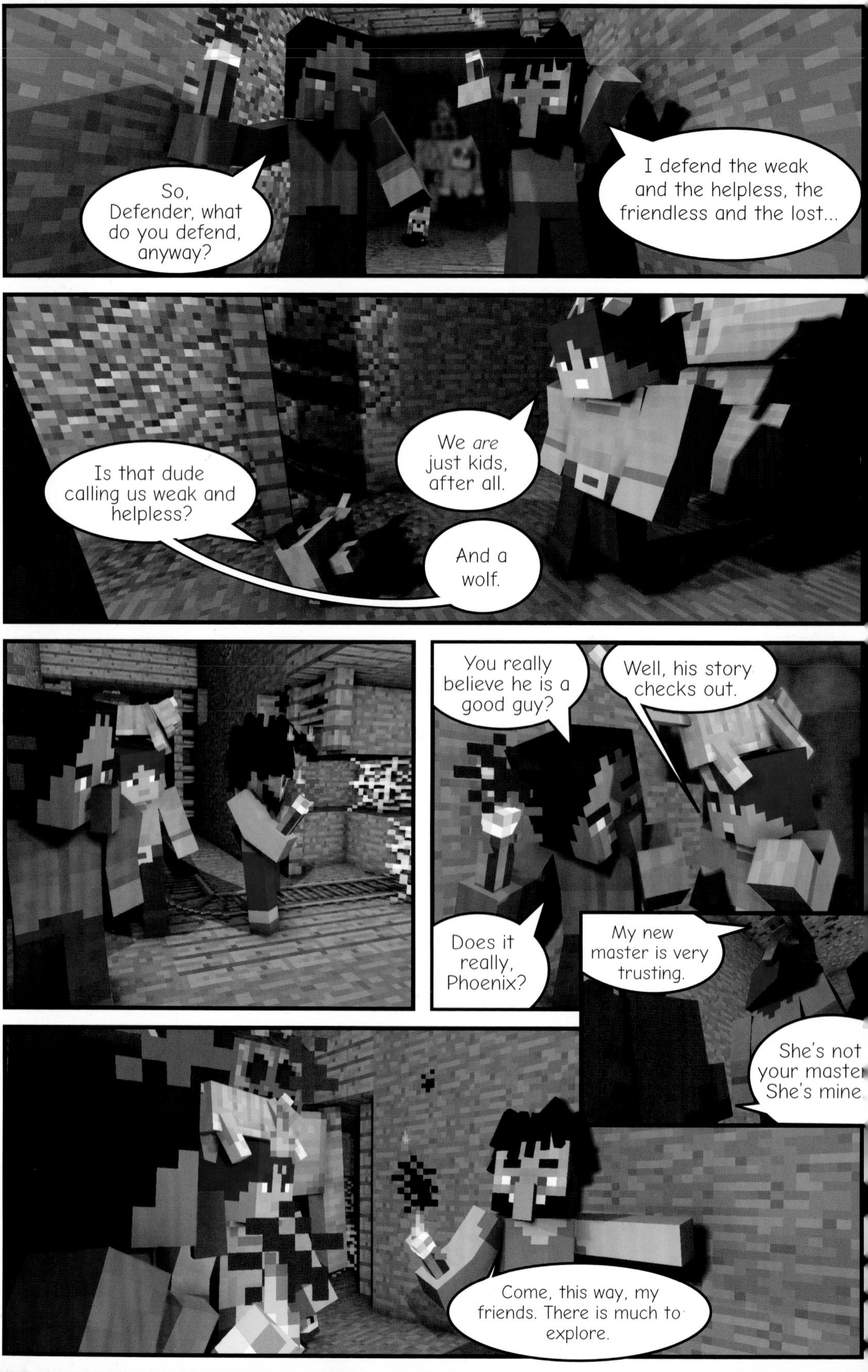
So, Defender, what do you defend, anyway?
I defend the weak and the helpless, the friendless and the lost...
We *are* just kids, after all.
Is that dude calling us weak and helpless?
And a wolf.
You really believe he is a good guy?
Well, his story checks out.
Does it really, Phoenix?
My new master is very trusting.
She's not your master. She's mine.
Come, this way, my friends. There is much to explore.

CHAPTER 9

THE CAVE OF DIAMONDS

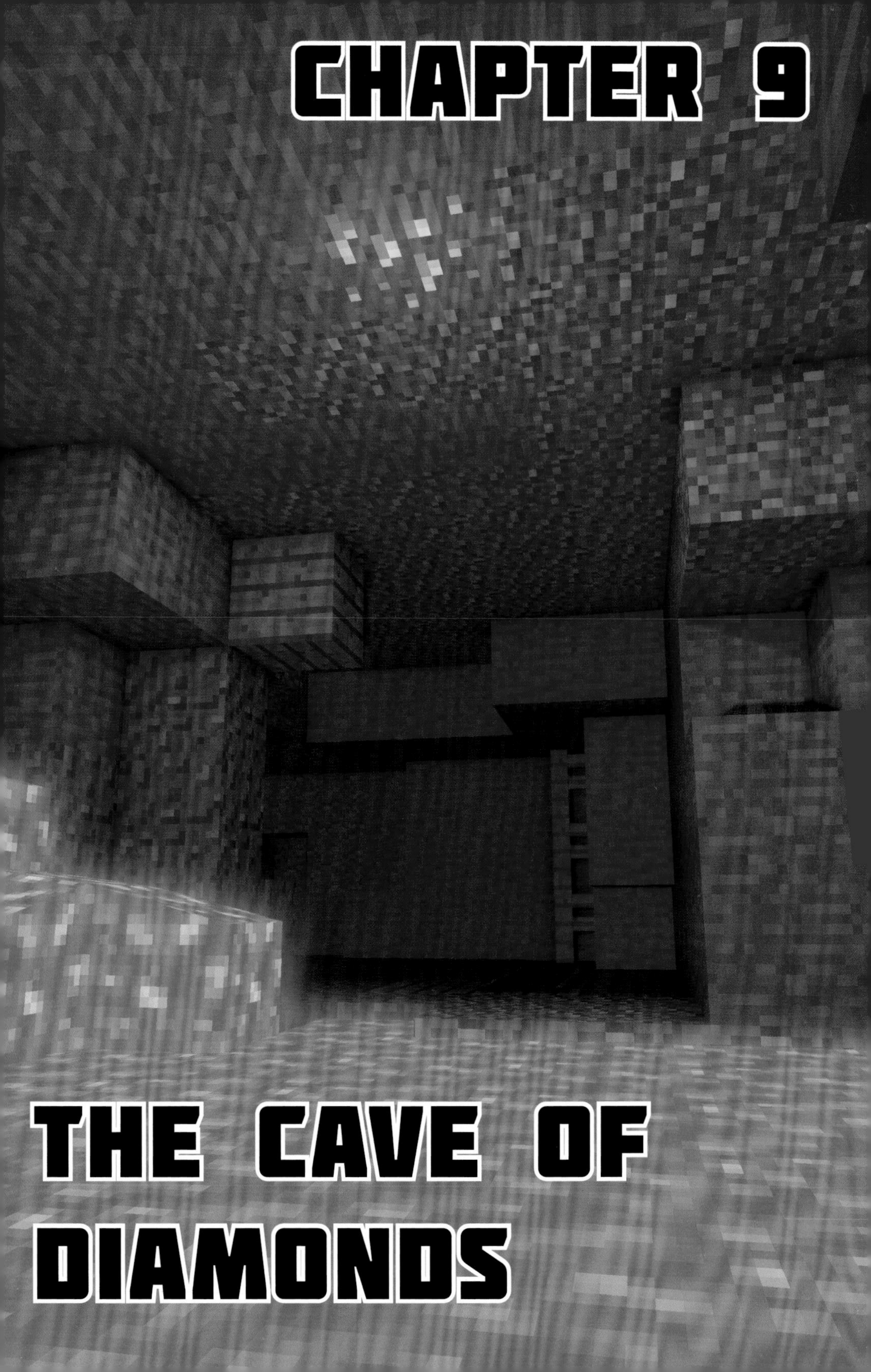

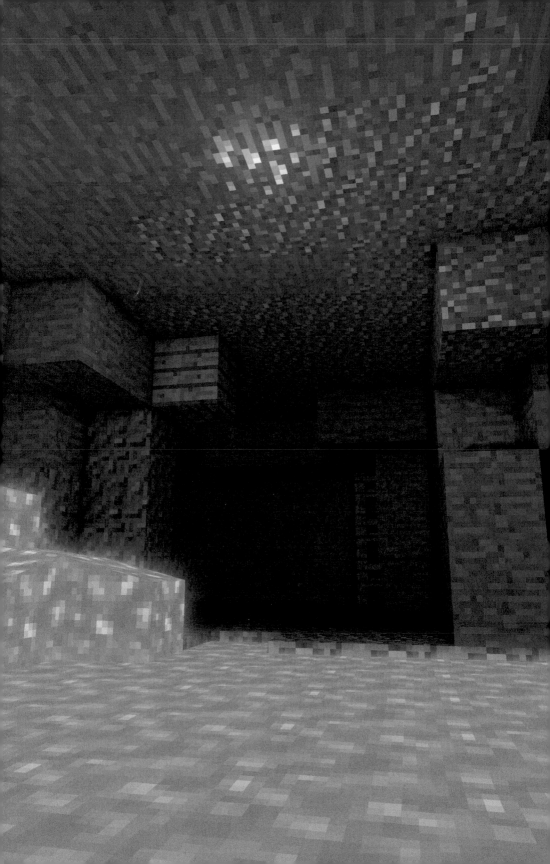

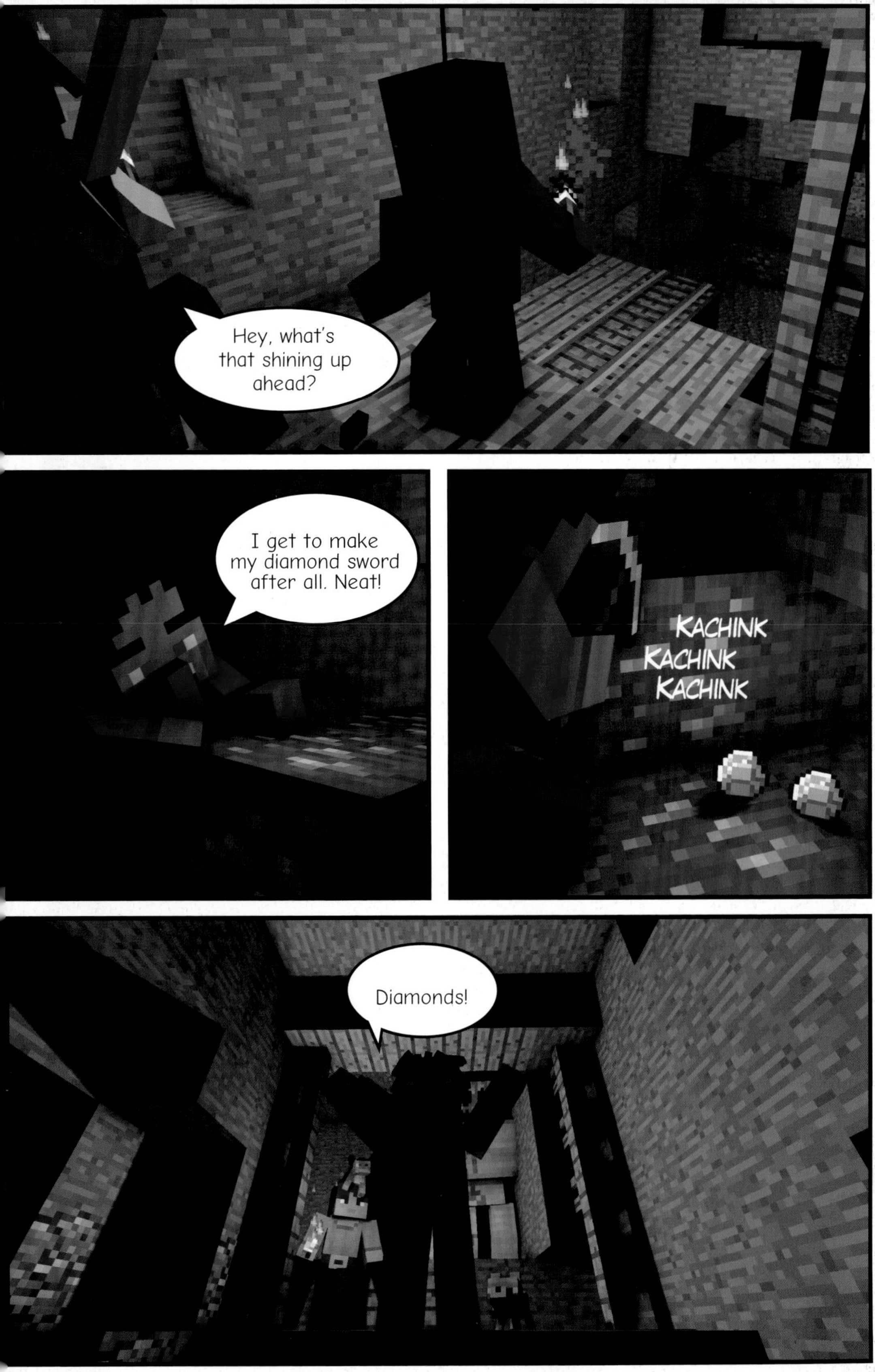
Hey, what's that shining up ahead?
I get to make my diamond sword after all. Neat!
KACHINK
KACHINK
KACHINK
Diamonds!

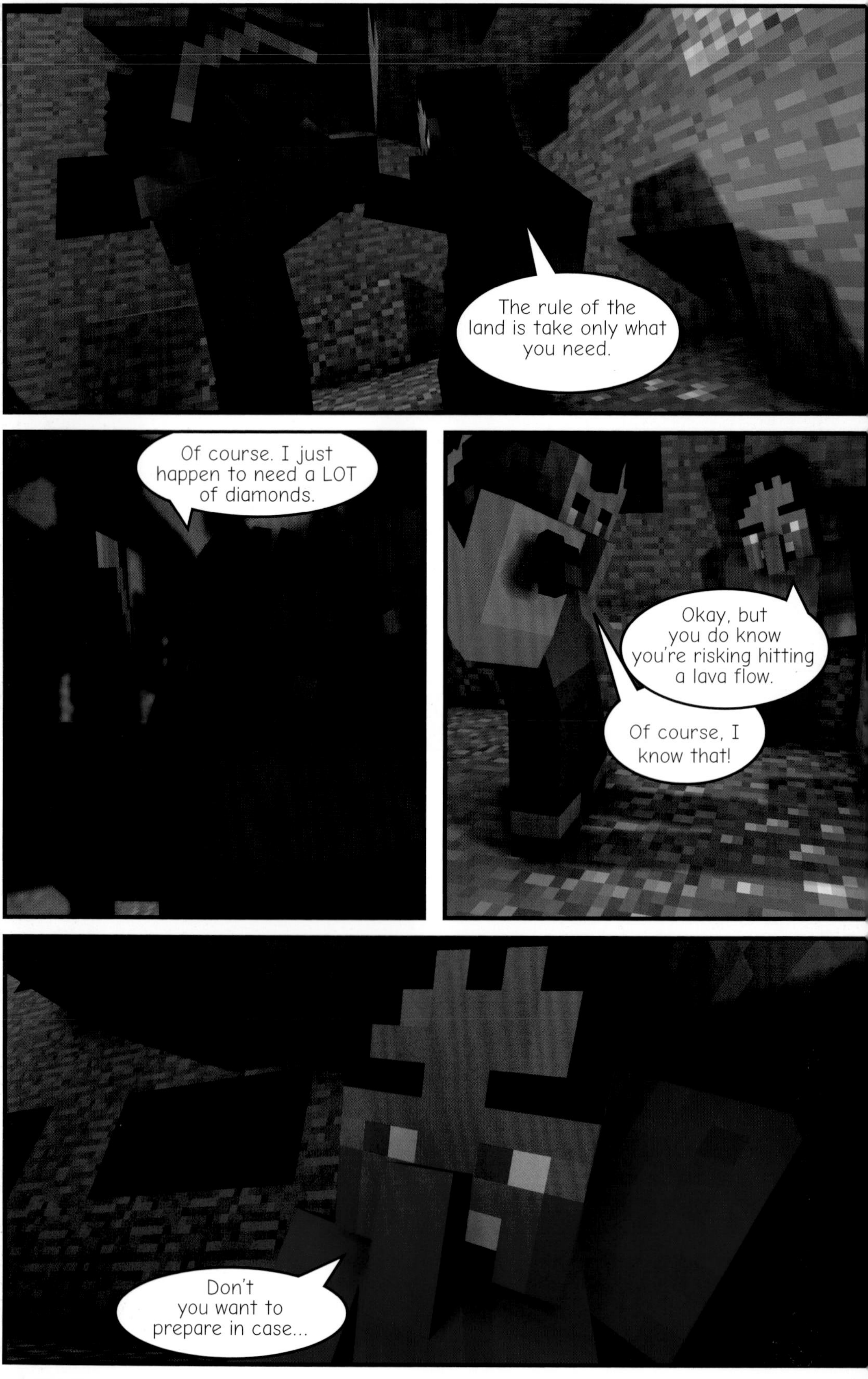
The rule of the land is take only what you need.
Of course. I just happen to need a LOT of diamonds.
Okay, but you do know you're risking hitting a lava flow.
Of course, I know that!
Don't you want to prepare in case...

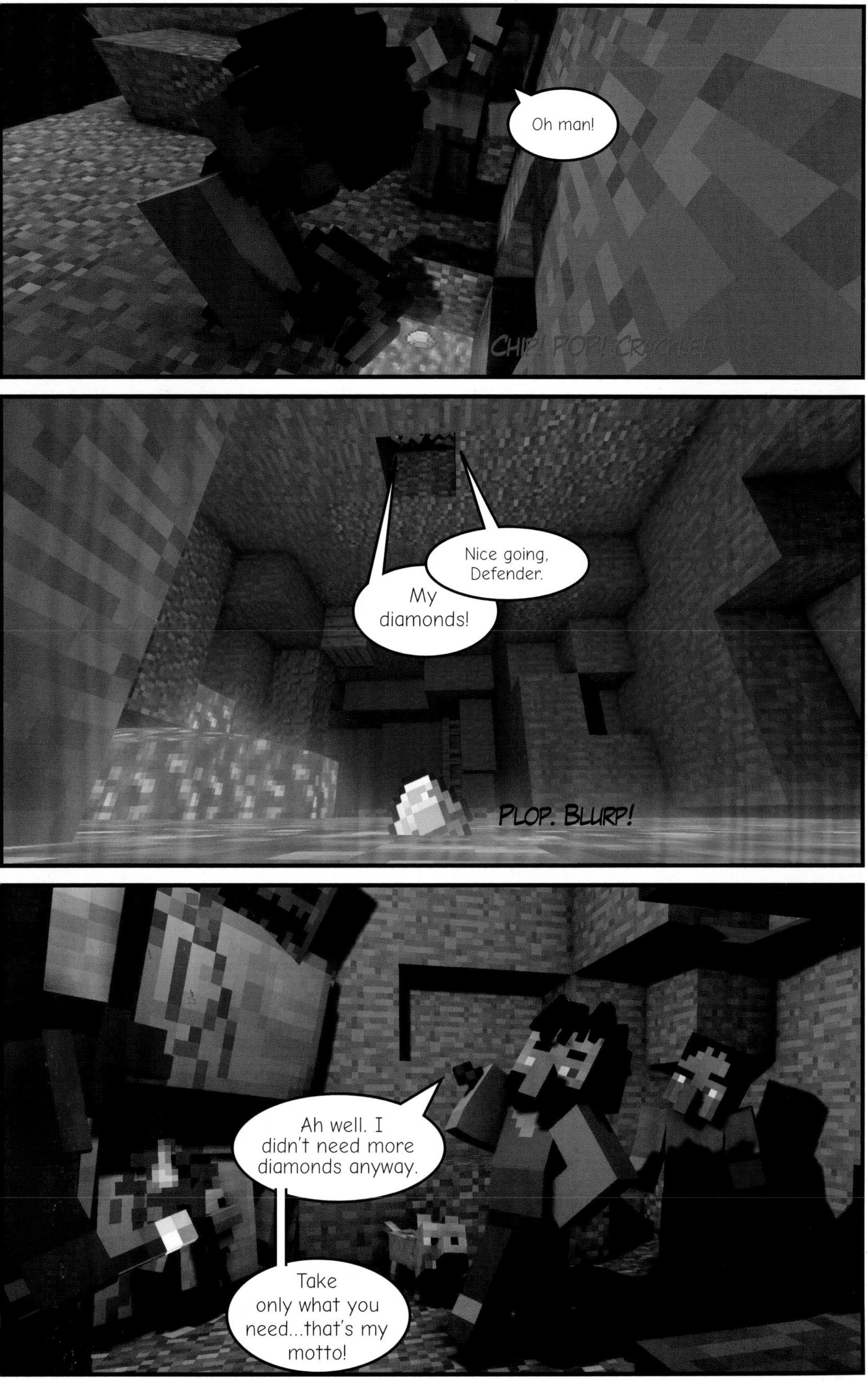
Oh man!
CHIP! POP! CRACKLE!
My diamonds!
Nice going, Defender.
PLOP. BLURP!
Ah well. I didn't need more diamonds anyway.
Take only what you need...that's my motto!

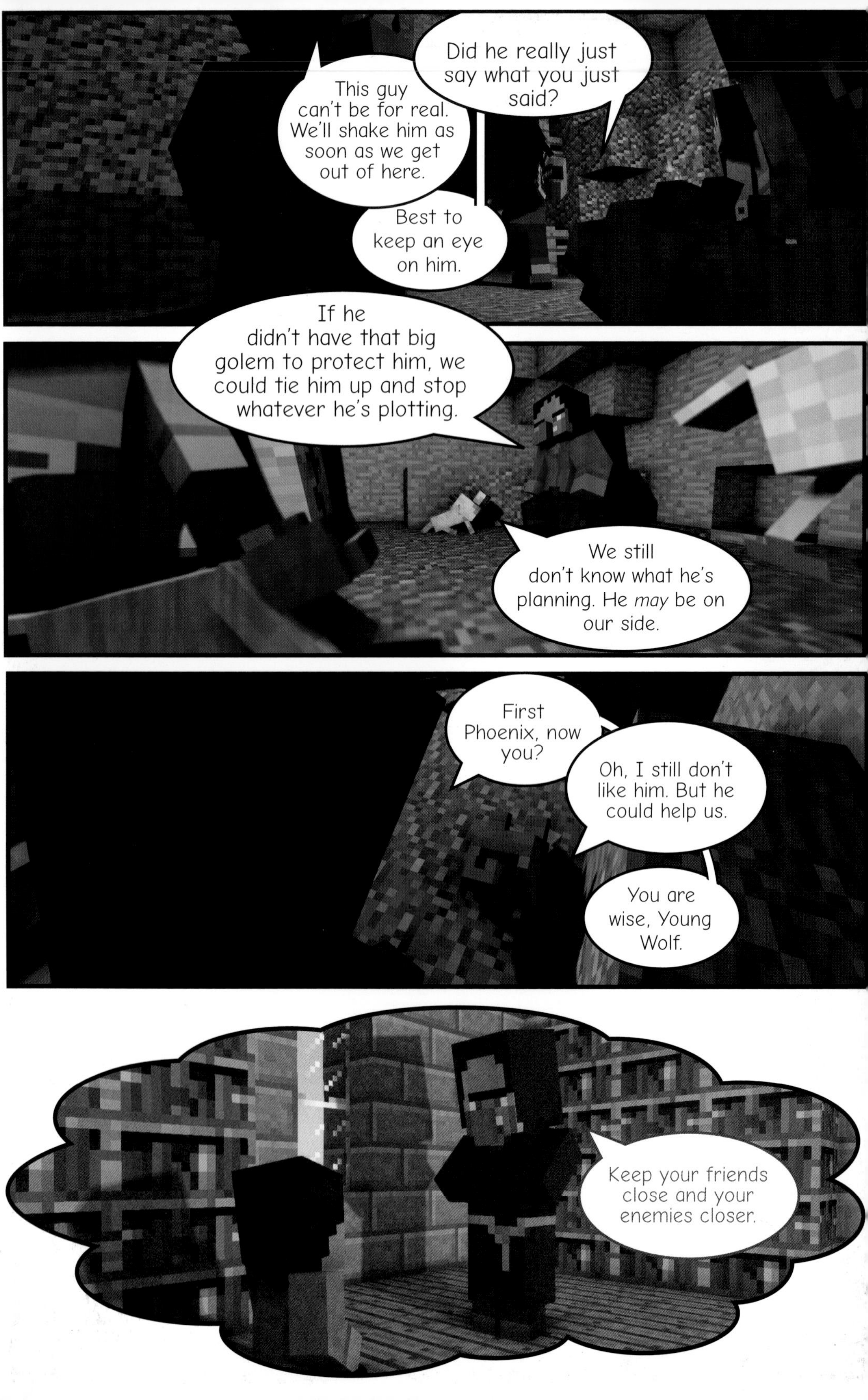
This guy can't be for real. We'll shake him as soon as we get out of here.
Did he really just say what you just said?
Best to keep an eye on him.
If he didn't have that big golem to protect him, we could tie him up and stop whatever he's plotting.
We still don't know what he's planning. He *may* be on our side.
First Phoenix, now you?
Oh, I still don't like him. But he could help us.
You are wise, Young Wolf.
Keep your friends close and your enemies closer.

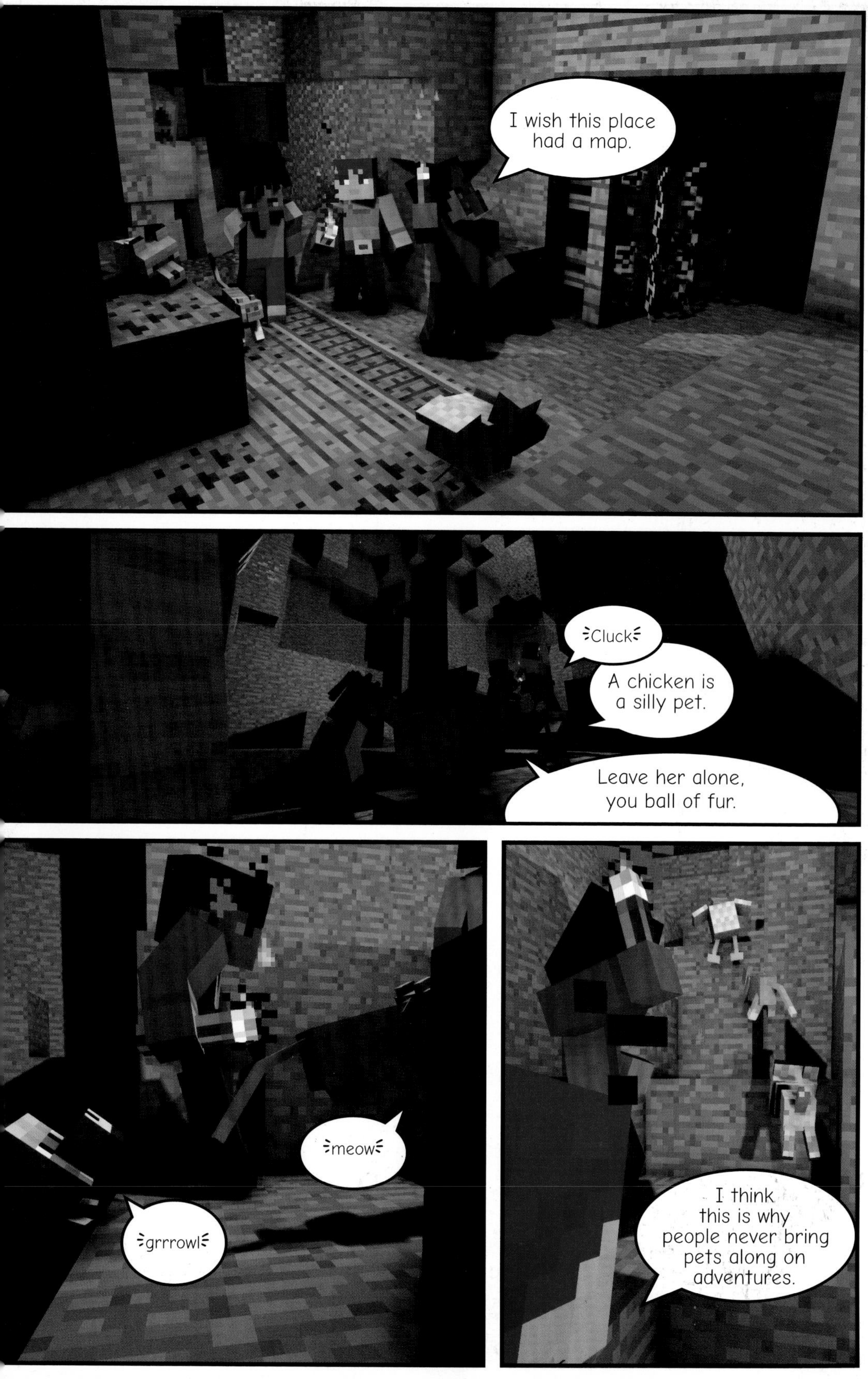
I wish this place had a map.
Cluck
A chicken is a silly pet.
Leave her alone, you ball of fur.
meow
grrrowl
I think this is why people never bring pets along on adventures.

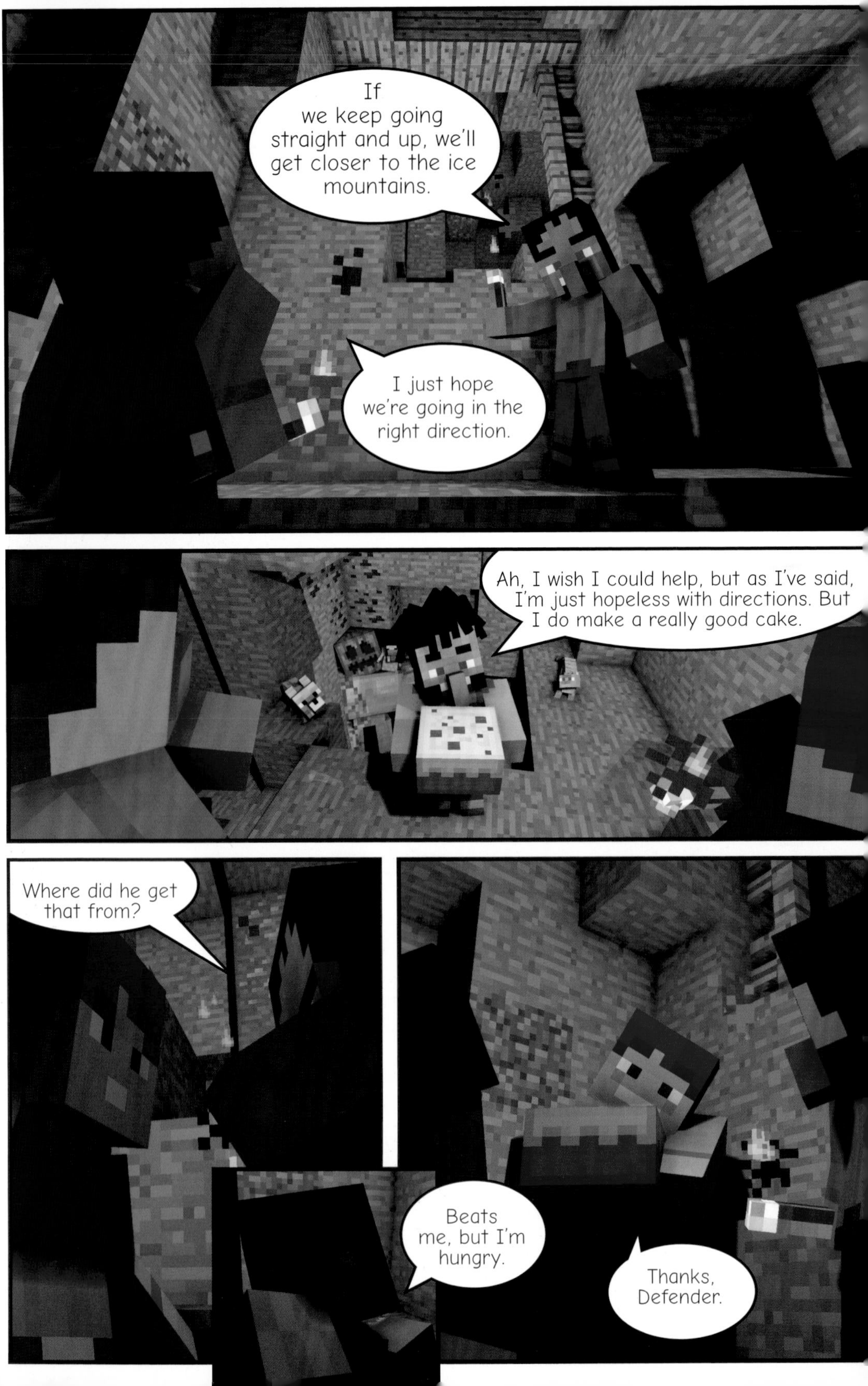
If we keep going straight and up, we'll get closer to the ice mountains.
I just hope we're going in the right direction.
Ah, I wish I could help, but as I've said, I'm just hopeless with directions. But I do make a really good cake.
Where did he get that from?
Beats me, but I'm hungry.
Thanks, Defender.

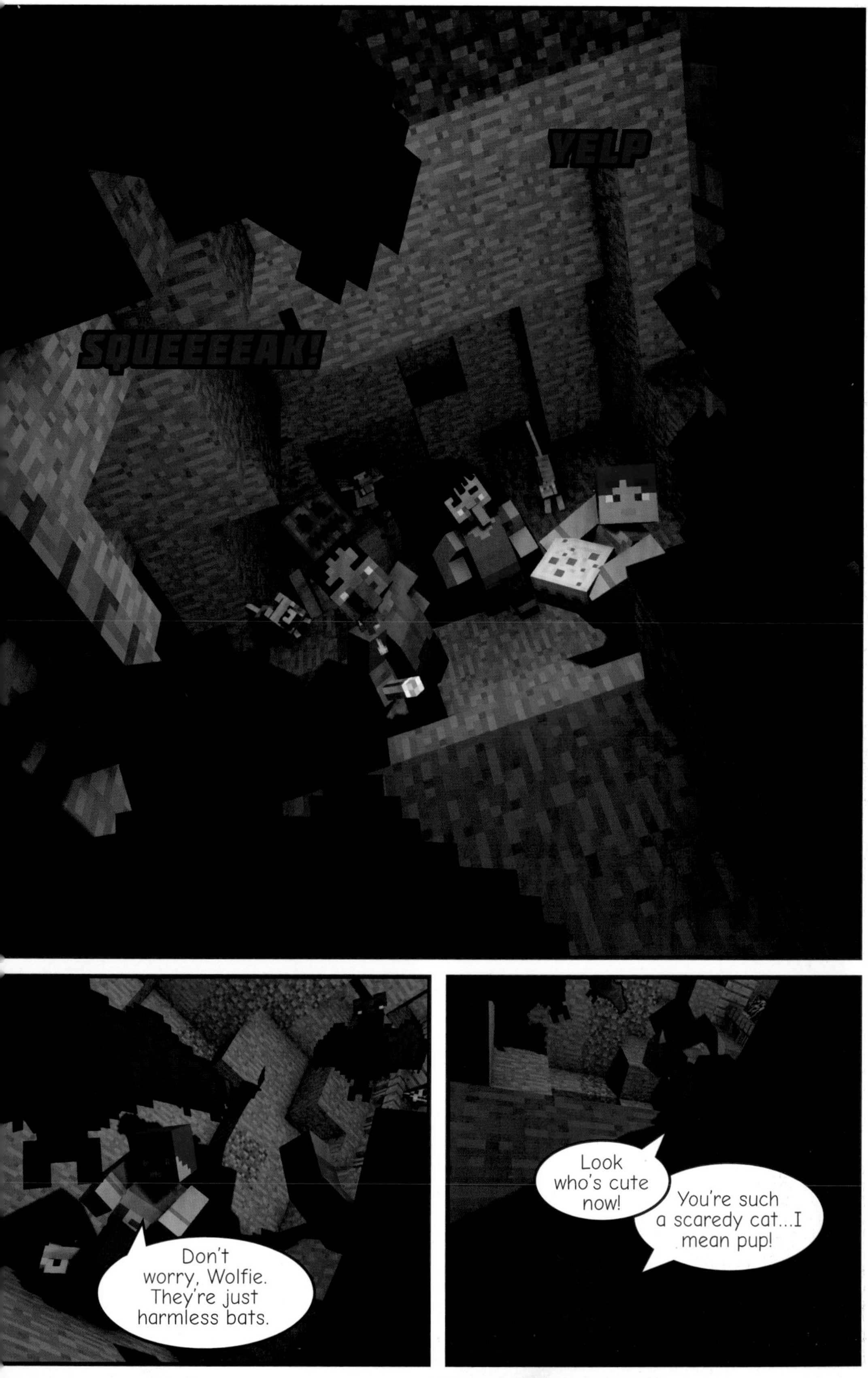
YELP
SQUEEEEEAK!
Don't worry, Wolfie. They're just harmless bats.
Look who's cute now!
You're such a scaredy cat...I mean pup!

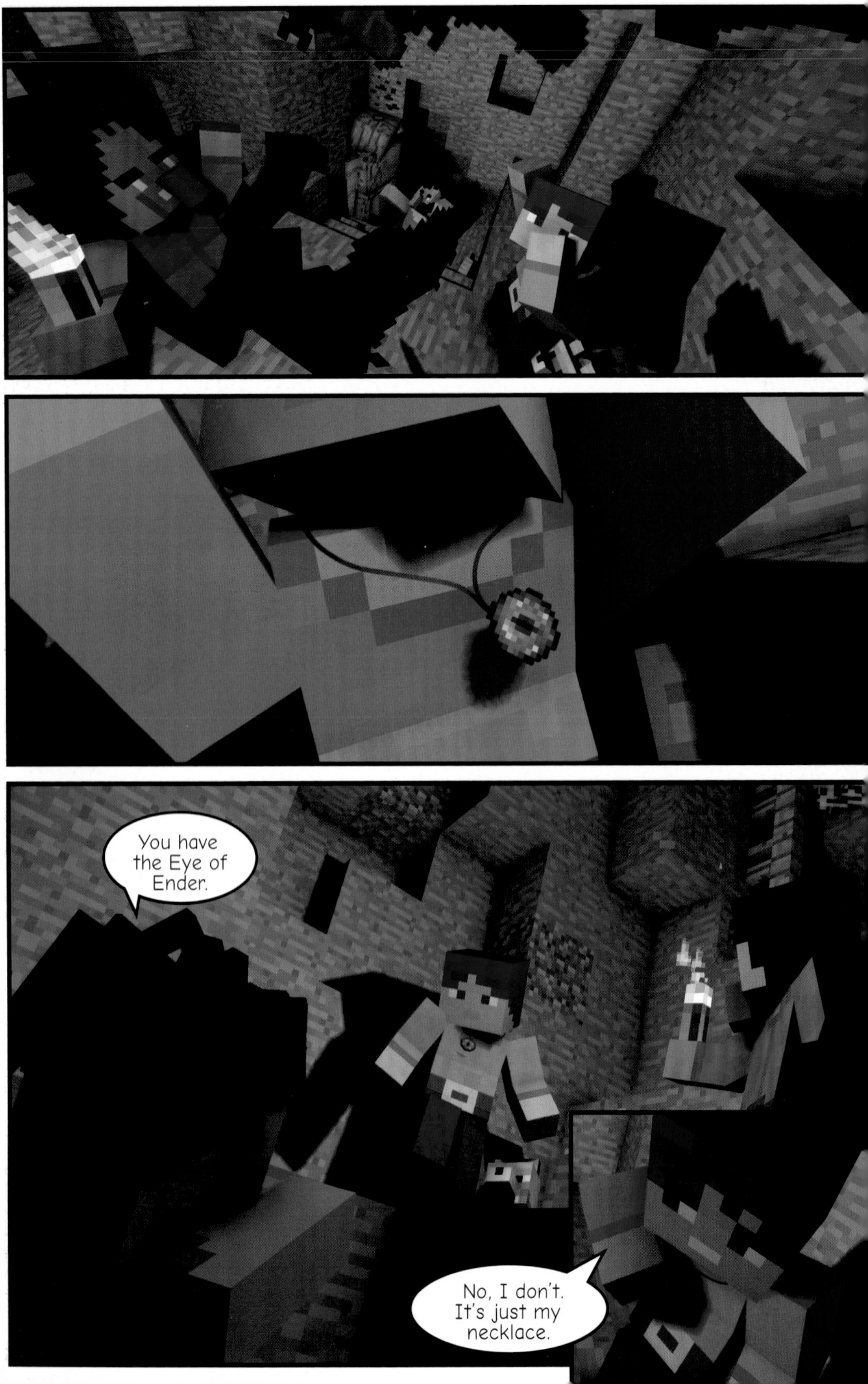
You have the Eye of Ender.
No, I don't. It's just my necklace.

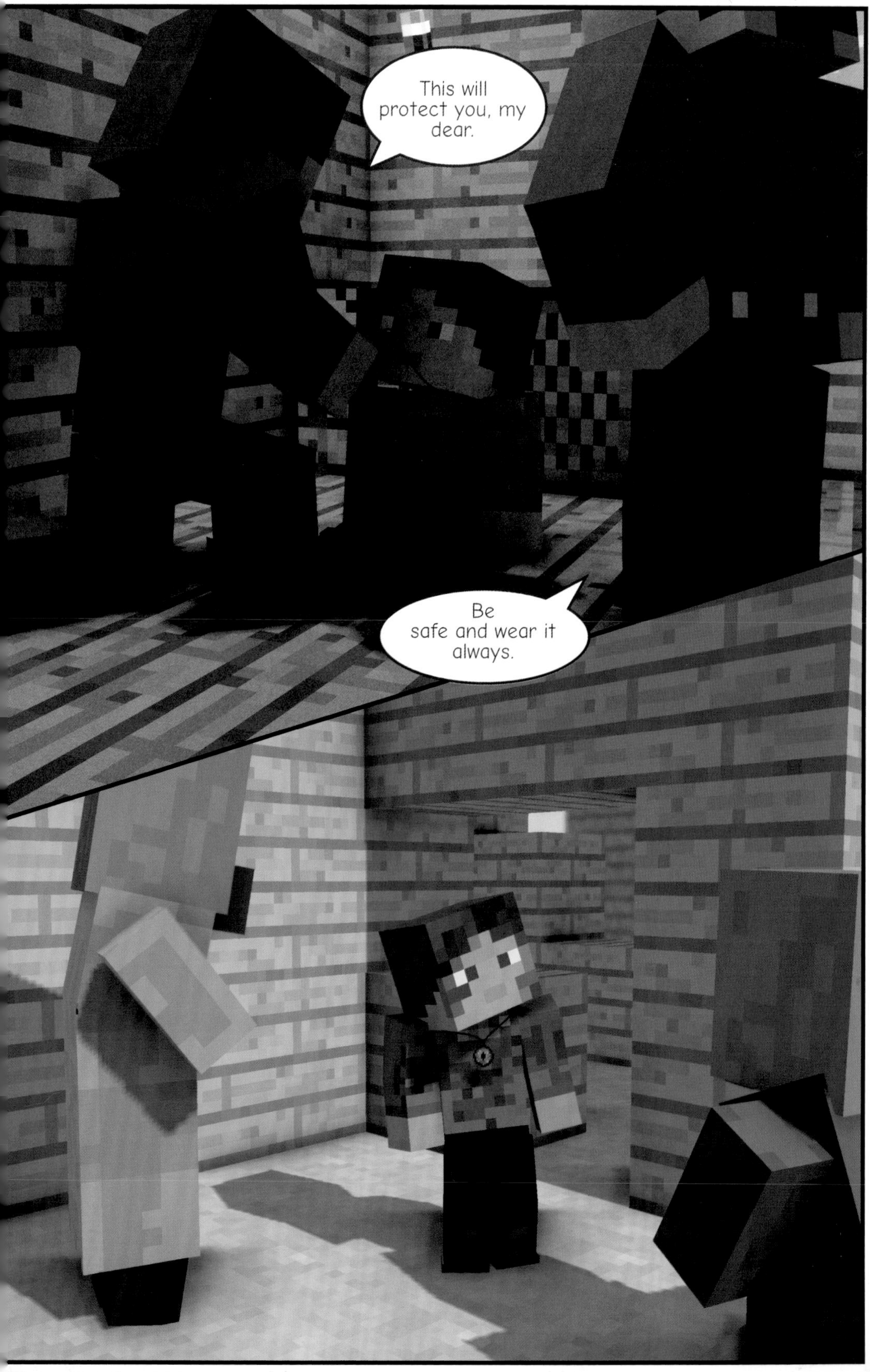
This will protect you, my dear.
Be safe and wear it always.

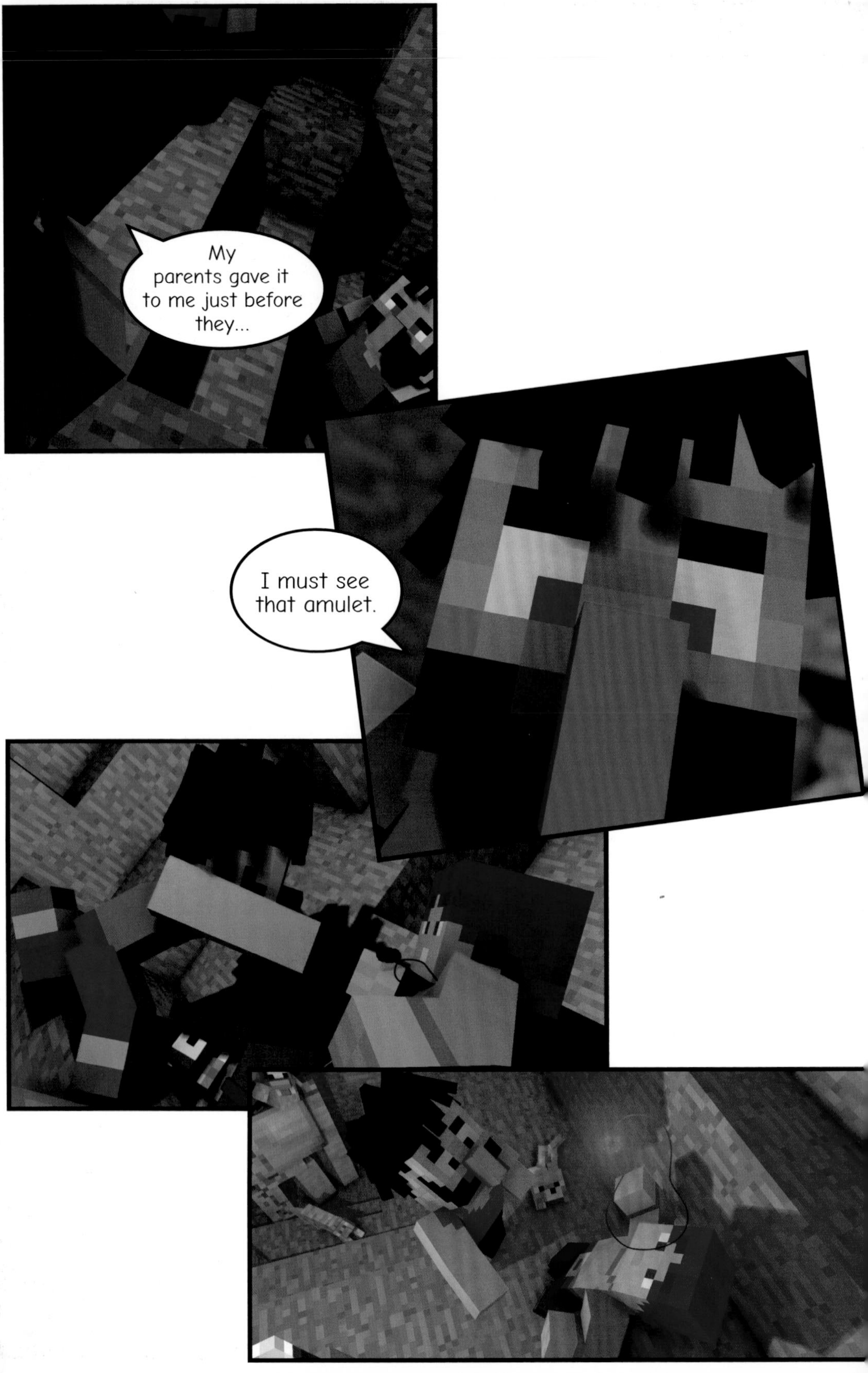
My parents gave it to me just before they...
I must see that amulet.

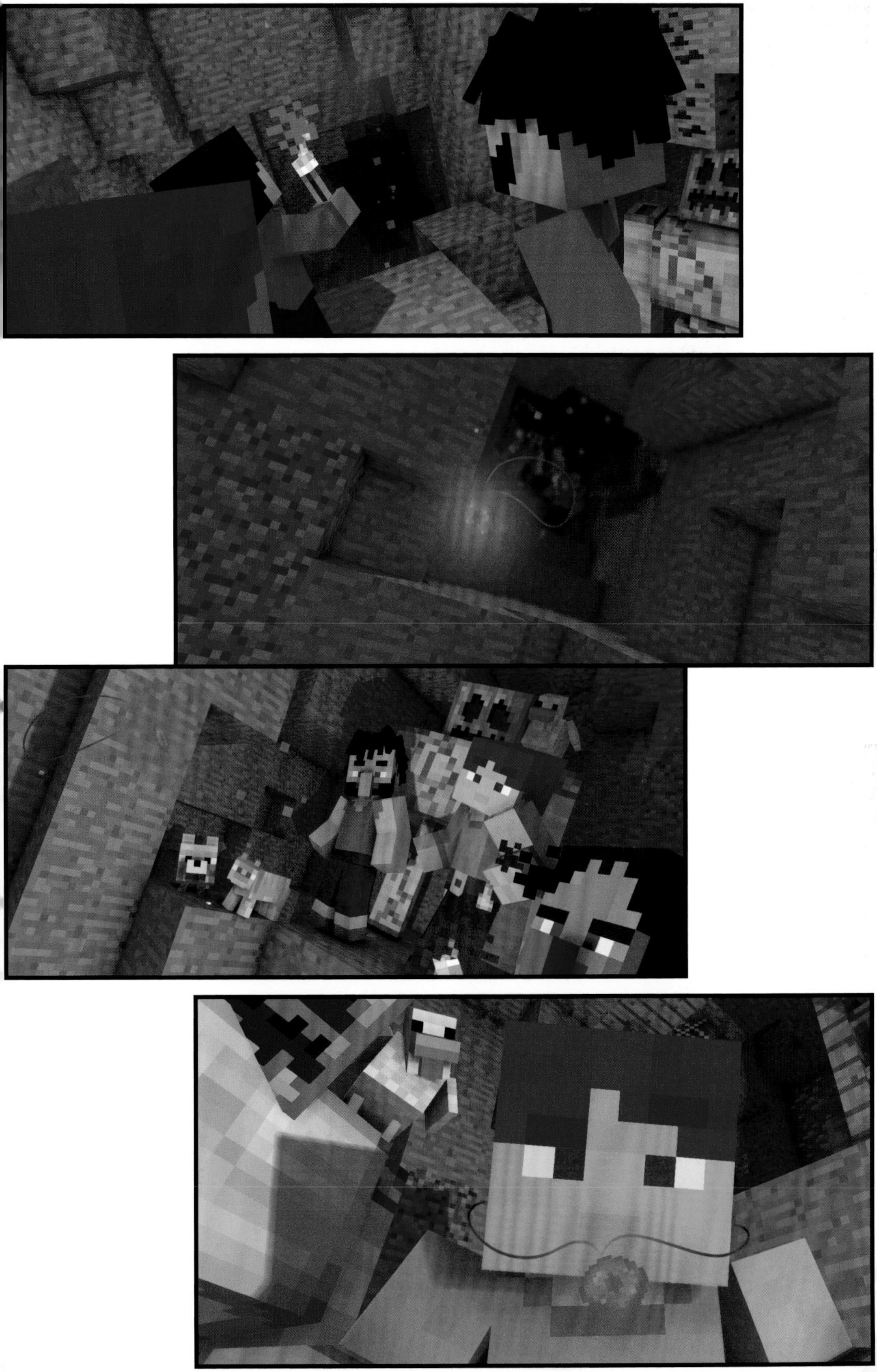

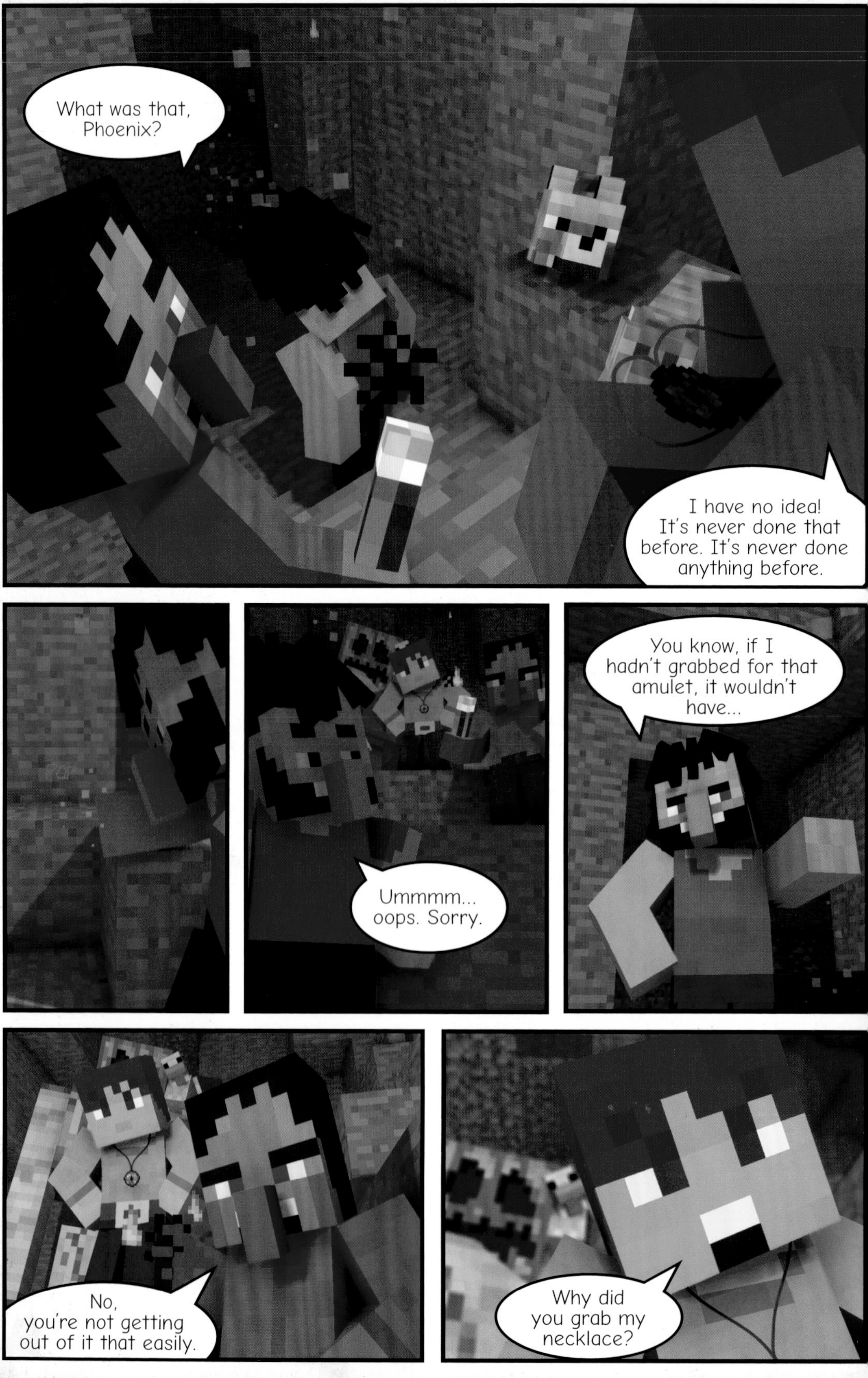
What was that, Phoenix?
I have no idea! It's never done that before. It's never done anything before.
Ummmm... oops. Sorry.
You know, if I hadn't grabbed for that amulet, it wouldn't have...
No, you're not getting out of it that easily.
Why did you grab my necklace?

CHAPTER 10

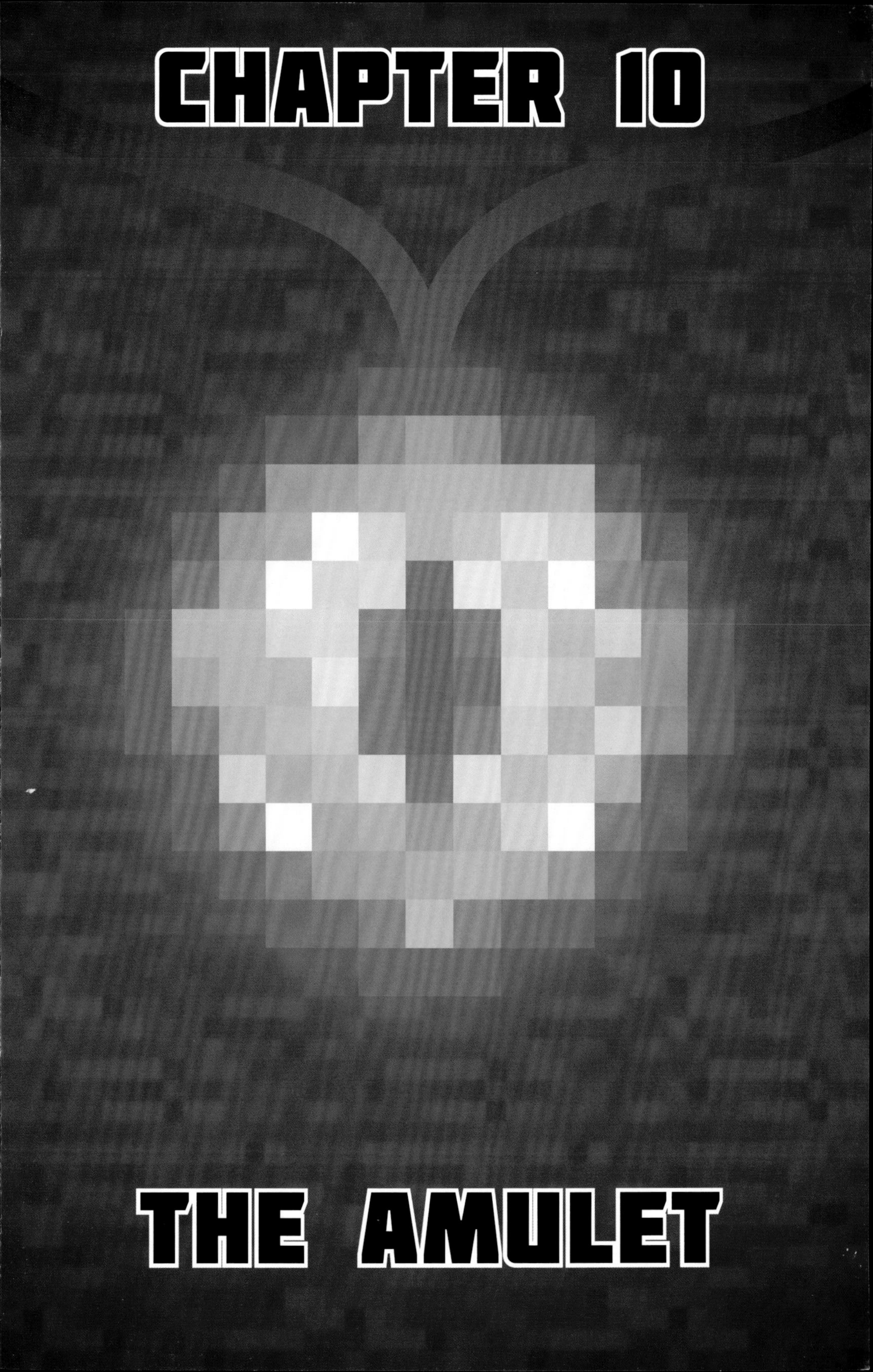

THE AMULET

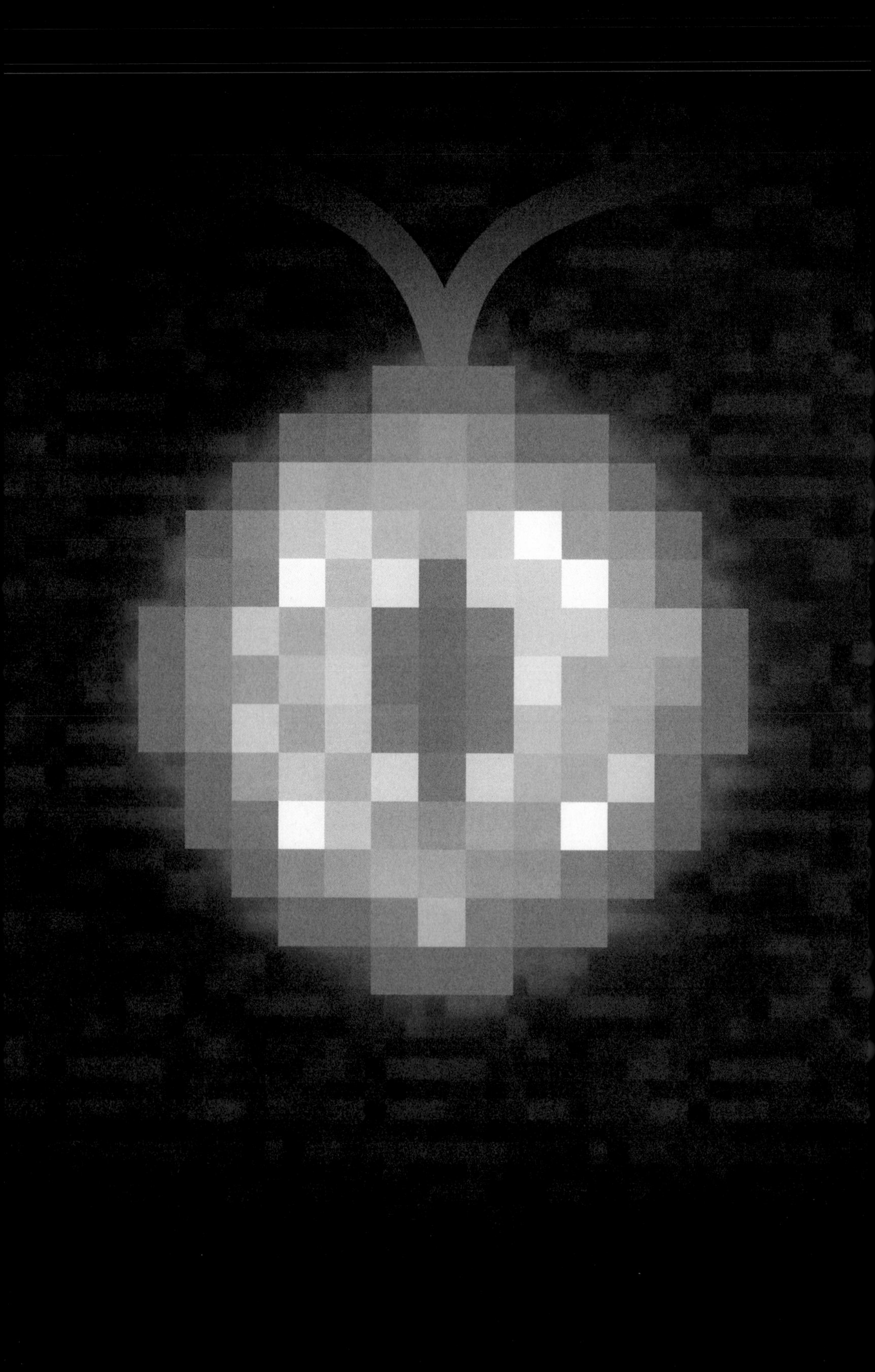

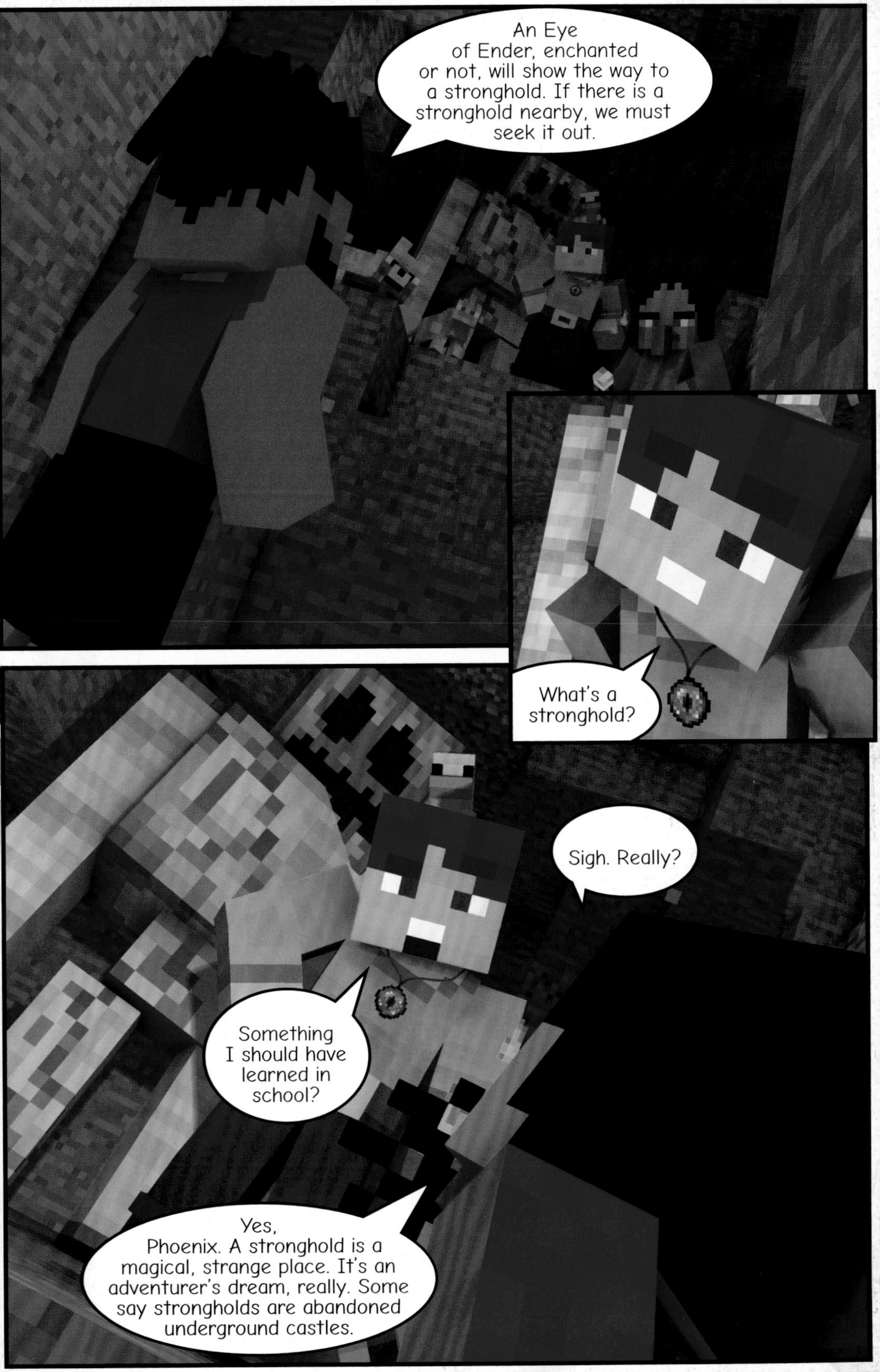

An Eye of Ender, enchanted or not, will show the way to a stronghold. If there is a stronghold nearby, we must seek it out.
What's a stronghold?
Sigh. Really?
Something I should have learned in school?
Yes, Phoenix. A stronghold is a magical, strange place. It's an adventurer's dream, really. Some say strongholds are abandoned underground castles.

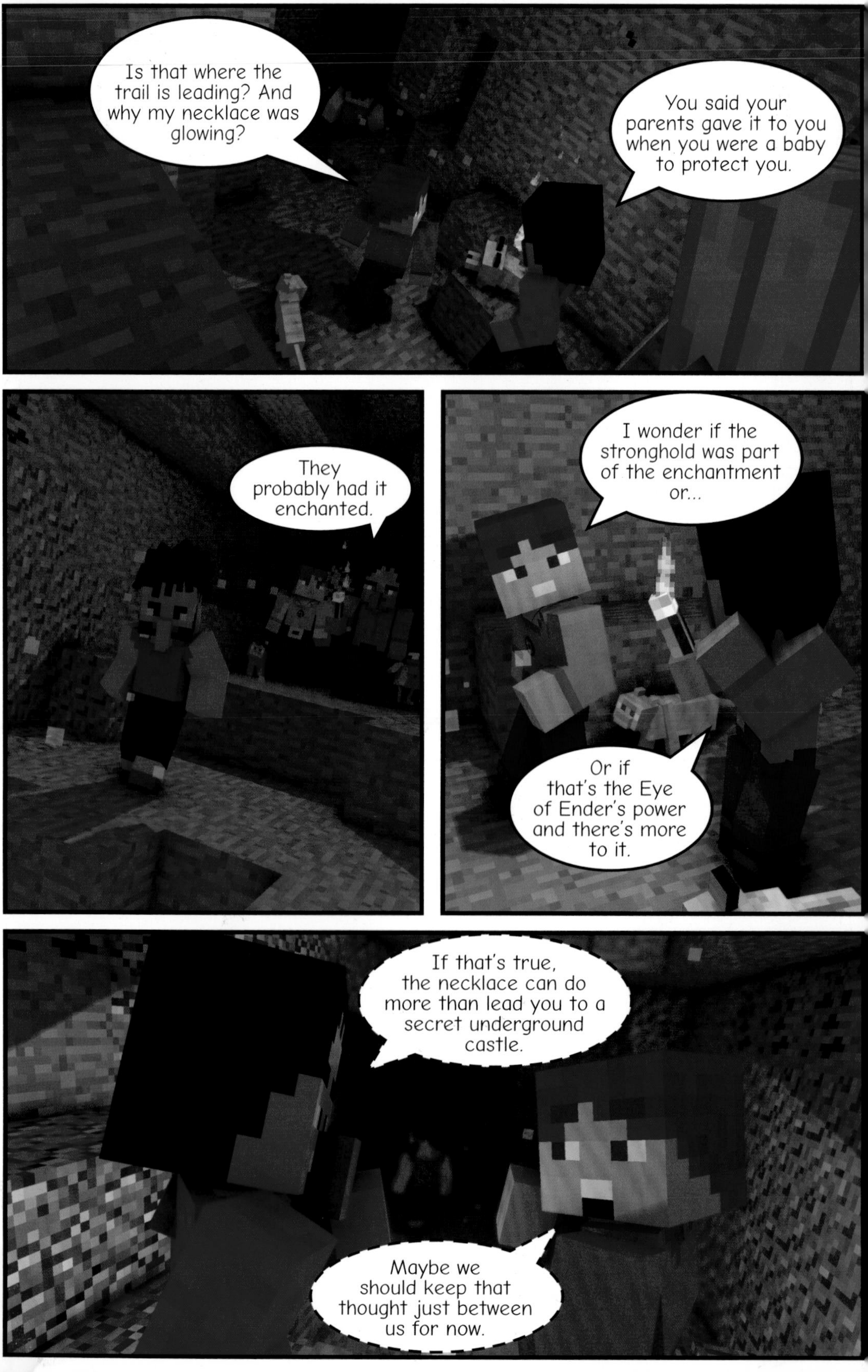
Is that where the trail is leading? And why my necklace was glowing?
You said your parents gave it to you when you were a baby to protect you.
They probably had it enchanted.
I wonder if the stronghold was part of the enchantment or...
Or if that's the Eye of Ender's power and there's more to it.
If that's true, the necklace can do more than lead you to a secret underground castle.
Maybe we should keep that thought just between us for now.

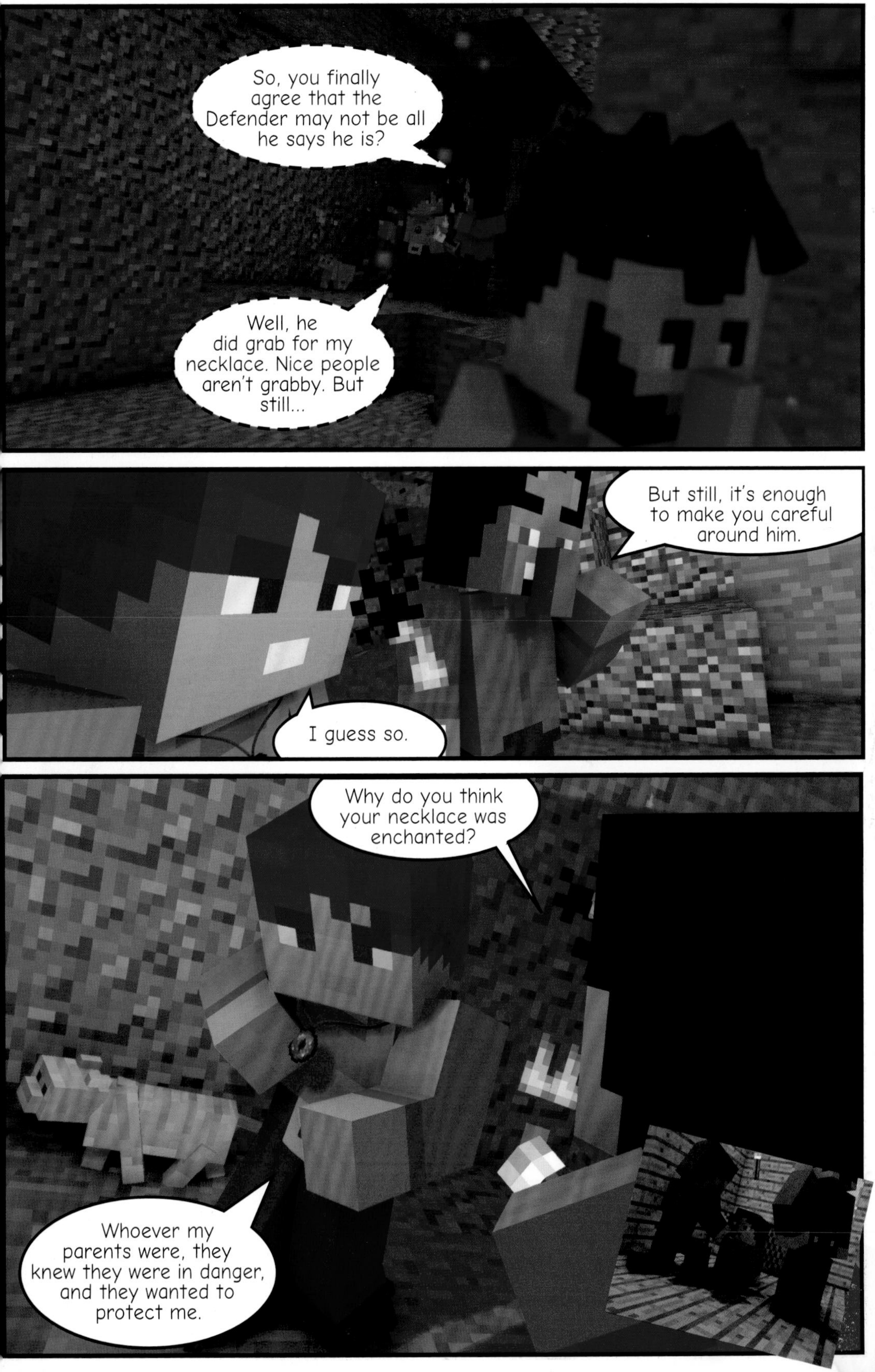
So, you finally agree that the Defender may not be all he says he is?
Well, he did grab for my necklace. Nice people aren't grabby. But still...
But still, it's enough to make you careful around him.
I guess so.
Why do you think your necklace was enchanted?
Whoever my parents were, they knew they were in danger, and they wanted to protect me.

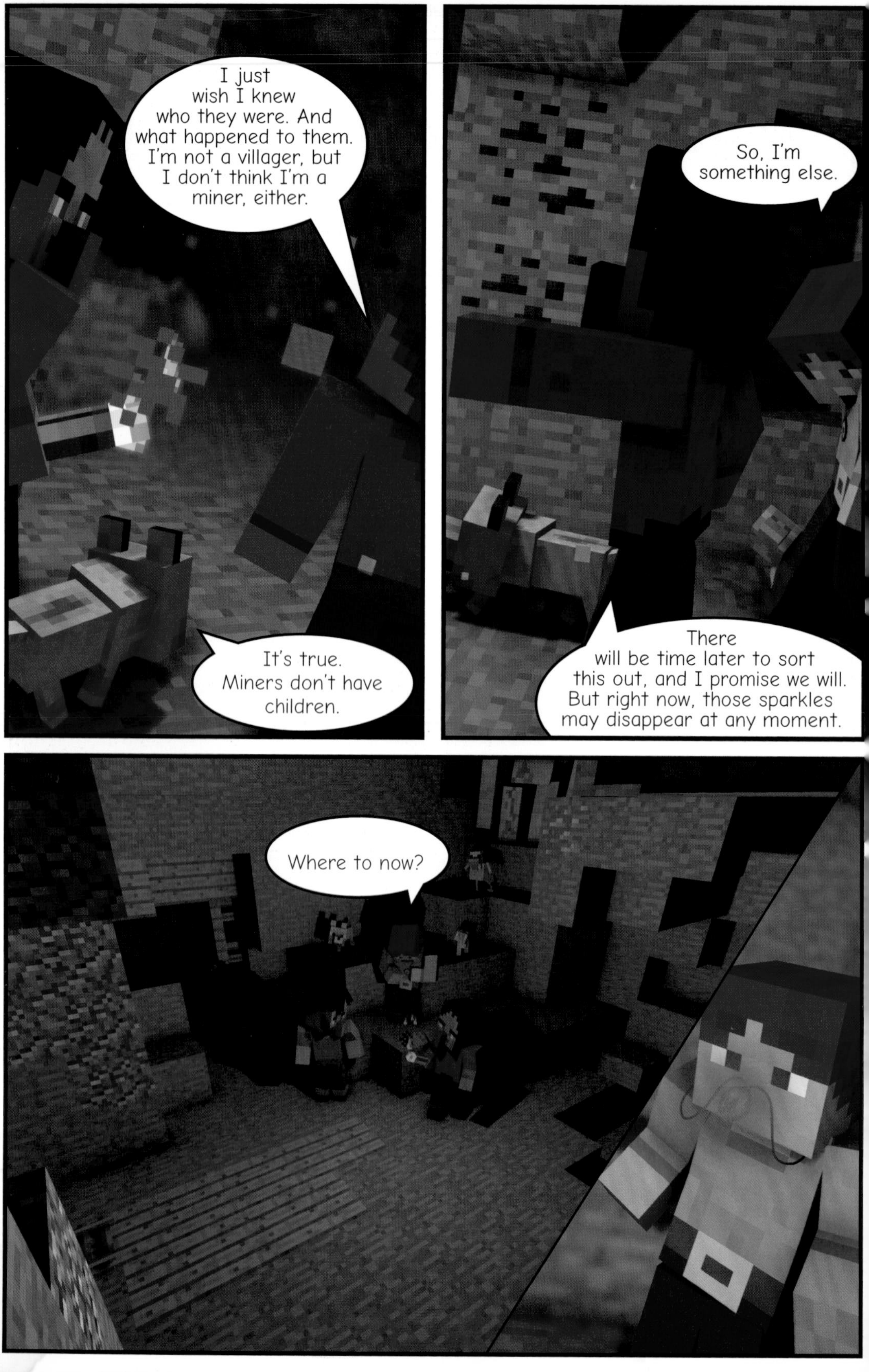
I just wish I knew who they were. And what happened to them. I'm not a villager, but I don't think I'm a miner, either.
It's true. Miners don't have children.
So, I'm something else.
There will be time later to sort this out, and I promise we will. But right now, those sparkles may disappear at any moment.
Where to now?

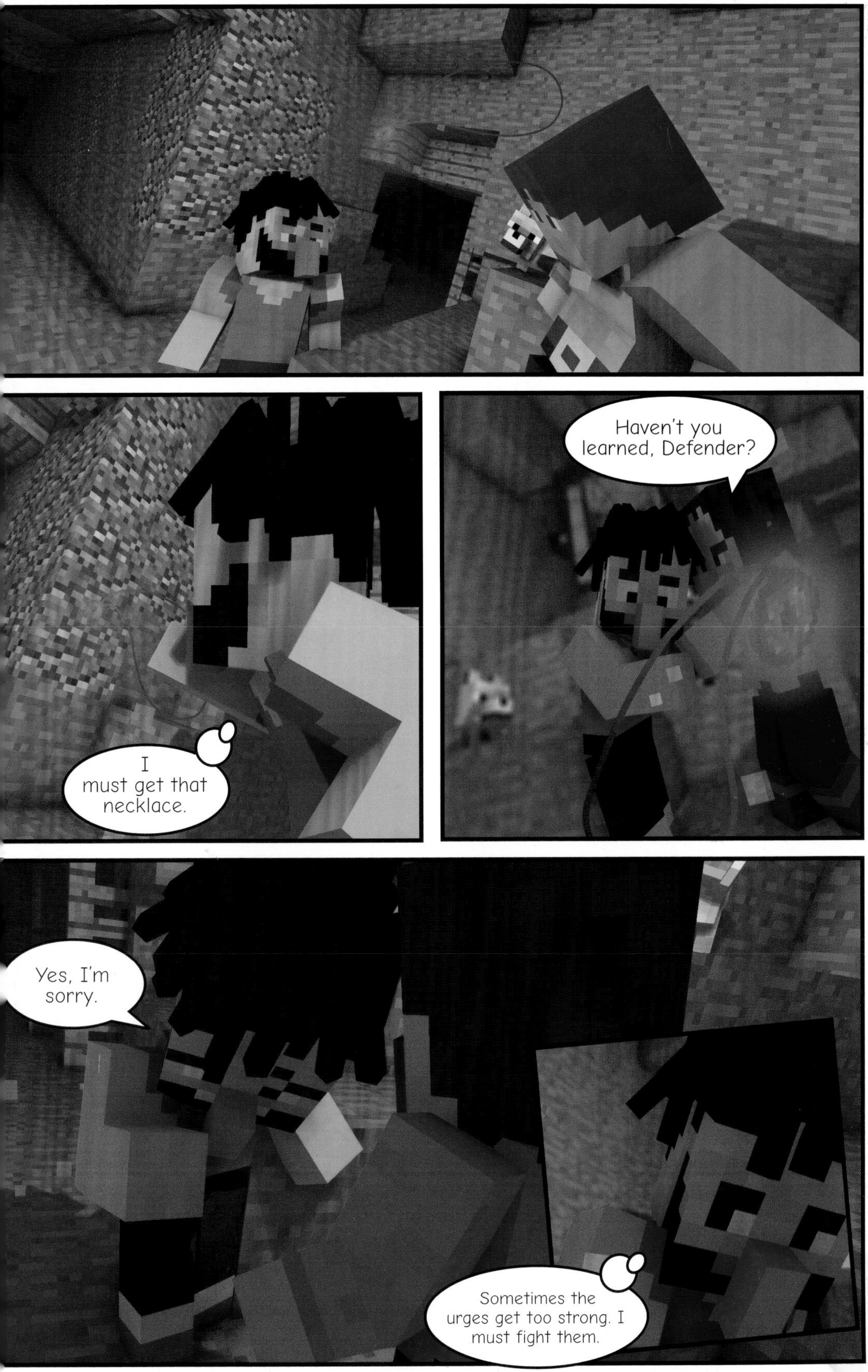
I must get that necklace.
Haven't you learned, Defender?
Yes, I'm sorry.
Sometimes the urges get too strong. I must fight them.

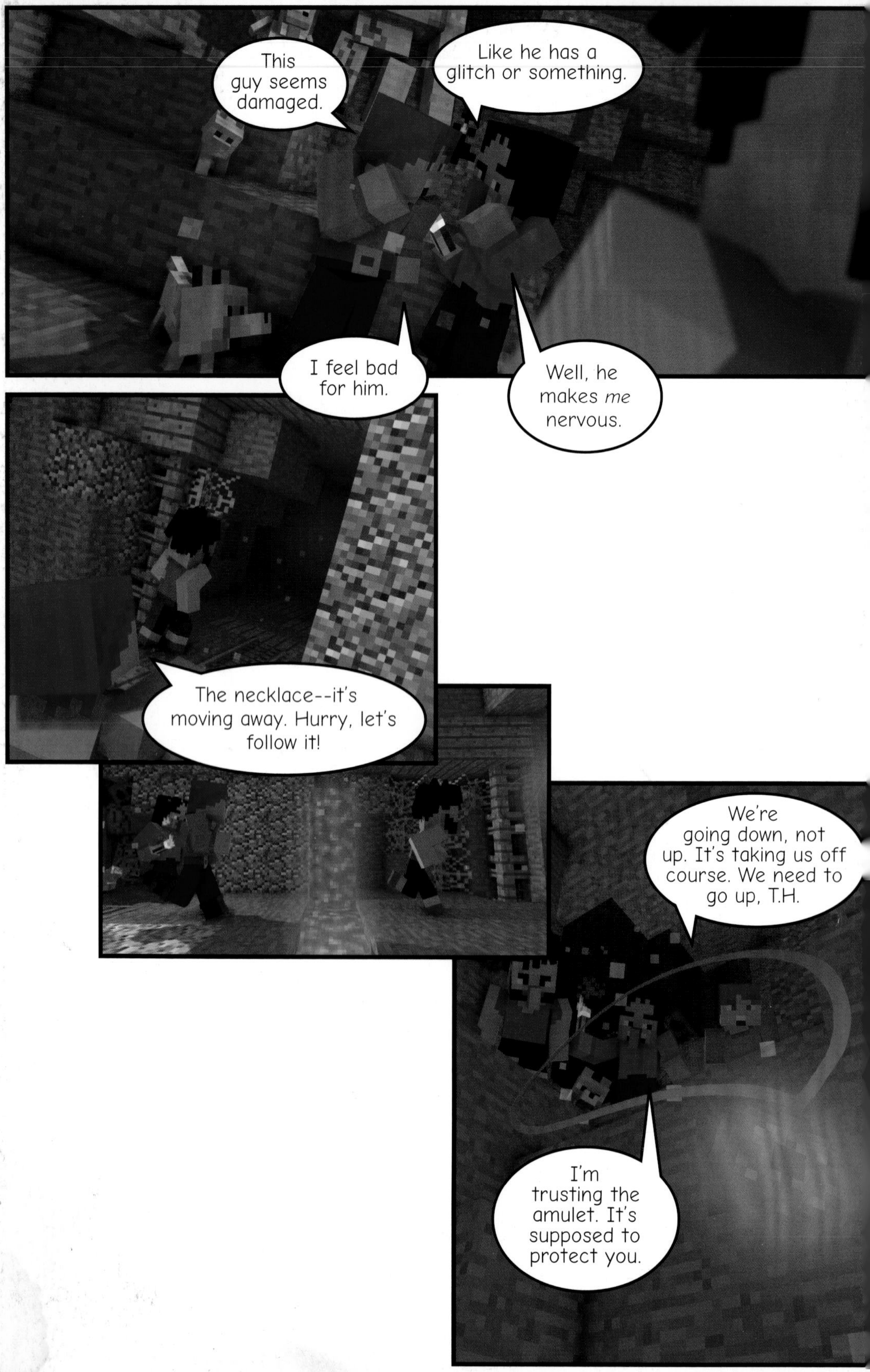
This guy seems damaged.
Like he has a glitch or something.
I feel bad for him.
Well, he makes *me* nervous.
The necklace--it's moving away. Hurry, let's follow it!
We're going down, not up. It's taking us off course. We need to go up, T.H.
I'm trusting the amulet. It's supposed to protect you.

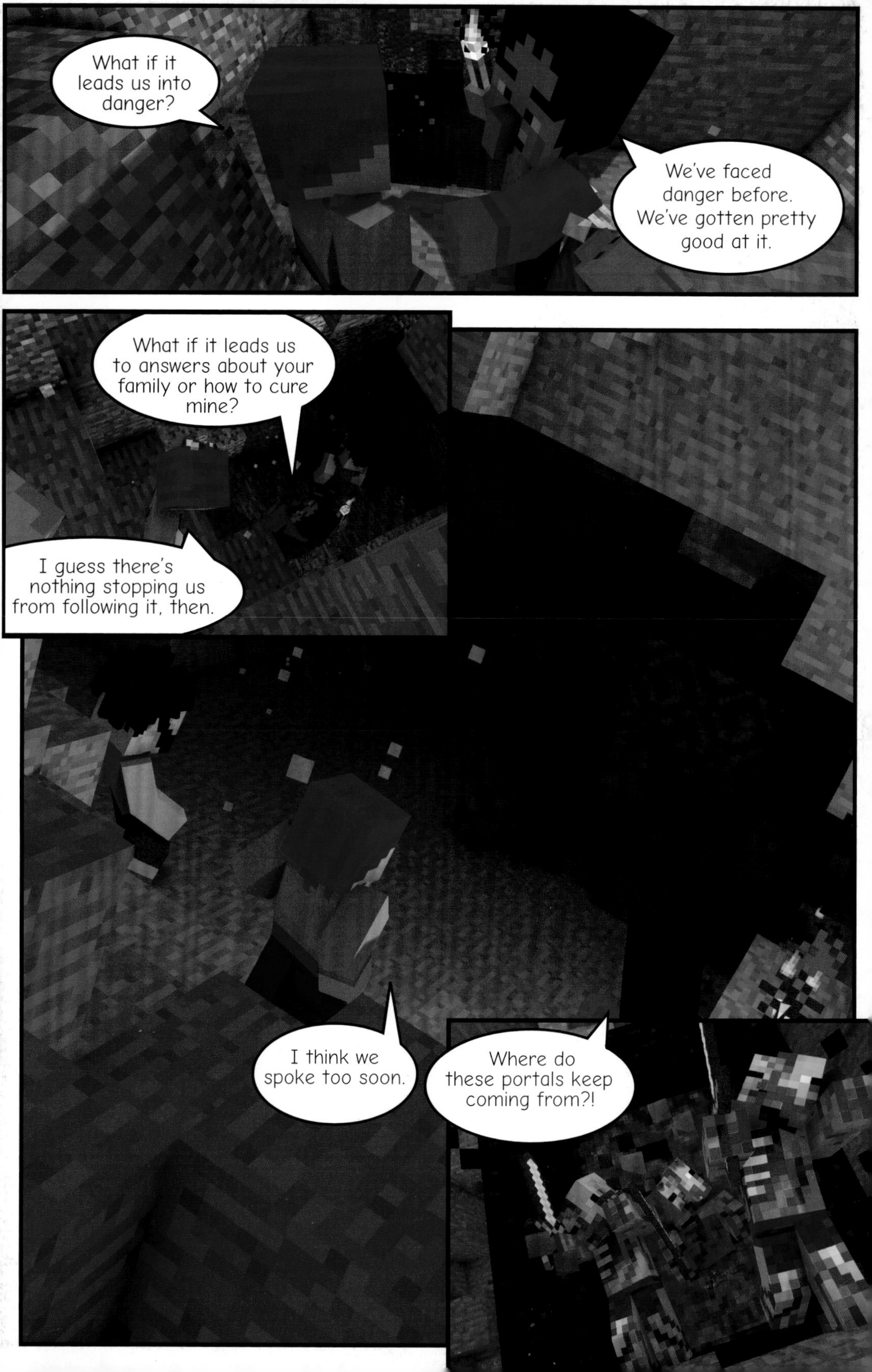
What if it leads us into danger?
We've faced danger before. We've gotten pretty good at it.
What if it leads us to answers about your family or how to cure mine?
I guess there's nothing stopping us from following it, then.
I think we spoke too soon.
Where do these portals keep coming from?!

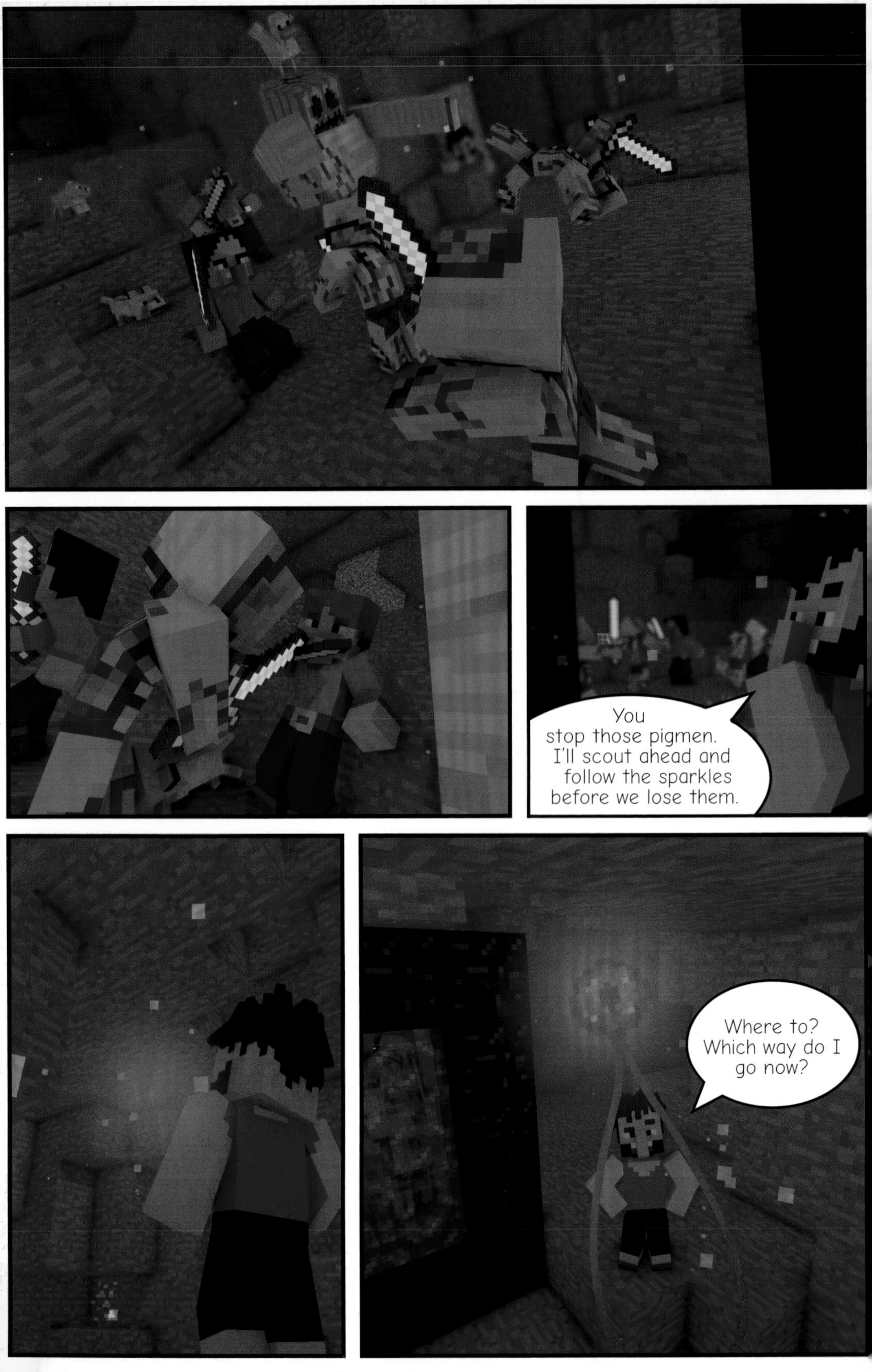
You stop those pigmen. I'll scout ahead and follow the sparkles before we lose them.
Where to? Which way do I go now?

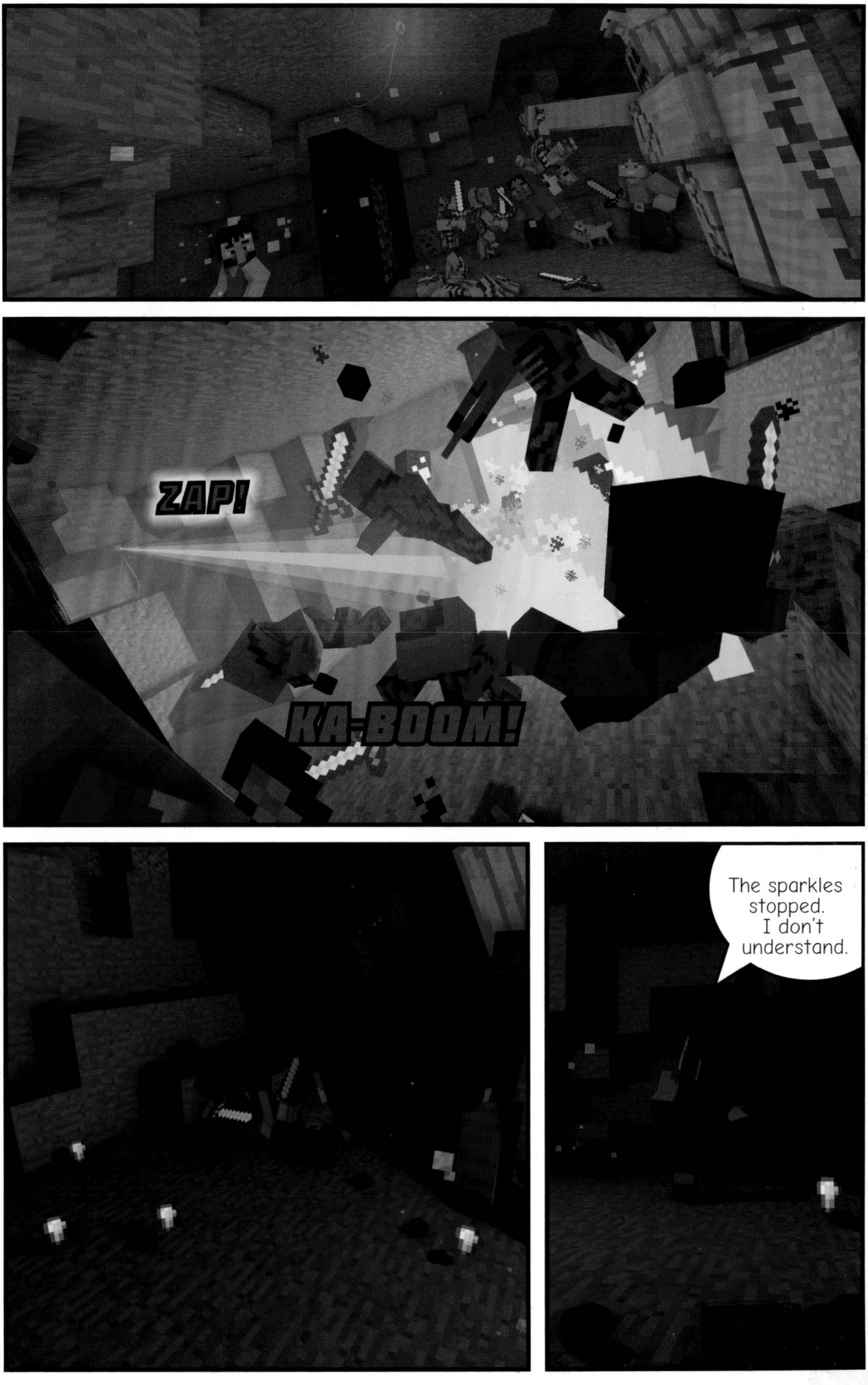
ZAP!
KA-BOOM!
The sparkles stopped. I don't understand.

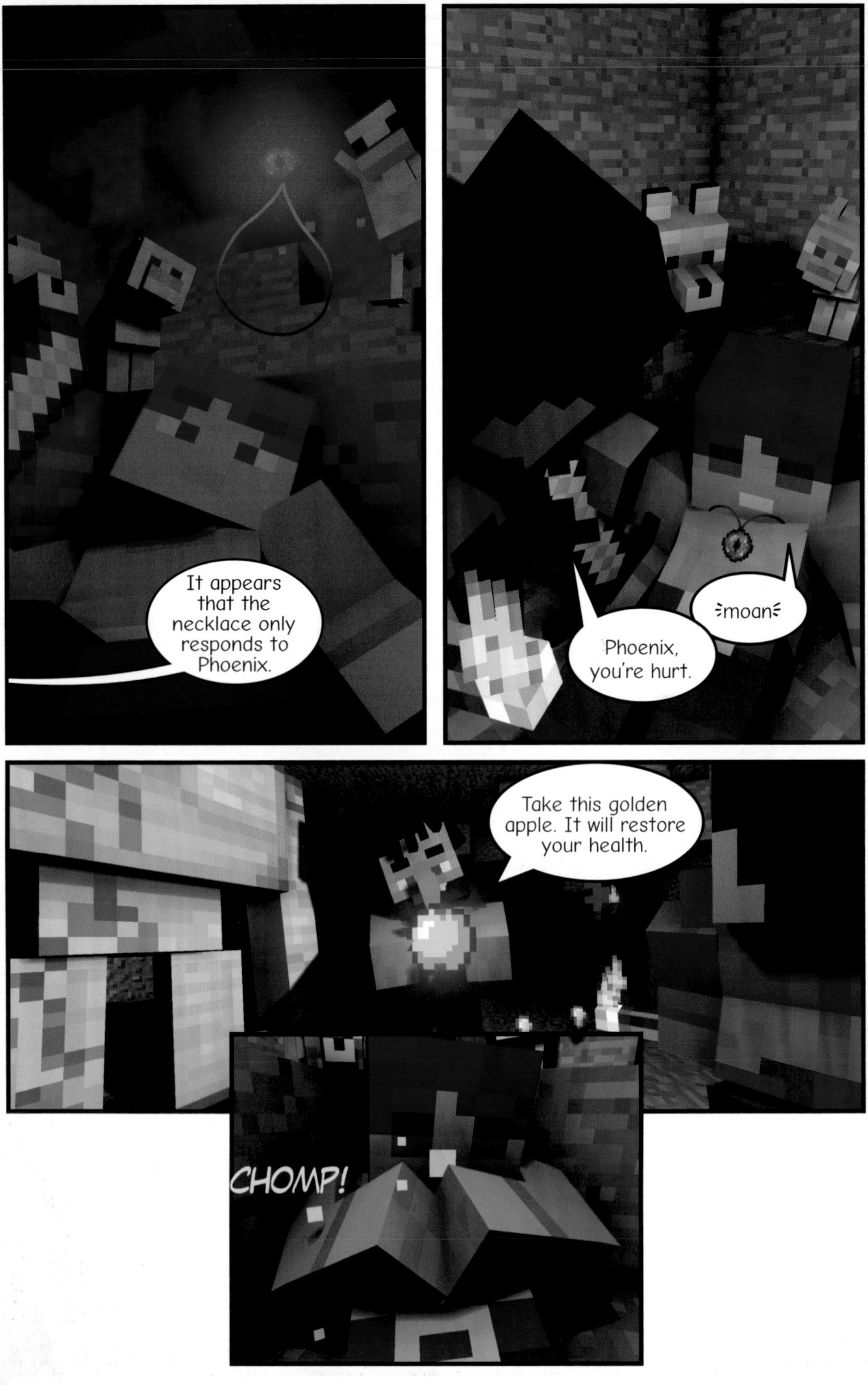
It appears that the necklace only responds to Phoenix.
Phoenix, you're hurt.
moan
Take this golden apple. It will restore your health.
CHOMP!

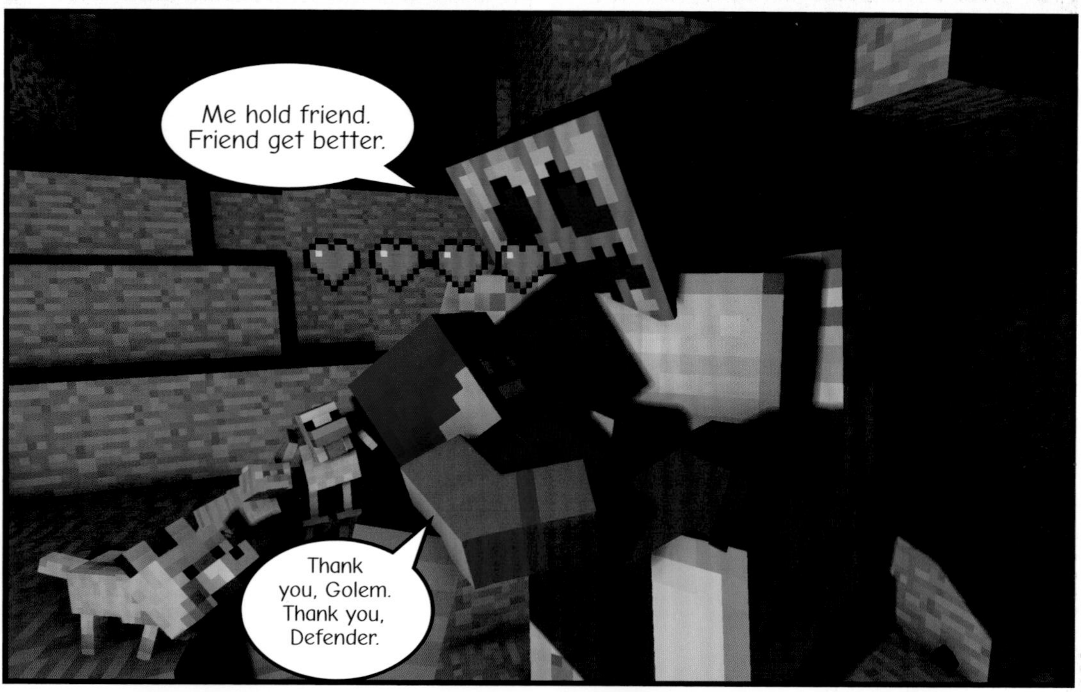
Me hold friend. Friend get better.
Thank you, Golem. Thank you, Defender.

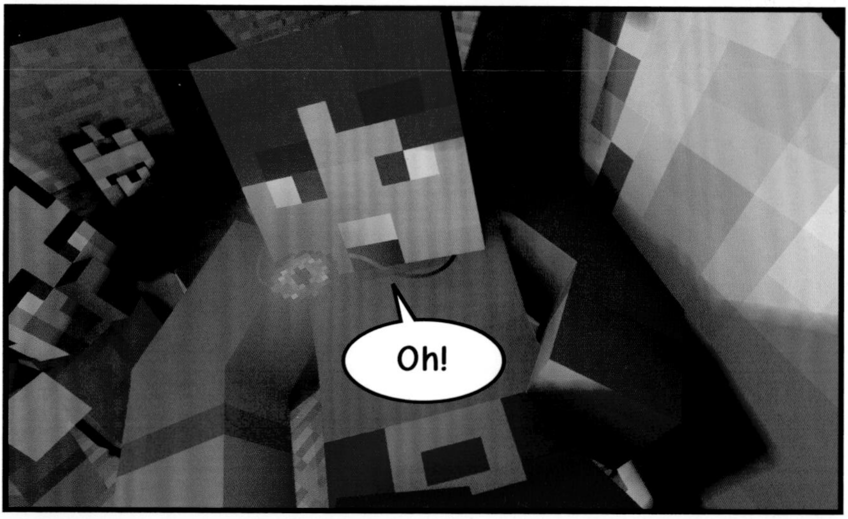
Oh!

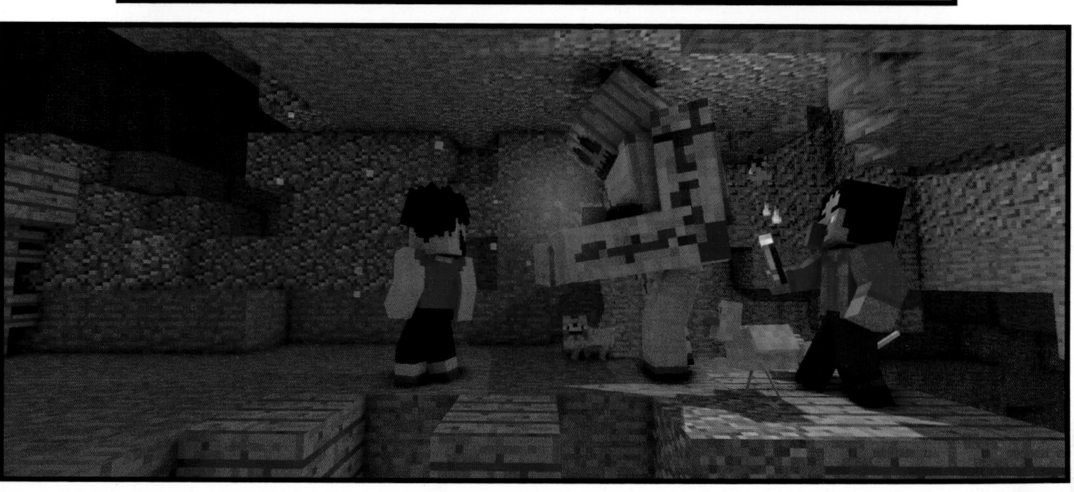

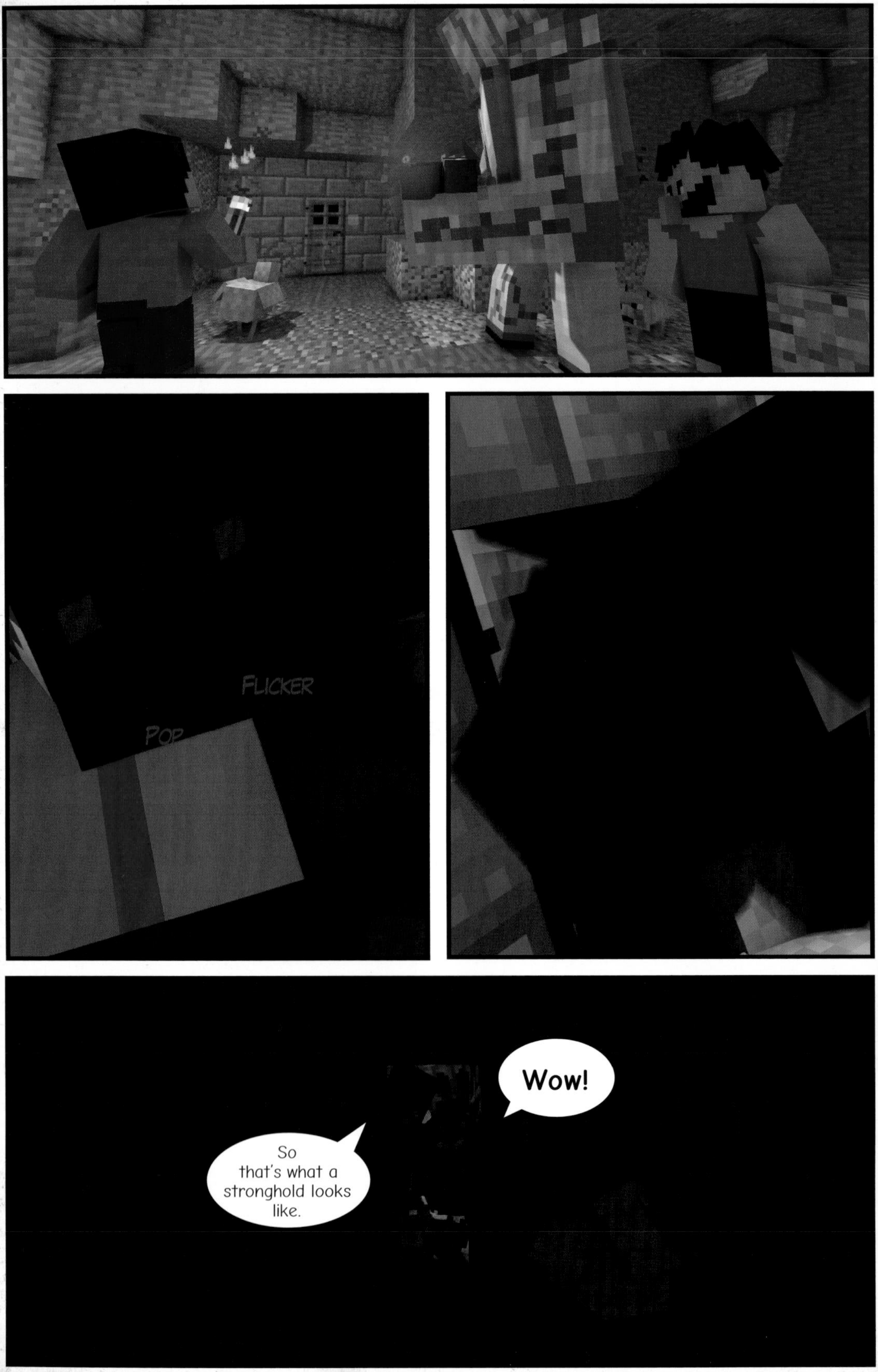
FLICKER
POP
Wow!
So that's what a stronghold looks like.

CHAPTER II

THE STRONGHOLD

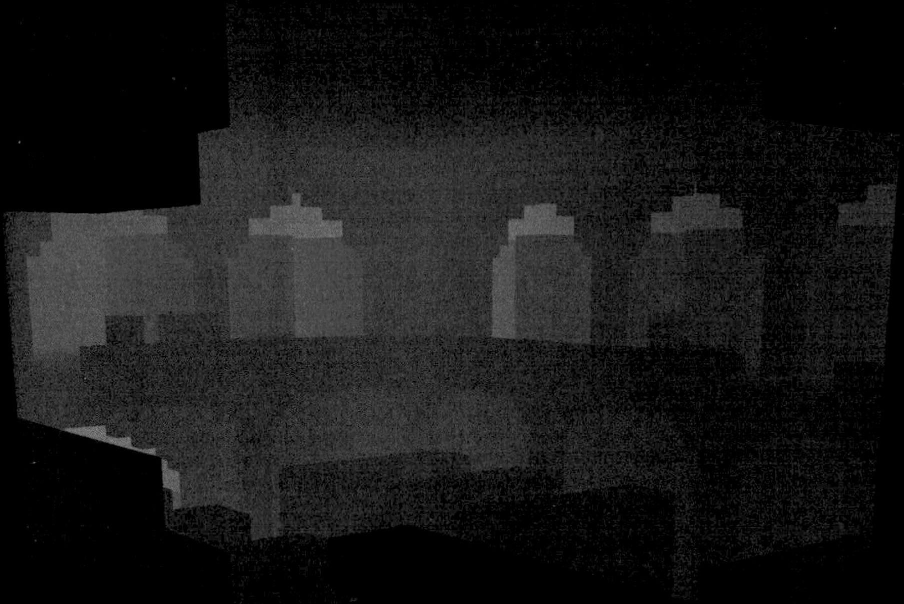

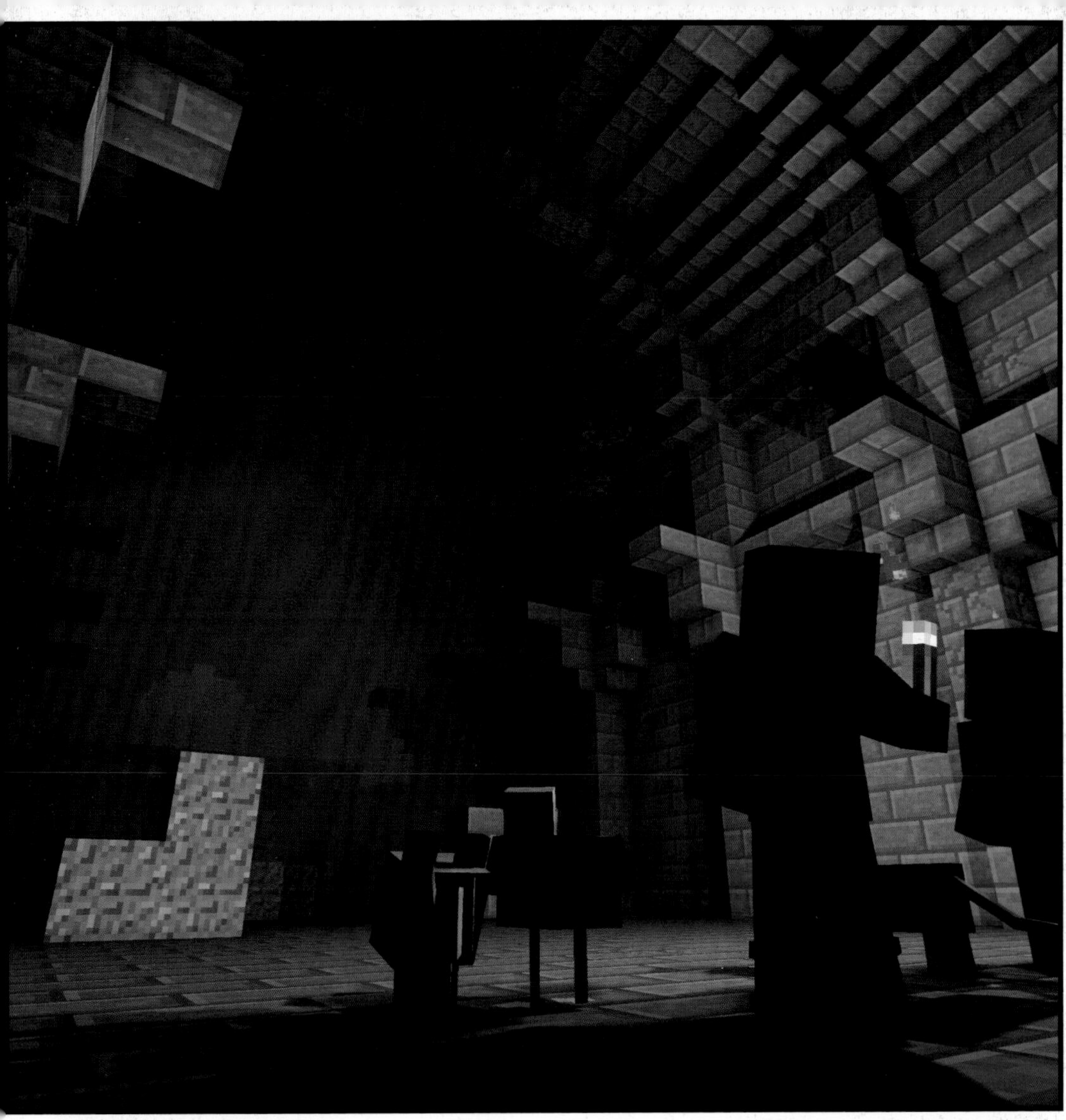

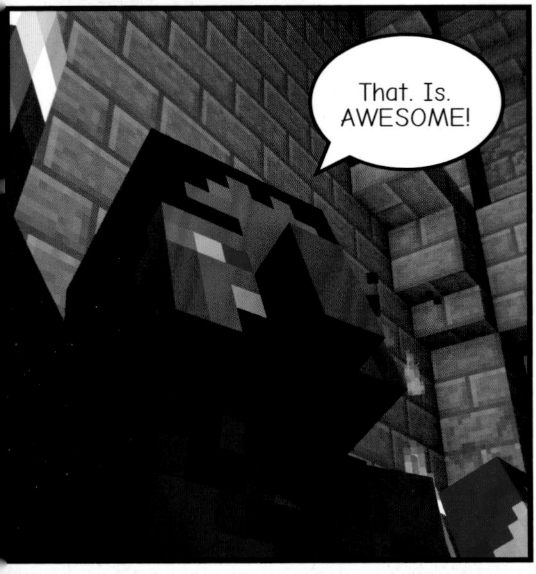
That. Is. AWESOME!

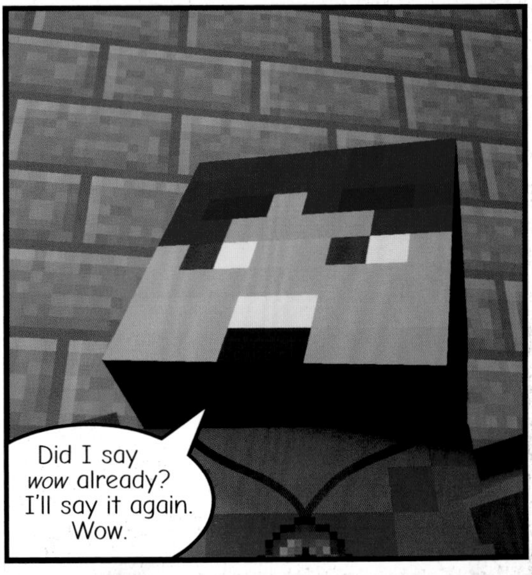
Did I say *wow* already? I'll say it again. Wow.

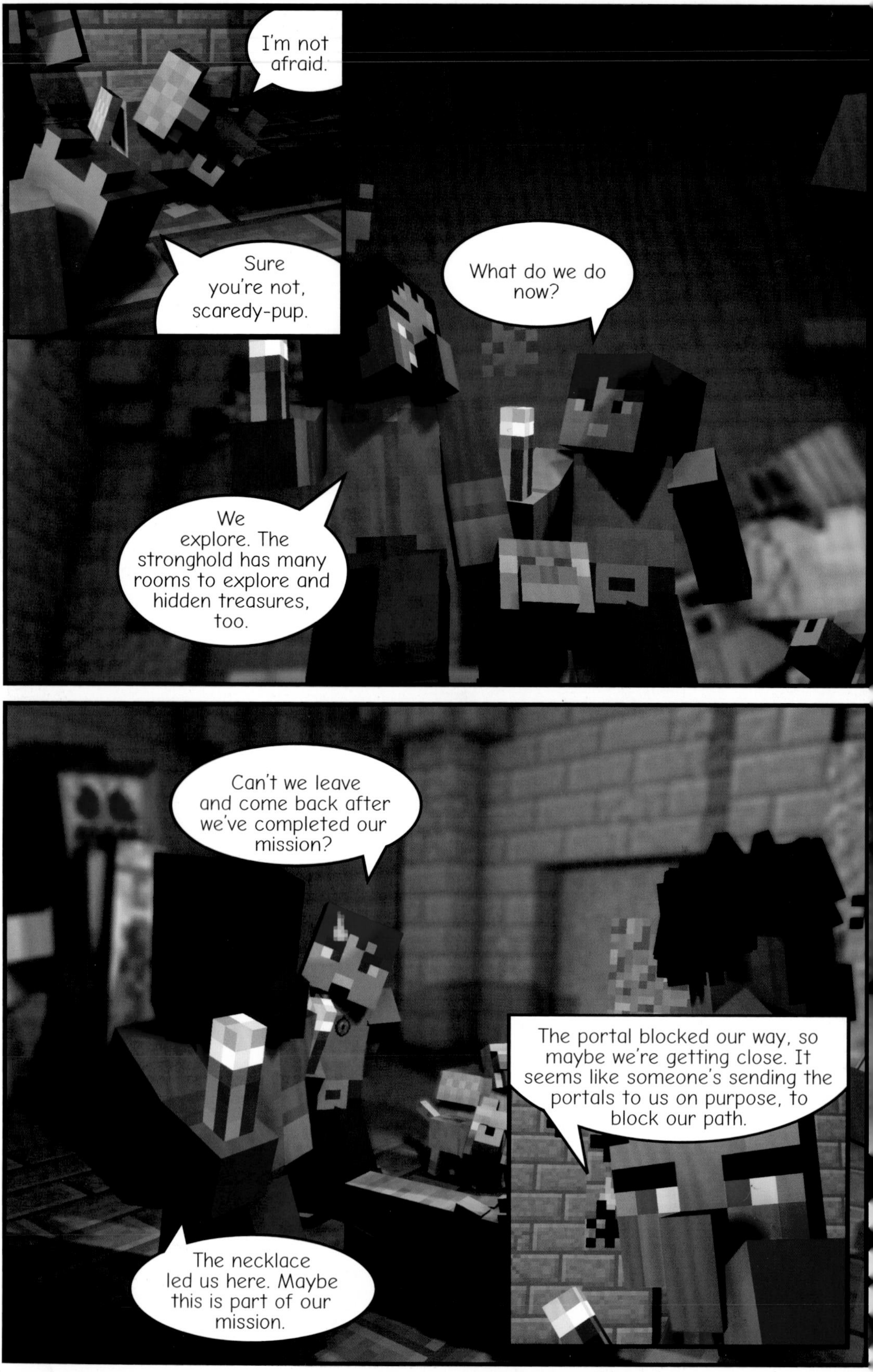
I'm not afraid.
Sure you're not, scaredy-pup.
What do we do now?
We explore. The stronghold has many rooms to explore and hidden treasures, too.
Can't we leave and come back after we've completed our mission?
The necklace led us here. Maybe this is part of our mission.
The portal blocked our way, so maybe we're getting close. It seems like someone's sending the portals to us on purpose, to block our path.

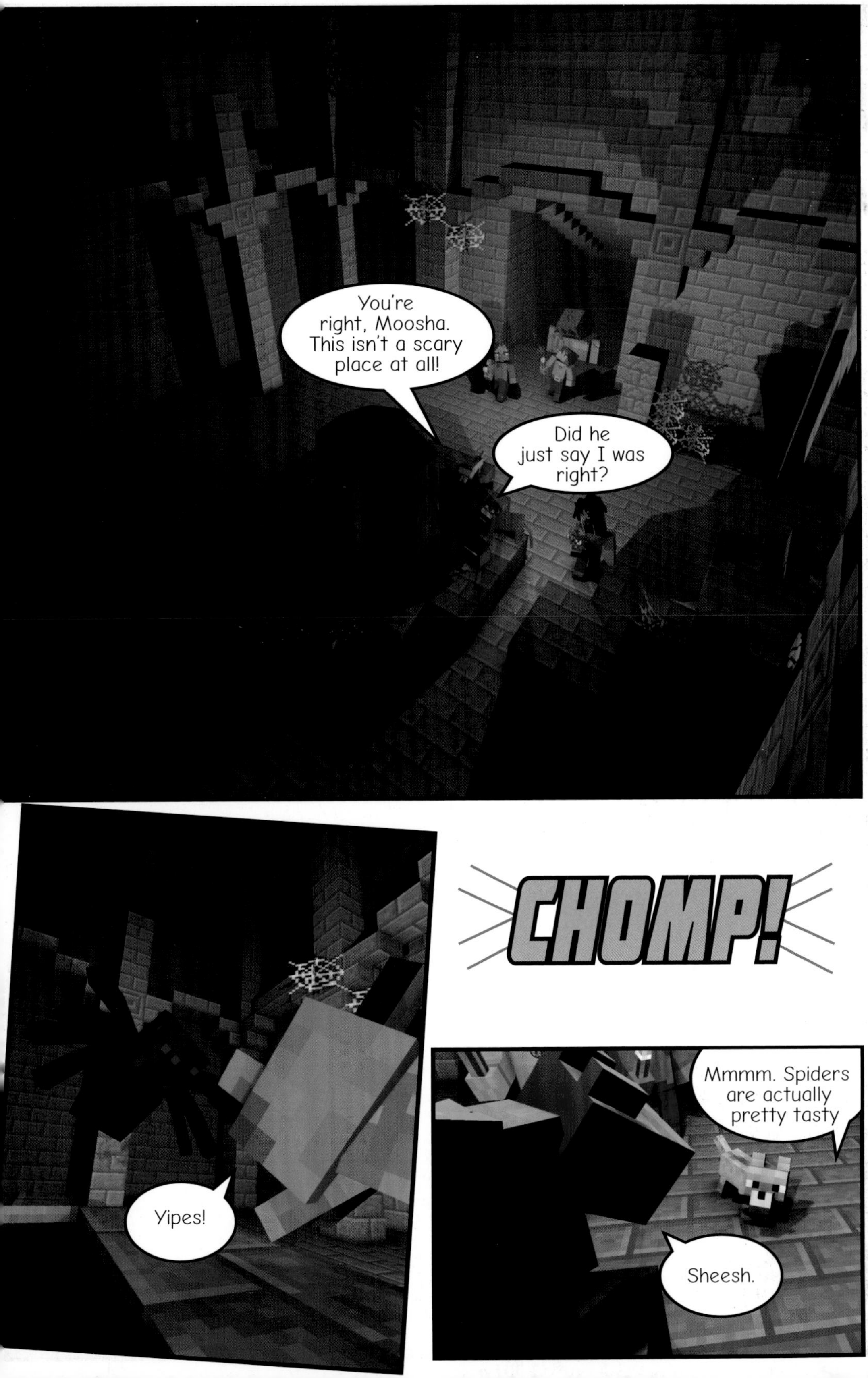
You're right, Moosha. This isn't a scary place at all!
Did he just say I was right?
CHOMP!
Yipes!
Mmmm. Spiders are actually pretty tasty
Sheesh.

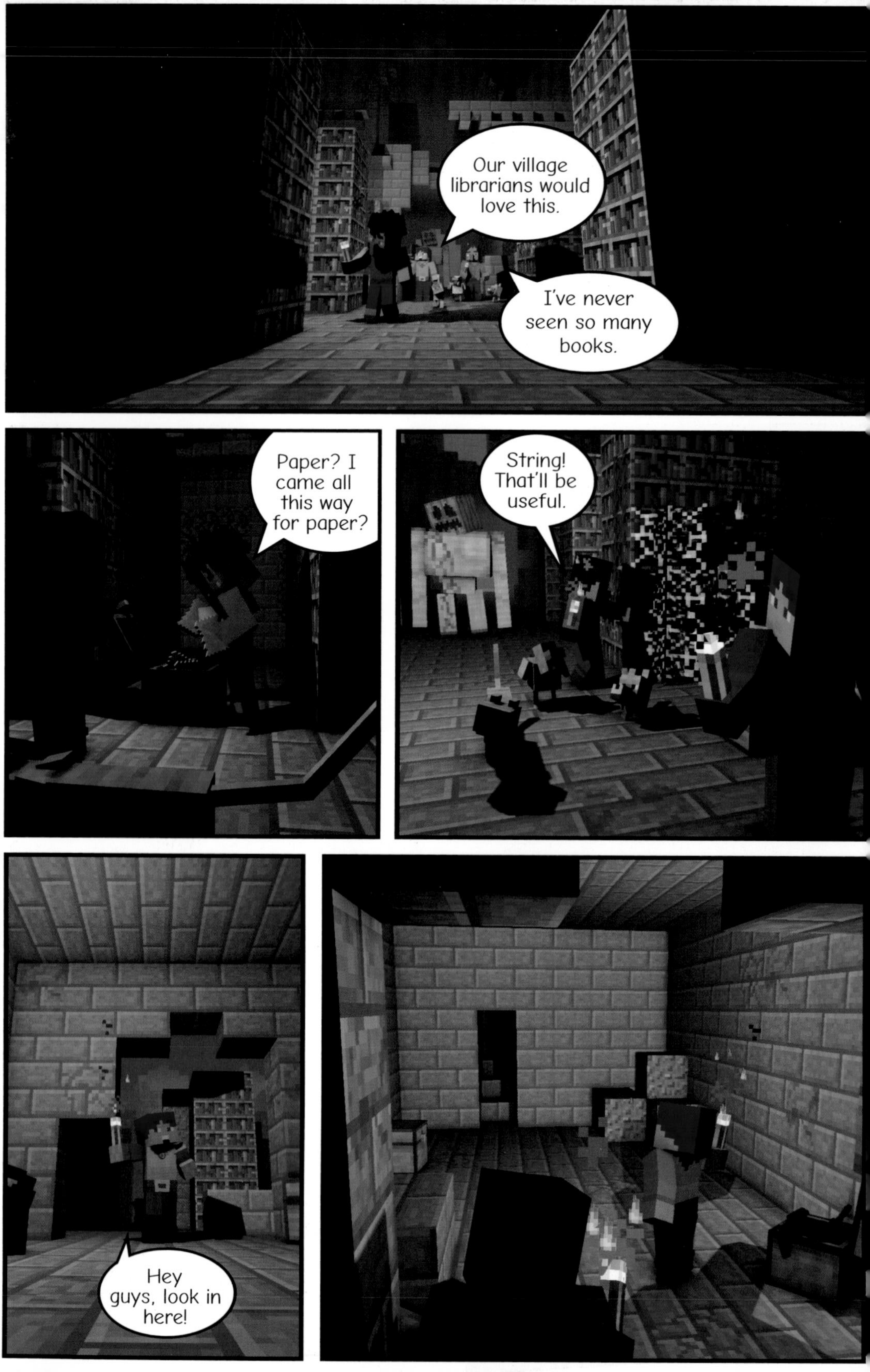
Our village librarians would love this.
I've never seen so many books.
Paper? I came all this way for paper?
String! That'll be useful.
Hey guys, look in here!

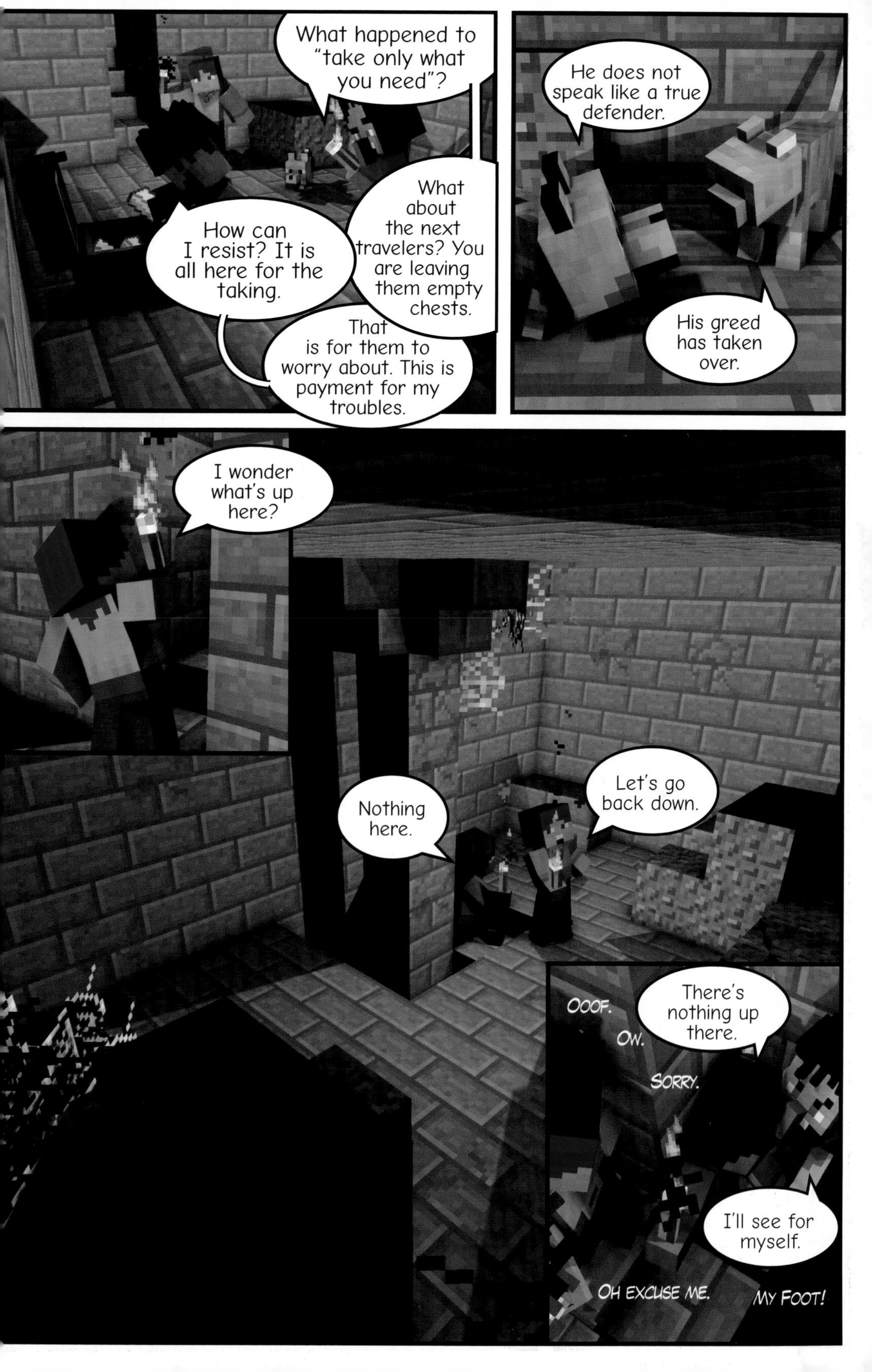
What happened to "take only what you need"?
How can I resist? It is all here for the taking.
What about the next travelers? You are leaving them empty chests.
That is for them to worry about. This is payment for my troubles.
He does not speak like a true defender.
His greed has taken over.
I wonder what's up here?
Nothing here.
Let's go back down.
OOOF.
OW.
There's nothing up there.
SORRY.
I'll see for myself.
OH EXCUSE ME.
MY FOOT!

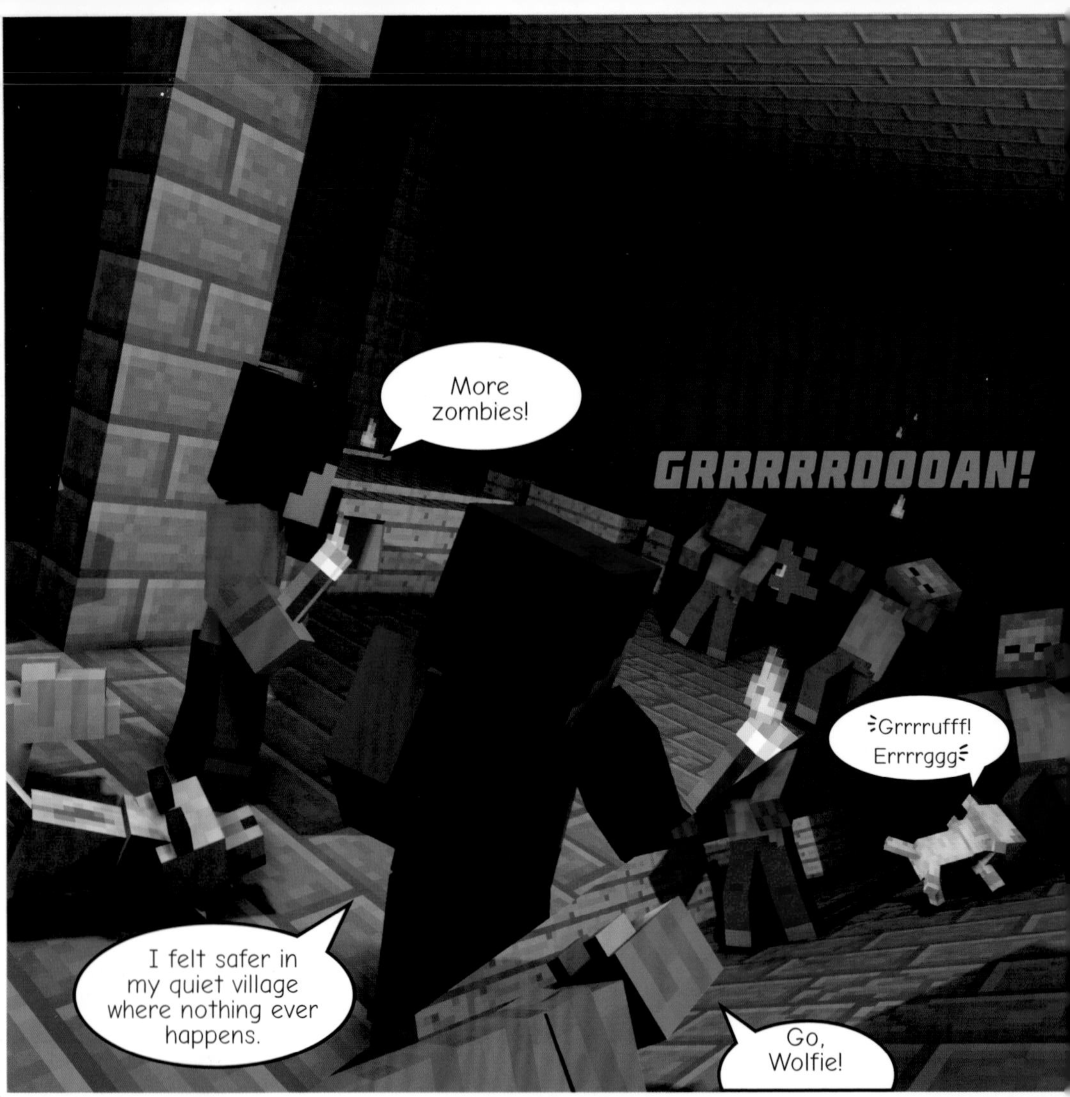
More zombies!
GRRRRROOOAN!
Grrrrufff! Errrrggg
I felt safer in my quiet village where nothing ever happens.
Go, Wolfie!

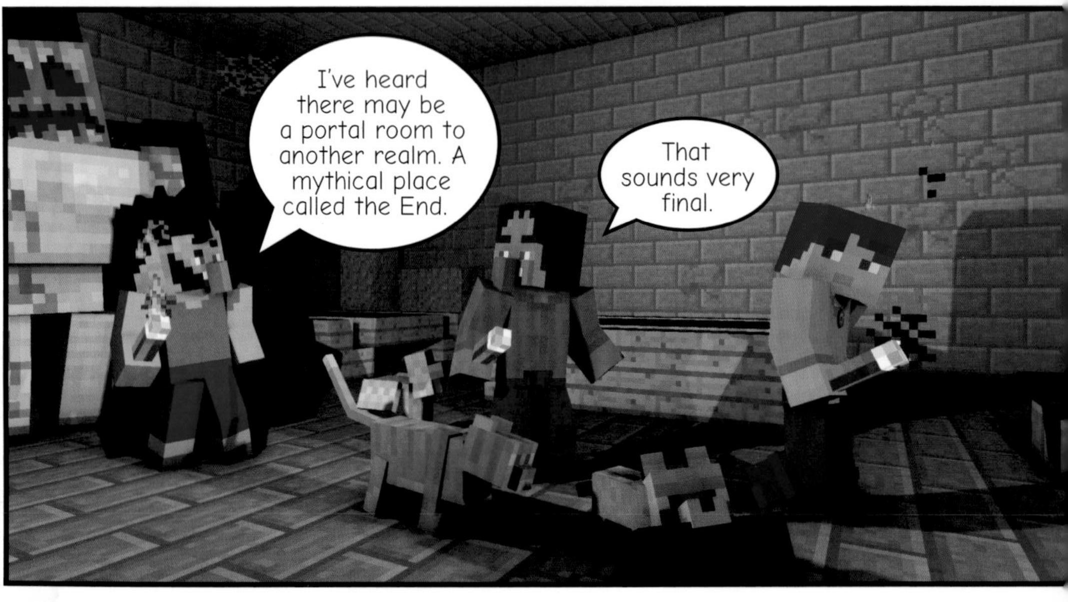
I've heard there may be a portal room to another realm. A mythical place called the End.
That sounds very final.

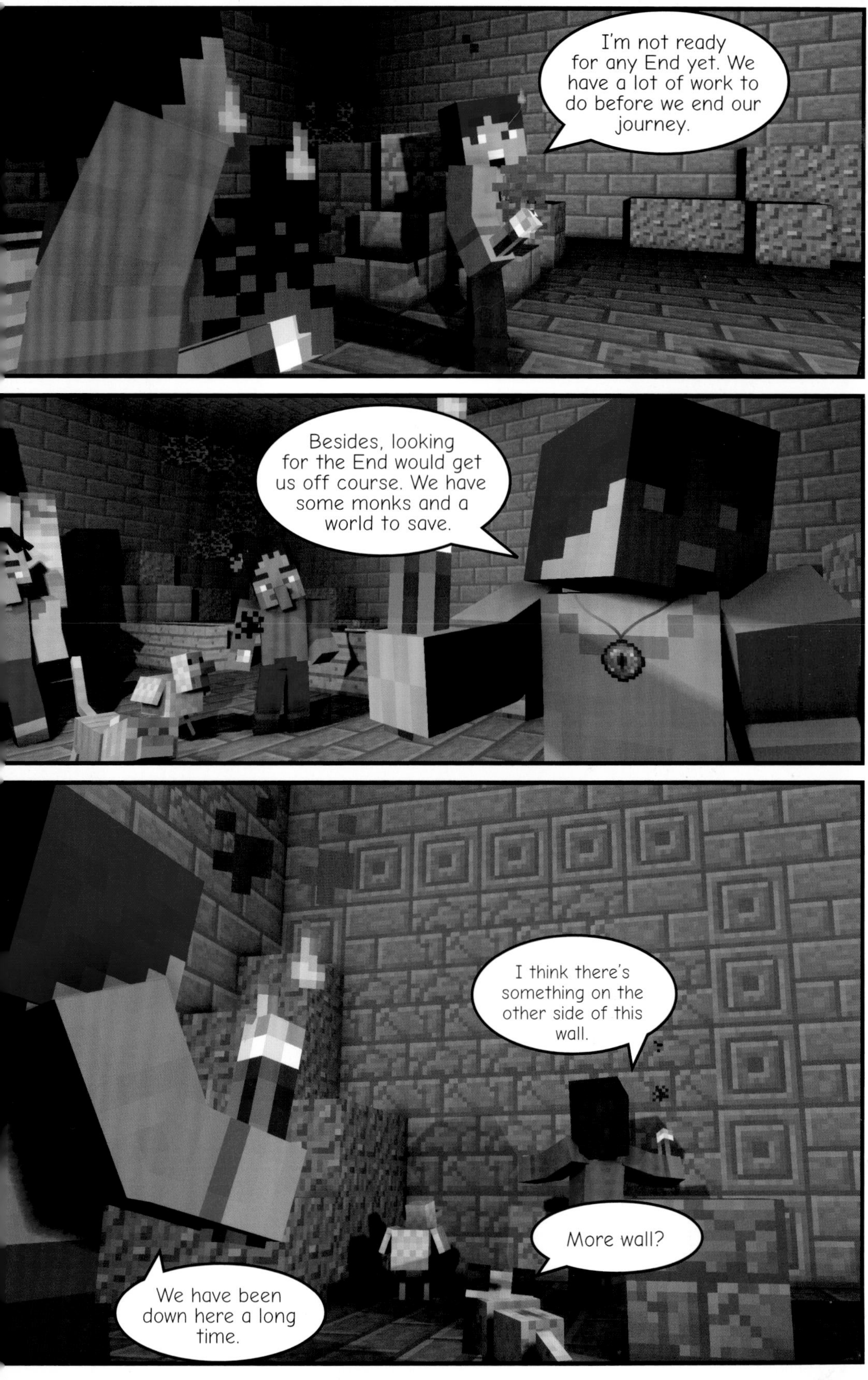
I'm not ready for any End yet. We have a lot of work to do before we end our journey.
Besides, looking for the End would get us off course. We have some monks and a world to save.
I think there's something on the other side of this wall.
More wall?
We have been down here a long time.

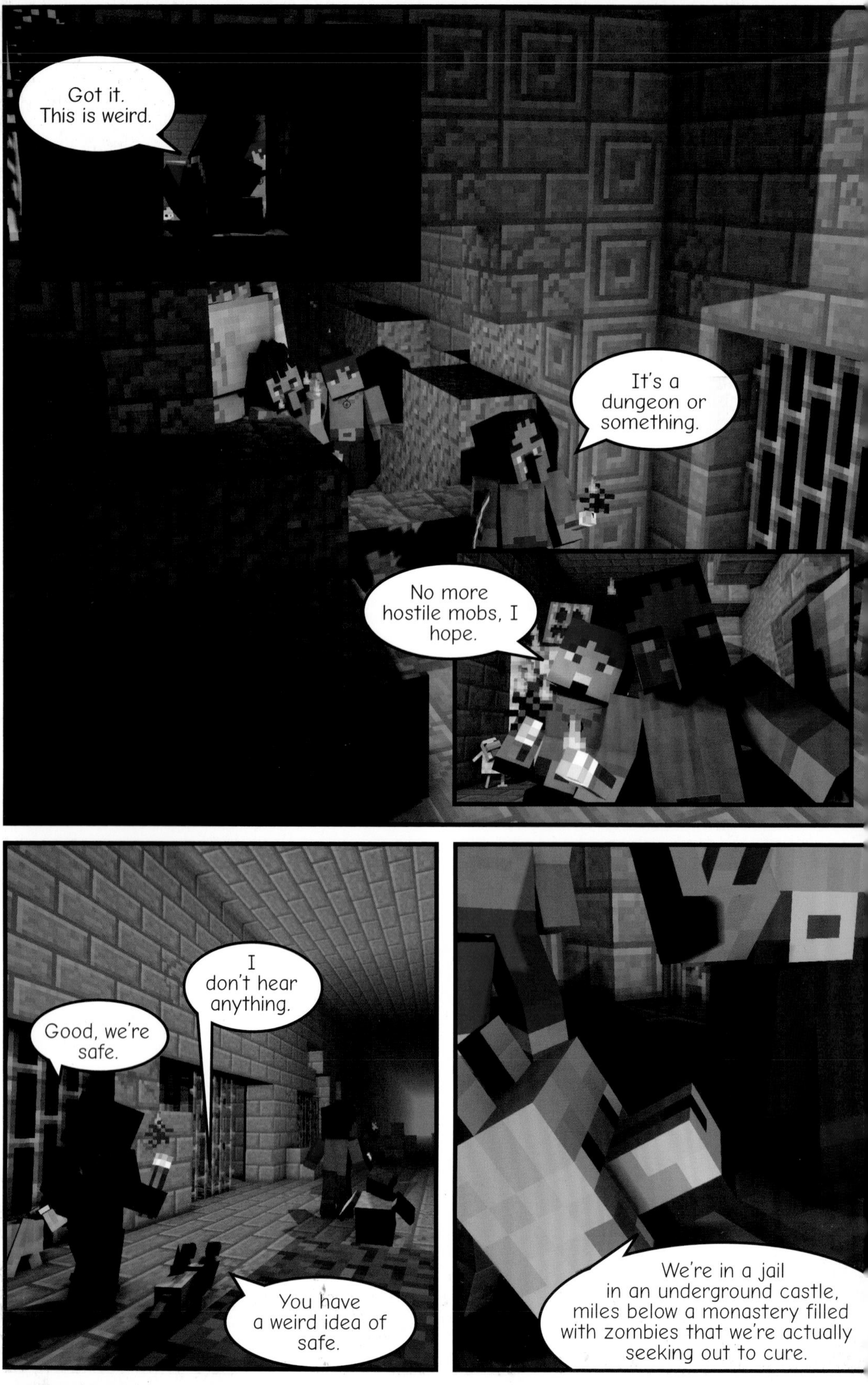
Got it.
This is weird.
It's a dungeon or something.
No more hostile mobs, I hope.
Good, we're safe.
I don't hear anything.
You have a weird idea of safe.
We're in a jail in an underground castle, miles below a monastery filled with zombies that we're actually seeking out to cure.

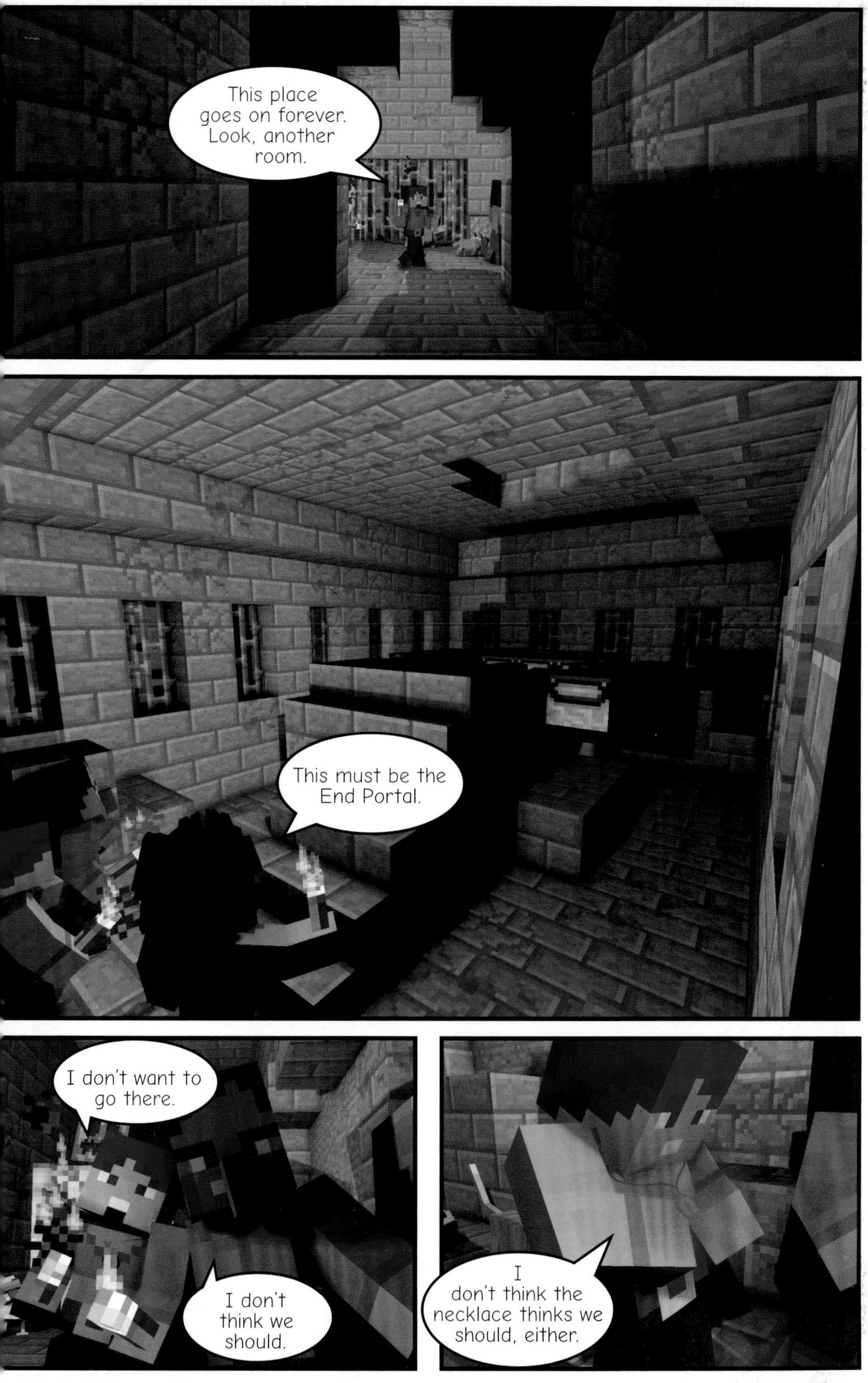
This place goes on forever. Look, another room.
This must be the End Portal.
I don't want to go there.
I don't think we should.
I don't think the necklace thinks we should, either.

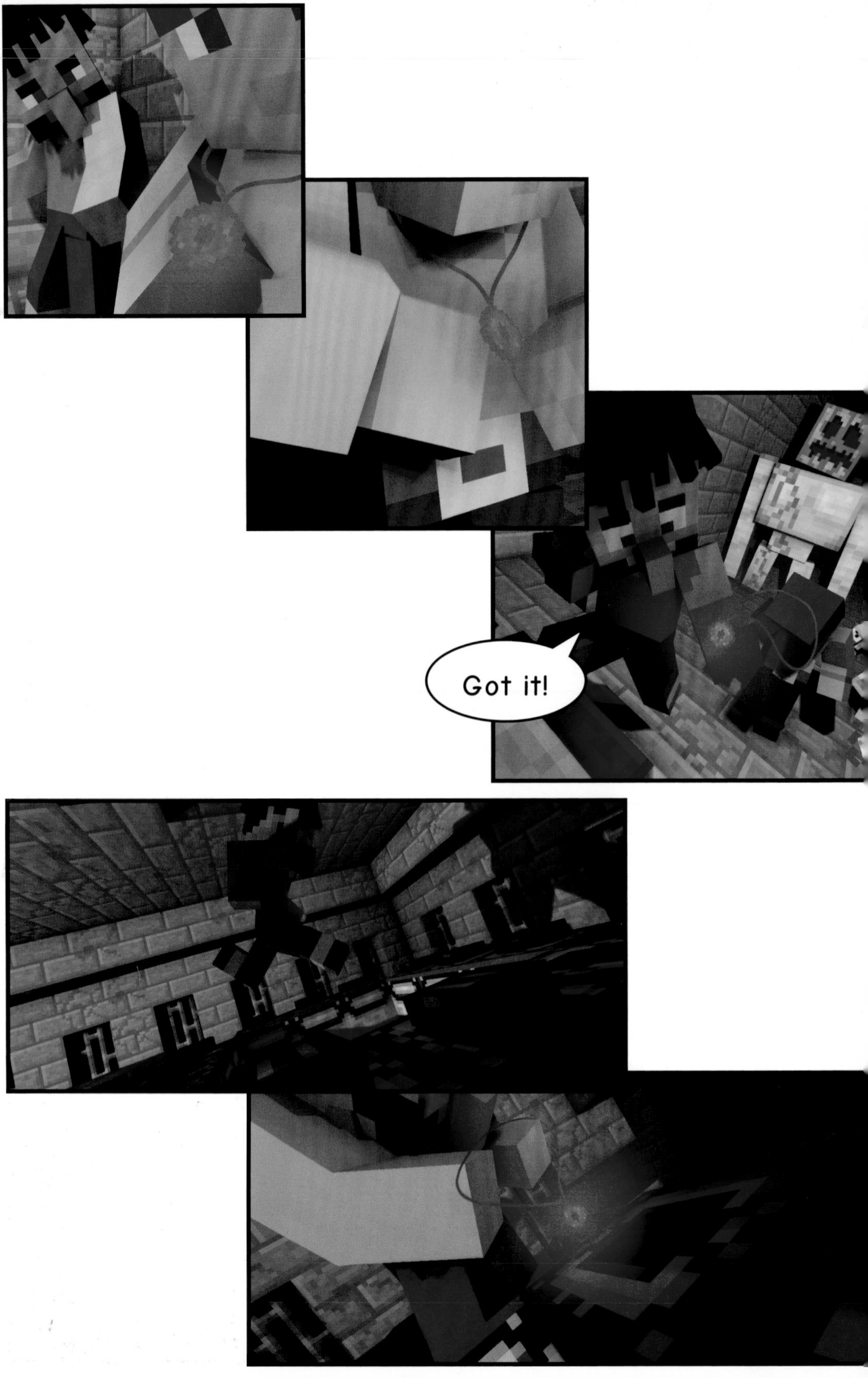
Got it!

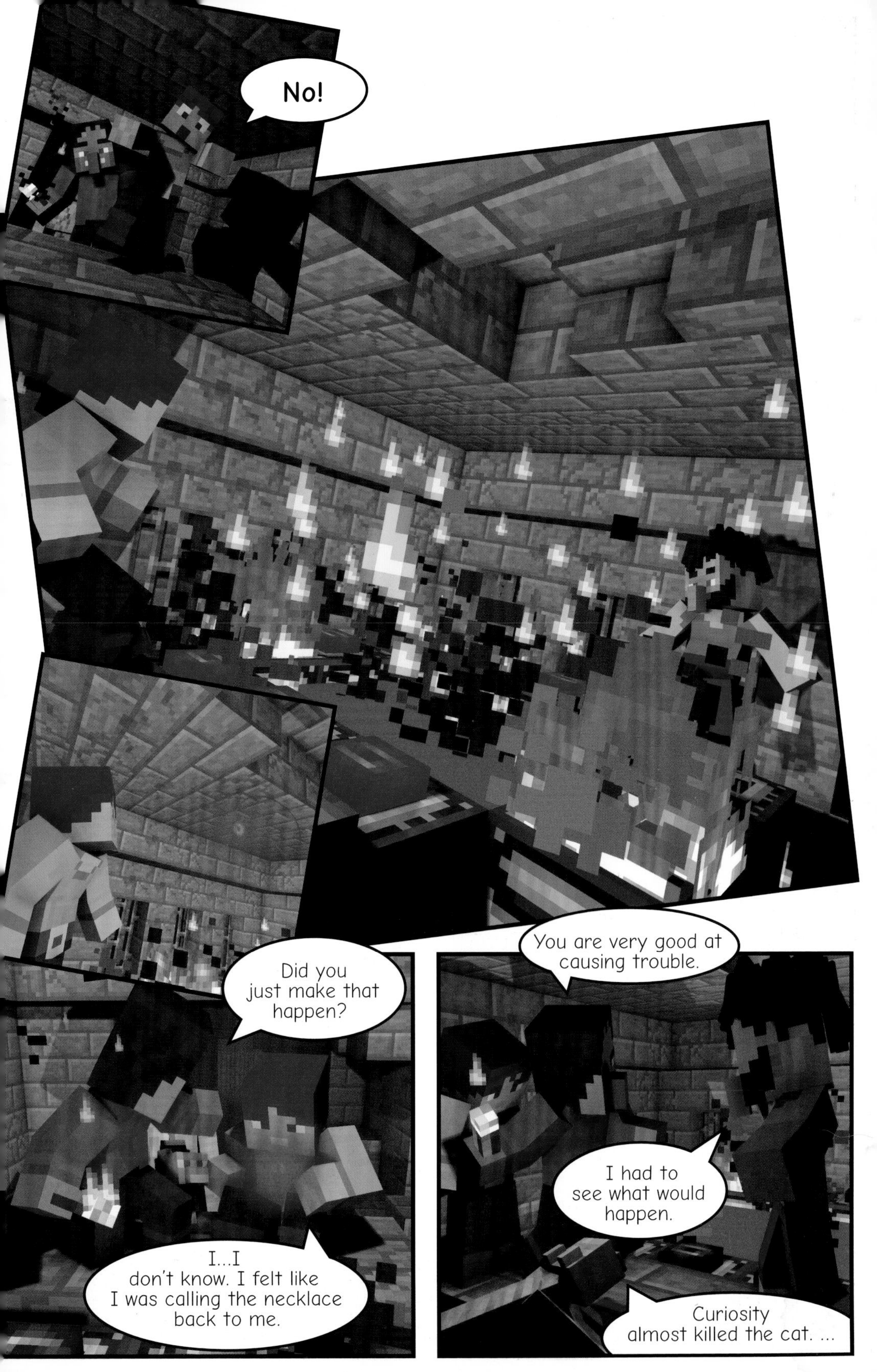
No!
Did you just make that happen?
I...I don't know. I felt like I was calling the necklace back to me.
You are very good at causing trouble.
I had to see what would happen.
Curiosity almost killed the cat. ...

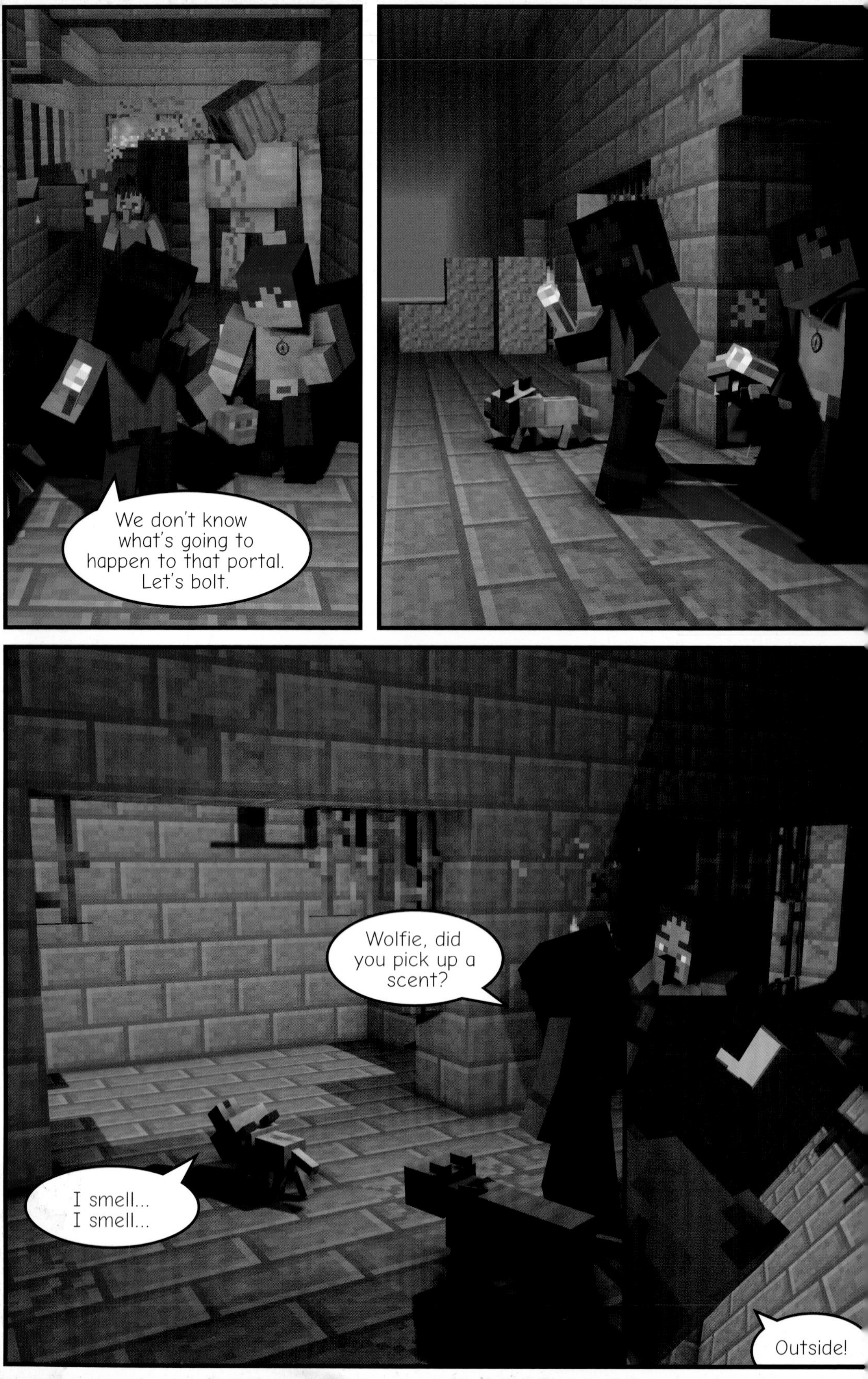
We don't know what's going to happen to that portal. Let's bolt.
Wolfie, did you pick up a scent?
I smell... I smell...
Outside!

CHAPTER 12

THE MOUNTAIN OF XENOS

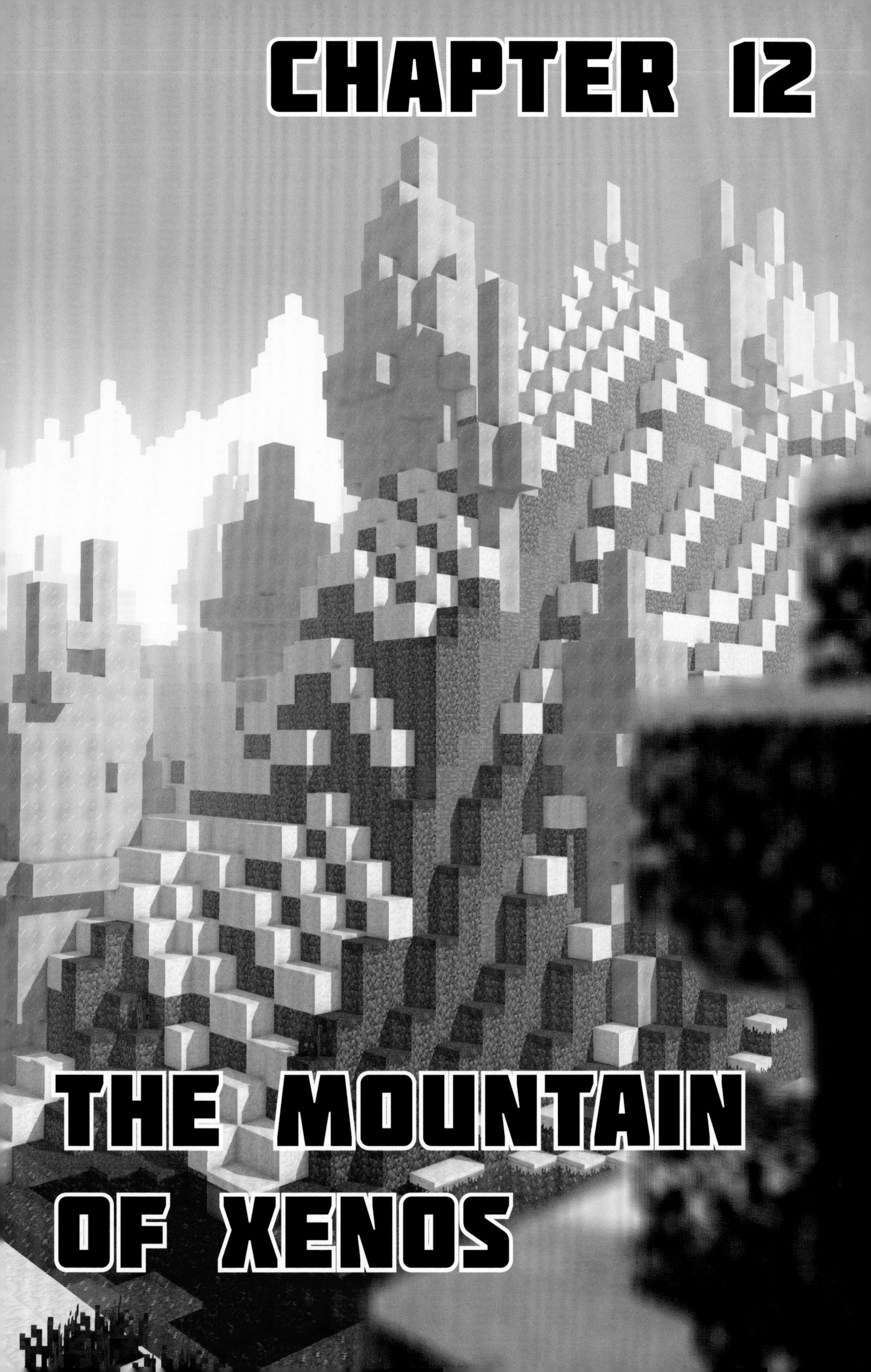

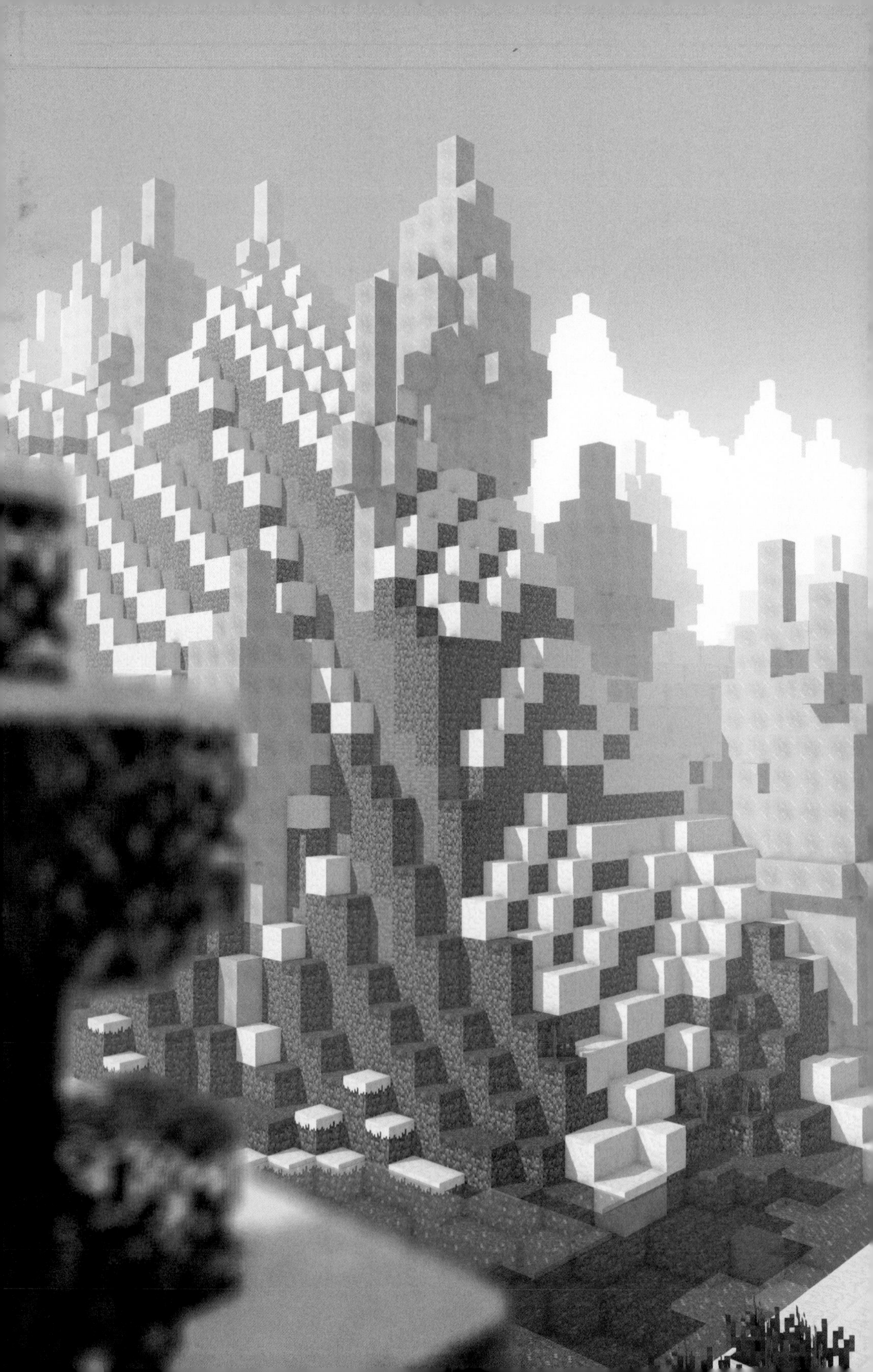

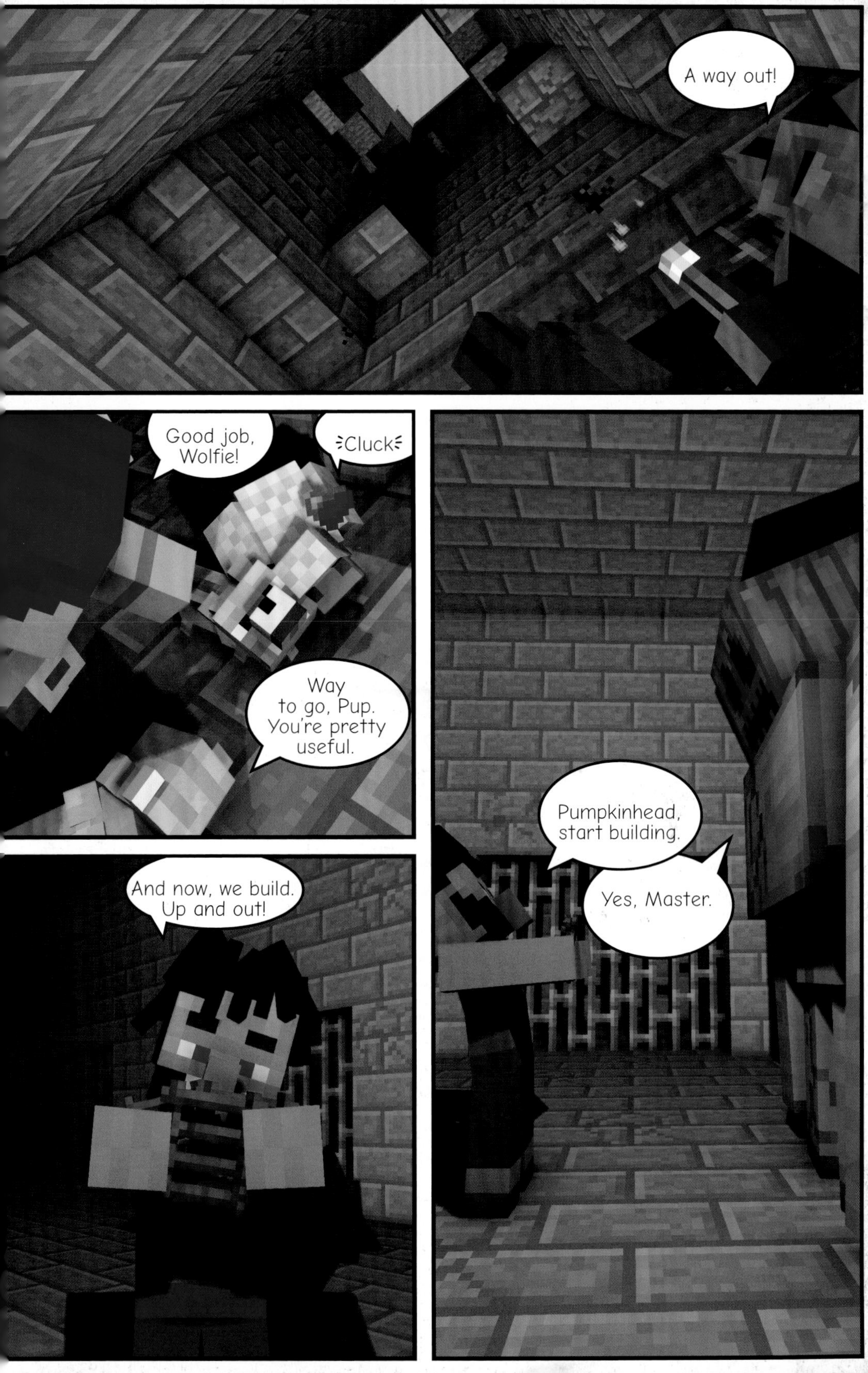
A way out!
Good job, Wolfie!
Cluck
Way to go, Pup. You're pretty useful.
And now, we build. Up and out!
Pumpkinhead, start building.
Yes, Master.

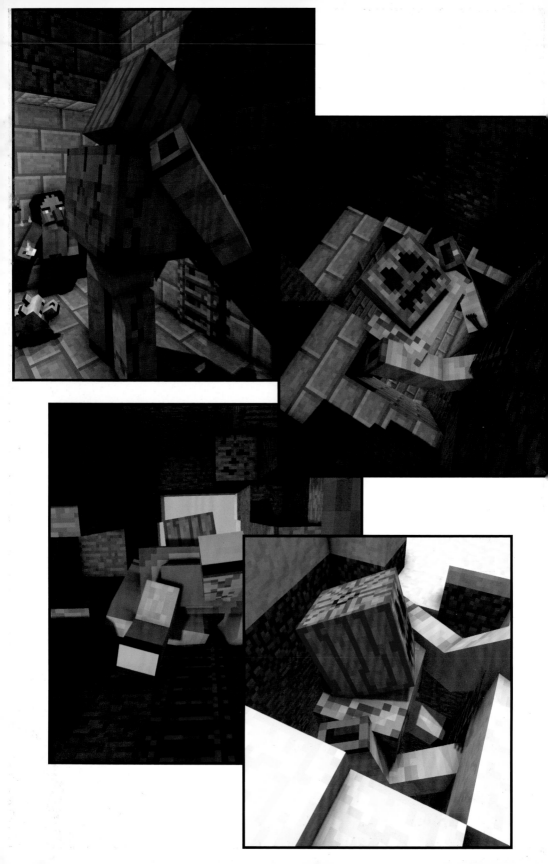

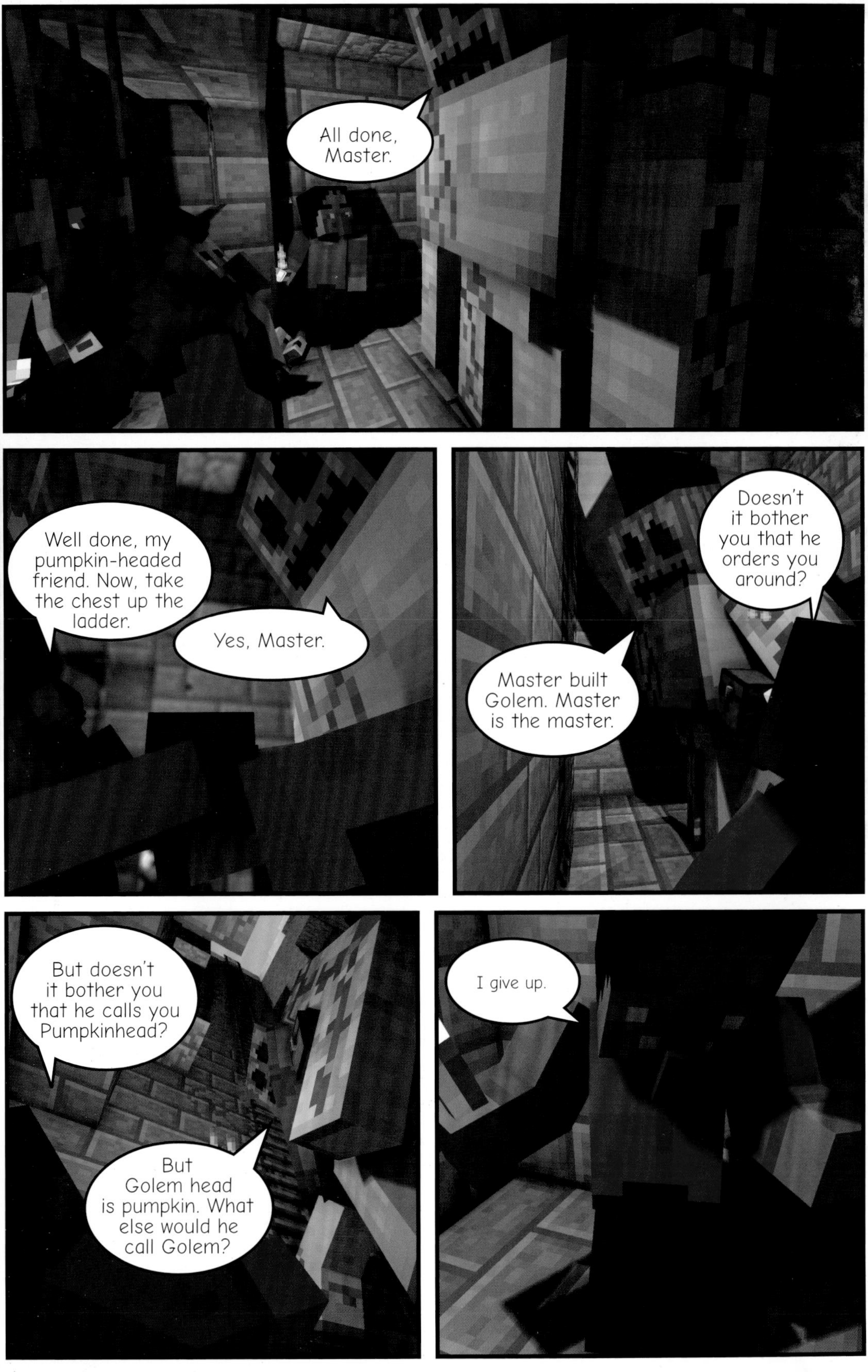
All done, Master.
Well done, my pumpkin-headed friend. Now, take the chest up the ladder.
Yes, Master.
Doesn't it bother you that he orders you around?
Master built Golem. Master is the master.
But doesn't it bother you that he calls you Pumpkinhead?
But Golem head is pumpkin. What else would he call Golem?
I give up.

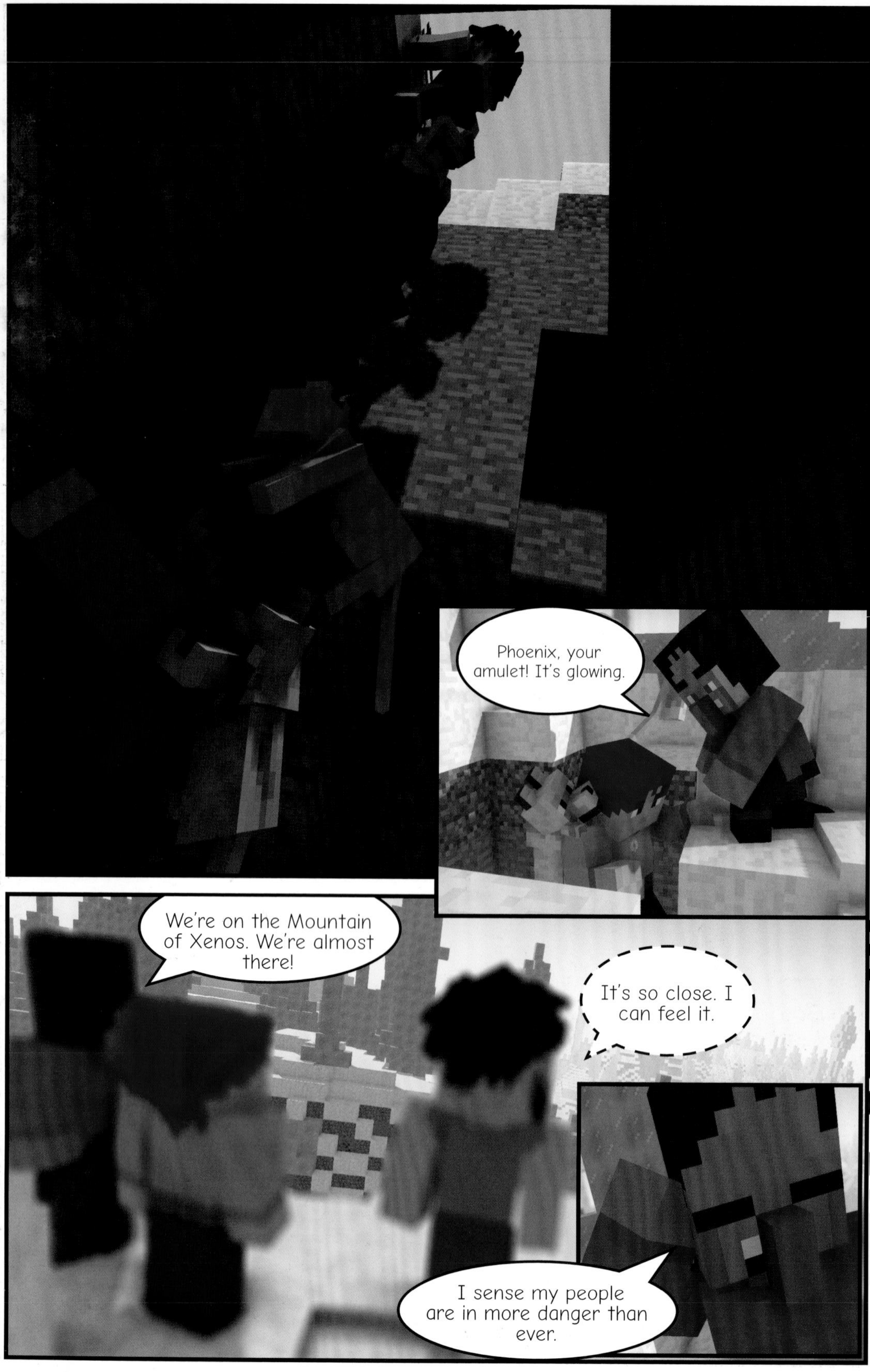
Phoenix, your amulet! It's glowing.
We're on the Mountain of Xenos. We're almost there!
It's so close. I can feel it.
I sense my people are in more danger than ever.

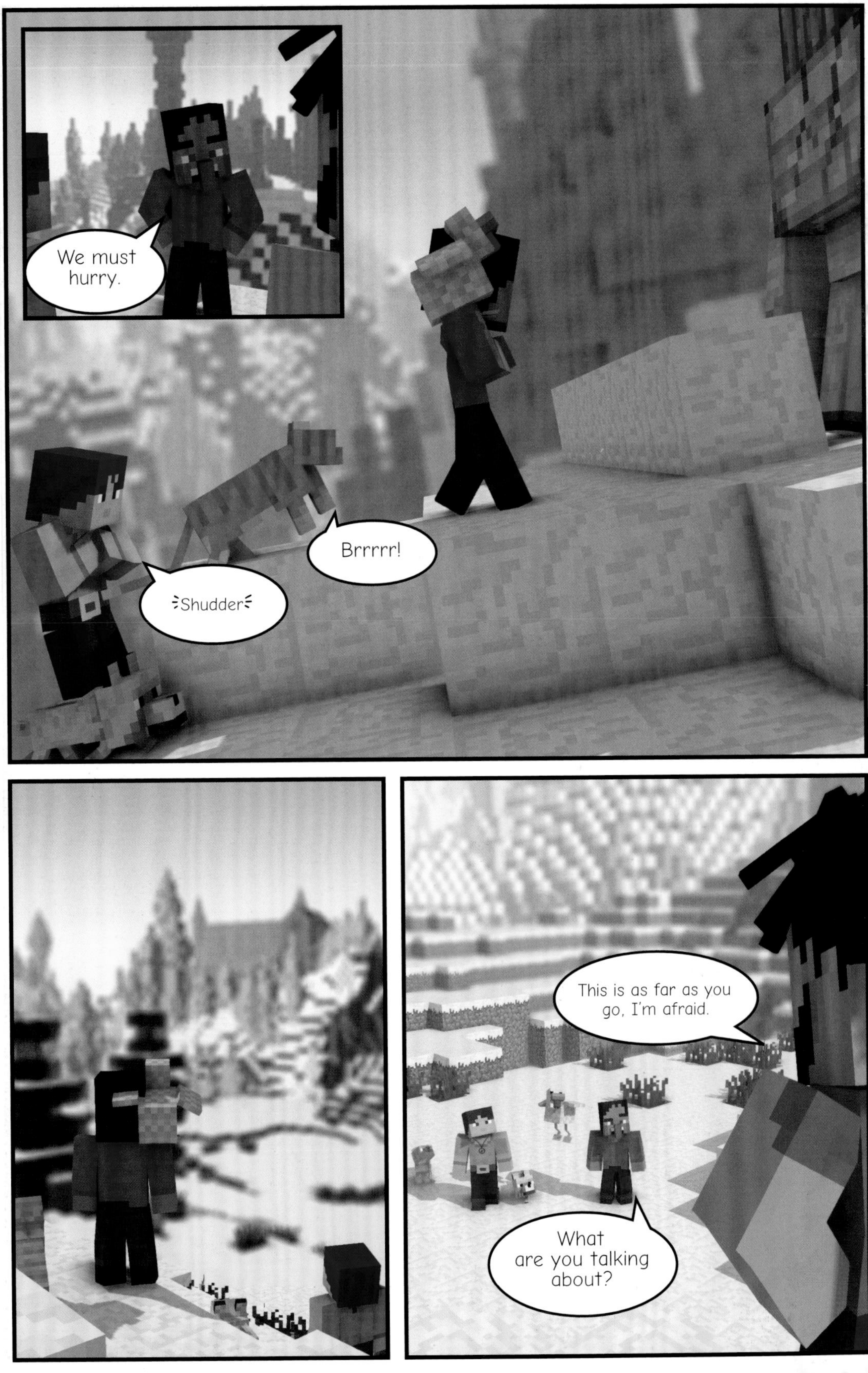
We must hurry.
Shudder
Brrrrr!
This is as far as you go, I'm afraid.
What are you talking about?

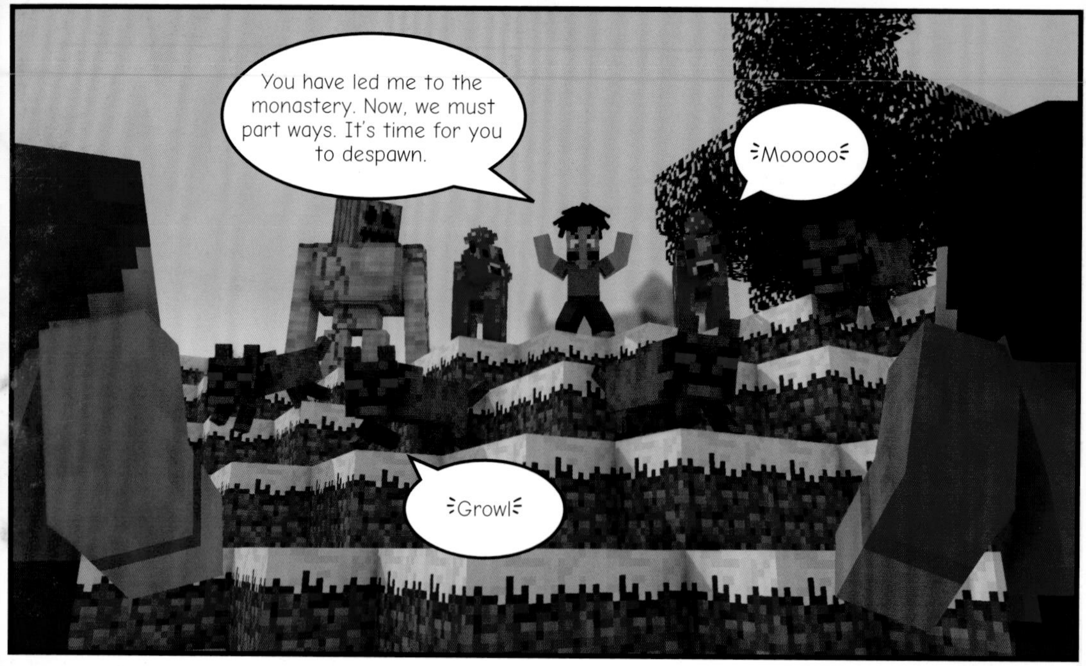
You have led me to the monastery. Now, we must part ways. It's time for you to despawn.
Mooooo
Growl

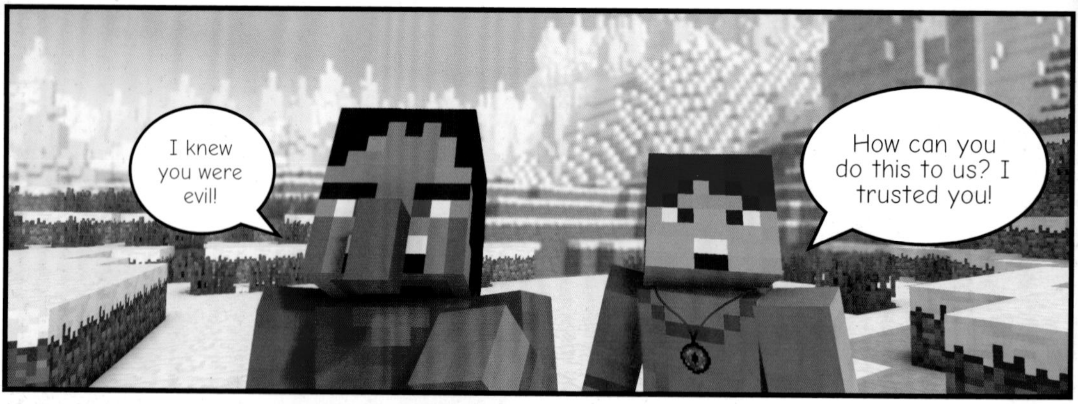
I knew you were evil!
How can you do this to us? I trusted you!

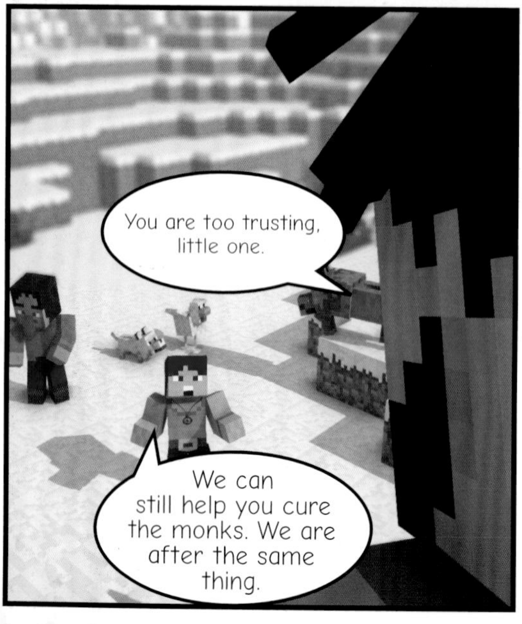
You are too trusting, little one.
We can still help you cure the monks. We are after the same thing.

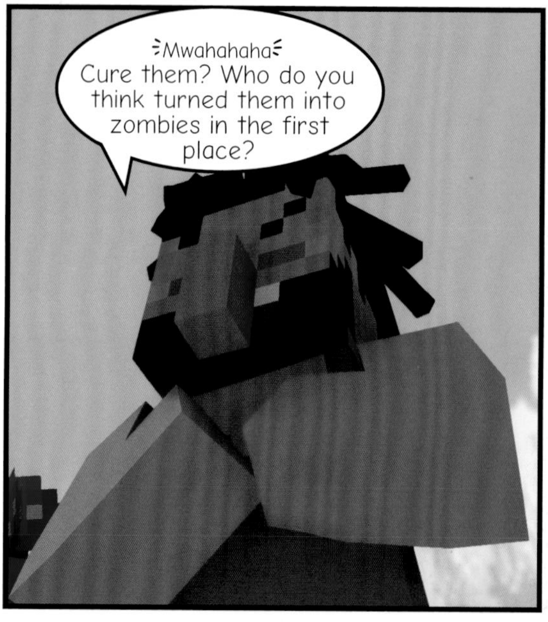
Mwahahaha
Cure them? Who do you think turned them into zombies in the first place?

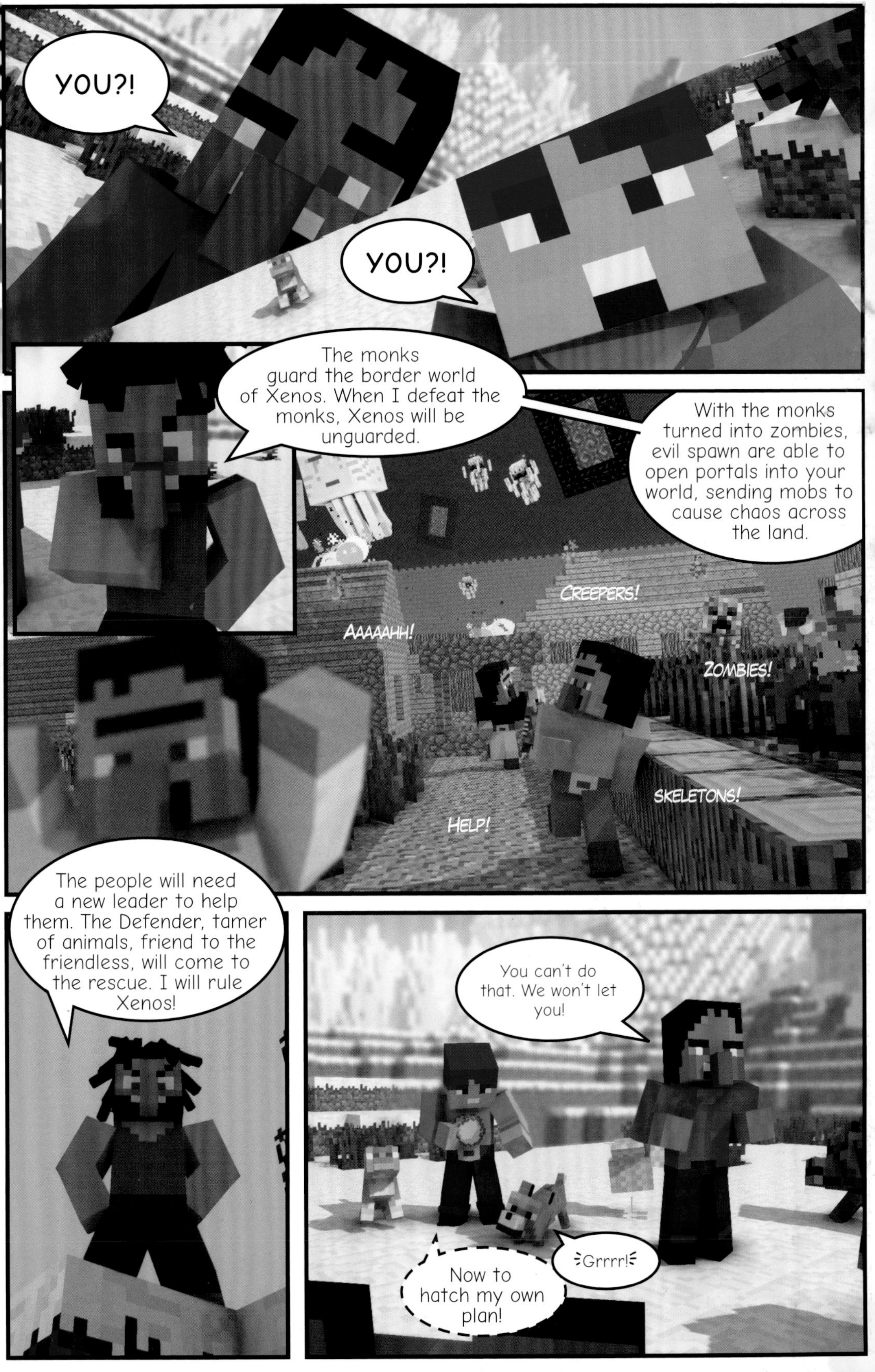
YOU?!
YOU?!
The monks guard the border world of Xenos. When I defeat the monks, Xenos will be unguarded.
With the monks turned into zombies, evil spawn are able to open portals into your world, sending mobs to cause chaos across the land.
CREEPERS!
AAAAAHH!
ZOMBIES!
SKELETONS!
HELP!
The people will need a new leader to help them. The Defender, tamer of animals, friend to the friendless, will come to the rescue. I will rule Xenos!
You can't do that. We won't let you!
Grrrr!
Now to hatch my own plan!

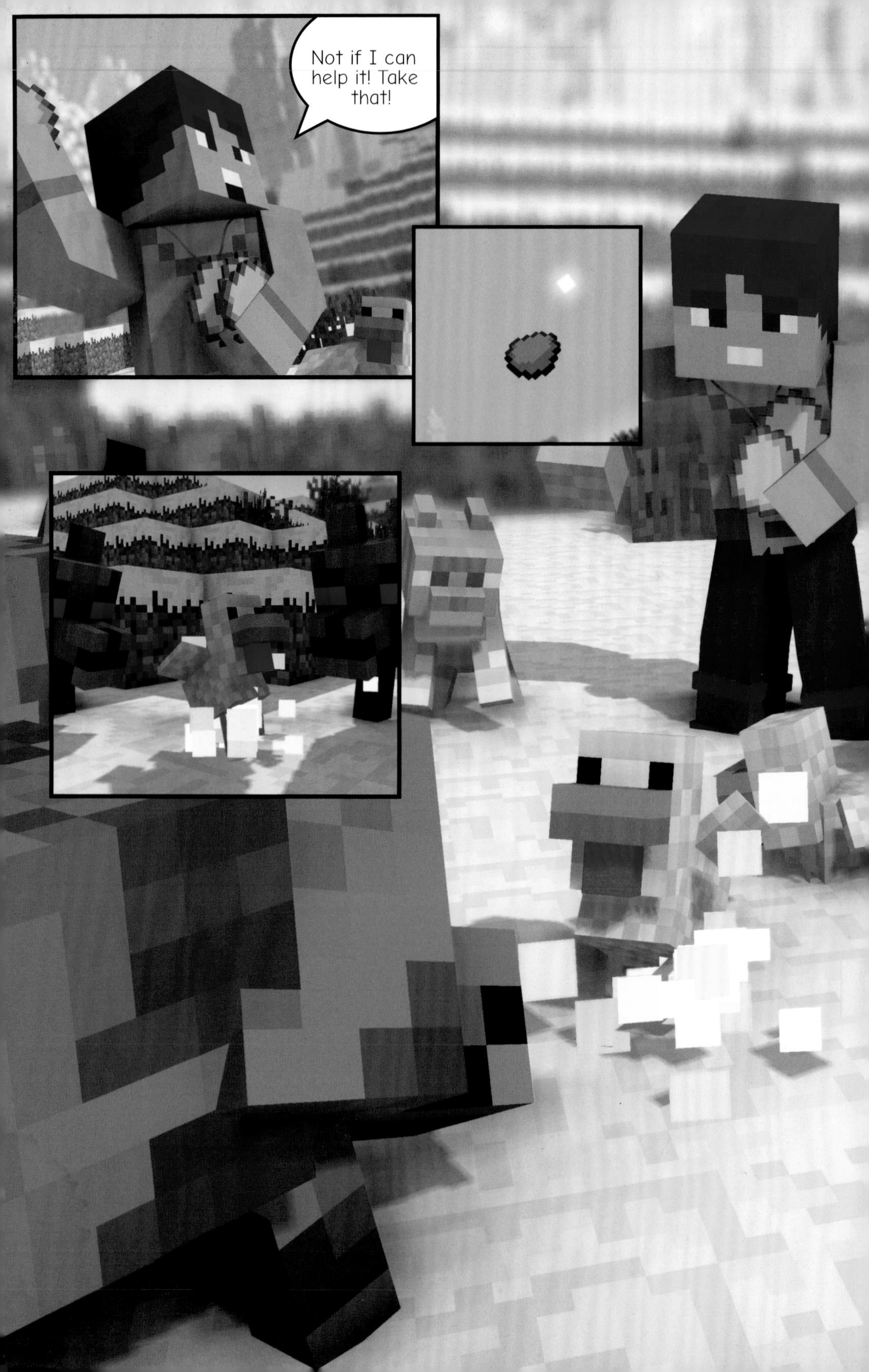
Not if I can help it! Take that!

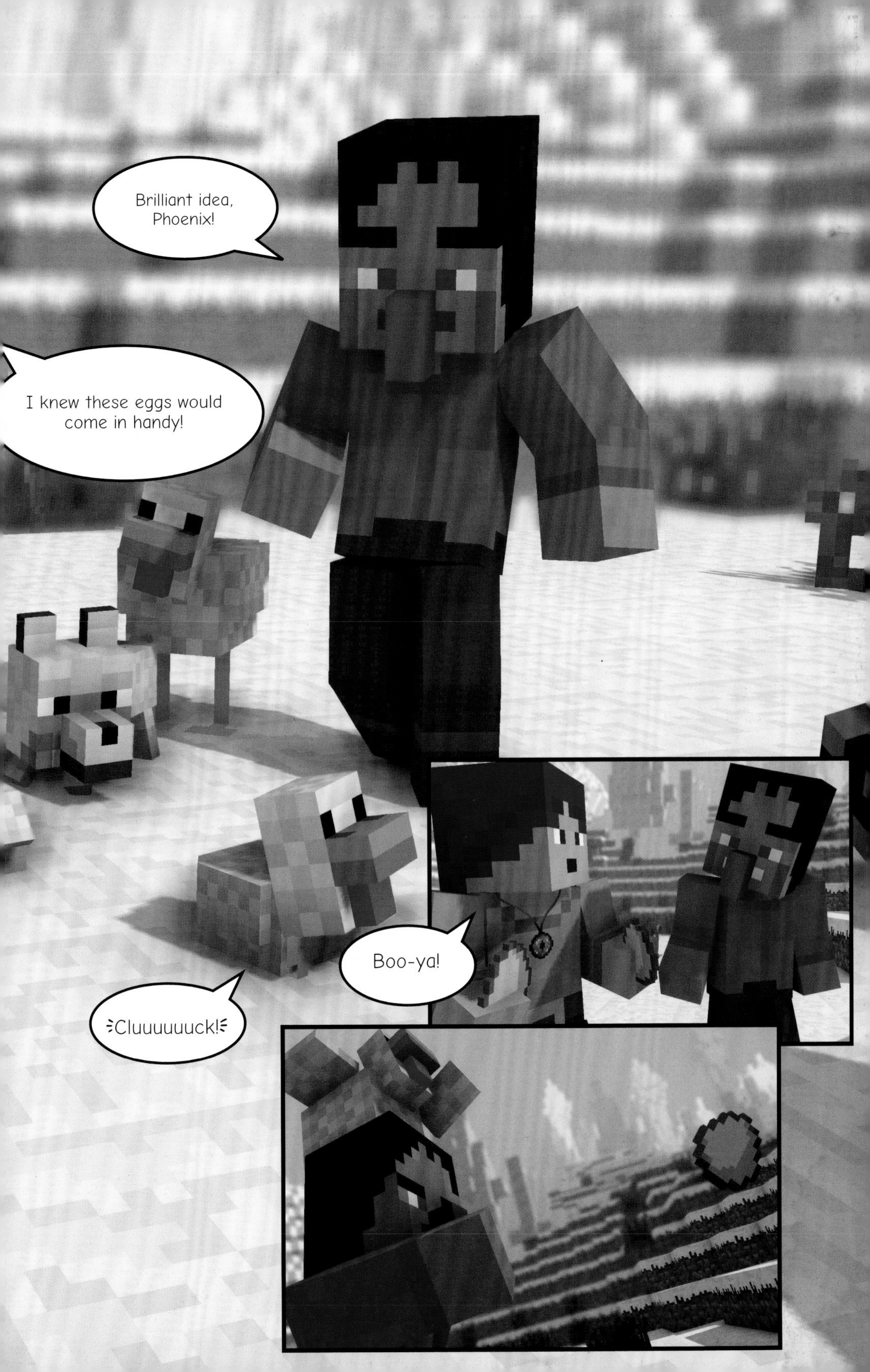
Brilliant idea,
Phoenix!
I knew these eggs would
come in handy!
Boo-ya!
Cluuuuuuck!

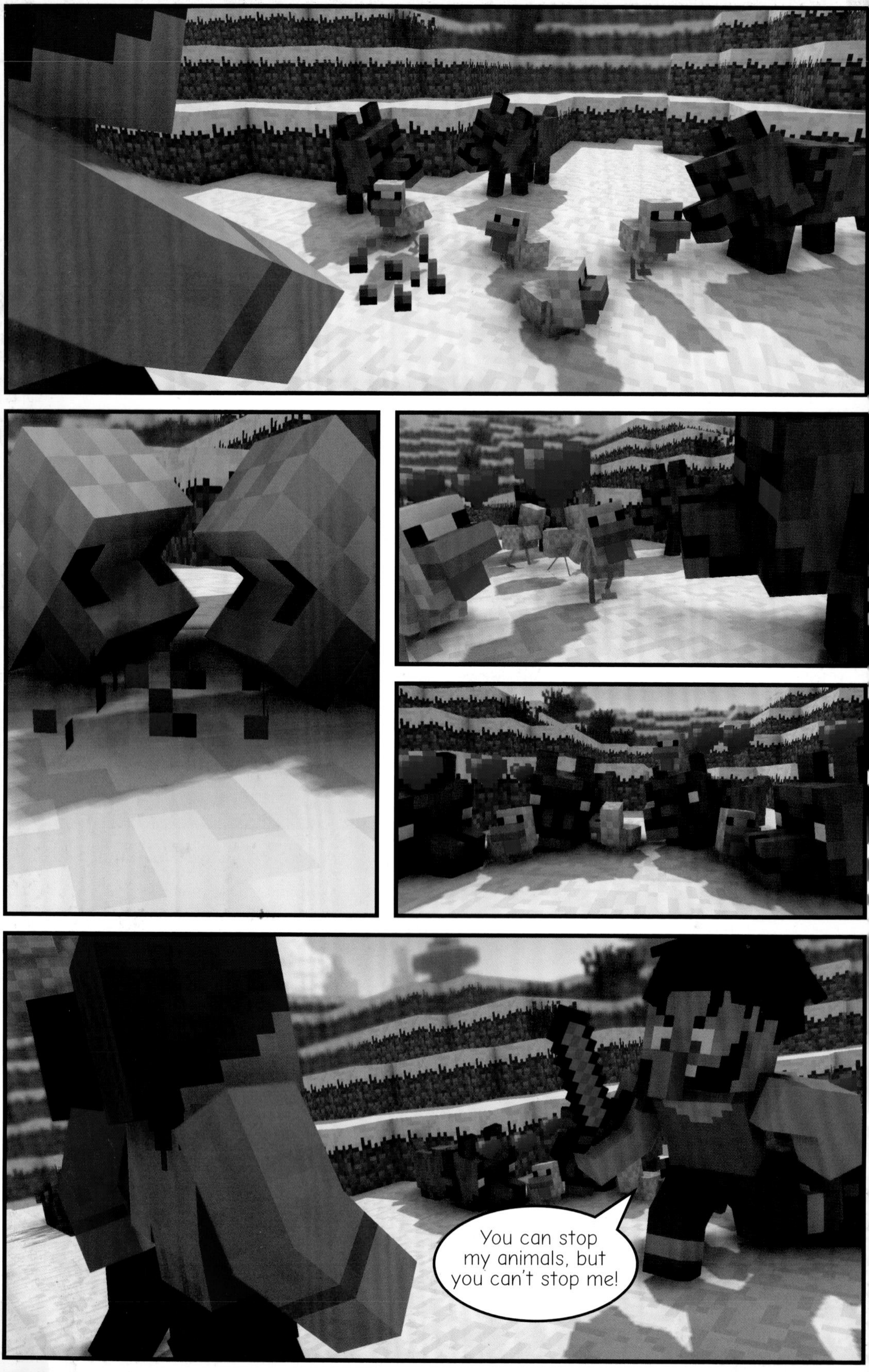
You can stop my animals, but you can't stop me!

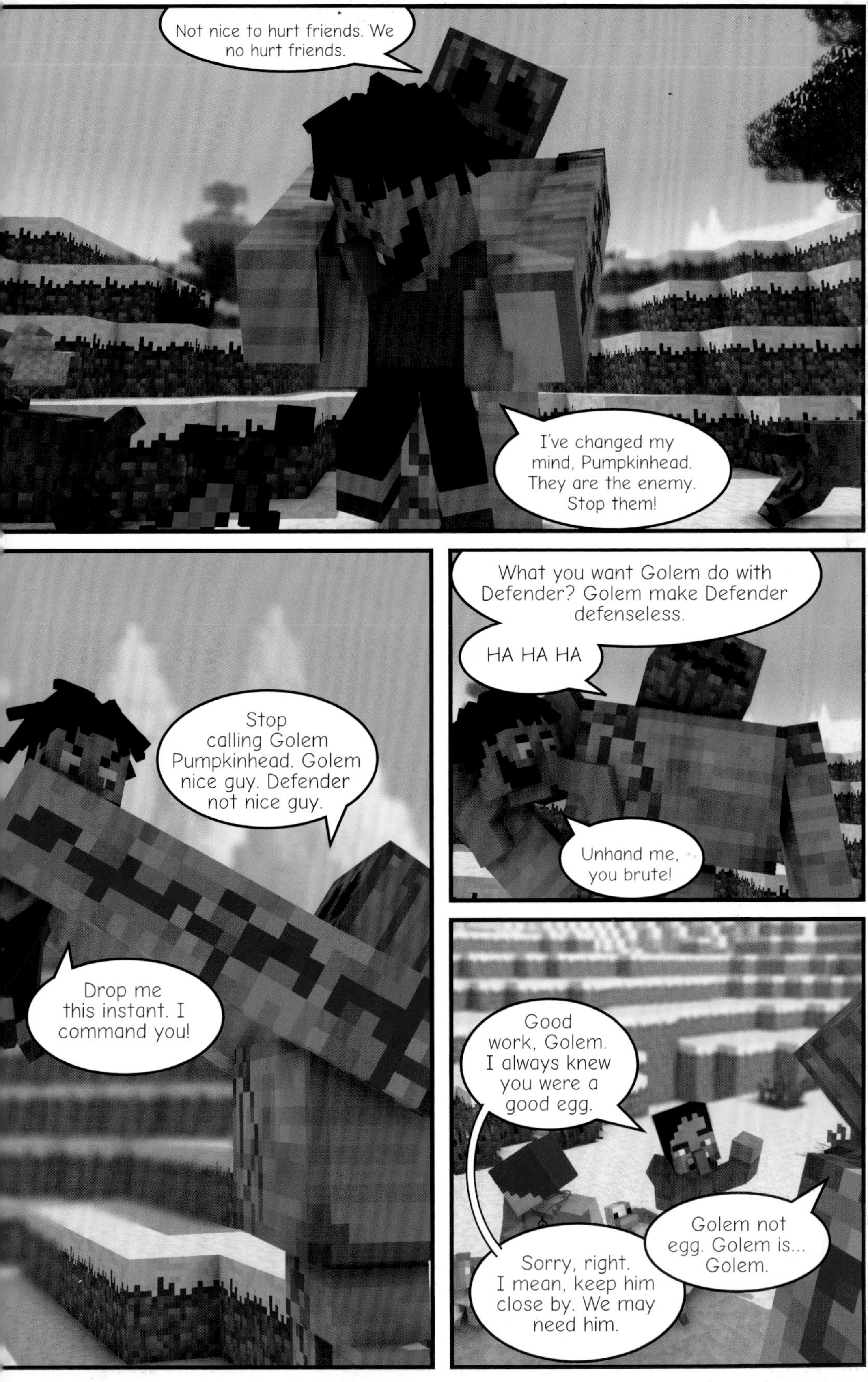
Not nice to hurt friends. We no hurt friends.
I've changed my mind, Pumpkinhead. They are the enemy. Stop them!
Stop calling Golem Pumpkinhead. Golem nice guy. Defender not nice guy.
Drop me this instant. I command you!
What you want Golem do with Defender? Golem make Defender defenseless.
HA HA HA
Unhand me, you brute!
Good work, Golem. I always knew you were a good egg.
Golem not egg. Golem is... Golem.
Sorry, right. I mean, keep him close by. We may need him.

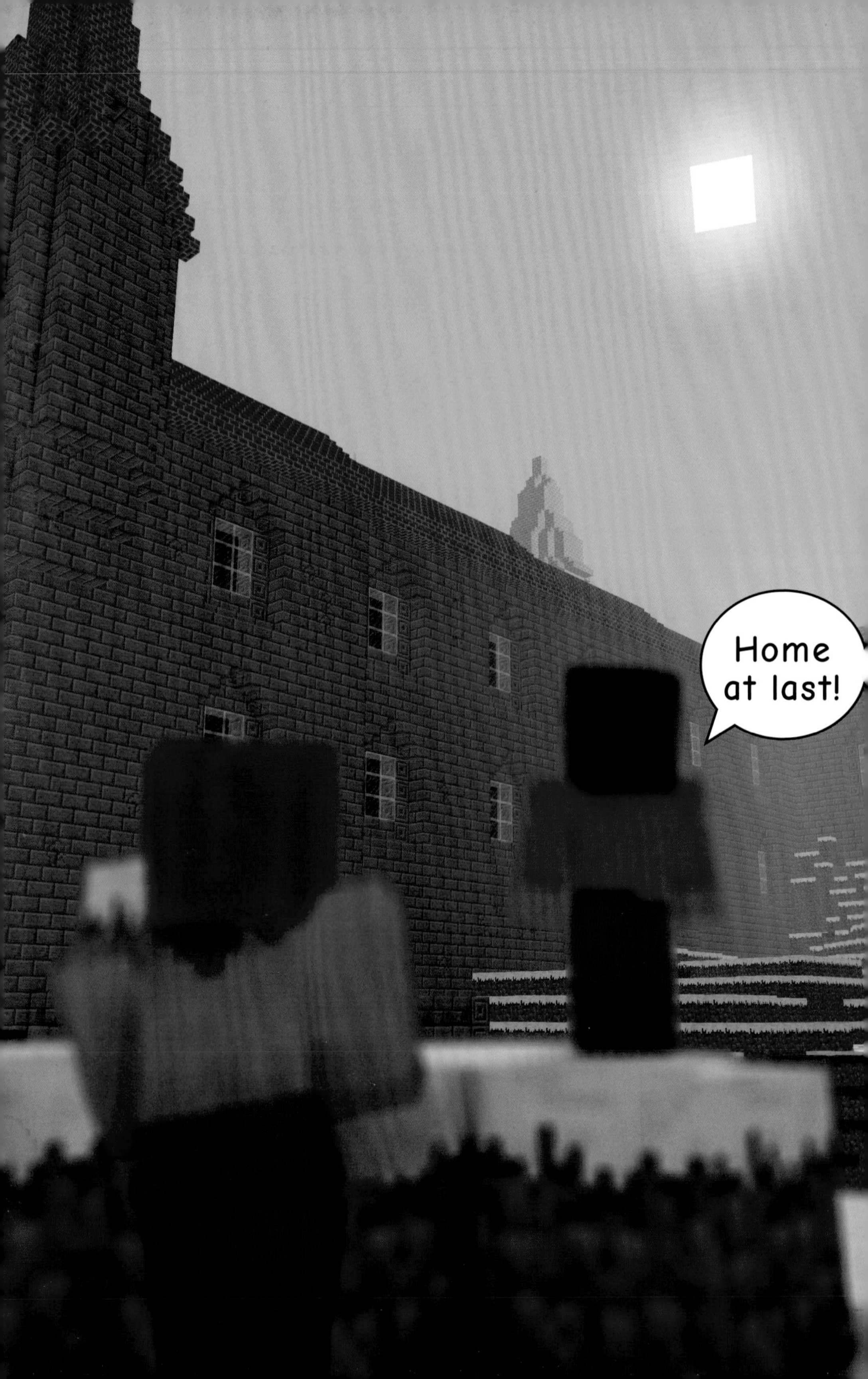
Home at last!

CHAPTER 13

ZOMBIES NO MORE

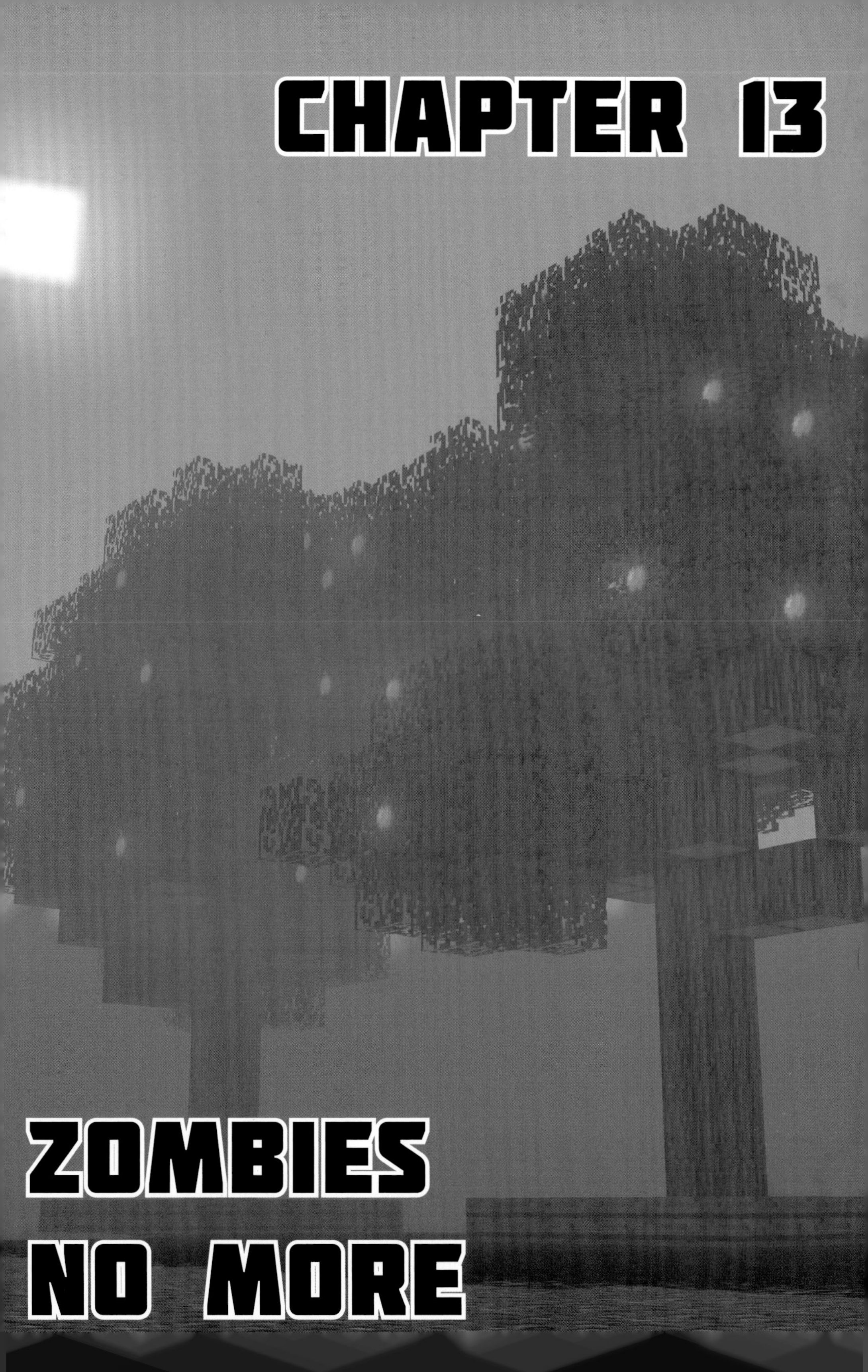

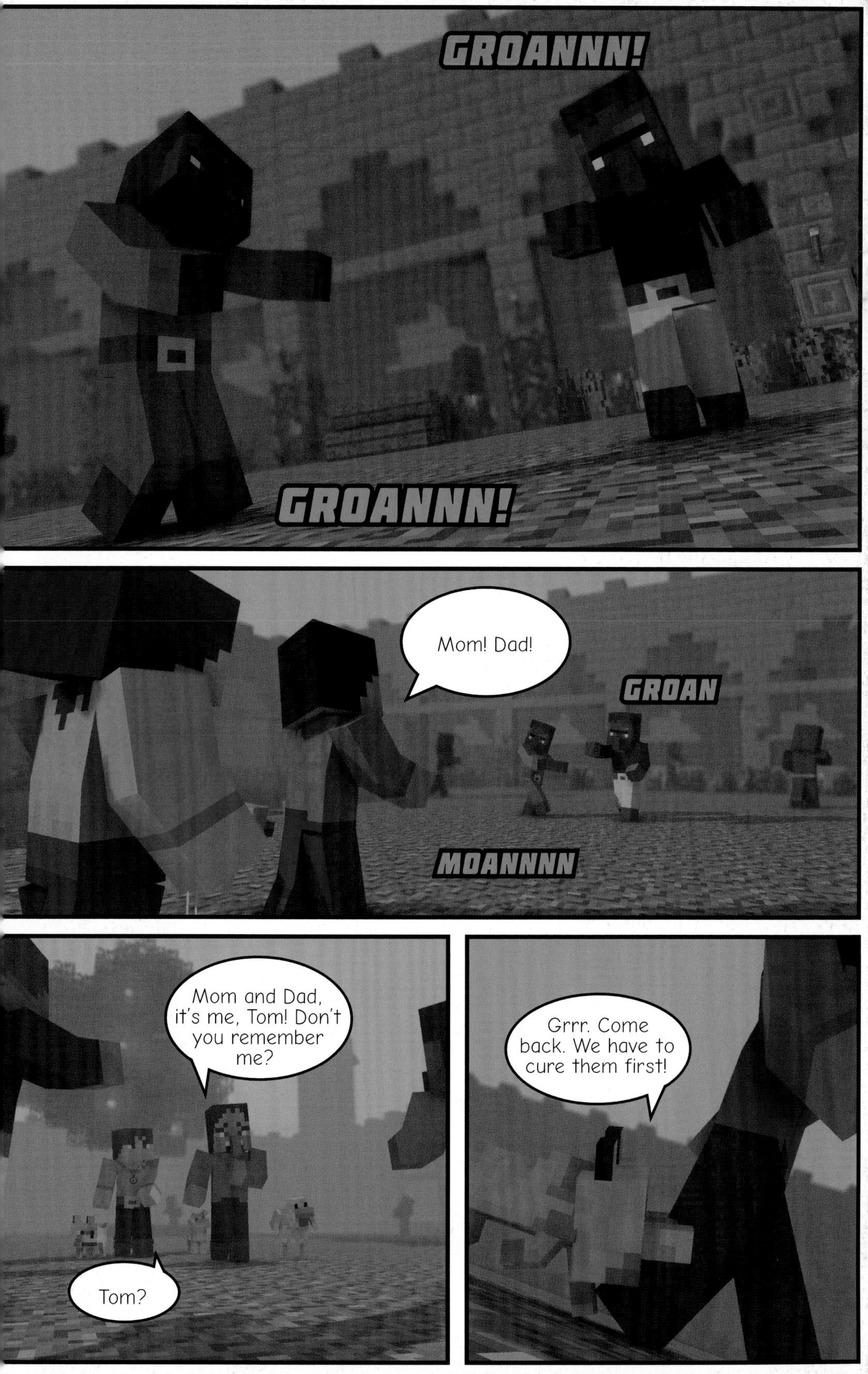
GROANNN!
GROANNN!
Mom! Dad!
GROAN
MOANNNN
Mom and Dad, it's me, Tom! Don't you remember me?
Tom?
Grrr. Come back. We have to cure them first!

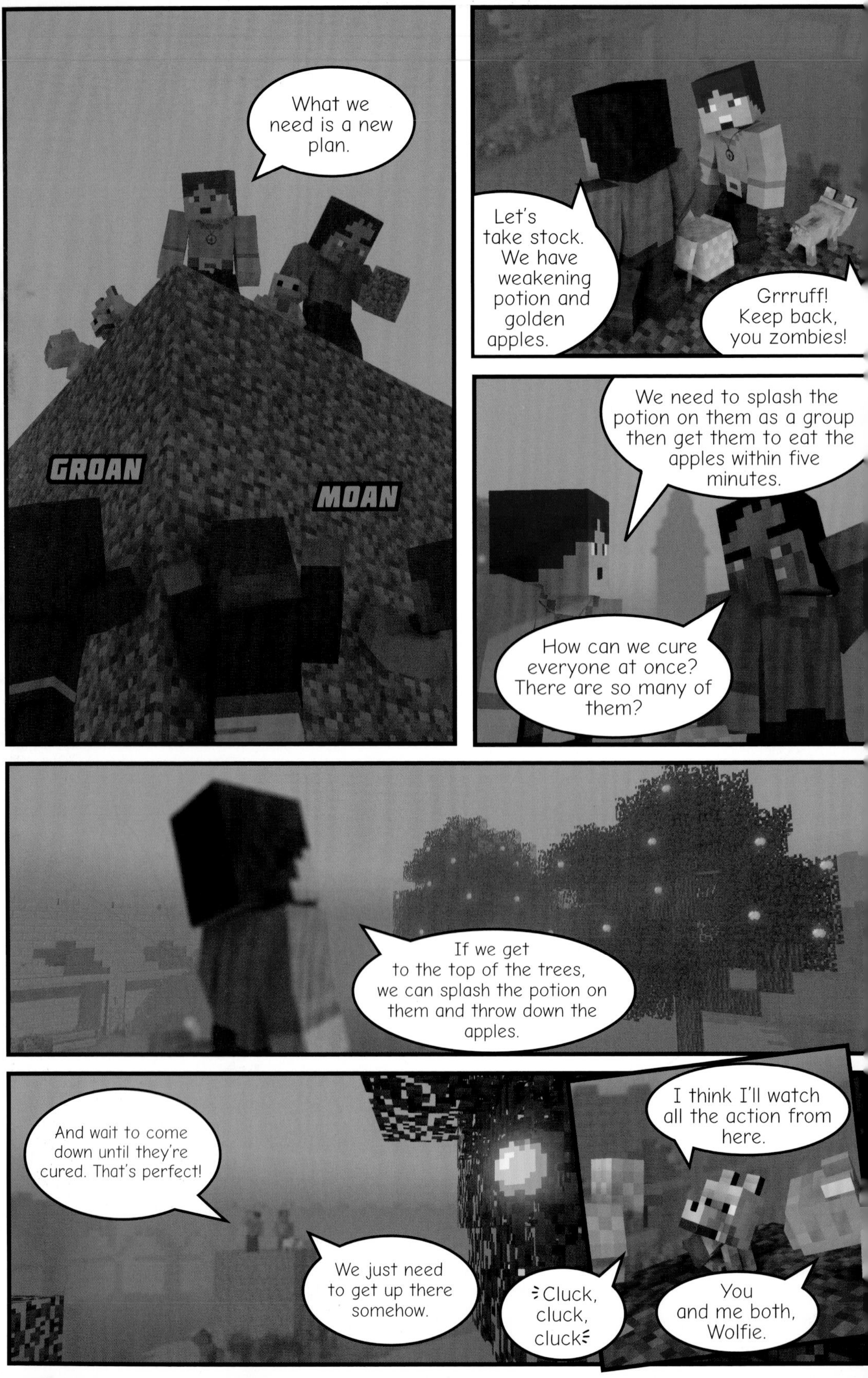
What we need is a new plan.
GROAN
MOAN
Let's take stock. We have weakening potion and golden apples.
Grrruff! Keep back, you zombies!
We need to splash the potion on them as a group then get them to eat the apples within five minutes.
How can we cure everyone at once? There are so many of them?
If we get to the top of the trees, we can splash the potion on them and throw down the apples.
And wait to come down until they're cured. That's perfect!
We just need to get up there somehow.
Cluck, cluck, cluck
I think I'll watch all the action from here.
You and me both, Wolfie.

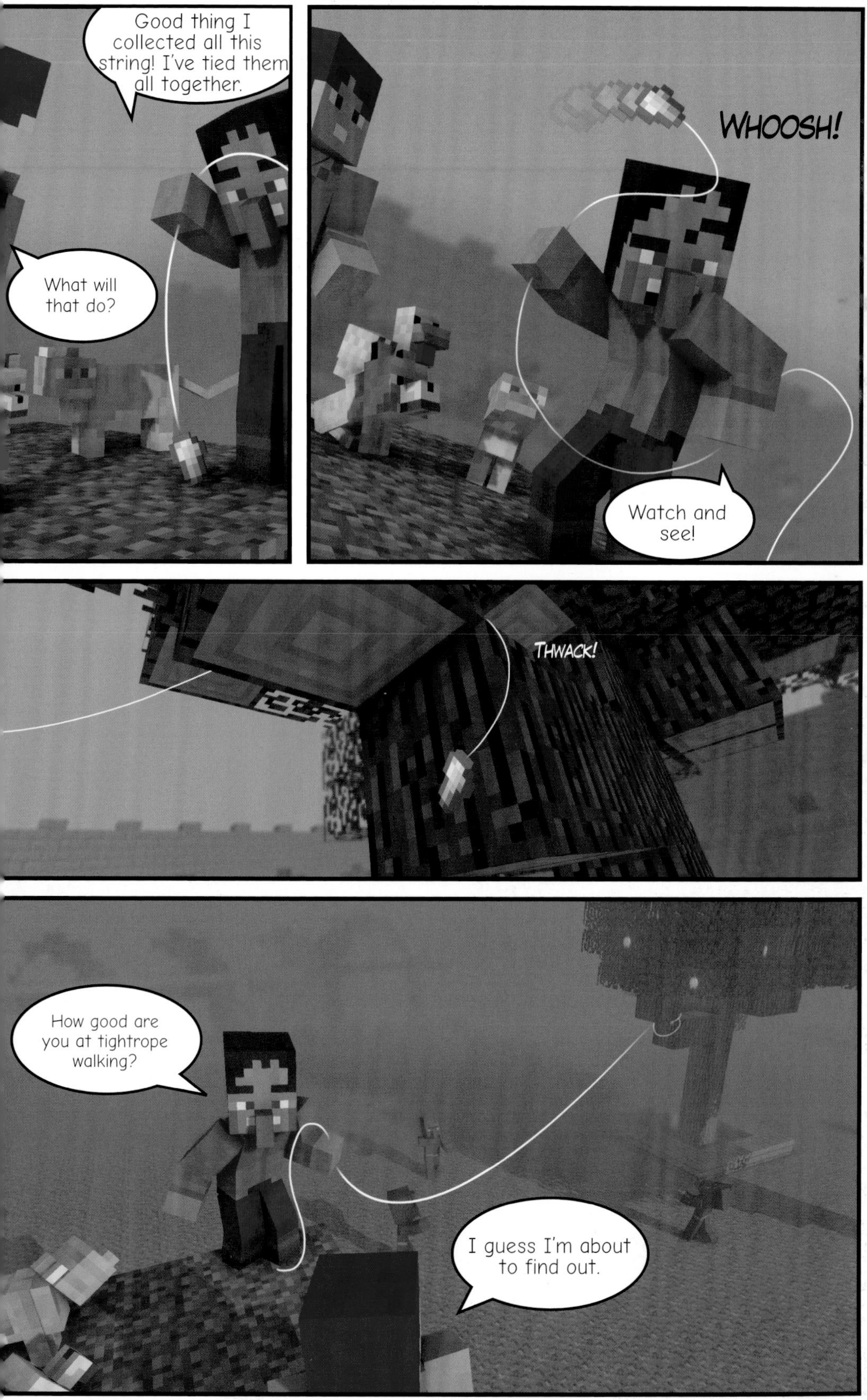
Good thing I collected all this string! I've tied them all together.
What will that do?
WHOOSH!
Watch and see!
THWACK!
How good are you at tightrope walking?
I guess I'm about to find out.

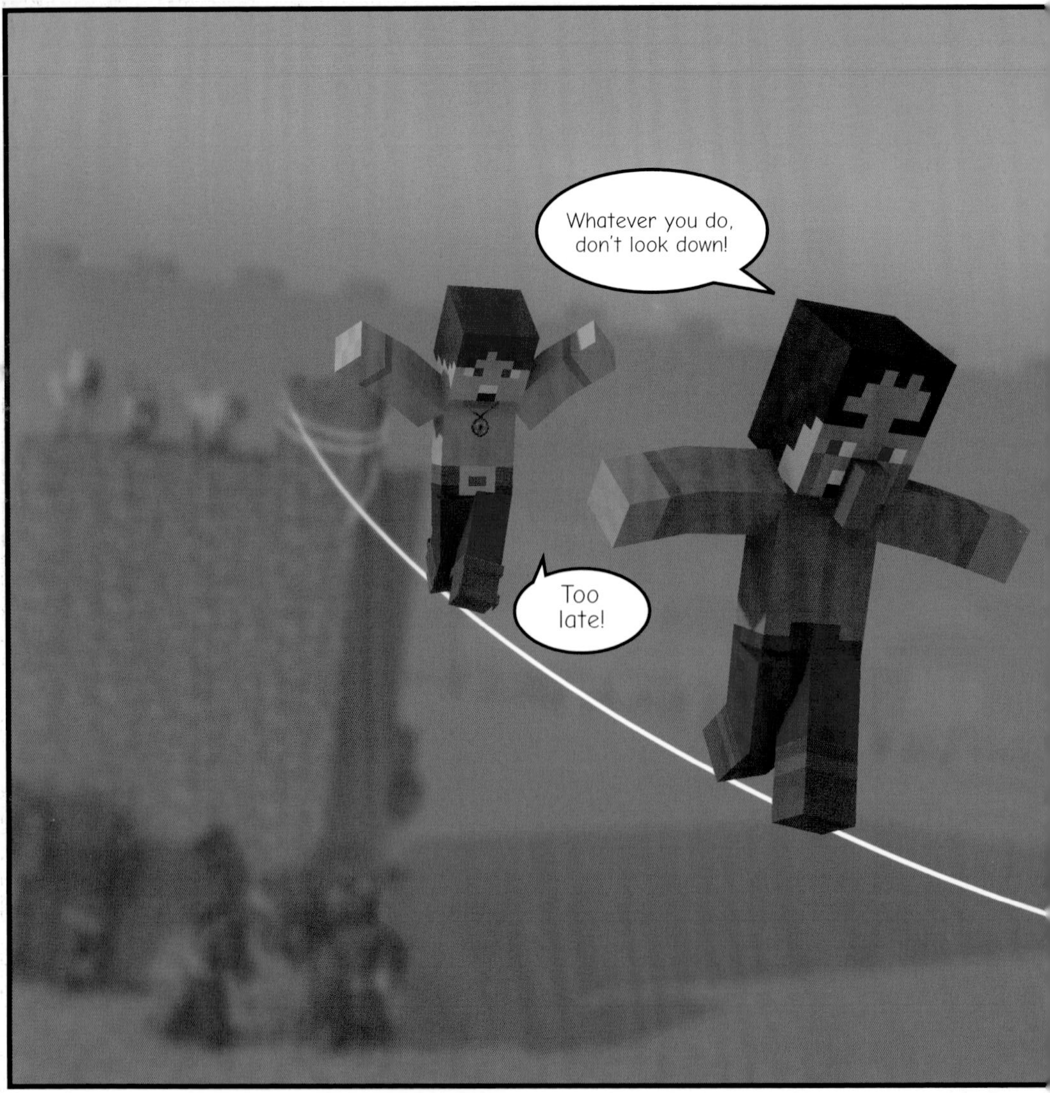
Whatever you do, don't look down!
Too late!

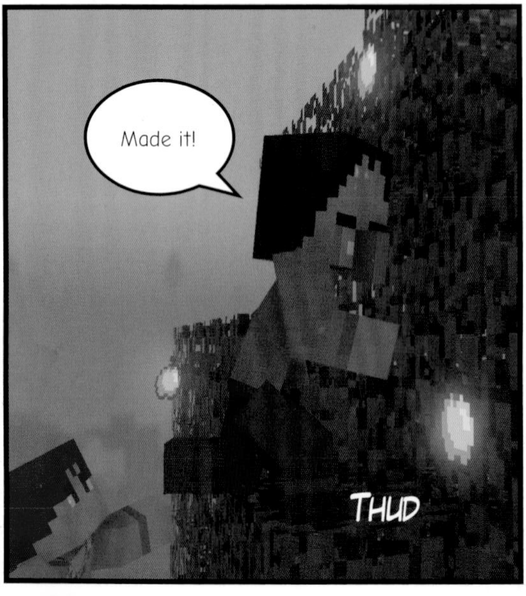
Made it!
THUD

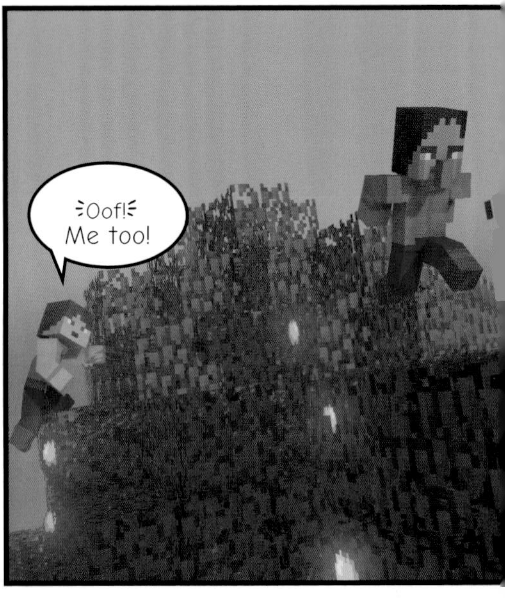
Oof! Me too!

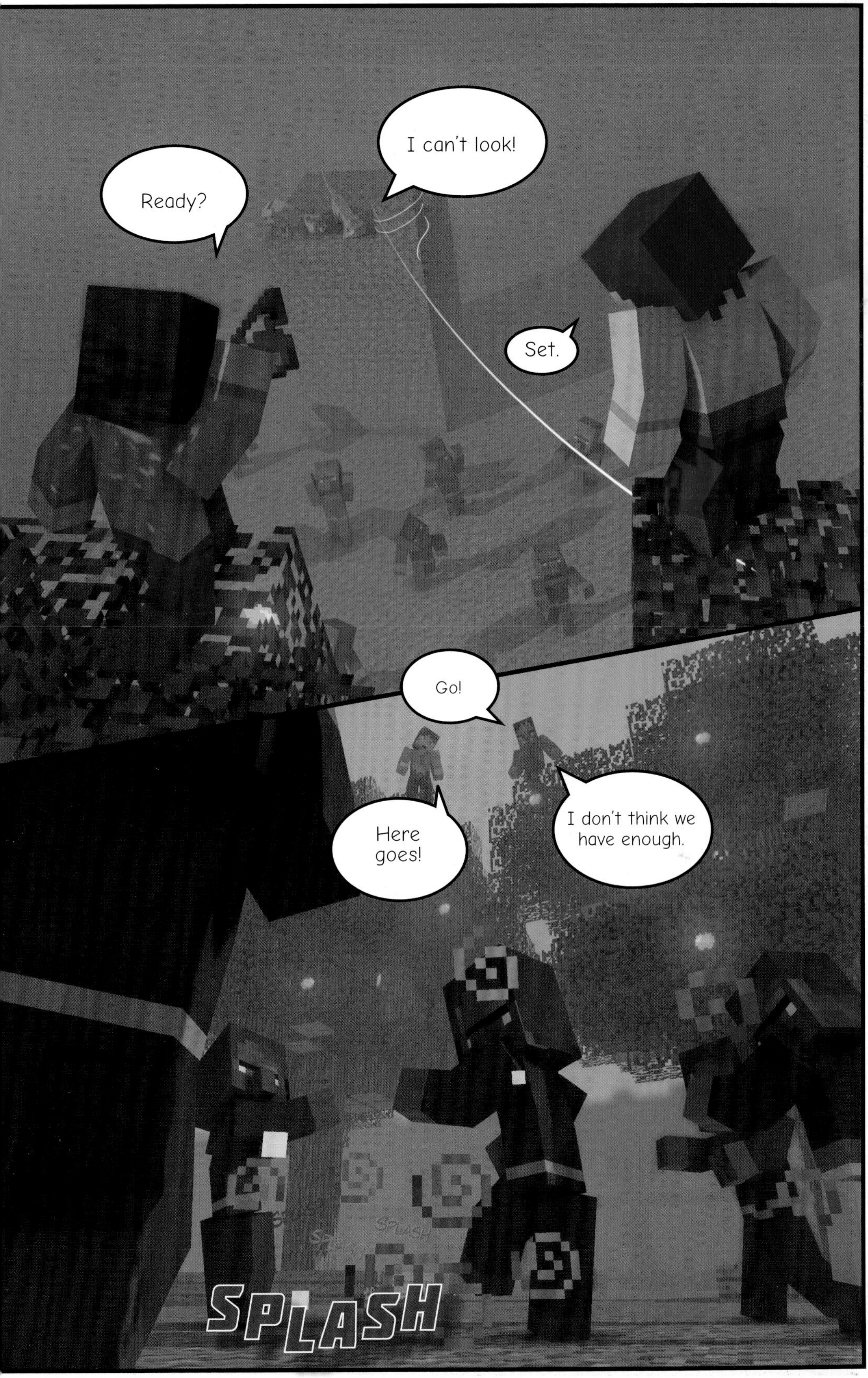
Ready?
I can't look!
Set.
Go!
Here goes!
I don't think we have enough.
SPLASH

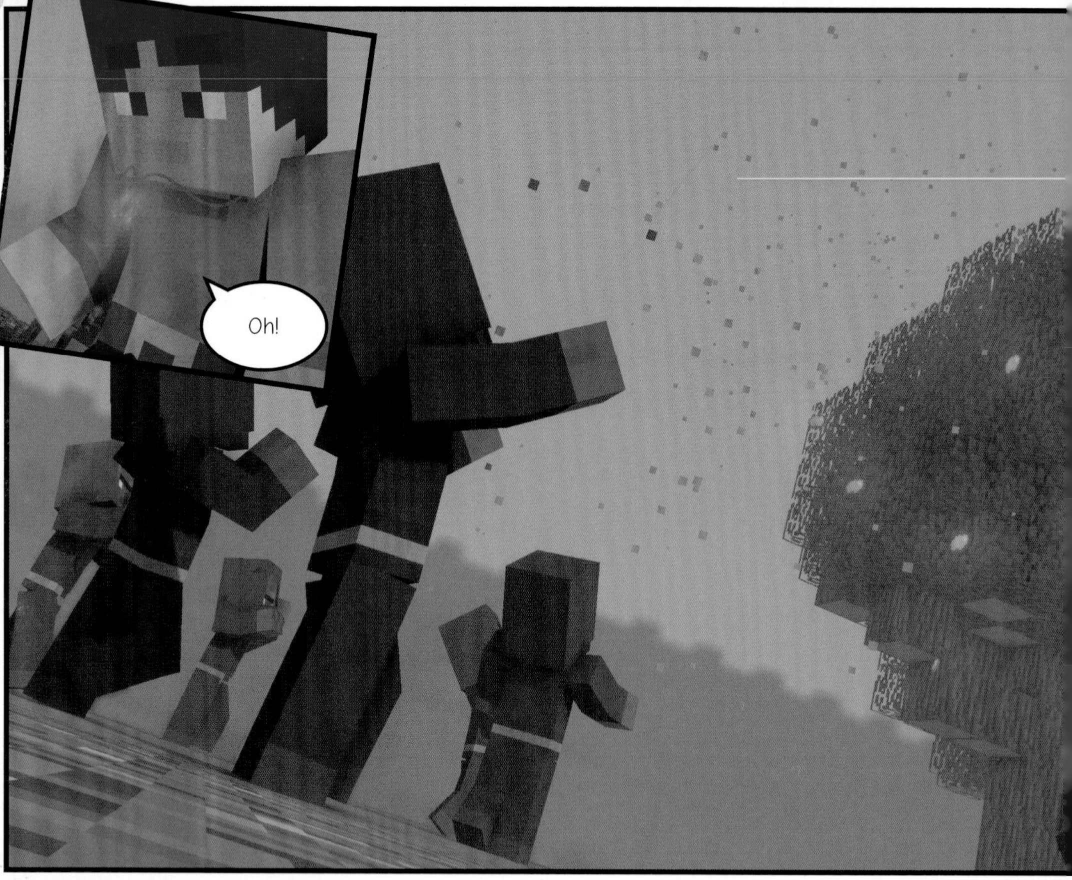
Oh!

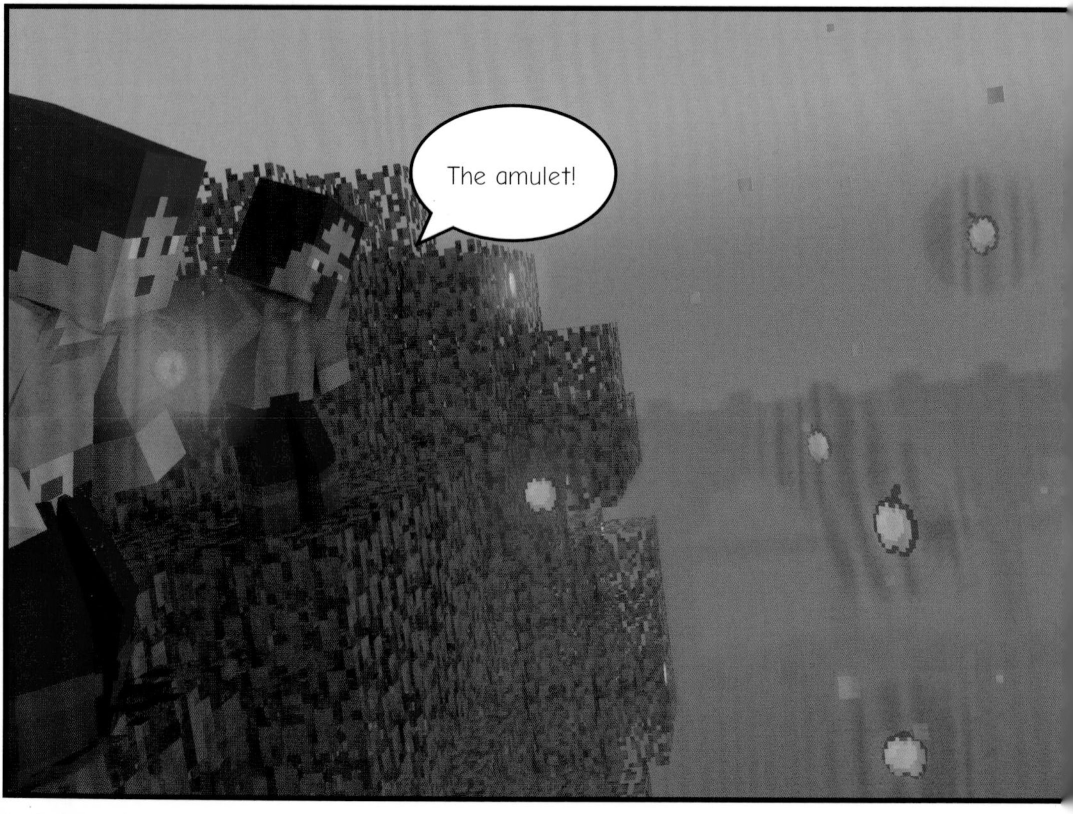
The amulet!

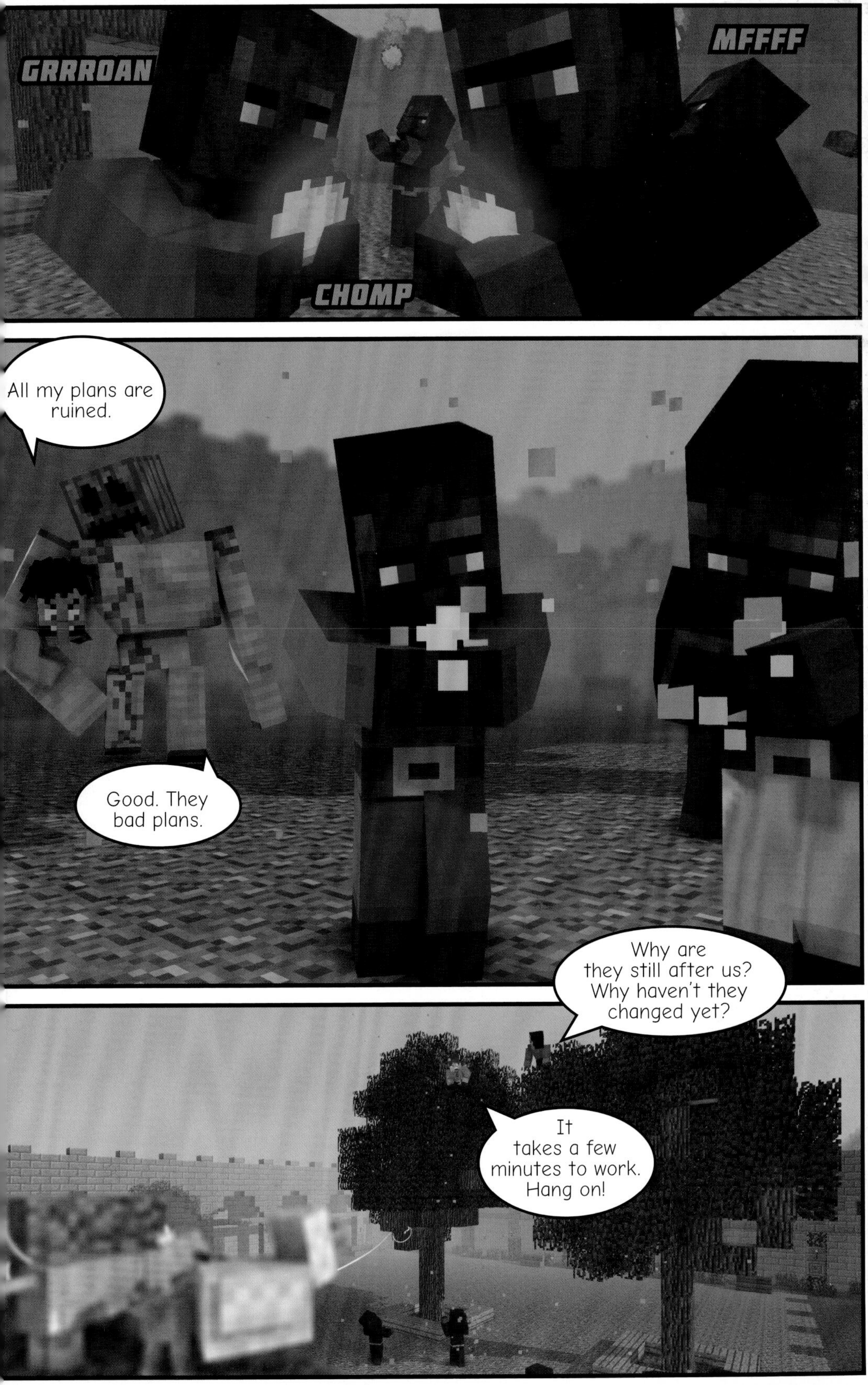
GRRROAN
MFFFF
CHOMP
All my plans are ruined.
Good. They bad plans.
Why are they still after us? Why haven't they changed yet?
It takes a few minutes to work. Hang on!

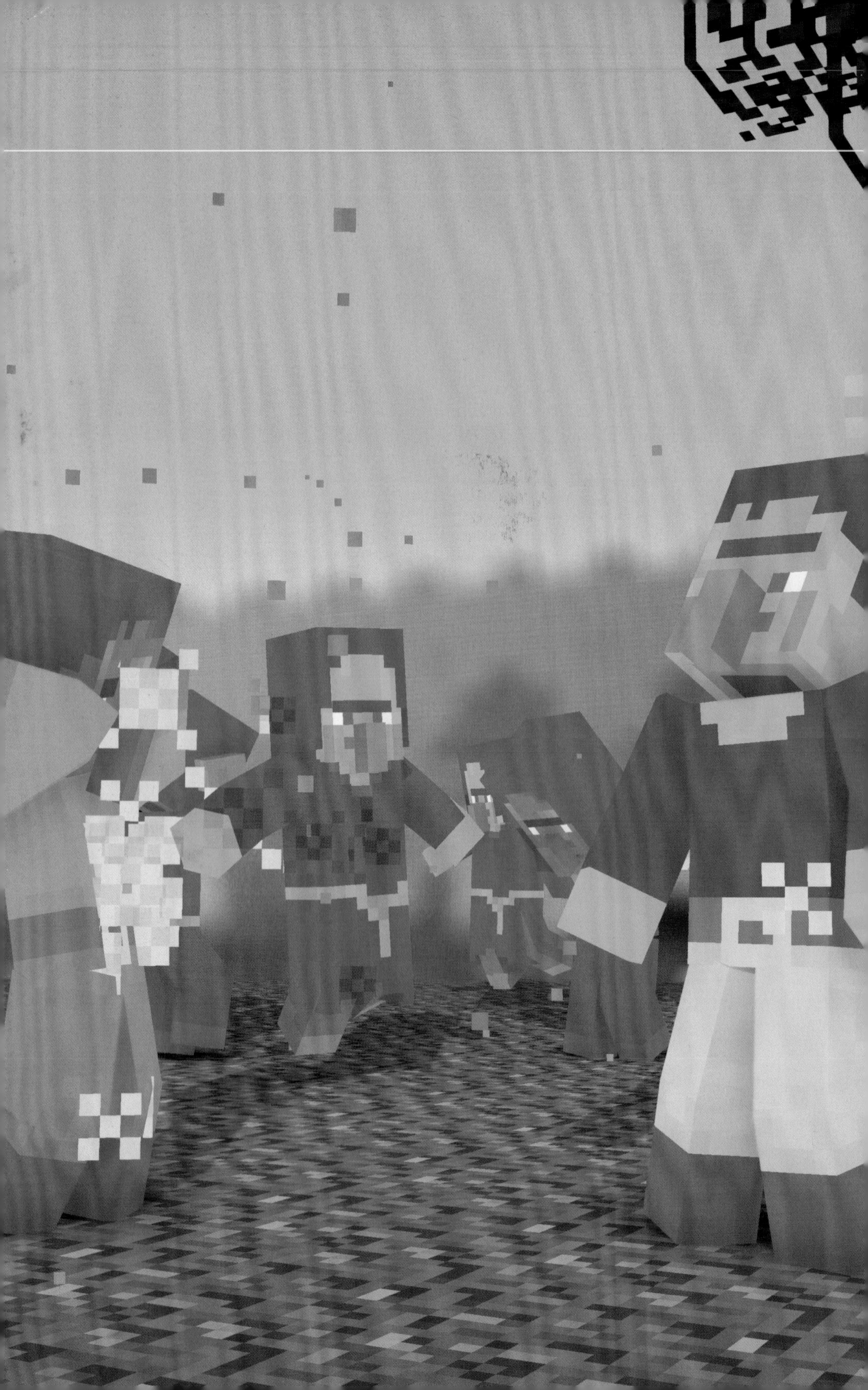

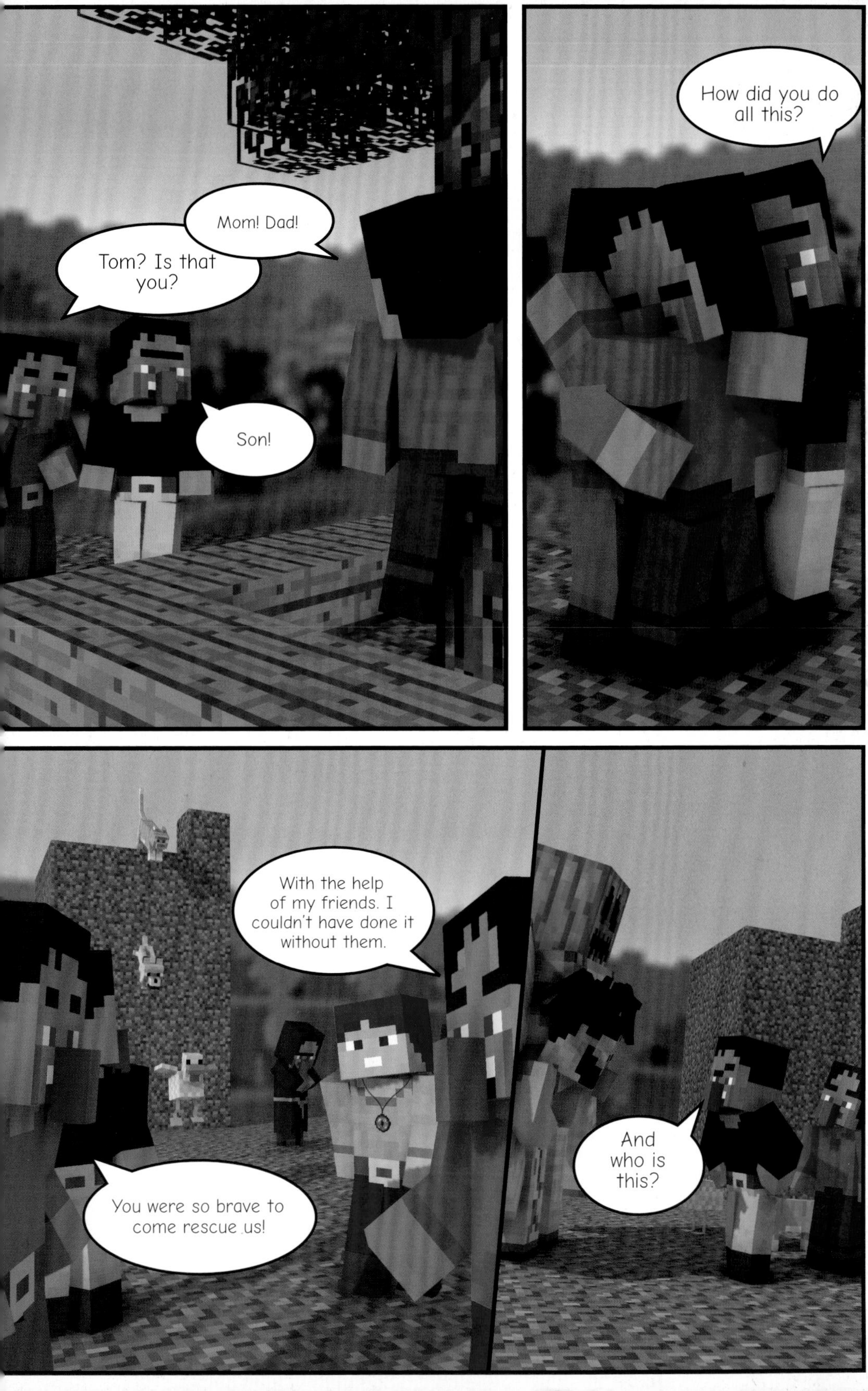
Mom! Dad!
Tom? Is that you?
Son!
How did you do all this?
With the help of my friends. I couldn't have done it without them.
You were so brave to come rescue us!
And who is this?

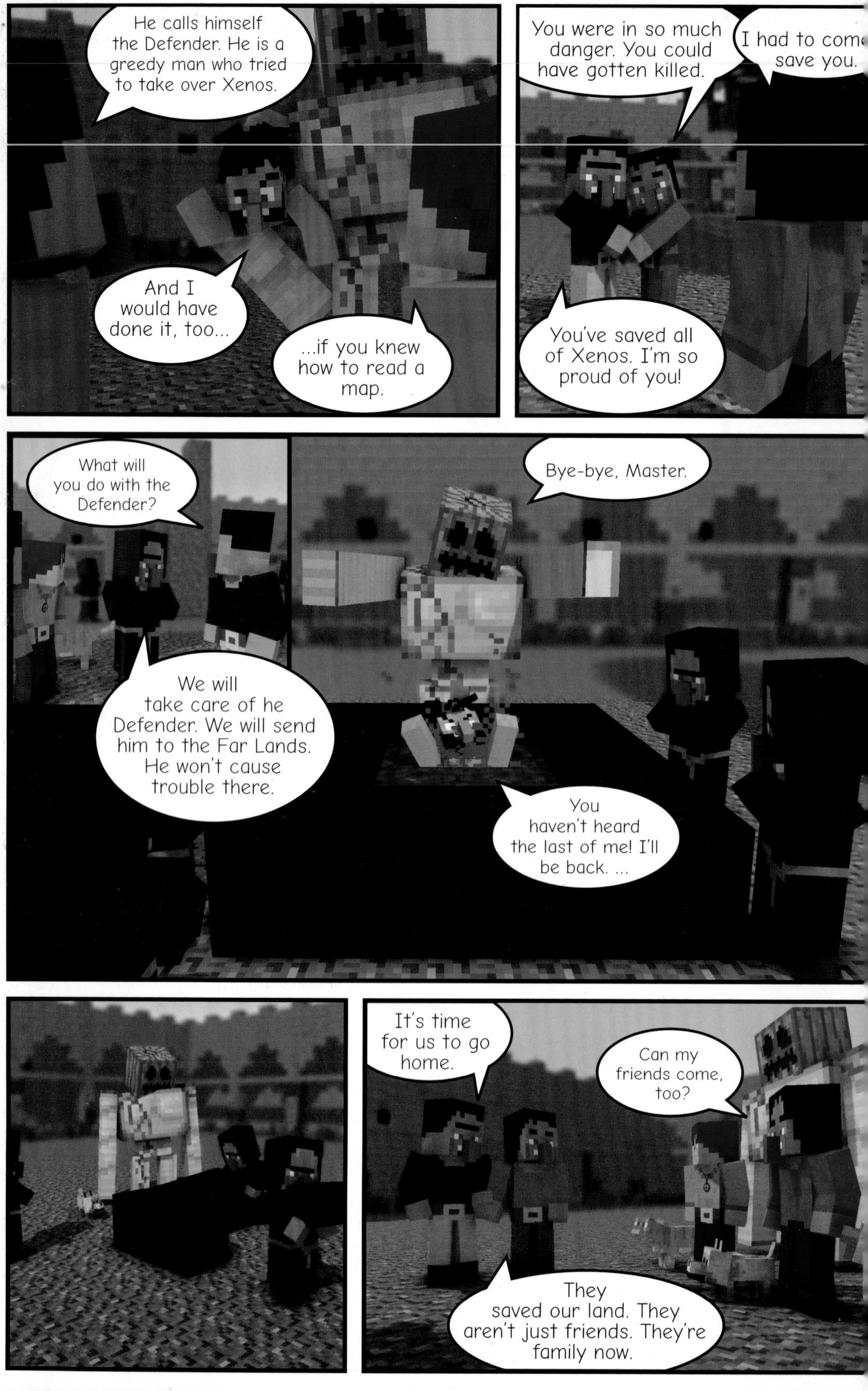

He calls himself the Defender. He is a greedy man who tried to take over Xenos.
And I would have done it, too...
...if you knew how to read a map.
You were in so much danger. You could have gotten killed.
I had to come save you.
You've saved all of Xenos. I'm so proud of you!
What will you do with the Defender?
We will take care of he Defender. We will send him to the Far Lands. He won't cause trouble there.
Bye-bye, Master.
You haven't heard the last of me! I'll be back. ...
It's time for us to go home.
Can my friends come, too?
They saved our land. They aren't just friends. They're family now.

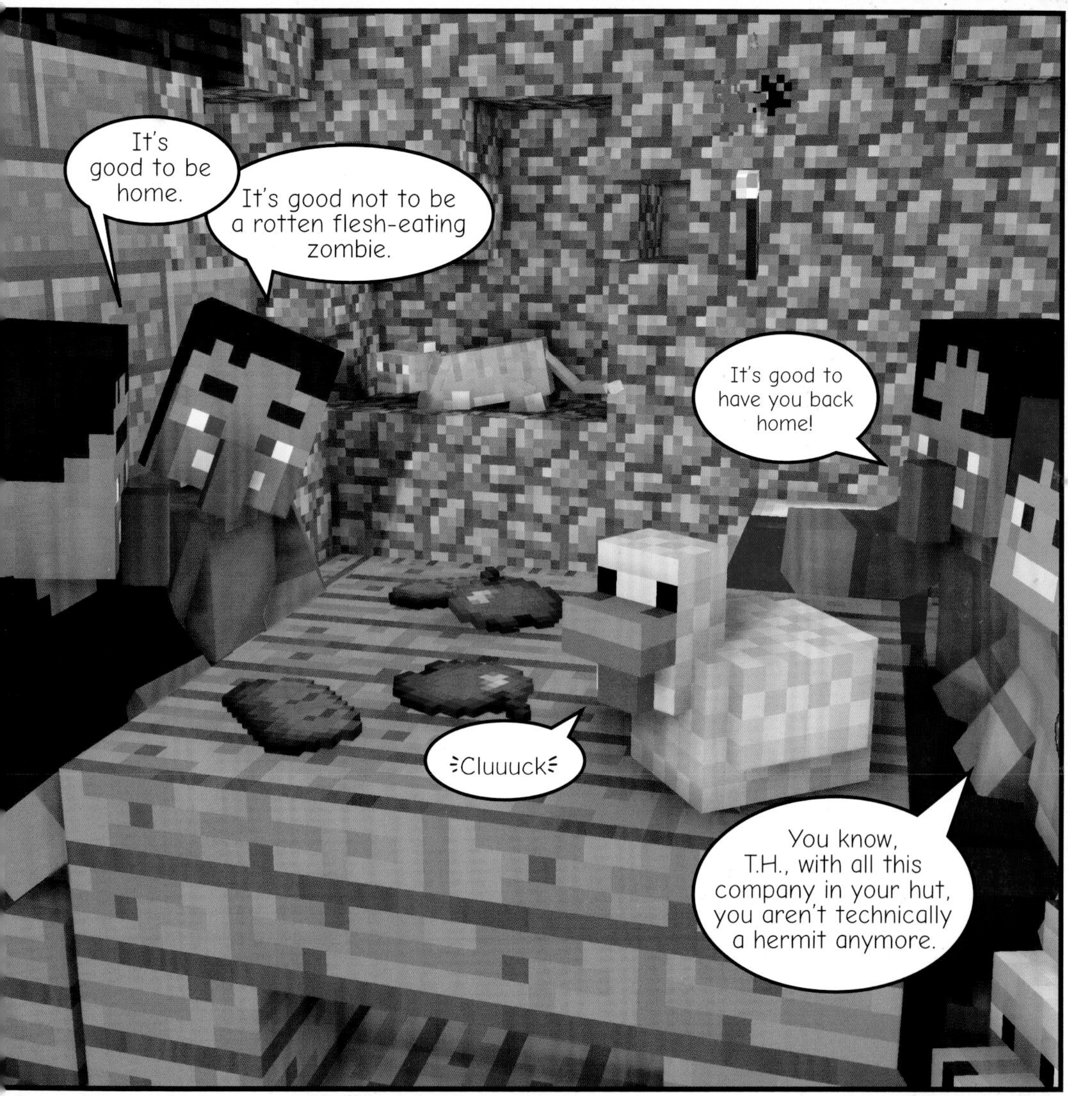
It's good to be home.
It's good not to be a rotten flesh-eating zombie.
It's good to have you back home!
Cluuuck
You know, T.H., with all this company in your hut, you aren't technically a hermit anymore.

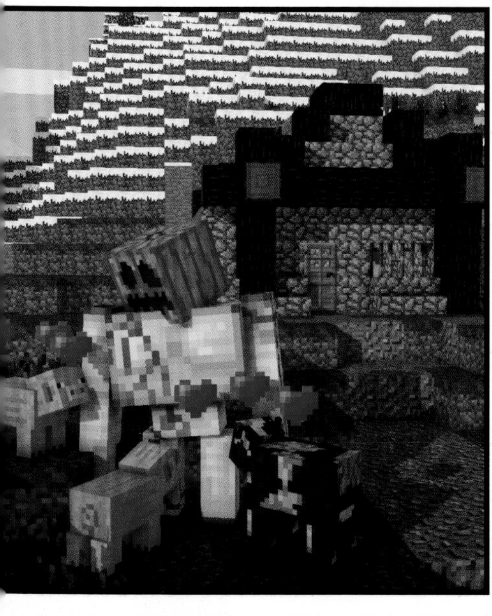

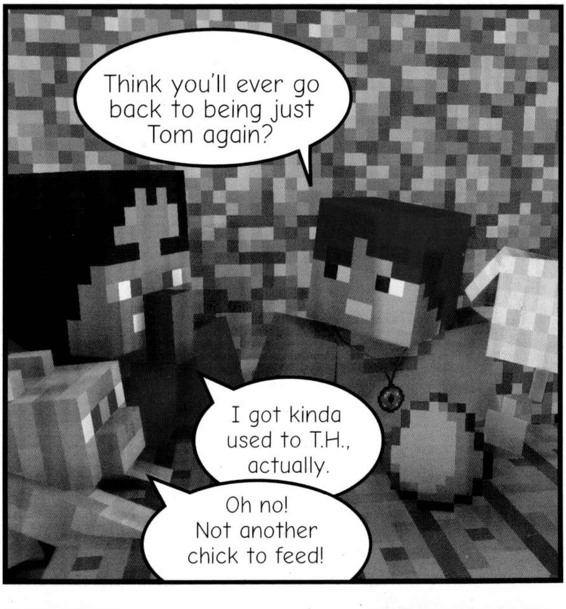
Think you'll ever go back to being just Tom again?
I got kinda used to T.H., actually.
Oh no! Not another chick to feed!

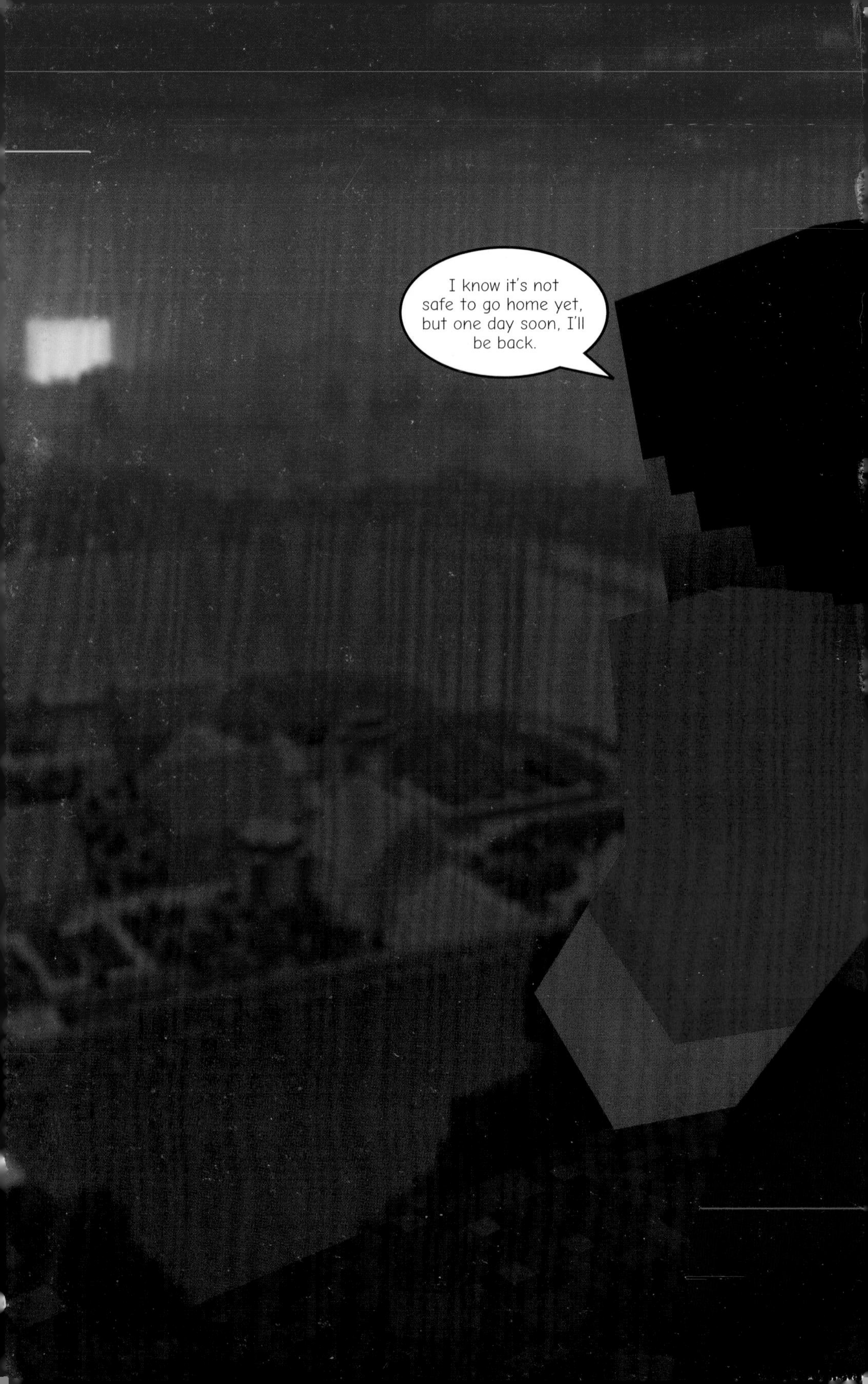
I know it's not safe to go home yet, but one day soon, I'll be back.